RISE OF

BOOK

HOPE

AURYN HADLEY

SPOTTED HORSE PRODUCTIONS

ISBN: 978-1-956455-60-1

Cover Art by DAZED designs (www.dazed-designs.com)

Edited by Sarah Williams

DEDICATION

No one can get there alone. Doesn't matter where "there" is. We all need a shoulder to lean on, a friend to cheer us on, and even an adversary to give us something to fight for.

Because life is nothing more than a story, and I hope yours is written in color.

Aunynn Hadley

MAP: OGUN - NORTHERN CONTINENT

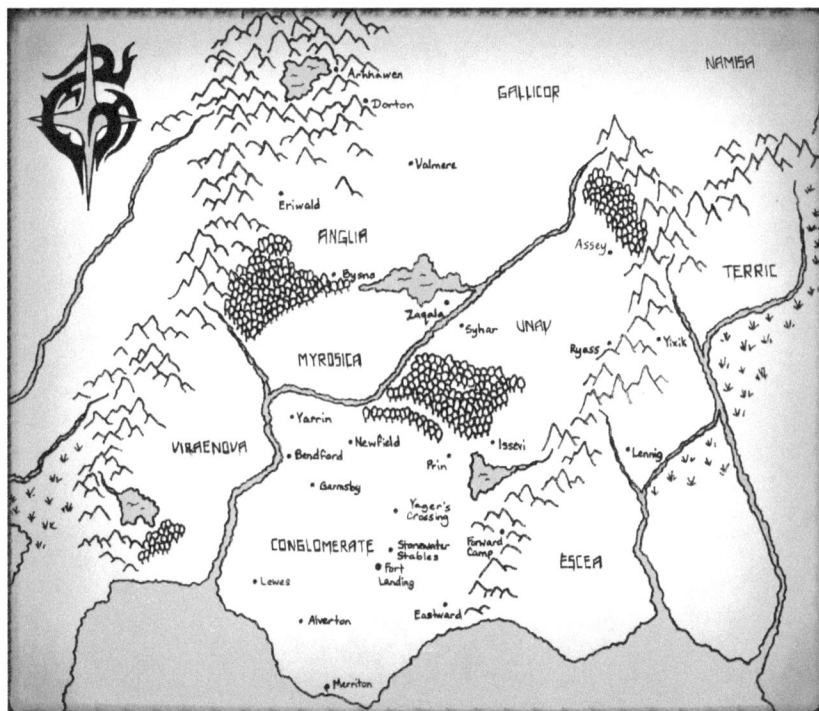

INTRODUCTION

The Terran war dragged on for a total of twenty-three years. No nation on the northern continent was spared. Lives were lost, but important alliances were made. Most of all, the iliri finally found the one thing we'd never had before: freedom.

But it came at a price, and one most humans couldn't even comprehend. Ayati, the pattern of all things, was gone. Since the end of the war, no prophets had seen a glimpse of the future. No visions had been foretold. One of the iliri's most powerful advantages had been lost, but it seemed a small price to pay in order to experience equality for all three species.

Finally, our people were free to live as they wanted, knowing their families were truly safe. Women could publicly acknowledge their mates. Children weren't for sale to the highest bidder. Iliri men weren't stolen from the streets and sold off to the military. Our people had the chance to eat the food our bodies needed and work for wages that allowed us to survive. For the iliri, it was an age of rebirth.

Yet our new world wasn't perfect. For so long, humans had grown accustomed to being in charge. Sharing that power was confusing to many, while others opposed it completely. Anglia, the new superpower on the continent, was struggling to change it all. The problem was that such things never happened quickly. Piece by piece, our traditions had to change. They held us back. Not just one species, but all of us needed to adjust because this wasn't equality if we all didn't enjoy the liberty of this new age.

So our leaders threw themselves into policy. Anglia was ruled by the King, Kaisae, and Orassae. Each one had been chosen by their people to represent their species. Combined, they made the final decisions and mutually beneficial laws. A council of three different cultures, brought together by war, thriving in peace.

They gave us hope.

Slowly, we were all learning to adapt. Humans began to use color in their writing to explain the meaning to iliri and grauori. The grauori had made an effort to speak the human language of Glish. The iliri balanced them both, lacking enough history to cling to anything besides the slavery and prejudice we'd survived. That was one tradition we were all willing to give up.

The question was how. While the three species coexisted, that didn't mean it was harmonious. Better was not the same as best, but was this why we finally had a Kaisae who'd lived through her final battle? Salryc Luxx had died for us. A human brought her back. A grauori taught him how. This Kaisae was the thread that bound the species together, and we all looked to her for answers about where to go from here.

Now, without ayati to guide us, we will need to forge our own path. The future is no longer mapped out. If the iliri are to move forward into peace, we must create a new pattern. One visible to all. Traditions, friendships, and families - they tie us together and erase the lines between our species. This time, we will need to make something filled with vibrant traditions and colorful dreams. A future tinted with the emotions of our words.

Pink - *fear*
Red - *anger/pain*
Orange - *joy*
Yellow - *pride*
Green - *life*
Cyan - *knowledge*
Blue - *faith/belief*
Purple - *hope/trust/passion*
Gold - *strength*
Brown - *disgust*
White - *love*
Silver - *fate/destiny*
Black - *death*

- Excerpt from *The History of Salryc Luxx*, by Ilus Molis Cernyn, professor of iliri history at the University of Arhhawen

CHAPTER ONE

ORANGE

*T*yr had one elbow propped up on the pillow, his palm holding up his head, while his other hand traced the new lines across Sal's back. It had been five months since the end of the war. For three of those, they'd been here in Arhhawen. In that time, many of the Black Blades had gotten their stories inked onto their bodies by Risk, but Sal's was the most beautiful.

The best part was knowing that the orange section was about him. The other guys were there as well, and the colors shifted between them all, but that bit right before the final battle? It was in orange, representing the moment he'd accepted the title of sixth mate, or Kernor. And while the others were adamant that Sal could have as many mates as she needed, he somehow knew he was the last. They were all she'd ever need. He would make sure of it.

Tyr let the pad of his finger follow it gently, careful not to disturb the woman sleeping across Zep's chest. He just wanted to enjoy this moment for a bit before she woke up. In his heart, he could feel warmth ebb and flow in time with her pulse. That meant it had finally happened. For months, she'd kept the link open between them, burning it into place the same way she'd done with Jase so long ago. This morning, Tyr hadn't needed to strengthen it. The bond was *there*, and he could finally feel her the same way the others could. He was now cessivi.

Just with Sal, though. Oh, she'd offered to link him with the others, but that had felt like too much. More than *he* could take, at any rate. Dealing with the iliri-ness of this whole situation was hard enough. To have five men running around in his emotional life? Tyr needed a little more time before he was ready for that. The best part was that the guys understood. Actually, it had been Jase who'd suggested burning the link open.

He'd said this way, Tyr could get used to the bond alone and add the others in when he was ready. He could take his time about it - since time was something they now had plenty of. It didn't matter if it took years to get there. This was peace, and what else would they need to worry about?

And it had *finally* happened. That bridge between their bodies was permanently in place. He could feel her relaxation. Behind that, he could also sense an echo of more, proving that she was tied to the others in this bed. Six men, one Kaisae, and they were all piled together like puppies. Well, like organized puppies.

The suite was made for the leader of the iliri in Anglia, and it had been renovated to plan for a harem. The bed was the largest thing he'd ever seen, in a bedroom big enough to swallow most of the houses Tyr had lived in. Originally, this area would've been used for meetings and filled with a table to hold at least fifty. On each side of the room was a door that led into smaller bedrooms for the harem. That gave them the option of personal time with her, or a place to heal and recover if sick - although that rarely happened to the iliri. They had healers for such things.

Then there was the rest of the suite. Across from the foot of the bed was a door that led to the main room. It had a fireplace, couches, and plenty of bookshelves. Most were filled with Jase's books. Attached to that was a complete kitchen. The wall between it and the living room had been carved out, connecting the spaces. If Tyr had to guess, he'd say that long ago, the kitchen had been for servants to prepare meals that were served to whoever used the massive room for meetings.

Besides that, there was a large bathing room, two smaller bedrooms for the kids, and, the best part of all, the balcony. Yes, Sal's suite had an entire patio placed above the entrance to Arhhawen - by a couple of stories - that allowed her to look out onto the valley below. Tyr had been in awe of the view. To both sides were the snow-covered peaks of the Ahnian Ridge, but straight out was Dorton. Supposedly, Sal could see the King's Palace. Tyr could only make out the town.

The whole thing felt like it was straight out of a fairytale. The room, the mates, and the tranquility of being able to sleep in. This bond with Sal was the final piece, and all that was left was the living happily ever after part.

He was leaning closer to kiss Sal's spine when a sound made him pause. Outside the suite was the rest of Arhhawen, a city built under a mountain. It was so much more than simply a palace or castle. This place was massive, but the main room typically buffered the noises from the bedroom, which was why Tyr paused.

Someone was yelling, and it sounded like it was coming closer. Years of serving in a war zone made Tyr tense. Beside him, Sal sucked in a breath, clearly feeling his concern. He was just about to tell her to go back to sleep when the entrance to their suite banged open.

As one, the Kaisae's mates woke up. None of them made a noise, but all of them moved. Kolt grabbed something from the air, then tossed it across the bed to Sal. Tyr caught the glint of her steel dagger. Zep rolled off the edge, aiming for where his own sword hung on the wall in a decorative display. Gage shoved the blankets back -

And the bedroom door opened.

For a split second, everything paused. Tyr saw Jase poised to leap. Sal was tensed. Blaz was halfway out of the bed on the far side. Gage and Kolt were ready to rush off the end. Zep stood beside the bed on their side, bare-ass naked, and Tyr had his body leaned across Sal's to shield her. But the man at the door wasn't a threat. In fact, his mouth hung open in surprise.

It was the King.

"Well," Dom chuckled, "that didn't go according to plan."

"Fuck," Zep groaned, his word relaxing all of them. "Now I'm dying to know what the *plan* was."

Dom made a feeble gesture toward the bed. "Catching her sleeping, actually, since she's done it to me often enough."

"We hear better than you," Sal grumbled before flopping back onto the mattress. "But I'm awake. What did you need?"

"And who was yelling?" Tyr asked.

"Arctic," Dom said, looking almost sheepish. "He said you were in your room. So I came in."

"Why?!" Sal demanded.

The King lifted a stack of papers in his hand. It wasn't a couple of pages. No, this was thick, as if it was trying to be a book. Just to make his point, he flicked them, causing the corners to fan out and snap back together.

"These are the reports of inter-species problems. They run from Bysno all the way up the ridge. Every city in Anglia has at least one report of cultural tension, and our allies will be here in *days*, Sal. They're going to notice that our idea of three nations isn't working as well as we hoped. If we want to make a case for recognition of iliri and grauori as independent and sentient people equal to humans, then this is a big fucking problem."

She nodded, the back of her head rubbing against the pillow it rested on. "Do I have to dress up for this?"

"It's just us, actually. The Shields are down at the stables talking to their friends, and my mates didn't come." Dom sighed. "Sal, I can't get Rragri. I mean, she answers, but she can't come. Not with Nya's condition."

"She's pregnant," Sal grumbled. "It's not a debilitating thing."

"She's three weeks overdue," Dom countered. "Rragri's frantic, worried that the pups will be too large."

Tyr couldn't help himself. "So, don't we still have human doctors?"

Everyone turned to look at him. Tyr tried to figure out why that was a stupid question, but he had nothing. The expressions on everyone's faces were all confused, and he had no idea why.

"What?" he asked. "I mean, iliri healing doesn't exactly do C-sections, but I'd think that Anglia would have at least one doctor who knows how. I dunno, maybe a vet if the doctors are scared of working on a grauori?"

"Shit," Dom breathed. "He's right. We've gotten so used to thinking away wounds that none of us considered it! If the kids are too big to fit, then there's no reason she can't have them surgically born, and then a grauori healer can put her back together!"

"Anesthesia might be a problem," Gage pointed out. "I'm not sure how their species handles the medicines humans use, and we already know that some stuff that is fine for humans will sedate a crossbred and poison Sal."

Blaz grunted in thought. "But Raast or I could knock her out. Sal probably could as well. I mean, it would be a communal effort, but I can't see why this wouldn't work. We'd just need to get Nya over the mountains and into Dorton."

"Dorton?" Dom asked.

Blaz slowly nodded. "That's where Jarl is, since Rragri banned him from the den until the pups come. Makes more sense than here."

"Rragri won't like that," Dom told them. "She says Jarl shouldn't be there so he can't refuse the kids. Pups. Whatever they'll be." He canted his head. "I'm pretty sure Jarl won't mind. That boy's gone stupid over this, but it's one more of those cultural divides that are fucking everything up."

"Says the man with no kids," Kolt grumbled. "Trust me, it's not easy waiting and worrying. Makes a guy feel pretty helpless."

"He'll feel a lot more helpless if Rragri tears him a new breathing hole in the middle of his neck," Dom pointed out.

"Then they can come here if that makes everyone feel better," Sal decided before waving it away. "I'll talk to Rragri about it later and sort it out. You wanted to deal with our policing problem. Do you mind if we do this at Tensa's? Because none of us can cook for shit."

Dom let out a heavy sigh. "I just walked *up* all those flights of stairs, and now you want to just go back down?"

"Welcome to Arhhawen," Sal told him. "Just remember that you picked this place for me."

"And she's starving," Tyr realized.

He'd assumed that hollow feeling was his own empty stomach, but he wasn't normally a big fan of breakfast. A couple cups of coffee were all he needed. Sal, on the other hand, ran on protein. And after last night, of course she'd be hungry. The seven of them had gone at it for a few hours. He smiled thinking about it, only realizing after a moment that Jase was staring at him.

"Ya can feel her?" the Ahnor asked.

Tyr's smile grew a little more. "Yeah. I went to strengthen the bond this morning, and there was nothing to do. It's wide open, and..." He looked over at Sal. "I think it finally happened."

Her eyes glazed over, focused on nothing for a moment before she smiled. "I can feel him!"

Immediately, the guys began to laugh, offer him words of congratulations, and Kolt even rubbed Tyr's arm. Among all of it, though, he could feel Sal's pride and happiness leaking through. There was some relief in there as well. It seemed she'd been hiding a fear that he didn't really want this, and that he'd change his mind before the link was truly formed. Now, it was there forever. No take-backs. Well, not unless she decided to cut his link for some reason, and she'd only ever done that when she thought she was about to die.

But death was no longer a daily concern for any of them. That had ended with the war. This? It was the happy ending, the boring bits. The Kaisae of All Anglia spent her days dealing with paperwork and her nights rolling around this massive bed with her mates. Why wouldn't he want this? And didn't she realize that the only reason he'd considered refusing her was to protect her? He'd said no because it was the only way he thought he could keep history from repeating, and now that wasn't a problem.

"I know," Sal said softly as she rolled to face him. "I do know all of that, Tyr, but knowing something and having fears aren't the same. Believe it or not, I still worry that I'm not enough."

"You, Sal, are more than enough." And he took the chance to kiss her.

Dom chuckled. "So much so that it takes six men to keep up. And congratulations, Tyr, but can you get her out of bed? Every minute, the Representatives of the Conglomerate get a little closer, and you know those assholes will use any excuse they can to swing this deal in their favor. I have no idea what Escea is going to be like."

"Viraenova and Myrosica should be easy," Sal reminded him. "And yes. Breakfast at Tensa's. Can one of you guys find me some clothes?"

"That's me," Gage said as he crawled his way toward the edge of the bed. "You staying to watch, Dom, or prefer to wait in the other room?"

Dom just leaned his shoulder against the door frame. "Staying to watch. Don't know how to break this to you all, but you make this insanity work. I'm taking notes for my own harem."

"Rayna's harem," Tyr corrected. "Hate to tell you this, sire, but you are *not* the one in charge anymore."

"Don't I know it," Dom said, but it was with a wistful smile on his face. "Which is part of what I wanted to talk to the Kaisae about. Clothes, people."

"And coffee," Jase grumbled. "Lots of coffee."

Kolt just groaned. "Which means I need to get Las ready to go see his grandmother."

"I'll help," Blaz offered. "And we'll probably be done before Sal's dressed."

CHAPTER TWO

BLUE

An hour later, Sal and Dom were sitting at a long table in Tensa's. Kolt and Blaz would be there shortly, after making sure their only live-in child was with his kauvwae while they worked. No, it wasn't exactly a diner, but it was close. Set in a long room just off the main entrance of the town, Tensa had recreated her restaurant from Prin. This time, however, there were no fees for the food. It was part of the deal. Everyone who lived in Arhhawen paid taxes based on their income. Those taxes covered the cost of keeping and restoring the underground city. The rest went to the necessities of life for the inhabitants.

Because while peacetime had helped a lot of the iliri get back on their feet, not everyone had a job. Those who needed assistance got it. Food was always offered at Tensa's, and the community often gathered here to socialize. In Dorton, they had evening events where the nobility showed off. In Arhhawen, they had a diner. Same idea, but Sal's version was a lot more functional.

So Tensa ran the place like a cross between a mess hall and her old restaurant. Each day, the menu was written on a long stone wall in chalk. The waitresses would go from table to table, taking orders and bringing plates. The options changed daily, depending upon what was available, but it was always good, and there was usually company.

For those who preferred to arrange their own meals, most rooms had kitchens. Like the free people they were, the iliri - and the humans who lived with them, claiming the species as their own nation - had the option to buy groceries and keep to themselves. Not many did. There was something about the communal aspect that appealed to them, and Sal was no different.

She also wasn't worried about her people listening in on her discussion with the King. Then again, he wasn't treated like nobility in Arhhawen. Yes, the iliri respected him for making their freedom possible, but they didn't grovel. They did, however, drop their eyes. The best part was that most of them called the man Dom.

Not Dominik. Not sire. Not Your Majesty. He was Dom to these people, and he swore he loved it. Made him feel less like an outsider, he said. Sal was pretty sure the habit started with the Devil Dogs, though. Since they called the King by his chosen name, the iliri mimicked them, and it worked.

But the color-coded uniforms were gone. Today, Sal was wearing a short red shirt with loose-fitting black pants. Red flowers had been embroidered down the legs, and her feet were actually bare. The men also wore bright colors, and yet each one had managed to include a piece of black with it. It didn't matter if that was simply the trim or their boots. Somehow, the Blades always found themselves needing that color in their wardrobe, as if it was a part of their identity.

Dom went the other way. His shirt was brilliantly white with silver stitching around the sleeves. Tyr was the holdout, replacing black with grey. The tattoo on his neck proved he was a Black Blade, but on his bicep, where few would see it, was another tattoo. One of a dog with its teeth bared: the official symbol of the Devil Dogs. Sal could just see the bottom of it peeking from under his short sleeve.

"You ever going to get the Kaisae symbol?" she asked.

He shook his head. "I haven't decided where. I mean, I said I should put it on my dick, since that's the part of me you like best, but Risk refused." He grinned to prove he was joking.

Gage chuckled. "Put it on your foot. You know, since you kept running from her."

Tyr answered with a middle finger, pausing as the waitress came over. Dom had his hand over his mouth, but he dropped it when he recognized the girl. She paused a pace away, lowered her eyes to the entire table, and smiled.

"Kaisae. Dom. Davas. What can I get for you today?"

"Lyzzi?" he asked, looking back at Sal. "Isn't she a bit young to be working?"

"I'm thirteen," the girl reminded him.

"And you deserve to spend some more time playing," Dom insisted, shifting his eyes to Jase. "You can't tell me you agree with putting *children* to work?"

"She needs ta learn," Jase told him. "She does na work long hours, but she needs ta learn how ta speak ta her people in our language, and this is the best place ta do it. That she earns a wage fer herself makes it feel less like a chore."

"And we mature faster," Sal reminded him. "Keep in mind, most of us were working from the time we were born. Lyzzi has her own rooms. Yes, they're next door to ours, but she's not a child, not by iliri standards. She's a young woman."

Gage leaned into his chair, draping one arm across the back. "Dom, you do realize that Tensa doesn't just make her serve customers, right? Lyzzi is reading her own language, speaking it, and learning how to detect situations by smell. She's learning what it means to be iliri from the people who already accept their quirks."

"And to defend," the girl said softly. "Tensa makes me practice my skills along with the orders. She says a Kaisae must know it all, and the only way to learn is to start at the bottom, because a leader works her way up like everyone else." She flashed a smile at Jase. "My davas got me a good job."

"Davas?" Dom asked. "Seems I've been in Dorton too long."

"Davas," Zep confirmed. "Her 'papas' are still trying to sell their farm, which is taking a bit, but she's family. That means we're all her fathers, and Sal is her amma."

Sal just lifted a finger to get the girl's attention. "Ask Tensa if we can have a sampler - and plenty of coffee, if you would?"

"Yes, Kaisae," she agreed, her eyes flicking across them. "Three humans?"

"Yep," Zep assured her. "I actually like the iliri food now that it comes on four legs instead of two."

"Yeah," Dom drawled, "which brings me to my next point. Now that you don't have access to fresh human meat, how are the iliri dealing with the mineral problems?"

"It's called a kraug," Sal told him. "The nuvani told us about them. Evidently, it's some kind of warm-blooded lizard-thing. They thrive on the upper peaks of the Ahnian Ridge, usually on cliffs, which make them hard to hunt. Well, unless someone is a fetcher. Considering the grauori prefer the taste of deer in most cases, they tend to sell the meat to us. Kraug are also high in iron and calcium from the rocks that are a part of their diet. Professor Doyin seems to think that they're native to this world, like the grauori."

Dom pointed at the meal board. "And which one is that? I know most words, but a few up there are new."

"Green swirls," Sal told him. "Kraug roast with caramelized apples. Most of our humans like it."

"I'll have it put on the sampler," Lyzzi assured him. "It'll be out in a minute."

She backed away just like the perfect waitress. Sal's mates were smiling at the kid, but Dom just shook his head. "I'm really not used to kids working like that."

"Farms," Zep pointed out. "Most shops. Pretty much everyone without a title to their name has to have the kids start working early to pay the bills. It seems odd, Dom, because you were raised with privilege. So was I, so I understand. Still, Lyzzi's happy with it, and I'd rather she knew what it was like to work hard than to end up leading an entire species as a spoiled and pampered brat who thinks everything should be given to her. We already saw how that worked with the Emperor."

"And didn't work with me," Dom reminded him. Then he waved it off. "Your kid, your pack, your city, your rules. But I think that proves my point. There are so many cultural differences, and this integration isn't going as smoothly as we'd hoped." He patted the stack of papers he'd brought with him. "I've got reports in here of domestic abuse because an iliri man bit his iliri mate. Grauori are poaching from farms because they always have before. Humans are pissed about monsters wanting to own houses. All sorts of things, and I have no idea how to make this work, let alone handle it before the ambassadors get here."

Sal pulled the stack toward her and began to look through it. Page after page, it was nothing but police and military reports of infractions. Some were minor. Others were serious. Just like all crimes, they ran the gamut, but the problem was that so many were between species. For the soldiers who'd served together in war, the integration was easier. Most of the civilians - of all three species - felt like they were being forced out of their comfort zone, and there was friction.

"First," she said, "we won't be able to solve this *before* the ambassadors get here, but there's a chance we can have a solution in place and working. To do that, we need something to unite them." Sal paused, nodding to herself as she thought. "Some situation they can all celebrate together, to figure out that we do share a few things. It's still early, so there shouldn't be the centuries of hate to overcome, but that doesn't mean I want to ignore it."

"Ok, what?" Dom asked. "And I'm pretty sure that one event won't solve the nation's growing pains."

"It won't," Sal agreed, "but it's a start. I dunno, maybe an awards ceremony for the heroes of the Terran War? I also think we should assign a trio of Peacekeepers to each town. Like an oversight committee for the police. A group that can work together to find a culturally sensitive solution when things get complicated."

"Ok." Dom gestured around Tensa's. "You honestly think these people will leave their home to take this on?"

It was Jase who answered. "If their Kaisae asks, they will. They are na scared of moving. They simply do na wanna be slaves again. Making them powerful? I am more worried that they will take it too far."

"The grauori may be harder," Sal said, mostly to herself. "Most of the ones who'd want something like this are the brerror. Rragri shouldn't mind them having a purpose, though. I'll talk to her about it when I mention the situation with Nya." She jerked her chin at Dom. "What about your humans?"

"Would the military be ok? Because I've got a lot of soldiers with no other assignments." He shrugged. "I'm just not sure if that would look like a problem."

"Make it a side promotion," Sal decided. "Military-organized, but civilian duties. Something between the police and a soldier, and an opportunity for those who want to transition out."

"Done," Dom said. "But I want a trio to head up the whole thing. Stationed in Dorton, I think. Since that's where the two of us are, and Rragri can move fast enough to make it feel close. But by my calculations, we need at least twenty-one triads."

Tyr tapped the table. "I'm thinking you need to start hiring, then. Because it's not just twenty-one people, but also matching those people to others who will complement them."

"I recommend Ryali," Zep said. "But she'll need a gentle human to work with or she'll close up."

Dom nodded, his eyes unfocused like he was thinking hard. "So, what if we pair her with that old guardsman she's so fond of - Henrik? I think that's his name. Then we can ask Rragri for a grauori to join them. Might even keep them here instead, if you're ok with that, Sal?"

"I am," Sal assured him. "But I think they should have their own offices and be separate from our chain of command to an extent. That'll prevent problems in future generations."

"Done," Dom said again, but this time he was smiling. "We just need a few grauori." And he leaned his head back to groan. "There are millions of them, but they're all focused on these pups. It's like the entire species has gone into hiding again, waiting to see what's going to happen."

"So we need a reason to pull them out," Sal said. "Something big. Something that can cover up the minor scuffles between species, because that's all this is, Dom. These reports? They aren't hate crimes -

for the most part. They're misunderstandings, confusion, and tension. It's a bunch of people with an economy that's booming, free time they can actually afford, and not enough options for relaxation. They don't know they should hate each other, so it's not ingrained in the population to do so. They're just confused, so right now, we need distractions. I know we missed the Spring Ball, but isn't there something else Anglia does at the end of summer?"

"We have harvest celebrations in the fall," Dom said, but then he paused. Like an iliri, the man's head tilted slightly while his eyes shifted to the wall. Slowly, a smile began to grow on his lips. "What about a wedding?"

"What?" Kolt asked. "Who?"

"Me," Dom said. "It would be a state wedding, and a *very* big affair. The kind of thing that every city in the country will celebrate. It always is when a sitting king takes a bride, but it hasn't happened in a very long time. My grandfather, his father, and his father's father were already married when they were crowned. The last time this happened, it was basically a national holiday. We're talking a multi-day thing. Not the actual wedding, but the events leading up to it."

Sal was shaking her head. "You do *not* want to marry Rayna for some political stunt. Trust me on that. She will not go for it."

"No!" he insisted. "I *want* to marry her. I also need a political stunt. I've been getting some crap from the nobles because an acknowledged queen means a direct line of succession. Her kids would be my heirs, and everyone knows she's fucking Shift. All they can see is the chance of Shift's kid being recognized as mine and inheriting the crown. I've told them she can't have kids, but they always say there's a chance, and I didn't want to have the fight about it. Rayna doesn't need her choices dragged out like that, but I will if I have to. If this can bring Anglia together, I'll force the issue."

"What will Rayna say?" Sal asked him.

Dom began to smile. "Well, I kinda think I should ask her first, huh? And not just her, Sal. If I'm getting married, then I'm doing it the right way. I'm marrying my Queen and her Consort."

"Which," Blaz said softly, "is just one more way of proving that the species can work together, but we'll all need to make compromises to our traditions."

"Exactly," Dom agreed. But he paused to laugh like he'd just thought of something. "I'm going to get married."

"To a man," Tyr pointed out.

"And a woman," Dom reminded him. "And my heir's about to have some half-grauori kids. Huh. I think this is *exactly* what we need."

He pushed his chair back, but Jase grabbed it, stopping him. "Eat first. Then ya can run off in yer daydream. But ya had better plan on making it a big thing."

"Very big," Zep agreed. "A Kaisae as the maid of honor kinda big."

"An Orassae as family kinda big," Kolt pointed out.

Dom was nodding his head with gusto. "The kind of thing that can bring three species together kinda big. Yeah. Fuck. I need to find rings! I don't even know what size Shift wears. Or Rayna!"

Gage just chuckled. "Yep, I'll get Shift's size for you. Tyr, you want to ask Pig about Rayna?"

"Size seven," Tyr said without needing to think. "Yeah, she's mentioned it a time or two."

Sal just leaned over and hugged the King from the side. "Congratulations, Dom. Welcome to the family."

His eyes got wide. "Oh, fuck. I didn't even think about *that* either..."

Blaz was sitting across from him, grinning. "And now, I think you see why the nobles weren't thrilled. You should do it, though. I think you *want* to, and that's pretty much all that matters, right?"

"Yeah, I'm doing this," Dom assured them all. "I've wanted to for a while, so yes. We are definitely *doing* this. We're going to have the wedding of the century, and right when all her friends will be here."

"Is it too early for champagne?" Sal teased.

"Not for coffee," Dom assured her, "And yeah, I'll fucking drink a cup to this!"

CHAPTER THREE

WHITE

*D*om didn't know why he hadn't thought about it before. Marrying his "mates" was the perfect solution to this. It would also tie all three nations of Anglia together. Well, it could. If Jarl was accepted as the extended family of the Black Blades, that gave the Prince a tie to the iliri as well. He'd end up wearing the human crown of Anglia. His children were half-grauori. In other words, this solved *all* their problems.

Because Sal had grauori children herself, and Roo had just given birth to a couple more - a pair of aufrio boys this time. Sal was mated to a few humans, and she was iliri. Rragri had the least ties, but it could still work. Her daughter was mated to a human who'd end up from an iliri pack. That counted, right?

The only problem was that it also meant restructuring their government a little, but he could live with that. The original idea had been to give each species autonomy, but none of them had expected things to end up as they had. No longer were they three different people, and their government should reflect that. Besides, no one really understood it yet, anyway.

He spent the rest of the morning with Sal and her mates, working out plans for the Peacekeepers. They'd discussed the idea back when they were heading into Terric, but it had never truly been activated. Since the army had returned, most of their time had been spent cleaning up the messes from the last year. Everything seemed ok, at least in the Dorton Palace. Things like certifying the laws Cillian Tor had written in Dom's absence had taken precedence.

Then Vanja heard about an iliri man in jail for biting his wife. The Verdant Shield immediately knew an iliri male would most likely be mated to a woman with more iliri - or nuvani - ancestry. The men tended to be drawn to women with more purity. That meant the woman would've most likely been into it. He'd brought it to Ilija, who'd learned that the neighbor had turned the iliri in for abuse. From there, the Shields had started digging.

Dozens of minor problems. A handful of major crimes. This wasn't a riot or a full-blown revolt, but it *was* a problem, and one the leaders needed to deal with. The moment Dom had learned about it, he'd packed up his guards and headed west to Arhhawen. Now, he was headed back, leaving most of the heavy lifting to Sal. She'd insisted, claiming he had a wedding to worry about. The problem was how to tell Ilija, so Dom decided to ease into it.

They were barely out of the Arhhawen courtyard before he had to try. The Verdant Shields all rode beside him, not caring about formation. The horses were used to this, and Dom had given up worrying about acting proper somewhere between Myrosica and Unav. These men were his own version of family. Unfortunately, that actually made him more nervous instead of less.

"So," he said, looking at his unit, "what did you all do while I was with Sal?"

Ilija chuckled, jerking his thumb back to Ricown. "Well, he vanished for an hour. Vanja and Dag looked over the new stable. The rest of us went to check out the school."

"Why?" Dom asked.

Ilija looked at the King as if he were an idiot. "Because I have two more kids who need a proper education?"

"I just wanted to see the books," Vanja admitted. "That one professor, the old guy?"

"The one with the teeth!" Danku said, proving he knew exactly who Vanja meant. "Molis is his name."

"Yeah, him!" Vanja snapped and pointed, proving that was who he meant. "Well, Molis has an entire library of the things, and Marin's helping to make copies of them. They're making a machine to reproduce them. It's pretty impressive."

"Nice," Dom said.

Ilija gave him a strange look. "You ok?"

"Yeah," Dom assured him. "Um... I mean, I hope so."

That had all of the guys' attention. "What's going on?" Ricown asked, nudging his horse forward.

Dom waved them all down. "So, Sal thinks we need an inter-species celebration. Something to help bring all three nations together and remind them of our bonds. Considering that we're about to be the host of the allied nations for a signing of a new set of international Conventions? Um, well, it seems like a good time, to um..." He blew out a breath, forcing his nerves to go with it. "I want to ask Ray and Shift to marry me."

"*And* Shift?" Tebio asked.

Dom nodded. "One relationship, so I think that's the best way to do it. I figure I can be the King, Rayna the Queen, and Shift can become the Consort."

"Yeah," Ilija drawled, "but if you call him your husband, everyone's going to assume you're fucking him."

Dom just leaned his head back, closed his eyes, and groaned. "Does it matter?"

"Uh..." Ilija just shook his head, clearly having nothing.

"It shouldn't," Ricown said. "And if the King can do it, then the iliri can as well. And if they can, then humans can, and we all know there are some humans who like their own gender."

"Perin," Dag mumbled under his breath.

"See!" Ricown said. "Tilso's another. I mean, he's a Blade, but human. Anyway, it's a good precedent."

"And I don't care," Dom decided. "What are they going to say? That I'm weak? That I'm too feminine to wear the crown? I don't see that happening."

"That Rayna's a man?" Ilija countered.

Dom blew that off. "And it still doesn't matter. Never mind that she might flash them to prove it, but still. She won't have children. Jarl's my heir. The succession is safe, so why shouldn't I do this? It solves our current cultural problem - or at least helps - and it gives me what I want. I won't have to hide that my iliri ambassador is spending most nights in my bed with his dick in my Consort."

Vanja huffed, proving he saw a problem. "They'll call her a slut."

"So?" Dom asked. "If it was anyone else, I could see your point, but Ray? She won't care. She'll even throw it back in their faces! If anything, she'll use it as a reason to point out that women can do the exact same thing as men, and we need that right about now."

"Ok," Ilija said, all but putting an end to the arguments the men were trying to make. "That just leaves one more question for you, then."

"What's that?" Dom asked.

The Colonel smiled. "When are we getting rings?"

"Yeah," Dom said, dragging the word out. "Now? I just have no idea what to get for a guy I'm *not* sleeping with, to ask him to marry me. Rayna? Well, I wanted to give her my mother's ring. It's simple enough for her. Since my father was a bastard, he couldn't really afford fancy gems, and she won't want them. Kayden?"

"*That* is Shift's name?" Vanja asked.

Dom shot him a disgusted look. "Yeah. Did you expect something else?"

"More weird letters, actually." The man grinned, making it clear he was mostly joking. "So I guess this means we should get used to him having a real name, though, and not just a call sign?"

"Probably," Tebio said. "Since Consort Shift wouldn't fly."

"Kayden Savis," Dom told them. "That's his name. So, I guess it would be Consort Savis?"

"Jens," Ilija pointed out. "Consort Kayden Jens, co-husband of the King of Anglia."

Dom was shocked enough to rein his horse to a halt. "What?"

"You're the King, Dom." Ilija shrugged. "If he's marrying you, and the three of you are a family, human customs dictate that they take your surname. Rayna Jens and Kayden Jens."

"But..." Dom was shaking his head. "He's got his own line. Men don't change their name."

"And grauori don't use last names." Ilija shrugged. "Jarl's kids still need to be Vayu to prove legitimacy. It's actually one of the laws, so if you want this to happen, there's nothing saying you can't marry a man. The only restriction, actually, is that you can't marry more than one woman. But your legal spouse, post-matrimony, must bear your surname. So you might want to let him know before he agrees."

"Fuck," Dom grumbled, squeezing his horse back into a walk. "I need a fucking ring for a man, a ring for a woman, *and* to convince both of them to change their name? How the *fuck* did Anglia end up so backward for so long?!"

Ricown just pointed to the mountains beside them. "We hid in the middle of those. Our country has enough resources to be self-sufficient, so we didn't need trade alliances like Myrosica or the Conglomerate. Unlike Unav, we didn't have other nations crossing through our country to get from one place to another. So, yeah, that's how."

"Help me?" Dom begged, looking back at the men he'd served with for so long. "I mean, what kind of ring would you guys want?"

"Something simple," Caein suggested.

"Maybe green?" Dag offered.

"No," Ilija said. "Shift's iliri. Green means life. It should be white for love."

"Rayna's should," Caein countered. "Shift? Green for life, since he's a healer. Black for the Blades. Silver for ayati. Blue for faith, if that matters in your relationship. Pink's out because that means fear. Red is anger, orange is joy, cyan is knowledge, and purple is hope."

"Black," Dom decided. "With an inscription in white and accents in green." He was nodding to himself. "It's even something I know how to write in Iliran without asking."

"What's that?" Ilija asked.

"Il bax genause," Dom said. "He matters, so his ring should say it. Rayna? Well, my mother's ring has an inset sphere of steel, set in white resin, so that works. Love and fate." He scrubbed at his mouth, thinking about it a little too hard. "That will work, right?"

"You want me to get the Consort's ring made when we get into town?" Ilija asked.

"How long will it take, do you think?" Dom asked.

"With enough money?" Ilija shrugged. "We should have it by tonight. Why? What are you planning?"

"Then I'm proposing tonight," Dom decided. "Every day means more time to prepare, and I want to do this while everyone's here. Guys, this is a state wedding. It's going to be a very big deal, and I want to make sure it's open to everyone. All the average citizens who want to watch, not just the nobles and ambassadors of foreign nations. I want this to be the kind of thing that our citizens can see and realize that it *is* ok. That Anglia is still Anglia, only better."

Ilija reached across the space between their horses and clasped Dom's shoulder. "It'll be perfect. Don't worry about that. And, so you know, the Shields are throwing you and Shift a bachelor party."

"And what does Rayna get?" Dom asked.

"That's up to Sal," Ilija assured him. "Let the women make a big deal out of her side of things, we'll let the guys do their own thing."

"In town," Vanja said. "Like commoners, Dom. We'll take the two of you to a pub, and fuck if anyone will get their hands on you."

"But," Caein pointed out, "that will bring it a lot closer to the commoners if that's really what you want."

Ricown added, "It will also be closer to what Shift would expect. Not that he's going to expect a *wedding*, but he's not noble, and the formal feasts won't be his idea of a good time."

"Not mine either," Dom promised.

For a while, that seemed to be the end of it. The Shields rode almost a kilometer in silence, but from the grins and glances, Dom knew the guys were trading thoughts and making plans. Thankfully, not a single one was trying to tell him that he couldn't do this. Sure, they'd listed the things he needed to think about, and the potential roadblocks he'd come across, but that was more like preparing for battle. Not once had they ever made him feel foolish for wanting to not only get married but also include a third person in his vows.

Which meant that this could work. If men who'd been born and raised in Anglia could accept the idea without disgust, then everyone else would learn to accept it eventually. Oh, not at first, and yes, there would be plenty who assumed the King was less of a man because of it, but that was ok. It was the price of leadership, and he wouldn't correct them. Shift could. If he wanted to make it clear that he was only interested in women, then Dom wouldn't stop him.

But if Dom publicly declared his affection for another man, then Perin would be a little safer in Dorton when he came to visit. And Tilso wouldn't need to change how he acted in public. If the King could do it, then every other man - or woman - in Anglia who loved someone that others thought they shouldn't could finally admit it. Didn't matter if that was a group relationship, their own gender, or even another species.

Because the lines had to blur eventually, and it would take a strong person to deal with the backlash. Dom knew he could, and he was convinced that Rayna would take this as a personal challenge. But Shift? Marriage wasn't something they'd discussed. Dom and Shift shared a woman. They shared a bed. They shared secrets. Yeah, Dom was fond of the man, but was love the right word for it? Would Shift be ok with this? Was Dom going too far?

Which all came down to one thing. With his eyes locked on his horse's neck, Dom said softly, "I'm so nervous."

"Why?" Tebio asked.

"What if he says no?"

The men all laughed, but it was the gentle kind, as if he'd just told a joke. Ilija gently rubbed Dom's shoulder. "Then you ask him why not. And if he has a reason, you respect that, but I don't see it happening. Look, you three love each other." He lifted a hand before Dom could interrupt. "The same way that Sal's mates do. The same way I love you, Dom. As family. All this will do is let the world know that you're not hiding it. Tell him that, and I think you'll be fine."

"And what if I'm not?" Dom insisted. "What if Rayna says no? I mean, she's never really been the kind to care about such things. What if she's against it? Thinks being a wife will take away her autonomy or something?"

Vanja answered before anyone else could. "Tell them you want to spend the rest of your life with them and share everything, including running this crazy-ass country we're making, and I have a feeling they'll be down for it."

"So why am I so fucking nervous?" Dom insisted. "I followed Sal into the Emperor's palace and wasn't this scared."

"Yeah, but this time the Kaisae's not planning it," Vanja pointed out. "But we got your back, man."

"No fancy speeches," Danku suggested. "Just ask. I mean, get down on a knee, but just lay it all out there."

"And at the same time," Caein told him. "So one doesn't feel like they have to wait for the other to answer."

"Not in food," Dag said. "Someone would choke on a ring."

And the rest of the way home, the guys kept offering pointers. Things from the obvious to the downright absurd. The best part, though, was that it really did help. The Verdant Shields had a plan, and this was going to happen. His men had his back, so he could do this. He was actually going to get married to two people that he needed in his life. Two people who could help him rule Anglia the right way.

Two people he fucking loved.

CHAPTER FOUR

CYAN

That afternoon, Sal headed over to the school. The first students had started showing up earlier in the week, and dorms were being assigned. For now, the professors had limited enrollment to only younger students. According to Molis, the class was two-thirds iliri, with most of the rest being human, plus Rhyx and Raast. Yes, Roo had been adamant that the girls *needed* a real education.

But it was a long walk up the hill to the building. Gage and Tyr wanted to go with her, mostly because Tyr was still enjoying the new sensations of the cessivi bond. Gage had always dreamed of being a teacher, but the students were currently too young for what he knew best: organizational management. Jase and Zep had headed down to the stables to make sure there was plenty of space for the herd of horses the Blades wanted to breed and sell. Blaz and Kolt had offered to go through the tenant contracts for her, because peacetime didn't mean life was a complete vacation.

The school was set against the tallest peak in this section of the mountains. That kept it isolated enough for the instructors to monitor the kids, but also close enough in case there was ever an emergency. It also meant the view was amazing. A long and winding trail led from the main entrance of Arhhawen all the way up to the Iliri Academy of Studies, as it had been named. Halfway there, Sal paused to look back at her home.

Arhhawen wasn't overly impressive from the outside, but it still looked nice. The courtyard was secured behind a high stone wall. The gates leading into the mountain were gorgeous, and the inscription on them was beautiful. *"Home is where our differences make us the same, and strangers can become a pack. It is one thing that can never be stolen,"* it said. Dom had those words carved for her. His own promise that this could work. Then there were the creatures carved along the front facade. They were supposed to be grauori, but they looked scarier than any Sal had seen before.

The rest of the city was underground. Unlike Dorton, Sal's home was meant to be a vault, built like a fortress. She had theories about that, but nothing had been found to confirm it yet. Still, anyone foolish enough to kidnap multiple grauori females should expect their packs to fight to get them back. The irony was that Dom had given this place to Sal in case the iliri ever needed to block out the humans. He'd picked it so that she could be safe.

Which meant they'd come full circle. For a moment, she stared out at the expanse of amazingly blue sky, still finding it odd that there was no pattern weaving across it. Blaec had said he wanted to change the cycle. Instead, he'd destroyed it, but if she looked hard, she swore she could see something shimmering at the edge of her vision. It was faint, but if she had to describe it, she'd call it orange.

"Do you see anything?" Gage asked.

"A world willing to let us live in it," she said, turning to smile at him. "No pattern, though. I think he wiped the slate clean."

"Which means," Tyr said, reaching out to claim her hand, "this can be the age of the iliri, right? The grauori came first, then humans took over. Now, it's your turn."

"Our turn," Gage countered.

Tyr just shook his head. "I'm still human, man. Not even trying to deny it. Blaz and Zep can pretend they're something else, but I'm ok with what I am."

Sal ducked her head, but she couldn't hide the smile. "It means he gets to look in my eyes," she explained.

"Fuck," Gage teased. "Then I want to be human too."

And he caught her chin, lifting her face so he could meet her gaze. Sal noticed that one side of his mouth was curled partly up as if he was fighting his own smile, but she loved it. The truth was that she didn't mind her mates meeting her eyes. There was never any challenge there. Just love.

"Do that more often," she told him.

Then Tyr nudged her from behind, pushing her into Gage's chest. Together, they pinned her between them, and Sal felt their heartbeats quicken. Just as Gage leaned in to claim her lips, Tyr's hands landed on her waist, and he pressed his body against hers. A moment later, she felt his mouth teasing the back of her neck.

Sal slid an arm around Gage's shoulders, holding herself against him. The other one reached back, pulling Tyr closer. These two liked to work together. They played hot and cold with her, keeping her worked up throughout the day until she fell into bed with all of her mates at night, and she didn't mind at all. Sal gave herself to the kiss, but sucked in a breath when Tyr's mouth moved higher, vanished, and then his teeth grazed the edge of her ear.

Gage smiled against her lips. "School kids. Young ones."

She groaned. "And you started this."

"Technically," Tyr whispered against her ear, "I did. Sorry. I just can't resist."

Sal stole a quick kiss from Gage's lips, then pressed her forehead into his chest and sighed. "It'd be a shame to walk all the way up here and never see the students."

"Mhm," Tyr agreed.

"And," Gage added, "you wanted to talk to Inessi."

"I want," she told them both, "to strip you naked and have my way with you on iliri land."

Tyr's mouth was still by her ear. "Later," he whispered. "It's more fun when we aren't rushed."

Gage grunted and rolled his eyes, but that did it. The mood had lightened just enough for them to let go of her. Sal couldn't help but glance down, not surprised at all to see Gage's erection straining against his pants. So she turned to check Tyr, and he was no better. One little kiss was all it ever took to get these men worked up, and she loved it. She also knew that not all iliri had been raised to think that sex was normal. The more time they spent with humans, the more they'd been trained to deny the most basic aspects of life. To be ashamed or scandalized by it.

So Sal stepped backwards, aiming toward the entrance to the school. "Old human women," she teased them. "Zep's naked ass."

"Nope," Gage said, but he was grinning, aware that she was listing off things that should cool them down. "Sorry, but Zep's ass usually gets *you* excited."

"And... cessivi," Tyr finished.

"Children!" Sal said, and she could feel that was working, but not for the reason she wanted.

"You sure you're ok with this?" Gage asked. "I mean, if you aren't, you'd tell me, right?"

Tyr gave him a confused look. "You mean because she can't have kids?"

"Yeah," Gage said softly.

Sal lifted both hands to calm them. "I never thought I'd have kids of my own, so I'm fine. Having Lasryn is more than enough. And Valri? Rhyx and Raast? Never mind Lyzzi! Now we have Roo's new boys, Wrasau and Wyron - if Risk will let anyone else play with them."

"He will when they start walking," Gage pointed out. "But those pups are the only kids those men will ever get too, Sal. Be patient, you'll get to spoil the boys soon enough."

She chuckled, knowing it wouldn't be much longer before she would need her baby fix. "Look, my point is that I've got kids. *We* have kids, and there's no way Roo can keep up with four of them on her own."

"And Shade's already tried again," Gage said. "At least according to Ghost."

Tyr shrugged. "Keeya's due in a few months. Pretty sure she and Pig would love a little help."

"See?" Sal said. "Plenty of babies. Just means I get to send them home when I want to cuddle with you two." Then she glanced at Tyr. "Did Pig ever forgive her for not telling him until the trip home?"

"Oh, the trip home?" Tyr asked. "Nah, she waited until they got a room here. Like, she was about three months along, and he thought she had the flu. But yeah, he was upset she kept it from him until she pointed out that he never would've let her into the Terric City battle - let alone allowed her to climb that tower - and he knew she was right. Still, can you imagine?"

"Piglets," Gage teased.

Sal gasped. "You won't call it that!"

"Her, actually," Tyr said. "Healers say it's a girl, and Pig's calling her the Piglet. Poor thing. Worse is that Keeya thinks it's cute."

Sal paused, thinking about that for a moment. "Are they getting married?"

"Keeya wants to wait until after the baby is born so she can wear a pretty dress. Pig said they could do it twice. Once in private, and then again for her family. And yeah... Her parents are coming to Dorton for the Alliance meeting, apparently."

Sal groaned, having heard about Keeya's feelings for her parents. "So we need to make sure they can't give her a hard time." She waved the men to start walking again. "Would giving Pig a title help?"

"Maybe," Tyr said, "but what title could you give him?"

"Advisor to the Kaisae?" she suggested. "I mean, I do trust his opinion, and besides the six of you and Arctic, he's the man I go to."

"Actually..." Gage said. "That's not a bad idea. Name Arctic and Pig as your advisory council. Give them the title of advisor in Iliran or something."

"Arctic is the Raewar," Sal said, thinking about it. "Maybe we should call Pig our Kalargi?"

"Brother?" Tyr asked. "I'm translating that right?"

"You are," Sal assured him. "Because the Dogs are our brothers, aren't they?"

Gage fake-coughed, "Lover."

"*I* am her lover. The rest of them?" Tyr shook his head. "She's got six of us. I think they can find their own girlfriends."

Sal grinned, jogging the last few steps toward the Academy door. "I think Tyr's jealous!"

Then she opened it before he could reply. The man still groaned, but he and Gage followed her in. Their footsteps rang out on the stone floor, and the sounds of kids could be heard in the distance, but not close. Unlike Arhhawen, this building was only partially made of stone. The walls had been covered in plaster, giving it a warmer feel. Wooden arches were spaced along the outer walls, with thick glass windows set inside them. As they passed, Sal saw that time had warped the glass, making the view look slightly distorted, but she kinda liked it.

She was here to talk to Inessi, but when they passed a pair of doors, both thrown open, she stopped in her tracks. Inside, Molis and Marin were bent over something. It was a machine, but like nothing she'd ever seen before. Jars of colored ink sat below the table, with hoses leading from them up into the top of the contraption. There, six arms jutted out like a star, and the men were adjusting it, proving the whole thing spun around a central axis.

"Is it working?" she asked, daring to walk into the room.

The older iliri man looked up, smiling when he saw her, even though his eyes never lifted above her throat. "It seems ta be, Kaisae. Did ya wanna see?"

"He has your books," Marin mumbled, clearly having heard about Molis's old habit of yelling at Zep. But he also waved her and her mates in. "Kaisae. Cinnor. Kernor. I think we finally have the ability to print the textbooks."

"How?" she asked, heading closer to see.

"This," Marin said, "is based on screen printing. They use it for fabric. The guy I worked for used the idea to print the covers of the Empress's books, but it seems to do well enough for Iliran writing." He held up a finger, placed a large piece of paper on the table, and then spun the contraption to the third arm. "Each panel is for a specific color. There are six of them for each page, which means it's still tedious, but doesn't require the same skill as handwriting them." Then he pressed a button.

Bright red ink flowed through the tube, filling a tray on the arm. Then, a blade swiped that across and back. When Marin lifted it, parts of Iliran words were visible on the page. Without waiting, he turned it again and repeated the process. This time, the ink was blue. Then came yellow, black, brown, and finally white.

When the last screen had been used, Marin raised the contraption and showed Sal a single page, but it was colored perfectly. Yellow had been laid over blue to make green, mixed with red to make orange, the brown muted some of the vibrant shades, and the black and white altered the intensity. To her eye, it looked almost as good as any book in Jase's library.

"That's amazing!" she said.

Molis gestured around the room. "We can add more a these, and run up ta ten pages a day on each one, if we have the staff. The hard part is ta make the screens."

"But," Marin said, "after that's done, anyone can do this. The Professor said there are still iliri without jobs? Well, if we use the basement as a printing room, we can actually produce a complete book every day, but that would take a few hundred of them. Both the page inkers and the iliri to run them."

"Whoa," Gage breathed. "It usually takes months to copy a book, doesn't it?"

"Yeh," Molis said. "Sometimes years. Ta get it right, they can na be sloppy, and the colors bleed."

"So," Sal said, "does this mean you can reproduce your entire library?"

"It'd take years," Molis said. "Decades, prolly, but yeh. And yer Ahnor has a book I do na. The one I sold ta yer Dernor fer him. Green, about a Kaisae."

Tyr was nodding. "I know the one. He has it in our suite, and the man is careful with it."

"I'm sure he'd let you copy it," Sal told Molis.

The old man grabbed a rag and wiped off his hands as he moved around the table. "There is also one I want ta write by hand, if ya will let me?"

"Ok?" Sal shook her head, not quite following.

"Yers," he told her. "The History of Salryc Luxx. Ya are the only Kaisae ta survive, and ya did na follow the rules, but I can na write it unless ya can tell me what has happened in yer life." He paused. "In all yer life. Fer history."

She let out a heavy breath. "All my life?"

"Sal," Tyr said softly, pressing his hand against her back, "you need to do it. From your earliest memory until now. Record it all, because in a hundred years, they won't understand what we fought for. We need to make sure that this doesn't happen again."

She nodded. "On one condition?"

"Anythan," Molis swore.

"You let Marin make a copy in Glish."

"But ya are ours!" Molis snarled.

Marin chuckled, not even flinching from the surly little man. "She's ours too, Professor. I'm a human of the iliri nation, and the King? She's kinda his too. The grauori speak Iliran, but not all humans do. Sal's the Kaisae of *All* Anglia, remember?"

"And not even all iliri read Iliran," Sal pointed out.

"Will ya write it right?" Molis asked his assistant. "Ya will na make her sound like a beast?"

Marin smiled at him. "Sir, I assure you that I have nothing but respect for *our* Kaisae. If I ever make her sound like a beast, it will be because there is no other way to describe the complete horror of being on the wrong side of her war."

Molis's mouth fell open, and he blinked at Marin for a moment before looking over at Gage, and then Tyr. "Yer mates. Yer friends. Do ya think they would help? Could I talk ta them about how they saw it all?" He stabbed a finger toward Tyr. "The man that fueled yer view of ayati." Then Gage. "The one that organized it all. Do ya mind? It is history, and it should na be fergotten."

Sal nodded at him, but it felt strange. The whole idea of her life being dissected and recorded like this? She didn't feel like she deserved it, and yet she knew Molis was right. How many things had Jase found from the other Kaisaes? Besides, she'd always known that there would be a book eventually; she'd just assumed she'd die before it was written.

"I actually think I'd feel better if you talked to them, so I'm not telling the story wrong," she decided. "So there's more than one opinion in there."

"And," Gage added, "I'm sure the King would *love* to be a part of this."

"A human..." Molis breathed. "There is na a Kaisae who had her story told by humans." Then he waved that off. "There is na a Kaisae like ya in history. Yes, I think that is perfect."

"Just tell me when," Sal assured him. "And, if you could direct me to where Inessi is hiding?"

Marin pointed to the right while Molis answered, "The office. She's assigning kids ta rooms, and there are lots a them."

Sal stepped back with a smile. "Which makes it sound like the school is already a success. Enjoy your books, Professor."

The man was already back at work, but she saw the smile. He was perfectly happy with this new life. For once, his love of books was treated with respect, and Sal couldn't be the only person who thought that felt really good.

CHAPTER FIVE

GREEN

*T*he group headed deeper into the building, and the sounds from the kids grew louder. Finally, they turned the last corner and saw the lines disappearing into a set of doorways. Boys were on one side, girls on the other. Most of them looked to be only a few years younger than Lyzzi. Closer to Lasryn's age, if Sal had to guess.

Tyr grabbed Sal's hand. "That's a lot of kids," he whispered.

Gage smacked his shoulder. "They aren't contagious."

Sal just giggled and kept walking. She also refused to let go of Tyr's hand, hauling him along behind her as they squeezed past the youngsters, through the doors, and into the office. Most of the children made room for the adults. The human ones all looked at her with wide eyes, as if shocked to see someone they recognized. The iliri simply whispered the words of respect like they'd been taught.

But when Sal was inside the office, it was even more crowded. On the far side of the room was a dark wood counter, and the professors were lined up behind it. She saw Ashir Doyin, the professor who'd scoured the records in the Arhhawen basement. Inessi was in the center. On her other side was Narnx, of all people. Oddly, he looked like he was in his element.

"Sal," he greeted her.

"Hey," she said, weaving through a few more kids to get closer. "What are you teaching?"

"History, actually." He looked proud.

Behind Sal, a kid grumbled, "That's the Emperor of Terric."

Another, most likely his friend, said, "Yeah. He's the reason my dava died."

"No," she said, turning around to see them. Her eyes landed on a pair of iliri boys, crossbreds who looked to be around ten years old. "Narnx is a Black Blade, my brother, and the man who risked his life to *stop* this war. He only took the title of Emperor because I *asked* him to. And if you're lucky, he'll explain why in his class."

A woman's chuckle made Sal look back at the teachers behind the desk. It came from Inessi, Jase's amma, and she was smiling proudly at Sal. "Ya know that will na stop them, so why do ya try? Kids will be kids."

"And heroes should be respected," Sal told her. "But I actually came to see you, Amma."

Inessi smiled brightly at being called Sal's mother. "But ya did na bring my boy?"

It was Gage who answered. "He's making sure the stables are ready for the horses from Dorton. With the allies coming in, Dom's going to need more room, and Tilso says we have bred mares, so we want to move them before they're too heavy to make the climb up the mountain."

She nodded, then waved them to a half door at the side of the counter. "Come. I think these two can handle check-in fer a few minutes."

Which explained the lines. In truth, Sal had no idea how the school was being run, just that it was handled. Slipping between a pair of children waiting their turn, she left her mates to follow or not, but she knew they would. Behind them, whispers were swelling, turning the line into a buzz of excitement and making Sal feel like a celebrity.

Once they were on the other side of the counter, Inessi led Sal's group further back, to a hall lined with offices. None of them were large, and most of them were still empty, but it was a start. The smell of freshly-cut wood proved that the construction was new, created simply to make the building useful as a school.

Inessi led them into the last door on the left, then turned to face Sal. "What do ya need, Kaisae?"

"Just Sal," she reminded Jase's mother. "And I actually want to pick your brain about iliri customs."

Inessi waved them to a set of chairs and then claimed the one behind a desk. "What custom?"

"Marriage," Sal explained, taking the seat in the middle. "I figure there has to be some tradition with the grauori at least. Something for when a child of one pack moves into another, or when two packs join together."

Inessi's eyes narrowed, but they were locked on Sal's jaw. "Is this fer yer Kernor?" She meant Tyr.

Sal shook her head. "For my brother, Shift. Dom wants to get married, but he wants to include Rayna's other mate in the bonding. Mostly because our country needs new traditions to bring the iliri and humans closer. With the grauori being so similar, and Jarl expecting half-grauori children soon, we think it will help ease some of the tensions."

"Or make them worse," Inessi pointed out. "Na a lot of people like change. Fer all we know, this could start a coup."

"I don't think so, though," Sal assured her. "I honestly believe that the problem is a lack of knowledge, not a lack of acceptance. The iliri were virtually unknown in Anglia until Jase and I came here. Now, there are thousands of us, and quite a few don't live in Arhhawen. Grauori are moving into towns, or simply traveling there for business - like selling game. I think it's culture shock, and seeing a king that they love accept this change can only help."

Inessi was nodding to prove she was listening. "Iliri do na marry. We could na fer so long. It has only been in the last hundred years or so that we were allowed ta be free in the Conglomerate. The nuvani may have a custom that works better, but the only thing I can think of is a binding of packs."

"And what does that entail?" Sal asked.

So Inessi began to describe it. The more she talked, the more Sal realized just how much the history of slavery had affected her people. There was no ceremony, simply an agreement that two distinct groups could come together as one. It had become the custom when slaves were sold in groups and needed to find a new leader once they'd been thrown together. Since fighting could damage the slaves, humans punished them for dominance challenges, so the iliri had found ways to be less obvious about it.

The problem was that it didn't quite fit what Sal needed. Dom wouldn't be giving her dominance over him, and she certainly wouldn't give him control of her people. That meant they'd need something else.

"Is there something for adopting a brother?" she asked.

And Inessi's face lit up. "Yeh. Just as ya adopted Ran ta be yer Sadava, there is a tradition of iliri making their own families. Na packs, because we were na allowed ta do that in public, but families. Often, the sisters - fer it was usually women - would blend their names inta one, taking their old last name as the middle. Humans do that, so it allowed us ta keep our lines."

"Ok," Sal said, thinking this was closer to what she wanted. "How is that done?"

Inessi glanced over at Tyr, then her eyes jumped to Gage. "They bite. It is an instinct. One we have na fought ta lose."

Which explained her mates biting each other. They claimed each other as brothers in a way that went beyond pack. Family. Co-mates. All of her men bore the scars of Jase's teeth on their shoulders, even Tyr. The problem was that Dom didn't have sharp enough teeth to leave a mark.

"So how do we make that work for a king?" Sal asked, looking at her men for help.

Tyr reached up to rub at his right shoulder, where Jase's teeth had scarred him. "Um, when I was a kid, some of the guys had a blood brother pact," he said. "Humans, you know. But we did it by cutting ourselves and then holding the wounds together. Usually a hand or the forearm. I don't think that cutting shoulders in a formal ceremony would work out very well."

"Wait," Gage said. "The point is to combine our cultures, right?"

Sal nodded. "That's what we're hoping for."

"So have Dom use a knife, Shift use his teeth, and clasp their different wounds together." He tapped the middle of his forearm. "Grab each other's elbows, and that should match, right? My life for yours type of thing, and both of them for Rayna."

"Do ya think the King would do it?" Inessi asked. "Is that na too bloody fer most humans?"

"Yeah," Sal agreed. "He's adamant that he wants to marry Shift as much as Rayna, because they are both mated to her, but that might upset the nobility. Can you do some research and find some words that they can add to a human wedding? Something for Dom's and Shift's bond, and then for Shift's and Rayna's?"

"I can," Inessi promised as a tap came at her door. "Come," she called out.

The door opened to reveal Ran, and his body tensed in surprise. "Sal?" he asked.

She couldn't help but notice a sweet scent coming from him. Not the typical smell of humans, but something more... floral. She flicked her ears forward and canted her head in an unspoken question. Ran's face began to get a little darker.

"Uh," he said, "I can come back later."

"You're not interrupting," Sal insisted, aware that he was trying to escape. "I was just asking for advice on how to get a king married to an iliri man and the woman they share. Have any ideas?" She curled a finger, beckoning him into the room.

Ran dropped his head and sighed. "Do not laugh at me," he grumbled.

Because when he pushed the door open enough to step through it, she could see he was holding a cluster of flowers in his other hand. Wild ones that he'd most likely picked on his way up from Arhhawen. Sal's eyes dropped to the bouquet, then back up to his face. The smell of embarrassment was pouring off him - which was rare for Ran. Then there was the smell of amusement from her mates, and something subtle from Inessi. Subtle enough that Sal had to breathe again to make sure it was really there.

"I, uh..." Ran lifted the flowers. "I thought these might brighten your new office," he explained.

Tyr snorted, clearly trying to stifle his laughter, and Ran shot a warning look at him. Gage, however, kept his face perfectly calm. Sal pushed her chair back and offered it to her father, but only because she saw something on one of the shelves. Making her way over, she claimed the piece of pottery, then brought it back to the edge of the desk.

"You'll need water to keep them alive, Amma, but they'll remind you of him each time you look. And they smell nice."

"But why flowers?" she asked.

It was Tyr who answered. "They're pretty. It's a human thing, and a compliment of sorts."

"A mating ritual," Gage told her.

And Ran sighed again, this time with a groan attached to it. "The three of you are not helping me at all."

"Dava," Sal said, moving to rub the shoulder closest to her, "if you've finally met someone worthy of chasing, then we all are happy for you. No need to smell like that."

"I was just being polite," he insisted.

Sal leaned closer to his ear, aware that Inessi would hear. "No, you weren't."

"And ya do na need ta," Inessi assured him. "But I will na have a male chase me. So, I will take ya fer lunch once the Kaisae is done and the kids are checked in." She looked over at Sal pointedly, clearly hoping the Kaisae would leave.

"Good luck," Sal told her dava before gesturing for her mates to get up. "Be gentle with him, Inessi. He's been alone for a long time, and he's still learning about our kind."

"He learns fast," Inessi promised. "But do na tell my son."

"No promises," Sal teased. "I can't exactly keep secrets from him." And she opened the door, leading her men out.

Gage was the last, closing it behind him. "Ran and Inessi?" he asked.

"It makes sense," Tyr said.

Both iliri looked at him in confusion.

"What?" he asked. "They've both been single for a *long* time. They both lost their mates to this war. They're both strong, both have children who are now grown - and mated - which makes it a little weird."

"Not that weird," Gage assured him. "Iliri can smell relations, which is how Sal knew she was Reko's sister."

"Ah." Tyr nodded at that. "Well, I hope she gives him a chance, because that was fucking cute."

"Yeah, it was," Sal agreed, just as she reached the main office again. "Hey, Narnx?"

"Yeah?" he asked.

"What age kids are you taking this year?"

"Up to twelve," he told her. "So Lyzzi is too old, sorry."

Sal shook her head, proving that wasn't why she was asking, and made her way to his side. "What do I need to do to get Lasryn on that list?"

"Kolt's kid?" He smiled. "Well, I'd need to have one of his parents sign the admission form." He reached to his side, grabbed a paper and pen, and set it on the counter before her. "Which means you."

"Yeah..." Sal breathed. "Hang on." And she reached out with her mind. *Kolt?*

Yeah, babe?

What do you think about sending Las to school this year?

What? Really? How often will I be able to see him? he asked.

"How often can parents visit?" Sal asked Narnx.

He shrugged. "Evenings after classes and the kids are allowed to leave campus on the weekends. Why?"

"Because his dava missed him. Kinda a lot." Holding up a finger, she told Kolt, *You can have dinner with him at the school every evening, and he can come home on the weekends. He'll also learn more from real teachers than we can ever teach him.*

Yeah, no, I agree. What do I need to do to get him in? Kolt asked.

Sal replied, *Well, I can just sign this paper in front of me, and we'll need to get him a room tomorrow, I think. I'll get all the details, but I wanted to make sure you were ok with it first.*

I am, Kolt assured her, *but thank you for asking. He's your kid too, Sal.*

And I didn't spend years wishing I could have more time with him. I just wasn't sure you were ready.

I'll never be ready for him to grow up, Kolt told her, *but I want what's best for him. So yeah. Maybe we can tell him tonight? Sounds like we're watching Valri, too. Joe's supposed to bring her over, since Ryali's being antisocial. I figured we could invite Lyzzi over and make a family thing of it.*

Sounds perfect, Sal agreed. *I'll be home soon.*

Then she grabbed the pen and scrawled her name on the page in Iliran, filling in all the details for the boy that she knew, which was most of it. She wasn't sure of his clothing size, though, yet when she slid it back to Narnx, he was impressed.

"If Kolt knows what he wears, that will help. Otherwise, we'll just make him try on a few uniforms until we find something that works. And he's an official Blade, right?"

"He is," Sal said.

Narnx scrawled at the bottom, "Black." Then he put the form on his other side. "We made adjustments so the kids can still show their family ties, even the humans." He looked at the next kid in line and waved him forward. "I'll be back in Arhhawen tonight if you both have any questions, but it would be best to get him signed in tomorrow or the next day."

"We'll make it happen," Sal promised. "Don't work too hard, brother."

"Never, Kaisae. And thank you for the chance."

As Sal and her mates left the school, she felt like she was living a dream. Even if Inessi's answer hadn't been exactly what she wanted, the school made up for it. An entire education system created for iliri, and a large amount of those human kids were girls. That meant women were finally getting the chance for their own equality.

In other words, Anglia was doing just fine. It might not be perfect, but their problems were manageable ones.

CHAPTER SIX

PURPLE

*W*hen they got back to Arhhawen, Sal headed to her office. She had hundreds of requests for land leases. So far, she'd been granting them to families who already lived there and until now had been under the territory of Dorton. That was the only problem with her new home. While being close to the King was good, it made splitting their land complicated. Then again, Dom said it was why the mountain city had been empty so long.

No other noble wanted to have control of an area that paid taxes to the King. Sal, however, wasn't a part of his "nation," so she could keep the taxes herself. The iliri didn't need much land outside the compound, but Dom had still given them a respectable chunk. Along with that came families who'd lived there for generations. Previously, they'd paid taxes to the King. Now, they paid them to Sal, but only if she agreed to let them stay, and she had.

But all the timber, rock, and other natural resources within her borders were also hers to sell off as she chose. Thankfully, Rragri had offered a little advice there. She'd warned Sal not to strip her land bare for a fast profit. Instead, Sal was planning for industries that would benefit the iliri as a whole. Mostly farming and ranching, because with all the iliri in Arhhawen, it meant they'd need a lot of food.

"What do we have?" she asked as she walked in.

Kolt looked up with a smile. "I've got seven more who can prove their families have been here for more than one generation," he said.

Blaz slapped his palm down on a stack of pages beside him. "These are offers you should consider." Then he pointed to another, much larger stack. "Those are ones to deny."

"Ok?" Sal moved toward her desk, taking a seat on the wrong side of it. "Do I need to do anything with them?"

Blaz shook his head. "If you have a stamp, I can deny them and send them back for you."

But Kolt was looking antsy in his chair. "So did they say anything?"

"About what?" she asked.

"Is Lasryn in? Are they really going to let him go to school?"

"He needs to show up tomorrow or the next day," Sal assured him. "But yes, he's in. They'll also make sure he can display his pack color."

Kolt sighed and leaned back, letting his head tilt toward the ceiling in relief. "Good. He's moved around so much as a child that he can't write Glish well at all, and the only history he knows is military."

"Inessi will be there to watch over him," Sal promised, "and we can visit him every evening."

He nodded. "I know you both think I'm crazy, but that's my only kid."

"We don't," Blaz assured him. "And he's a good boy. A bit cocky, but I think he gets that from his sire."

"Mm," Sal said, holding up her hand before Kolt could reply. "If we're doing a family dinner tonight, who's trying to cook?"

Kolt just pointed at Blaz. "He's the best."

"Fuck that," Blaz said. "Gage is better."

Then both of them looked at Sal. She just ducked her head and groaned. "The closest I ever got to a kitchen was washing the plates. They thought we'd steal meat, remember? And then I was in the military, which provided our meals. I have no clue how to cook."

"Maybe we can teach you?" Kolt asked.

"Please?" Sal asked. "Believe it or not, it's something I always wanted to try."

"Wait..." Blaz said. "I bet if we offer to watch the new pups, Roo will help. And Hwa can even steal a nap. Poor guy's gotta be exhausted with four kids now."

"Never mind that the girls are also leaving for school tomorrow," Kolt said. "So yeah. Let's make a night of it? Invite the whole pack if they want?"

"You," Sal said, pointing at Kolt, "invite them all. I need to get in touch with Rragri, and then we have the rest of the evening to ourselves."

"And me?" Blaz asked.

Sal pointed to her desk just in front of him. "In that drawer is a stamp. You can start denying all the applications you said wouldn't work, and send them back."

"Can do." But first, he stood and walked to a cabinet at the side.

Without asking, he poured a tall glass of mead, a small one of whiskey, and another of rum, then carried them all back. The mead went to Sal, the whiskey to Kolt, and Blaz kept the tumbler of rum for himself. When he sat back down, his eyes found Sal's, and he smiled. It was the most comfortable thing she could imagine, so she smiled back even as she reached out for the leader of the grauori with her mind.

Rragri? she asked. *Do you have a minute?*

I have a few, the Orassae assured her. *My daughter is no closer to birthing, and the healers say the pups are not ready.*

Human gestation is just under ten months, Sal reminded her. *Iliri is just over nine. Grauori tend to carry for only eight. It's not surprising that the babies are still forming. They're part human.*

But she's so large she waddles, Rragri replied. *She cannot care for herself now, and what will we do if the babies won't come out on their own?*

That's what I wanted to talk about, Sal soothed. *It's a common problem in human women. Their children sometimes don't turn the right way, or their heads are too large. So many reasons. Because of this, they have a surgical option. If the birth is complicated, they cut the children out, and a grauori healer could repair the wound.*

Grauori can't! Rragri sounded frantic. *Nya is my only child, Sal. Her twin was stillborn, and I've never had another litter. I can't lose her!*

Which explained the Orassae's panic. Rragri had suffered her own birthing complications and had lost a child because of it. Nya could've inherited the problem - or it could've been a fluke. There was no way to know, but it explained why the Orassae was frantic. Sal honestly couldn't blame her.

So bring her to Dorton, Sal suggested. *Let all of us help. Raast and Blaz have both offered. I talked to Dom this morning, and he said he'll bring in the best doctors in Anglia. Between all of us, we can take care of her. How far along is she now?*

Nearly nine months, Rragri said. *And how will she get there? Nya's too large to climb the mountains. Never mind that the father's there, and who knows how he'll react to these pups.*

Humans don't do that, Sal reminded her. *Jarl knows that they'll be different. We all do. Humans don't reject their pups, and they certainly don't kill them. At worst, they walk away.*

Rragri's response sounded almost hopeful. *Really?*

Honestly, Sal promised. *I'm not saying all humans are good fathers, but they do not have the same instincts we do. As for getting her here, why not use a carriage? There are passes, and if she doesn't need to walk, then it won't matter if the trip takes longer, right? I'll even send iliri to assist, so if there's a problem, my own people will protect her.*

No, Rragri said. *I will bring our packs. That will be enough. We'll still need to get her down from the cliffs. Our den is high enough that humans can't reach us. It's how we survived.*

What about soldiers? Sal offered. *Maybe one of the units you worked with?*

Dalyr, Rragri immediately said. *I do not mind him and his men knowing how to get into our home. He's grauori.*

Which was another thing Sal hadn't thought of. Dalyr Trant was still legally grauori, and he had no intention of changing that. The problem was that he and his wife - not to mention all of the men who served with him - couldn't live among the people they felt comfortable with. A grauori den was typically built into a cliff. The species had four hands for climbing, and they'd learned to use it to their advantage when humans began hunting them.

So I'll tell Dom to send him, Sal said, *but have you considered creating a place where your grauori humans can be comfortable with their adopted families?*

No... Rragri admitted. *Do you really think they'd want to? I always assumed that once the war was over, they would go back to being humans, but Dalyr still claims to be mine. He says his service isn't done.*

Bonds are formed through strife, Sal reminded her. *The man is proud to be grauori, so ask his opinion. If we want to live together as equals, we have to include those who can't scale a cliff.*

Like you have in that mountain? Rragri teased. *Although it seems to work.* And Sal could almost feel the woman relaxing. *I'll ask him. Tell him to send a carriage, and ask if he can come with it. I heard his own wife is expecting now.*

What is with all the pregnancies? Sal asked.

Rragri's amusement flowed across the link. *The war is over. The iliri are finally safe and well-fed. The grauori are no longer hunted. The humans were away from their mates for long enough that they needed to make up for it. There are always a lot of children after a war. I assumed that was why you built a school.*

I honestly didn't expect this many women to be pregnant at once, Sal told her. *Did you know Pig's mate, Keeya, is pregnant? Shade recently went through estrus again. Roo just had two boys.*

Nacione? Rragri asked, meaning solid white.

Aufrio, Sal told her. *Although it's a pale grey. Roo says she wants at least two more litters. I think she's planning to breed an entire pack herself.*

She impressed me, Rragri admitted. *As did her mate. I am glad you saw their worth.*

Mm, speaking of worth, Sal said, thinking about the Peacekeepers, *we need a few grauori volunteers, and I'd really like your recommendation for them. Do you remember how Ryali and the iliri women protected the human crown?*

I do.

Well, Sal continued, *Dom and I want to make a police force to protect the relations between our species, called Peacekeepers. I know we talked about this briefly, but it's been crazy since we got back. Representatives of all three species who can work together and are willing to spend time in the city they're assigned to. Our goal is to have them dismiss crimes that don't apply, such as an iliri male biting his wife - which had the guy charged with domestic abuse.*

I see. Rragri sounded like she was thinking. *What traits do you want in these Peacekeepers?*

Wisdom and calm minds, mostly, Sal told her. *Because they will see things that will upset them. I also need people who can work with the other species, and who may not be near their packs. My plan is to pair one human, one iliri, and one grauori together, and their decisions will basically determine which set of laws the accused will be tried under, or if there's even a crime at all. Hopefully, they can also help ease inter-species relations by acting as representatives of our kind in places that haven't seen much of us.*

But they will not have a pack, Rragri repeated. *I do not know the brerror well enough to recommend most of them, but how many do you need?*

Ideally, twenty-two, Sal told her. *One of those will work with Ryali and Henrik here in Dorton. They will have the final decision over the others, like a commanding officer.*

I know the perfect male for that, Rragri said. *And I will bring along thirty others, so we have options. They shall serve as my daughter's guard on the way there, so if any humans think to hunt us for our hides, they will not get close to her.*

And you'll have Dalyr, Sal reminded her. *I'm sure Jarl will be thrilled to hear Nya's coming. Dom said the boy's beside himself with worry for her. He's excited about the kids, too.*

Those two aren't more than pups themselves, Rragri grumbled.

Which is why they have us to help them get this right. Sal chuckled, knowing Rragri would feel it. *Those children - whatever they end up being - are going to be spoiled. They're basically the tie that binds Anglia together.*

But we cannot spoil them too much, Rragri reminded her. *They will not live long if they are too soft to hunt for themselves, or too arrogant to listen to advice. But...* She paused, cutting off the thought.

What? Sal asked.

I hope they are iliri, Rragri told her. *This may be rude, but I like the idea that if you cannot have children, then maybe my daughter can help your species recover from what the Emperor did. It feels like it helps us repay our debt for allowing you to be kept as slaves for so long.*

There is no debt, Sal assured her.

There is, Rragri countered. *We knew about the nuvani. We'd heard about iliri, but we did nothing. We left you to fight for yourselves, but you are our cousins. We should've done more.*

And the humans would've killed you for it, Sal told her. *Ayati needed more time for the pattern to be complete.*

Yes, Rragri said, *but now ayati is gone. It is just us, trying to do our best without any idea of what the future holds, or which choices to make.*

Kinda like the humans, Sal reminded her.

And an entire group of people whose abilities are no longer useful? It just feels like there's got to be something we're still missing. Why would we have prophets who can't see the future? What good is that skill if there is no pattern to see?

I think we need to make one, Sal told her. *It's just this feeling I have, but Blaec kept saying that he wanted to change the pattern, to end that cycle. I can't help but think that means there will be another, but we have to make it.*

How? Rragri asked.

I have no idea, Sal told her, *but maybe we can make this one peaceful?*

I hope so, the Orassae thought. *I honestly like this peace thing. I like feeling safe when we leave the den. I would love for this to be what my grandchildren know for the rest of their lives.*

Me too, Sal agreed. *So how about we start with getting Nya to Dorton. I'll let you know when I have Dalyr and a carriage headed to you, if that works?*

It works, and I will pick thirty grauori who I trust to represent our species. Tell the King we are coming.

In time for his wedding? Sal asked.

Rragri paused for a little too long. *He is getting married?*

I hope so. He plans to propose to both Shift and Rayna tonight. A ceremony to bind our species together, with the hope that Jarl will bind the grauori with these kids. Human, iliri, and grauori, and we'll all be publicly joined as equals.

Then I will be there for the wedding, she promised. *Even if I have to chase the horses to make them run fast enough. We will definitely be there.*

CHAPTER SEVEN

ORANGE

*I*t didn't take long to finish up the applications for land leases, and in truth, Sal was getting excited about the Blades spending an evening together. It had been too long. While they lived close, it still felt different not having her brothers in her back pocket all the time. Giving up on being responsible, she called it a day just as the sun started to set.

The three of them - Sal, Blaz, and Kolt - walked into their suite to an absurdly high-pitched squeal, followed by the sound of men laughing. A couple more steps and she understood why. Valri was chasing Lasryn around the main room with a toy dagger. The thing was made of cloth and stuffed with wool, but that little girl loved it, and Las was always willing to be her villain.

Zep, Jase, and Gage all sat on the floor, doing their best to make her life a little harder. They attacked like grauori, tackled her like humans, and anything it took to gang up on her. The whole thing was just cute. Jase was a natural father, making his play into a lesson for the kids. Zep went the other way, always making time to spoil them and show the kids how much they were loved. It was Gage who surprised her. The man was a mush with Valri, but always treated Lasryn like a young man, even though the boy wasn't even eight.

Sal was spotted quickly. "Amma!" Valri squealed, forgetting all about Las as she rushed toward Sal.

"Hey, kid," Sal crooned, bending down to scoop the toddler up. "Where's your dam?"

"Gone," Valri said.

Zep huffed at that. "Ryali and Joe asked if she could spend the night. Seems there's a rumor going around about a family dinner, so Joe thought that maybe he could show Ryali what a real date is like."

Sal grinned at that. "So you're spending the night with us, sweetie?"

Valri just nodded her head emphatically. "Mhm!"

"I can share my bed with her," Lasryn offered.

"Uh..." Kolt made his way over to one of the couches. "Actually, I kinda wanted to talk to you about something."

"Dad, she's a baby," Las shot back.

Kolt glanced at Valri quickly, shook his head, then back to his son. "No, I mean about school. Sal got you enrolled."

Surprise took over the boy's face. "I get to go to school?"

"Is that what you want?" Kolt asked him.

Las nodded quickly. "Yeah. I mean, everyone wants to. They say we're going to take classes with the Emperor, and that Kauvwae Inessi will be teaching us proper Iliran, and that Professor Doyin teaches the same kind of sciences that humans get!"

"Not quite the same," Sal told him. "He's one of the top scholars on the formation of iliri. What little we know, so it's more like cutting edge science that most humans can't get."

"See!" Las said, waving his hand at Sal. "And all my friends are going, but I didn't think you'd let me."

"Why didn't you ask?" Kolt wanted to know.

Las let out a heavy sigh and flopped onto the seat across from Kolt. It was on the other side of the room, but placed so they could see each other. Still holding Valri, Sal moved beside Kolt, and Zep scooted over to lean against the couch beside her legs. Seeing this was going to be a real discussion, both Jase and Blaz claimed a spot as well, and all eyes were on Lasryn.

"I didn't want you to think that I wasn't happy to see you, ok? I mean, you all just got back from the war," Las told them, looking from one adult to the other. "But while you were all fighting, I made friends here, and they're all going to school."

Kolt leaned over his knees. "Well, I happen to think that school is important, and I'd prefer it if you didn't have to pretend to be a human to get an education."

"Is that what you did, Dava?"

Kolt nodded. "My own amma taught me how to fake it, and since I have dark enough skin, I could."

"He filed down his teeth, too," Zep added. "I can't imagine that felt good."

"Hurt like a bitch," Kolt admitted, flashing a smirk at his son. "So when Sal asked me if I thought you should go, I asked her to enroll you. That means you need to get a room tomorrow, if you're up for it."

"I am!" Las promised. "I heard that we'll learn knives and stances too. And that there's a class for both Iliran and Glish. Plus two different histories, and the science class."

"And homework," Blaz added. "Studying, good grades, and all those other things."

"Yeah, but it'll be fun," Las insisted. "You wouldn't understand since you're human, but it would be!"

Although, speaking of humans, Sal glanced around the room. She counted five of her mates, but one was missing. "Where's Tyr?"

Zep waved that off. "He's with the Dogs. Said he'll be back for dinner. But Sal, did they tell you what Las needs to take up there with him?"

"Just the basics," Gage said, answering for her. "He'll be supplied a uniform, but I'm guessing he'll want his own clothes for the evenings and weekends. Toiletries and such, of course, but that's about all."

"It is na all," Jase said, pushing himself to his feet.

Without another word, the little assassin headed into their bedroom. Sal wasn't the only one grinning. All of his cessivi could feel what he was doing, but Las would have no idea. Kolt shoved a hand over his face to hide his own smile, but Las noticed, and the boy narrowed his eyes.

"What are you all doing?" He pointed at Sal. "I blame you."

"Nah," Jase said as he walked out of the room. "This time, ya blame me. Ya are a Black Blade, and ya do na leave the den without a weapon. Yer too big fer the ones ya had as a boy. It is time fer yer next set."

And he passed over a sheathed dagger. Once, it had been white, but time, dirt, and blood had stained the hilt to an ivory color. The decorative grooves carved into the ceramic had become dark, making it look beautiful, but Sal knew what was on the blade. Just like she expected, Lasryn pulled the dagger part-way out - and paused.

"This is yours," he said.

"And now it is yers," Jase told him. "Ya are my boy too, so ya need a weapon ta keep ya safe when yer pack can na. Once ya know yer stances, I will get ya a second. A black one made just fer ya."

Clutching the blade in his hand, Las stood and dropped his eyes. "Thank you, Ahnor." But a smile broke through. "And I'll give it back when the semester's over, Dava."

"That is yers," Jase told him again. "Ya are the only son I will have, so I have ta make sure ya do na embarrass me."

Kolt groaned. "He's not going to be an assassin."

"Na," Jase agreed, "but ya are na either, and ya do na embarrass me. I think Las will be a lancer."

"Like on horses?" Las gasped.

Jase nodded. "If ya make good grades, ya can have one of the foals born next spring. It will be ready ta ride by the time ya are ready ta learn."

That was enough to make the kid forget his manners. Rushing forward, he wrapped his arms around Jase's waist and hugged with enthusiasm. Sal found herself pulling Valri closer while she watched. Maybe she couldn't give her mates children, but they didn't need her to. Kolt and Zep had done that for them.

And so long ago, back when she'd clutched a slip of paper in her hands hoping for a place to belong, she'd never even dared to dream of this. She'd hoped for a unit that would let her die with dignity. Instead, she'd found a family where she could live proud instead. Maybe they were pieced together from what had survived the Terran War, but that was ok.

Seeing Kolt's son hug one of the most deadly assassins on the continent without fear proved just how far they'd all come. Jase had found a place where he could be himself. Zep had changed into the one thing he'd always wanted: an iliri. Kolt no longer had to hide who he was. Gage had learned to relax, and Blaz had found a way to finally be happy. Tyr still fought being iliri, but no one cared. He was allowed to be proud of his species.

But most of all, they'd all found love. Like freedom, it came in many sizes and shapes. Family, children, and mates, they were finally free to care about whomever they wanted to; however they chose. This had been a dream too big for Sal to even imagine back then, but she'd still fought for it. Mostly, so that kids like Las and Valri wouldn't need to know how much it hurt to be called a scrubber.

"Ya look sad, Amma," Valri whispered.

Sal shook her head. "I'm happy, little one. My boy is going to school, and he's going to learn to be an impressive ilus. And one day, you'll do the same."

The little girl scrunched up her nose. "I wanna grow up and be a Kaisae."

"Doesn't work like that," Zep told her. "You get born a Kaisae."

"Then I wanna be born a Kaisae," Valri told him.

Zep chuckled as he reached up to grab her little foot. "Pretty sure your sire messed up your chances of that."

"But you're my sire!"

"Mhm," he agreed. "And I'm pretty proud of my little girl. You're the prettiest iliri in Arhhawen."

Sal gasped in mock-shock. "Prettier than me?"

"Oh yeah," Zep teased. "You're all white and pasty looking. Valri looks like her dava, and he's pretty handsome."

"Like you?" Valri asked.

Sal leaned closer to the child's ear. "You look more like your Amma Ryali. Dava Zep's just trying to take credit for it."

"But Dava Zep's the Dernor of *All* Iliri," Valri said. "And I'm the baby of all iliri."

"Yes you are," Lasryn told her before anyone could reply. "And I agree, you're prettier than Amma Sal."

"Hey now," Sal said. "Someone needs to tell me I'm pretty, or I'm going to start feeling bad."

"Beautiful," Kolt assured her. "Although I am looking forward to seeing you cook."

"What?" Gage asked. "Sal's cooking? Do I need to get something sent up from Tensa?"

"No!" Sal groaned. "Roo's going to help teach me. Guys, I never learned how, and I figured it'd be fun."

"Cooking is *not* fun," Zep promised. "It's like work, but the tedious kind. Trust me, there's a reason I don't do it."

"I'll help," Las offered.

"You will not," Kolt told him. "You're going to go into your room and start packing, because if you want to go to school tomorrow, then you'll need to have your things ready tonight."

"Dava..." the boy grumbled.

"I'll help," Kolt offered, "but I waited a little too long, so we need to make sure this happens tonight."

Lasryn looked over at Blaz. "Do you know what kids take to school?"

"Nope," Blaz said. "I went to military school. My dad was a soldier, so I learned at a human school where we went home every afternoon. Nothing like the Academy."

"Would Tyr know?" he tried.

The door creaked open a second later. "What about me?" Tyr asked. "And I heard family dinner?"

"Yes to family dinner," Sal told him. "I'm learning to cook."

Tyr just jerked his thumb over his shoulder. "So, I should probably eat with Ryek, huh?"

"Fuck off," Sal said, but they were both smiling a little too big. Mostly because Sal could *feel* that he was joking.

"I asked," Las said, "if you knew what I'd need to take to school."

"Zep would," Tyr said, "But me? Nah. I went to military school."

Blaz leaned back to see Tyr. "You too?"

"Oh yeah. We were too poor to afford the nice schools, but human kids had to go until they were sixteen in the CFC. Dropped out as soon as I could."

But Lasryn had latched onto that one bit of advice. "Zep, you went to school?"

The big guy let out a heavy sigh. "Yeah, I did, and while I'm scared to ask, why?"

"Because I don't know what to take," Lasryn told him. "I don't want to take the wrong things!"

"Take what you need," Zep told him. "Not what you want, but what you need, and if you forget something, then we can always bring it up that evening. How's that?"

"Really?" Las asked.

Kolt just nodded at him, but he sent a thought to his mates as well. *I think he's nervous.*

Of course, he is, Blaz replied. *His first day of school.*

I would na know, Jase admitted. *My amma taught me.*

It's intimidating, Zep explained. *All the other kids will judge him, and he knows it. Plus, he's a Black Blade, and that will either get him noticed or the others will try to dominate him.*

Shit, Kolt thought. *How do I prepare him for that?*

You can't, Sal told him. *You just tell him that it's ok to not always be the meanest. Sometimes, there's nothing wrong with dropping your eyes.*

Not really something I've learned, Sal. Maybe you can talk to him before he goes? Kolt begged.

Sal caught his eye. *If that's what you want, although it might sound better coming from you. Just try, Kolt. You're a good dava. Just tell him to do his best, and I think he'll surprise you. He's a good kid.*

Ok. And Kolt pushed himself to his feet. "You ready to get started?"

Las just shrugged, but he headed into his room with Kolt following him.

CHAPTER EIGHT

SILVER

asryn's room was large. It was also filled with everything his pack thought a kid his age might want. As soon as the Blades got settled into Arhhawen, they'd all made a point of spoiling the family members who'd been left here during the war. Most of those were kids. Lasryn was no exception, but he'd kept his things from back when he'd lived with Kolt in the CFC as well.

Like the hand-carved figure of a Kaisae in black. That was sitting beside the boy's bed, right in front of his lantern. Kolt couldn't help himself; he reached out to pick it up. Gently turning the toy in his hand, he noticed the wear spots in the paint, and the dull tip on the sword.

"You kept this?" he asked.

Las had his head partially in his wardrobe. "The Kaisae? Yeah. It was the last thing you made for me before I had to move here. I dunno. I thought that maybe... You know, if you didn't make it back..."

"Yeah," Kolt said, not needing the boy to explain any more. "You know this was supposed to be Sal, right?"

"And that I'm named for her," Las said. "Yeah. So, I guess she forgave you for messing up, huh?" Impishly, he glanced back to flash a smile at his dava.

"Actually, she never blamed me for leaving her there," Kolt assured his son. "Doesn't mean that I don't. That's the thing in relationships, Las. We don't always agree. We also don't always get it right, but we do work to make it better."

"Dad..." Las paused. "Dava," he corrected himself, proving just how long he'd spent in the Conglomerate. Then he sighed. "How'd you make her love you, anyway?"

"Sal?" Kolt asked.

Las nodded, but the boy's ears were turning pink. Kolt quickly turned his eyes back to the toy, not wanting to embarrass his son. It was rare enough for the kid to ask his advice, and he didn't want to make it harder for the next time. Las was in awe of Jase, and he respected Gage. He hadn't figured out how to deal with Zep yet, while Tyr was closer to feeling like Las's older brother than a father figure. Blaz tried, and Las had been nothing but polite to him, but the boy hadn't started treating him as family yet, so Kolt really didn't want to mess this up.

"Well, the truth is that I don't really know." Kolt carefully put the toy back beside the lantern where he'd found it. "But when she needed me, I helped - and I didn't expect anything for it. I did what was right, and tried to let her see the kind of man I wanted to be. Not the kind I was, because the truth is that I wasn't the best iliri out there."

"But you were a good human," Las told him.

Kolt shrugged. "I pretended to be, but I'll never be human, and so that meant I was always lying about it. When I was alone with Sal, helping her get back to her pack - our pack now - after the Kaisor died, I stopped lying. That's pretty much it. And if a girl likes you, then she needs to like the real you, because you can't always put on an act. It will wear you down."

"Yeah, but..." Las paused, grabbed a couple of shirts, and then carried them over to the bed so he was standing beside his dava. "What if the girl I like doesn't know what she likes yet?"

Kolt knew that was phrased carefully. Too carefully, if he had to guess. "But you don't want to tell me which girl, right?"

"Right," Las said.

"Can I ask why not?"

Las's answer was little more than a mumble. "Because you'll laugh at me."

"Not in a million years, Las. I mean, who would've thought that *I'd* be meant for a Kaisae? A lot of men laughed at me for even thinking she was real, and look how that turned out?"

"So, like, if I like a girl, and she's not old enough to like, does that make me weird?"

Kolt eased himself down on the side of the bed and patted the spot beside him. "Well, how do you like her?"

"I always want to be around her, and she smells *really good,* Dava. Like, better than maerte kinda good. And I don't care when she's annoying because she'll laugh with me, and that's kinda all that matters, you know? But my friends say I'm stupid for liking her."

Kolt just nodded. "Do you feel like you need to protect her? I mean all the time, even when there's nothing to protect her from? And do you get worried when you can't see her?"

"Yes!" Las hissed. "That's exactly it, and they said I'm just worried I'll end up a brerror."

"Well, could be," Kolt admitted, "but sounds like how I felt when I was near Sal. You know I'm meant for her, right?"

"Yeah... Kinda why I asked." And Las looked up with his big amber eyes. "Dava, I think I'm meant for Valri."

For a moment, it felt like all the air vanished from Kolt's lungs. Of all the females Lasryn could've been bound to, that was the last one he'd expected. Mainly because of something the boy's kauvwae had said long ago.

"Do you know the prophesy Nimae gave you?"

Las nodded. "I'm going to stand at the left of a powerful Kaisae who will rule in peacetime. That means I'll be her mate, which is why I can't be meant for Valri, right? I mean, she's my sister. Well, not my *real* sister, but my pack sister. So I'm just being a good ilus, right?"

"I can't tell you that," Kolt said. "Las, you're the only one who will know how you feel - and your cessivi, if you're lucky enough to have one - but right now, it's just you. So trust what you feel. But if you're meant for Valri, you know that's a very long wait, right?"

"For what?" Las asked.

Kolt wanted to groan, because he was not about to have an in-depth talk with a seven-year-old boy about sex. He also didn't want to make light of what his son was telling him, so he decided to go for something in the middle.

"You know about the iliri male curse?"

Las rolled his eyes. "Everyone knows about that. Men can only mate with women who are more iliri than they are."

"Valri isn't more iliri than you," Kolt pointed out. "You're more than half. She's less."

"But she doesn't smell like it," Las insisted. "Dava, that's what I'm trying to say. Valri smells like..." He let the words trail off.

"Go ahead," Kolt encouraged. "Try to explain it to me. I promise it won't sound silly."

"She smells like when you'd come home for leave. Like a present on New Year's day. She smells like..." Again, the boy paused, but this time he shook his head. "Like hope, Dava."

"Fuck," Kolt breathed as he reached out for someone with more knowledge. *Jase, is there any way to tell if a child might be a Kaisae?*

That professor is trying ta make a test from our blood, but normally we can na until puberty. Why? the Ahnor asked.

Because Las just said that Valri smells like hope.

So does Lyzzi, Jase said.

Yeah, and Sal, Kolt agreed, *but Valri doesn't smell like that to me. What about you?*

She is na old enough ta smell like more than her dam and sire. Could yer boy be saying what we say? Thinkin' it means somethan it does na?

I'll ask. And he looked at his son. "Did you know that Kaisaes do not smell different until they are about twelve? So Valri can't smell like hope yet. Are you sure it's not Sal you're smelling on her?"

"I told you that you'd think it was stupid," Las grumbled. "Dava, she smells like hope. Not like Sal's hope, but like a different hope. Like, Sal smells like possibilities, and Valri smells like laughter, but that sounds dumb."

"Doesn't to me," Kolt swore. "I'm just worried that if you're meant for a girl as young as her, then things will be rough for you. When your friends are flirting with girls and being asked out, you'll be waiting for Valri. When others are having their first kiss, you'll be playing heroes and villains. When you're close to finishing school, she'll just be starting. She's six whole years younger than you."

"Yeah," Las agreed. "And if I go up there, then she can't come, and I don't know how I'm going to take care of her."

"Are you linked with her?" Kolt asked. "Maybe you can tell her a bedtime story every night before she goes to sleep? It will help, you know. And if you find that you no longer want to, then it means you aren't meant for her. Because when a man is meant for a woman, he wants nothing more than to make her happy."

"I'm linked with her," Las admitted. "And we talk all the time. I mean, she talks about food and toys, mostly, but still. I can help with those."

"Ok. Then while you're at school, I'll take care of Valri for you, how's that? If you need me to check on her, you just ask, and I'll do it, then send you a memory of it. And if that's too hard, we'll figure something else out, ok?"

"Ok."

"And give Blaz a chance," Kolt told his son since they were trading advice. "He's a good man, and one of your davas. He's trying really hard to get it right."

"He tries too hard! He's always treating me like I'm a kid."

"You *are* a kid," Kolt reminded him, "and seven is a lot younger for humans than it is for iliri. Just tell him. He'll be embarrassed, but he'll do better the next time. I mean, you're the only son Blaz is likely to get, you know, and I think it hurts him that you keep shutting him out."

"But he's human," Las said. "He doesn't understand."

"He's my mate," Kolt told him. "And he's a Black Blade, which means he's your brother, too. Besides, Tyr's human and you like him. I promise Blaz is a good man."

Las shrugged. "He's not as fun as Tyr."

"He's a better horseman," Kolt countered. "And if you want to learn about horses, he's the best in the Blades. Better than Zep, even."

"Really?"

Kolt nodded sagely. "Definitely. Blaz knows as much about caring for them as Tilso, and more about riding. I bet if you asked, he'd even let you ride Rax. If you're *lucky* he might start teaching you how to do it the right way. I mean, if you're going to grow up and be a lancer, it's kinda something you'll need to know, right?"

Las started folding his shirts. "Maybe the first few times, Dava Zep can come too?"

"Sounds like a plan," Kolt agreed. "Now, what are you taking besides clothes?"

Las jerked his chin at the toy Kaisae. "Sal. And there's a bag of candy in the drawer beside the bed that Tyr got me. Um, and can I take my pillow? I like this one."

"Because Sal got it for you?" Kolt teased.

Las shook his head. "Because Valri always sleeps on it, so it kinda smells like her."

"Then your pillow can go." Kolt stood, heading for the closet to pull down a travel bag from the top shelf. "And I'll get another pillow for Valri to use when she comes over, then trade out with you. How does that sound?"

"Really?" Las asked. "Dava, why are you being so ok with this?"

Kolt grinned at the wall, knowing his son couldn't see. "Because I waited many years to be with the woman I was meant for. You're going to do the same, if you're right about this. I just want to make it easy on you. It's what davas do, believe it or not." Then he looked back and smiled. "Well, and because I'm proud of you for telling me."

Las didn't look up from the clothes in his hands. "Thanks for believing me. I was worried that you'd say I was making it up like everyone else does."

"Never. Even if you're wrong, Las, I'll still believe you. There's no shame in making a mistake."

"Just own it," Las said. "Admit when you're wrong, and do your best to fix it. Kinda like you did when you left Sal in Merriton, right? When you failed her?"

"Exactly. And I'll spend the rest of my life making sure you don't ever have to know what that feels like. Now, make sure you get some pants in that bag. And you can't always wear black."

Las chuckled. "Yeah, I can. Only Blades wear all black, and we're Blades. I'll be the only kid there in this color, since my sisters have fur!"

Kolt tossed the bag at his son. "Just remember that everyone thinks their pack is the best."

"Yeah, but *my* pack is inked in silver," Las said. "Kinda proves it."

CHAPTER NINE

GREEN

*A*n hour later, Sal and Roo were in the kitchen. Lyzzi was leaning over the counter watching. Everyone else had gathered in the main room. Arctic, Shade, and Ghost had arrived. Risk, Perin, and Tilso said they'd be there soon. Las, Valri, Rhyx, and Raast were on the far side, talking and playing amongst themselves. Then there were the new pups.

Wrasau and Wyron, Roo's new pups, were in high demand. The boys weren't simply twins like Rhyx and Raast. They were identical. Both of them had a soft grey tint to their ears and a silvery mane down the back of their necks, but otherwise, they were white. Including their eyes. Caught somewhere between the coat color of their sisters and their sire, they were beautifully unique, and all of their davas wanted a chance to hold them.

"They're cute," Sal said, flicking her eyes to the men.

Roo whuffed in amusement. *I told Hwa that we will have to have more since you cannot. He thinks we should start once the boys are weaned.*

"Oh, *he* thinks that, does he?" Sal teased.

Lyzzi giggled. "More pups means we all get to spend more time with them, right? I'm ok with this idea."

See? Roo said. *I'm just giving the pack what we need. And yes, it was Hwa who said we should start again. I just did not disagree.*

Sal continued cutting the meat before her, but she couldn't stop the grin. Everyone had been so worried about her not being able to have kids, but she'd had a feeling this would happen. Shade had forced her body to cycle again, since her first estrus hadn't resulted in a pregnancy. However, Raast had done some healing which they both felt would make it easier for Shade to get pregnant - although she said it might also increase the chances of twins.

Which meant that next year, Arhhawen would be filled with children. The Blades weren't the only ones who wanted to start a family. Nyurin from the 97th Pikemen had moved to Anglia with his mate, Marnia. She was human, but being pregnant with an iliri crossbred allowed her to emigrate without repercussions. Granted, Nyurin was no more iliri than Shift, but in Arhhawen, that didn't matter. Their baby was a couple of months old now, being one of the first born in Arhhawen.

And now, with much better nutrition, less stress, and safe working conditions, more women were able to conceive. It had only been a few months since the war ended, so there weren't too many large bellies yet, but Sal had a feeling it would be common soon enough. Each time she left her room, she could smell it. In other words, the iliri weren't done. Far from it.

"It's weird," Sal finally said.

Lyzzi looked up. "What is?"

"This." Sal gestured to the completely happy gathering in the other room. "There's no threat. We're not going to die in the morning, so we aren't desperately trying to make memories. We're just..."

"Living," Lyzzi finished for her. "Kaisae, this is what normal life looks like. It's all I've ever known, and there's nothing wrong with it."

"Yeah," Sal breathed as the door opened to admit a few more guests, "but I'm just not used to it."

"Used to what?" Perin asked as he walked in.

The smile on the man's face made Sal's lips curl to match. "Peace," she told him. "Although, it does look good on you."

Perin reached behind him for Risk's hand, even as he stepped over to make room for Tilso. "Not having to hide my choice of love is what looks good, Sal." Then he sniffed. "What are we eating?"

Sheep, Roo answered, sending the thoughts into their minds. *I thought that would be safe for everyone, and not too strange of a taste.*

"I actually like the lizards," Perin admitted.

"Yeah," Blaz agreed, moving over to make room for the new guys on the couch beside him. "I was worried it would taste weird, and the meat is dark and red, but it's good."

Then we will have kraug next time, Hwa said from his spot on the floor. *And I think someone should figure out how to breed them.*

"Huh," Perin said. "You know, that's not a bad idea. I mean, wild game tends to be tougher, right? And we can use the fatty layer for oil, so it's not a bad idea."

Zep chuckled. "Sounds like you have a new gig for Dark Heart."

Perin just shook his head. "I'm actually retiring next month. Passing the unit to Jad."

"Not Hax?" Tyr asked.

Perin gave him a look that proved the question was a foolish one. "Hax is a good soldier, but I wouldn't recommend him as a leader."

"Has he found his skill yet?" Sal asked.

Perin just shrugged. "The guy's so wrapped up in that new mate of his that he never talks to the rest of us."

"She intends to move out west soon," Risk said. "To the wildlands of Anglia."

Sal looked over and met Jase's eyes. "We should let them," she said.

"First iliri town?" he asked.

Sal canted her head. "We need one, and it would get them out of Arhhawen. If it happens before the allied nations arrive, I will not complain at all."

"Yeah," Zep said, "but what kind of specist group would he make?"

Arctic looked up from the pup in his lap. "So send some humans with him. Make him a lord or whatever the iliri equivalent will be."

"No," Sal said. "That would be his mate."

"And her title?" Ghost asked.

"It used ta be kaisae with a small k," Jase told them. "But I do na think that will work now. Na with us having two Kaisaes again."

"He means me," Lyzzi told Perin.

"Trust me, kid, we all know." And Perin reached an arm out. "Someone hand me one of those boys?"

Shade clutched the pup in her lap tighter, so Arctic handed over the little boy he was holding. Perin cradled the child in his arm like he'd done it a million times.

"Hello, Wyron," he said softly.

"And this," Ghost teased, "is proof that I deserve to hold at least one of them. I can't tell them apart yet."

"Wrasau told me his name," Shade admitted, but she begrudgingly offered the pup to her mate.

Ghost moved the baby onto his lap and leaned toward Shade so she could still see him. Sal watched it all. Seeing her pack together like this felt good. No, it felt *right*. At the counter beside Sal, Roo stood up on her hind legs to peer over the top. She also nudged Sal to continue cutting the meat. Dinner wouldn't get done until this part was finished, and it was the only part Sal felt like she understood.

Put it in the oven, then you can talk to your family, Roo reminded her. *Or if you want, I can finish for you.*

"No," Sal said, smiling down at her sister. "You've cooked for me enough times. I want to return the favor at least once."

Ok. Then you need those spices rubbed into the meat. A pinch on each side. The oven is warm now, so once the meat is flavored, you can put it on the heat. This is easier than fighting, Sal.

"So you say," Sal replied. "How do you know what spices to use, anyway?"

I use the ones my pack likes best. If they smell good together, they often taste good together, but sometimes you have to try and fail to be sure.

"Ya know," Jase said, proving he'd moved closer to lean beside Lyzzi, "most women do na cook fer their men. They let us cook fer them."

"And this is Anglia," Sal pointed out. "Women can do men's work, men can do women's, and all species are equal but different. I want to do this, Jase."

"I know, kitten. Ya look cute in the kitchen."

Like a fish out of water, Roo teased.

Sal stuck her tongue out at her friend, but leaned closer to Jase and lowered her voice. "Did you ask everyone?"

"I did, and they do na mind. They said he's a brother already, so he deserves the invite."

"And Risk? Tilso?" Sal asked.

Jase's smile turned into a grin. "They were excited. They said he's a mate, and he will na leave, but Risk wants ya ta ask."

"Ok." Sal rubbed the last piece of meat with the dried herbs and then started stacking them on a ceramic pan. "Let me just put this in to cook, ok?"

"Yeh." But Jase leaned a little further and crooked a finger for her to do the same.

Sal matched him, just for Jase to steal a quick kiss. As he pulled back, his eyes met hers one more time, glancing into each one, before leaning back. He'd been doing that more often, and every single time, it made Sal's heart beat just a bit faster. The problem was that all of her mates knew it. Thankfully, they didn't say a thing.

While Jase returned to the main room with the pack, Sal placed the meat into the oven. It wasn't large, but being so old, it was made to be efficient. The inside was lined with ceramic, and small bricks of charcoal were burned in a tray underneath the main cooking area. That kept much of the smoke and soot off the meat, and kept the temperature more consistent than the fires they were used to using. Someone had told Sal that there was an entire network of vents for the cooking smoke and water heating in Arhhawen, and that the moving heat kept the air circulating deeper in the city as well. Efficient, he'd called it, and Sal was willing to trust him.

"Ok," Sal said once it was cooking. She wiped her hands on a clean cloth and headed into the living area to get her own chance with one of the new pups. "So, I wanted to talk about something, but I need one of my boys first."

Perin lifted the child he was holding, offering him to her. "I think I've spent more time with him than you have."

"Thank you." She snuggled the child up against her chest, breathing in the scent of young grauori. "Perin, I have a question for you."

"Ok?" he said.

Sal was standing right before him and didn't move. "This isn't the most formal way of doing this, but it feels like the right way. I wanted to know if you'd be interested in joining the pack. I know you're with Dark Heart, but I'm not sure if that's your unit or your family, and if becoming a brother is something you'd even want?"

Without looking away, the man's hand moved to find Risk's. Their fingers laced together, and slowly, Perin began to nod. "Sal, I've been chasing Risk for years. He's always told me no. He said he loved a human, and that his mate wouldn't understand. I countered that I did, so his lover would, but Risk wasn't so sure."

"He's always expected people to judge him for being onsyc," Tilso said.

"Because of how I was raised," Risk explained. "The humans who owned me had very strong opinions about two men sharing a room in their tavern. Most of them were beaten before they were tossed out in the middle of the night. Knowing what Blaec and the 62nd did to get me out? They took a huge risk on me."

"Hence his call sign," Tilso added.

"But my pack was not onsyc," Risk explained. "We did not talk about those things back then. Our goal was to appear as human as possible, and my coloring made that hard enough. Being with men instead of women? I worried that would be too much, so I just... didn't." He looked up at Sal. "Until you came along."

"I think that was more Tilso than me," Sal pointed out. "And now Perin."

"Risk," Perin said, "I would've fought for you, even back then. I would've dared anyone to say we weren't fit to be soldiers, and I'm human, so it wouldn't have ruined your reputation." He leaned to look right into Risk's face. "I get it, you always thought I was joking, but I wasn't. I just thought you were the most beautiful man I'd ever seen, and your unit mates made it clear you weren't interested in women. I always assumed you just weren't interested in me, either."

"I was," Risk admitted. "I just didn't know how to navigate a world where I was allowed to make my own choices. Besides, if we'd ended up together back then, I wouldn't have met Tilso," Risk pointed out.

"It worked out," Tilso told them. "And I have to say, I'm kinda glad I got included. Not just with you both, but all of the Blades."

Perin looked over at his other mate. "Yeah, that's the whole ayati thing you people talk about, right? Things happen for a reason, and while it isn't always pretty, it works out the way it should."

"Has to," Sal corrected. "It works out how it has to, and sometimes that isn't pretty, but I want it to be. This time around, I want the iliri to have good lives. I want us to have happy choices as well as hard ones. I don't want our lives to be too easy, but I want them to matter, and to be the kind of important that we get to live long enough to enjoy."

"Then yes," Perin said. "I want to be a part of that, so yes, I will join the Blades. I'm not leaving my mates regardless, and I'd be proud to wear their family name on my throat. Dark Heart is just a group of soldiers. The Blades are a family, and one that I really want to say is mine."

Risk leaned in to rest his head on Perin's shoulder, and Tilso cupped Perin's cheek, but that was as far as it got. A yip from Roo interrupted them before the men could kiss in celebration.

Sal turned towards the threat and her heart froze. Rolling from the oven was nothing but dark smoke, and the smell of char was quickly making its way into the main room. In other words, dinner was ruined.

"Take the kids outside," Jase said. "Raast, ya need ta get Valri inta the hall. Blaz?"

"Right behind you," Blaz agreed.

But Zep was laughing as he dropped an arm around Sal's shoulder. "It was a good try, demon, but I think everyone screws up cooking the first time. How about we move this party down to Tensa's?"

All she could do was sigh, because he was right. But at least she'd gotten a new brother out of all this.

CHAPTER TEN

PINK

Over in Dorton, Dom was rummaging through his mother's jewelry box. All of her gems had been put in here for his future wife, but they were the kinds of things Rayna wouldn't be interested in. Large gems, ornate resin settings, and flamboyant displays weren't her style. His mother, however, had used any excuse to prove that marrying a bastard hadn't weakened her province or her power.

And the truth was that Valmere had been *her* province. Granted, back then, the laws wouldn't allow a woman to inherit, and Dom's mother had been the eldest daughter, with no brothers. Dom's father knew she'd needed a marriage to keep the titles and life they'd grown used to, and a king's bastard was as good as a minor noble for that. The man had increased his own power by taking advantage of his wife's weakness.

Which was why Dom wanted to change things now. He'd been raised in a loveless home, to absentee parents. The only person who'd ever been proud of him was his grandfather, King Jensen. Looking back, however, Dom knew that the man's pride was based on his favorite son making something of his life. Born from love instead of responsibility, the King adored Dom's father, and Dom had been proof that a bastard with a good mind could become more.

And now Dom intended to tear all of that down and make it even easier for the next bastard to step up. He paused, thinking about how much Anglia had changed since the crown landed on his head. When he'd been notified that he was the next in line for the throne, Dom had thought it was a joke. Then he'd panicked when he realized it wasn't.

He could still remember his coronation so clearly. He'd been scared to death of the responsibility he'd just been given. Never mind that it wouldn't take long before someone decided to put a dagger in his back to claim his crown, but Dom's father had taught him how to play politics. Make friends with the worst men, listen to the best, and let them play against each other. Never let anyone see weakness, because that was the first thing they'd exploit.

But Sal hadn't cared. When she'd landed before him, Dom had seen her white eyes, and he'd known. Not completely, but he'd been sure that anyone brave enough to run through the fully guarded Palace was doing it for the right reason. Otherwise, the risk didn't justify the reward. And the moment she'd pulled off her helm, Dom had understood.

Not just an iliri, or a pure iliri, but also a woman. That she'd escaped harm was impressive. But it was her words that hit him. She'd said the iliri needed him. When he'd asked her why she'd risked her life, that had been her answer, and it had felt so raw - so *honest*. Now, Dom understood why.

Shift had told stories about life before Anglia. Rayna had told him others. Initially, he'd assumed that Sal couldn't lie to him. It was rumored that iliri didn't lie well - but that was only part of the story. Iliri couldn't lie in their minds, and their ears often gave them away. Sal's had. But she could still lie, and had when it was necessary. What bothered him was that she'd ever needed to learn that skill.

As his fingers finally found the white resin ring he was looking for, Dom paused to imagine Arhhawen filled with iliri who told things as they saw it, and who couldn't remember a reason to lie. He tried to envision what a group of laughing iliri children would sound like, but he couldn't. He'd never had the chance to hear it, but only because his time in Arhhawen was usually for business with Sal. Thankfully, he'd heard a lot of women laughing lately, including her.

Because a female leading the military broke a lot of barriers for other women. Brisa was only one example. The woman had been the King's whore for a long time. She'd spread her legs for half the soldiers stationed in Dorton. Now, she was a respected soldier and treated as their equal. When they'd returned home, Dom had gone to check his men one last time and had caught some of the men who hadn't marched across the country trying to push her around. He'd almost stepped in, but he hadn't needed to. The veterans who'd served beside her had done it first.

And now it was the grauori who were getting their own chance at equality. That would be a little harder - but not much. Rragri's actions at Barton Meadow, back when Terric had tried to invade Anglia, had made it clear that they were not people to mess with. Unfortunately, that meant humans now feared them, but again, the soldiers were helping. Months of living together had a way of tearing down those boundaries between people.

During the war, they'd taken it all for granted, but now, it mattered. These people had stood up to protect his kingdom. He'd taken Anglia to war to protect them, and yet they'd still managed to give back. It was a cycle he very much wanted to continue.

So all that was left was this. A wedding to bring the species together again. Dom slipped the white ring onto the first knuckle of his index finger and turned it until he could see the inlaid piece of steel. Maybe it was simply iron, but his mother had always called it steel. To Rayna, those colors would have even more significance. White for love and the silver of the steel for ayati. It was Dom's way of saying they were meant to be.

He was still admiring the ring when Ilija slipped into the empty suite and knocked on the door frame behind him. "Dom?" he asked.

Dom glanced back. "I found it."

Ilija held up a small velvet bag in his hand. "I have the other. Want to see?"

"Yes!" Dom hissed. "I don't exactly plan on doing this again."

"And to think, it wasn't long ago that divorce wouldn't have been possible either," Ilija said while he opened the bag.

"Yeah, but it's not something I want to try personally," Dom told him.

"Pretty sure that won't be a problem for you." Then, without warning, Ilija tossed over the ring. "It's a little wider than you wanted, but thinner to make up for it. Had to make sure the symbol was large enough to be read."

"Il bax genause," Dom whispered as he looked over the ring. Then he held it up beside Rayna's. "You know they'll want to get me one, right?"

"And they can talk to me about where and how," Ilija promised. "I already know the colors, the design, and the size. All you have to do now is get the two of them to say yes."

Dom let out a heavy breath. "What if they say no?"

"They won't."

"But what if they do?"

Ilija shrugged. "Then you continue on as you are. Rayna stays your Consort, Shift is your iliri ambassador. There's no need for your proposal to ruin anything, and it could fix a lot."

Dom grunted and shook his head. "I am not asking them to marry me because it will make a political point. I'm asking them to marry me because..."

"You love them," Ilija finished. "And you're going to need to learn how to say that, even about Shift."

"I love them," Dom whispered.

Ilija stepped closer to slap Dom's back in approval. "See? That wasn't hard. As for proposing? Now that's the hard part. Your balls are going to crawl up into your throat, it will feel like it takes an eternity to get an answer, and every movement they make will feel like it's the wrong one. Just remind yourself that nothing is a refusal until they flat out say no. Just give them the chance to process this, and remind yourself over and over that they love you. You love them. This will be ok."

"Was it this bad when you asked Vanica?" Dom asked.

Ilija grinned at him. "Worse, because I had the entire country watching. You, at least, get to do this in private. Now, explaining it to the nobles if they say yes? Well, just remember that I'll be with you."

"I'm holding you to that," Dom told him.

"Kinda the point," Ilija promised. "Now, how are you asking them?"

"I was going to get down on one knee and ask if they'd marry me." Dom shrugged like that should've been obvious.

But Ilija was shaking his head. "You need a grand gesture. Something for them to tell Jarl's kids about. So, I suggest you hold out a ring to each of them, get down on a knee, and then tell them *why* you want them to marry you."

"Because I love them," Dom said, like that should've been obvious.

"No," Ilija groaned. "Tell Rayna that she makes you stronger. Tell Shift that he's your best friend. Tell Rayna that you can't imagine life without her. Tell Shift that you respect him more than anyone else you've ever met - besides Rayna. Tell both of them that they complete you, and that you want to give them everything, including your name. Tell them that you love them, and you want them to spend the rest of their lives with you making Anglia a place to be proud of."

Dom blew out a tense breath. "I'm never going to remember that!"

"Not that, you fucking idiot. Something like that. Whatever it is that you feel, tell them. Tonight is not the time to save your pride. It's the one moment in your life to show all of your vulnerabilities. Let them see that you don't just want them around, but that you can't *live* without them, and that you want everyone to know. Dom, talk to them the same way you did every noble-born woman that was thrown at you, but use the words that you mean."

"Rayna does make me stronger," Dom agreed. "She also makes me smarter. She's the common sense that I was never allowed to learn. Shift makes me wise, and he pushes me to be more. He makes me realize that I don't need to be big, strong, or rich to be a good man. I just need to be *good*. He's an ear when I need it, and a partner when I'm in the mood to get into trouble. Rayna is the glue that holds us together, though."

"That's it," Ilija told him. "Keep going."

"She challenges me. She shows me what it means to be noble, and Shift shows me what it's like to be humble. And yet neither of them are too good for me - "

"No," Ilija said. "Too good is not something you want to say. Maybe that they ground you? Or that they should be out of your reach, and you can't believe they aren't. Don't insult them when you propose."

Dom nodded his head to prove that he'd heard. "I'm going to fuck this up, man."

"Then it'll be a funny story," Ilija assured him. "Remember, those two know you better than Sal and I do. They're your soulmates, right? The pieces of your puzzle that are missing?"

"I'm using that!" Dom decided.

"Use away," Ilija assured him. "Just make sure you kneel before them, preferably between them, and hold out those rings. Even if you can't get any words out, the rings will say enough."

"You think they'll like them?"

Ilija nodded. "I think they'll like anything you give them. Dom, Rayna isn't in your bed because of your title. In fact, that almost made her stay out of it. Shift? He respects you. Not what you've given him, or what you could do for him. He respects the man who learned how to ride a horse into battle and who never once shied away from the tough decisions. Even when you didn't know the answer, you were still there, trying to learn how. You let Sal and I lead when it made more sense, rather than trying to take all the credit yourself. Shift respects you because you *are* a good man. And after being in the CFC with them, I can assure you that he's seen his share of bad ones. This will work."

"I just want them to say yes," Dom admitted.

"Then you have to start by asking," Ilija said. "Bare your soul, man. Those two have given you everything they have. It's now your turn. Give it all back, and use your words to prove it. Show them just how much you love them."

Dom glanced down at the rings, one on each of his index fingers, clutched tightly so he wouldn't lose them. "I love them," he whispered to himself. "I love them both, and I don't care if anyone else likes it. I love them enough to change the entire fucking world if I have to."

"That," Ilija said. "That's what you need to tell them."

CHAPTER ELEVEN

WHITE

S hift was in the King's suite, setting up a game of chess. It was an ancient game that had been discovered in the basement of Arhhawen, and both he and the King enjoyed it. Rayna found it boring. She preferred reading before bed to relax. Currently, she was rummaging through the bookshelves, looking for something a little more interesting than the current laws of Anglia.

"Where'd he go?" she asked almost absentmindedly.

"He said he'd be back in a few minutes," Shift told her. "He didn't say where, though. You think the council's giving him a hard time again?"

"Or there's something going on with the iliri," Rayna countered. "He went to Arhhawen this morning, and he hasn't said why yet."

Shift pulled in a breath, smelling something he didn't expect, so he decided to call her on it. "You worried he's seeing a crossbred on the side?"

Rayna's hands paused. "He'd tell us, wouldn't he?"

"Or Sal would," Shift assured her. "And I promise that nothing happens in Arhhawen that doesn't eventually get back to her. Maybe it's a surprise for your birthday that he's working on?"

"My birthday was a few months ago," Rayna pointed out.

Shift flashed her a smile. "Which Keeya told us about since you didn't. I'm just thinking that he could be making up for you keeping secrets."

"It's not that," Rayna insisted. "I just don't want to celebrate that day. I mean, Sal doesn't even know her real birthday."

"She does," he assured her. "Granted, she found it on a piece of paper, but she knows it. She also prefers to celebrate the New Year as her birthday. It's not really a thing most iliri worry about."

Rayna just jerked her chin at him. "Why not? Maybe because so many of you don't know? Because the ones who do don't want to rub it in for the ones who don't? Yeah. Kinda why I'm not interested."

Shift just cocked his head in acceptance. "Fair 'nough. That's why the Blades always made a big deal out of the New Year. A fresh start, and it's the legal birthday for most of us."

"You?" Rayna asked.

Shift tossed her an impish smile. "Oh, I know mine. I was born free, you know."

"Yeah?" Rayna asked, giving up on the books to walk toward him. "So when is it?"

"Fourth day of autumn," he said, leaning back in his chair as she moved before him. It was the only way he could look up enough to see her face without breaking his neck.

So Rayna bent until her lips were inches from his. "That changes every year."

"Mhm. But that's my birthday. Calendars are a human thing, Ray. Many of us never learned to read them."

"Because they weren't in Iliran," she said, proving she understood. "I just don't want to rub in my good fortune and make you, of all people, feel bad."

Shift reached up just a bit more. "No, Ray. You make me feel good." And then he pressed his mouth to hers.

Rayna's lips curled into a smile, but it didn't stop her from kissing back. What started as a stolen peck quickly turned into more. Shift grabbed the waist of her shirt and pulled her lower, sparing his neck, but also so he could tease the seam of her lips. Granted, Rayna wasn't the meek and gentle kind of lover. She slipped her tongue into his mouth, taunting him for just a little more. Shift sucked on her lower lip, allowing his teeth to hold it just hard enough to prove they were sharp.

Then the door to the suite opened, and they both jumped back as if burned. Dom walked through, his eyes flicking over them, but he didn't stop. Oh, he had to know they'd just been kissing, but he'd never cared before, and yet this time, he looked almost sick from worry.

"What's wrong?" Rayna asked.

"You ok?" Shift said at the same time.

Dom just walked right to them, and then sucked in a big breath. Slowly, he looked from one to the other, and then back a few times. Shift could smell the fear rolling off of him, but also something else. It smelled a bit like Sal. Like hope.

And then the King of Anglia dropped to his knees beside the chair and held up both hands. "Marry me?" he begged, proving why he was so terrified.

Clasped in each hand was a ring. Shift felt his brow wrinkle in confusion just as Dom cursed under his breath, swapped the rings in his hands, and then held them up again.

"I want you both to marry me," he said. "Rayna, I love you. You make me strong and smart, and brave. And Kayden, you are my best friend. I can't imagine ruling this country without you. I know I'm fucking this up, but I'm so nervous, and I know one of you will say no, but I want to marry both of you, and I want everyone to know that we're together. All three of us. You're the missing pieces of my soul, like a puzzle, and without you, I can't imagine this. Living, I mean. Not that I'd die, but I just can't imagine it."

Rayna pressed her hand over Dom's to stop his panicked rambling. "You want to marry us? Like, in secret?"

"No," Dom said. "I want a big state wedding while the allies are here. I want your friends to come, and his family. Kayden, I want to be your co-husband, but the law says you have to take my name. Rayna too, but women do that more."

"He doesn't mean it like that, Ray," Shift said.

Dom groaned. "I meant that the law says that I can marry one woman. It says nothing for or against a man, just that anyone I marry must take my name. Because I'm the King, we have to do it Anglian style, or at least part of it, but I want to be married to both of you. I want this to be something we don't need to hide. I want you to be my soulmates."

Shift knew Dom was begging. He might not be using the right words, and he was definitely fumbling in a rather impressive way, but the King meant this more than anything else in his life, and the man had already risked everything to save the iliri. That he wanted to marry Shift more than he wanted to make this easy? It was enough.

Reaching out like Rayna had, Shift closed Dom's fingers around the black ring on his palm. "I'll marry you both, if Rayna's ok with that."

"Iliri don't get married," Rayna reminded him.

Shift canted his head in a weak shrug. "Humans celebrate birthdays. You get to pick which thing you're giving up, and I'll give up the other."

"Birthdays," Rayna said as a smile began to grow on her lips. "No more birthdays, because I'll marry you, Dom."

"Will you marry me too?" Shift asked.

"Yes!" she hissed.

Shift grinned at her for a split second to prove he was being devious, then turned his eyes to Dom. "You're a given, Ray. I actually meant him, not you this time. Will you marry me back, Dom? Co-mates?"

"Co-husbands," Dom clarified. "You'll become Kayden Jens, Royal Consort."

Shift's eyes narrowed. "People will think you're fucking me."

"Or you're fucking me," Dom agreed. "I don't care. If we can do this, then Tilso, Perin, and Risk can get married. Or anyone else who does things differently. And like I told Sal - "

"Ah-ha!" Rayna said. "I knew you went to Arhhawen for something!"

"It wasn't this, actually," Dom admitted. "But while I was there, it came up, and the thing is that I want to marry both of you. More than anything, but Sal said that what we need is an interspecies celebration to bridge the gap between our cultures, and I decided that was the perfect excuse to push this through the noble council. It's easier to claim that we're doing this for the country than to replace all the nobles who won't agree, or to make an argument that love shouldn't be restricted, you know? But we need this, and I want this, and I'm not really sure if you're both agreeing because you want to, or because you think you have to."

Rayna dropped down to her knees before him, the pair just before the chair Shift was sitting - trapped - in. "I want to get married in a beautiful ceremony with my friends present. I've wanted that since I was a little girl, and being a soldier doesn't mean I can't. I just wanted to do it once, and with someone I love. Not just like, and not tolerate, but someone I love enough to die for, and I'd die for both of you."

And they both looked at Shift. All he could do was shrug. "I've never wanted to get married. I wanted to find a mate I could lose myself in, and brothers who I trusted. Dom, you're everything I could ask for in a partner, and Rayna..." Shift moved his hand so Dom's fingers could open again, then he claimed the ring. "I just want to be with you. Any way I can. If that's in secret, then I'm willing to sneak around - and I'm good at it. If that's like this? I'll gladly marry you with Dom. But you, beautiful, have to put this on my finger."

Rayna took the ring and paused long enough to examine it. "When did you make this?" she asked.

"Ilija had it done today," Dom admitted.

So she showed it to Shift. "You matter. To me, to him, and to all of Anglia. You, Kayden, are one of the men I love, so will you marry me?"

"Yes," Shift said, holding out his hand so she could slide the ring onto the third finger of his offhand.

But his mind was stuck on that word. She said she loved him. She'd never said that before. Not that way. He'd always assumed she loved him like she loved Sal. They were friends. They were partners. He was the odd man out, and humans didn't keep multiple mates.

But did it really matter? No. Shift loved her more than he could put into words. Dom had become one of his closest friends. More than just a brother, although he was that as well. Things between them were hot, they were intense, but in the back of his mind, Shift assumed he was being included just to make their sex lives a little more interesting. He was the buffer between them in many ways, and if that made all of this possible, then he could accept it.

After all, this was his own idea of a happy ending.

Rayna thrust her own left hand out for Dom. "And you get to put that on me."

"You'll have to do it again in front of everyone," Dom pointed out.

"I don't fucking care," Rayna told him. "This, right here and right now, is the moment that matters to me. The rest is nothing more than us showing the world what we already have between us and bragging about it. Put that on my hand, Dominik. Otherwise, I'm not taking your last name."

Dom moved the ring to his right hand, and then pushed it carefully onto her finger. His hands shook the whole time. The man was also smiling. The look on his face was so honest that Shift wanted to hug him. For Dom, this moment mattered a lot. Shift had never truly understood the human concept of marriage, but he could tell that both Dom and Rayna put importance on it.

Never mind that they were already mated, and that the three of them had shared everything. The only thing Shift could think was that making it public was somehow important. Since humans couldn't smell that they'd both been in Rayna's bed, it made sense, but at the same time, he couldn't stop thinking about how Dom had included him in the proposal and how he fit into this relationship.

Dom didn't just want Rayna. He wanted Shift as well. He was saying that the three of them belonged together. Slowly, Shift reached up to touch the tattoo along his throat as the reality hit him. Dom was asking Shift to be his legal brother. The same way the Blades had so long ago. Thankfully, Shift didn't need to leave his pack to do it, but instead, Dom was using a human method to join them together. To join the King of Anglia with the Kaisae of Anglia. To heal the rift between their species.

And Shift had said yes. Not because of all that. He'd said yes because he loved his mates. Dom had asked because he loved his mates. Rayna had agreed because she loved her mates. They were already a family, so none of the rest mattered in their decision, but it would in the execution. This, a legal and formal marriage between more than two people, would change Anglia a little more. It would also show that there was nothing at all wrong with being iliri.

It was a *big fucking deal.*

"Dom?" Shift said softly.

"Yeah?" Dom asked.

"I think you're the bravest man I've ever met. I never realized..." But he shut his mouth before he could finish the thought.

Rayna didn't have that problem. "You never realized that a human could be as strong as a Kaisae?" she asked.

All Shift could do was nod, because she'd phrased it better than he would have, but his stupid part-human eyes were starting to sting. "I know why he's doing this."

"Because I love you both," Dom said. "Differently, but I do, and fuck anyone who thinks that's not ok. And if us being in love can make Anglia better, then shouldn't we use it? Don't we owe it to all the people in this country to fight this battle for them the same way we did in Terric City?"

"I'm in," Rayna said. "Partly because of that. Mostly because I do love you both. I love you so much, and I never knew I was allowed to feel like this about more than one person at a time. I love you both so much it hurts."

Shift felt his heart skip a beat. "You *love* me?" he whispered. Because that didn't sound brotherly at all.

"I love you," she said again. "Not just as a friend, a brother, or an easy fuck. Shift, I haven't kept you around because I need to get laid. I care about you. I can't say I love you more than Dom - or less. That doesn't change that..." She tapped her chest, right over her heart. "I have fallen in love with you, and I want to spend the rest of my life with you just as much as I do him."

"Me too," Shift told her. "I love you, Ray. And Dom? You're all I could ask for in a brother. I love you too, man."

Dom let out a heavy sigh. "So we're really gonna get married?"

"Yes, we are," Rayna promised.

Shift just laughed once. "I never thought this was something I'd do, but yeah. I'll get married. There's just one thing you both need to know."

"What's that?" Dom asked.

Shift looked over at Rayna. "I *am* iliri enough that I won't change my mind. You're the one for me. I may not be meant for you, but there's no going back. I love you, Rayna Jens." He smiled to make sure she noticed his use of her new name. "I will love the pair of you for the rest of my life."

"May it be a long and comfortable one," Dom said softly.

"Yes, ahnor," Shift agreed.

Dom clasped Shift's knee. "Dernor," he replied, proving that he accepted his role in this family.

Because it didn't matter how they made it work or what they called the tie that bound them together. Marriage or mating - or some warped combination of them both. This was going to work, because *this* was Anglia.

CHAPTER TWELVE

PURPLE

"**S**o how long do I get to plan this?" Rayna asked.

Dom ducked his head to scratch at the back of his neck. "Is a month long enough?"

"No!" Rayna hissed. "Oh, Dom, no. That's not nearly long enough."

"Really?" Shift asked.

Rayna pushed herself back to her feet. "This is an official state wedding we're talking about. All of the Anglian nobility, representatives from our allies, and pretty much everyone on the continent who's important will be there. That means they need enough time to travel - "

"And they're already on their way for the Alliance meeting," Dom reminded her.

But Rayna had moved back enough for Shift to stand. His hands closed on her upper arms, making her look at him. "Who's missing?" he asked.

Her eyes lost focus and drifted to the corner of the room. "Sal and Pig will be there. The Dogs. The Shields." She huffed out a breath. "My family hasn't talked to me since I ran away to join the military, so not them. Fuck them if they only like me when things are good." Then she glanced up, meeting Shift's eyes. "But I kinda hoped Kesh could make it."

"He'll be there," Shift promised. "Lightning Brigade is one of the units coming with the allies. So is the 112th. The 43rd and Vanguard aren't, though. Is that a problem?"

Rayna shook her head. "All of my friends from the 43rd have moved on or retired. And the Vanguard wouldn't be allowed in Anglia yet. Not after we stole most of their best units." A little smile flashed across her lips. "But I guess that means everyone will be here." Then her lips fell open in shock. "Fuck, I'm going to need a dress!"

"Cillian's wife knows the best tailors," Dom assured her, moving to stand between them. "You can arrange for a dress, tell her it's a rush, and we'll set the date for a week after it's done. How's that?"

Rayna was nodding, but the look on her face proved that her mind was still going. "I know I'm forgetting something. Oh! I know..." She grabbed Dom's hand. "Who's officiating?"

"Did you have someone in mind?" he asked.

"No, but I want Pig to give me away. Ilija, maybe?"

"My best man," Dom countered. "I mean, since I'm marrying Shift."

"Cillian?" she suggested next.

Shift was nodding. "I like Cillian."

"Then him!" Rayna decided.

Dom was grinning. "And you'll need bridesmaids. I assume Sal will be one of them."

Rayna was nodding. "And Tyr?"

"He's not exactly a maid," Dom countered.

"No, but he's always been there for me, and if we're fucking everything else up, would the two of you mind?" she asked, looking between her men, her eyes pleading.

"Tyr's perfect," Shift assured her. "I just want Arctic beside me. He's my brother, and I think he represents the rest of my pack."

"Ok," Dom said. "And we can have Nava and Valri as flower girls? Sal promised to find me a ceremony for the iliri side of this so that Shift isn't being bound to us with only human traditions. I mean, if we're a mixed-species trio, we should have a mixed species wedding, right?"

"We'll need a rehearsal dinner, so we all know our places, and um...." Rayna just shook her head. "Dom, this is never going to work. Something's going to go wrong, and it'll fall through, but that's ok. I'm fine with trying, just so you know. I'm fine with being just your Consort, but mostly because I know you mean this. I just don't think it's going to be that easy."

Dom's answer was to cradle her face in his hands and lean closer. "I am a fucking king, Rayna, and believe it or not, I can make miracles happen. This is *going* to happen. If I have to turn into a pampered noble, I will. If I have to throw things, then I will, because I am *going* to marry my two best friends, and we are *going* to live happily ever after. The iliri aren't the only ones who got a fresh start with the end of this war, you hear me?"

And then he kissed her. Hard. His shoulder pressed into Shift's chest, but none of them cared. Shift just used it as an excuse to move around Rayna enough to reach her neck. While Dom worked her mouth, kissing her passionately, Shift swept Rayna's hair to the side and grazed his teeth across the back of her neck. She reached for him, grabbing at Shift's hip to pull him closer, until both men had her pinned between them.

The scent on the air changed. The fear was gone and the desire was taking over. Rayna moaned into Dom, and Shift could feel it against his lips. She writhed, pressing her ass against his pelvis and her breasts against Dom's chest. Not once had she ever been shy about her needs, and right now she was intentionally turning her men on.

So Shift pressed himself a little closer, grinding his dick against her ass. Yeah, he was hard, and getting harder by the second. "Bed," he suggested.

Dom chuckled as he pulled his mouth from Rayna's. "Oh yeah. Shift, make sure you tell the Kaisae that we're getting married." And then he spun Rayna in place and nudged her toward their bedroom.

Shift paused long enough to adjust himself and reach out for his sister. *Hey, Sal?*

Yeah? she replied immediately, almost like she'd been waiting.

We're getting married. No date yet, but Dom proposed, and Rayna and I said yes. I have a feeling you knew about this?

I did, she assured him, *and I've got Inessi looking for some stuff that will work for the ceremony.*

Good. Tell me about it tomorrow. I need to get laid.

Sal's amusement came back clearly. *Congratulations, brother. We'll talk about it tomorrow. I'm happy for you.*

Then she was gone, making a point of closing the link between them. That was Sal's way of saying she understood, but it meant he didn't need to excuse himself or get left behind. Dom already had Rayna out of her shirt, and he was kissing his way down her chest while he stripped away her pants, and Shift had no intention of being left out.

Yanking his shirt over his head, he tossed it on the ground, and then locked the bedroom door behind him, because this moment was going to be private. This was their celebration. This was his chance to show his mates how much he loved them. Both of them.

The moment Rayna was naked, Shift pushed between her and Dom. "Strip," he said, giving the King a chance to get out of his clothes, as Shift's hands found Rayna's waist and he lifted her just enough to toss her onto the bed.

She bounced a bit on the mattress and giggled, but Shift followed, crawling his way onto the bed between her legs. Rayna let her knees fall open and reached for him. Her hand clasped his bicep, drawing him closer, but Shift wasn't aiming for her mouth. He bent to kiss the inside of her thigh, then the spot where her legs met her body, and finally the folds right between her legs.

Rayna moaned, releasing Shift's arm just to grab the pillows over her head. When his tongue slid across her, she arched her back and pressed herself closer to his face, her hips lifting from the bed. He grabbed her hip and held her where he wanted, lapping across her slit until he found that hard knot. The one that made her gasp, and she gasped loudly.

Rayna wasn't a silent lover. She never did anything partway. Each time he sucked at her clit, she bucked, giving herself completely to the pleasure. Skin to skin, he could feel her, and that open link was right there. Shift just had to push at it a little more, and he felt her emotions begin to leak into his mind.

He wasn't a linker to bind them together, but he could force the mate bond. It wasn't as easy as it was for the men with more purity, and it didn't happen as fast, but that was a good excuse to take his time. Rayna felt the connection and reached for it while Shift drove her higher until he finally began to feel her pleasure as if it were his own.

"Yes!" Rayna said once the connection was in place. "Oh, Kayden, that's it."

"My turn," Dom said, grabbing Shift's shoulder in a plea for him to lift his head.

The moment he did, Dom took his place, but this was the trick. Being with two humans was harder. They weren't meant to share their emotions like this, so Shift had to force it, but he could, would, and always did. As soon as Dom had Rayna lost in her own pleasure again, Shift leaned in. His mouth found Dom's shoulder. His hand cupped the far side of the King's neck. Then, finally, his teeth closed on the tendon at the side of the man's neck, just where it met the shoulder.

Shift bit, and he bit hard enough to pull Dom in with them. The King surged into their link with a rush of excitement and the throbbing of his dick against the bed. It was intense enough to break Shift's mouth free, but the link stayed. Three bodies, three minds, one bond. Together, they worked, and Rayna was close. With his chest pressed against Dom's back, Shift reached between them to slip his fingers inside their woman, working her while Dom licked and sucked at her clit, and their lover watched, enjoying the view.

"Guys," Rayna panted. "Harder."

So Shift thrust. Using two fingers, he fucked her with his hand, and Dom rode the woman's movements, reaching up to grab her breast. That helped pin her down, but pinching and flicking at her nipple brought their woman even closer. Close enough that Shift changed the position of his hand, curling his fingers to hit that sweet spot while Dom sucked.

Rayna exploded, heaving her body off the bed as she cried out her orgasm, and the intensity of it hit both men. Dom reached down to squeeze himself, and Shift understood. It felt like he was about to cum, but that was her, not him. No, they weren't quite done.

"Yours," Dom said, rolling over Rayna's leg to let Shift take his place.

But Shift had other ideas. He crawled his way up her body, kissing her belly, her sternum, pausing to suck at one breast, then her neck, but he didn't enter her. Instead, Shift slid one arm beneath her shoulder and turned, rolling onto his side and pulling Rayna over to face him.

"I love you," he whispered as he reached for her lips.

And she kissed back, not caring that his mouth tasted like a combination of her and Dom's sweet skin. Rayna's fingers slid deep into Shift's hair, holding him to her, and the woman flexed her hips, angling herself until he was right there, teasing her opening - and she wanted it. She didn't have to say a word. He could feel how much she needed him inside her.

Shift pushed. Hot, wet, and so soft, she surrounded him, bringing forth a primal grunt. No matter how many times he was with her, he could never get over how good she felt. It was almost too good, the way he swelled to fill her, and she squeezed around him perfectly. Good enough that he had to pause.

"Don't finish without me," Dom teased as he moved behind her.

"Lube," Rayna told him.

Dom chuckled. "I know."

A rush of cold flashed through their minds, but that was Rayna. And then, positioning himself behind her, Dom pushed into her ass slowly. Again, Shift groaned, but this time it was closer to a growl. The difference in angle was good for her, but even better for them. He could feel Dom inside her body. The King's dick was all but pushing against Shift's as the man eased himself in.

"Fuck me," Rayna begged.

Dom obeyed. Slowly but deliberately, he began to pump into her body, grinding himself against Shift inside her. Unable to help himself,

Shift thrust, meeting him, and Dom reached out for his arm. His hand closed on Shift's bicep, but Shift was grasping Dom's forearm for leverage, and they both began to move.

For a moment, the world seemed to fade away. It was just the three of them, bound together in one woman's body, lost in the pleasure they could make. Every breath, every moan, and each movement felt better than the one before. Dom had his other hand clutching Rayna's shoulder. Shift had his teeth buried in the side of her neck. The blankets were crumpled beneath them. The bed creaked in protest, and each thrust became a little harder, a bit more intense.

Then Dom's hand released Shift's arm to land on the back of Shift's head. Just as the pleasure of their lovemaking reached the breaking point, the King met his best friend's eyes over his lover's body. "I love you," he whispered, the words meant for all of them.

And Rayna exploded, her body clamping down with her orgasm, wringing the men to completion. Shift forgot to respond, but with his mind open, he knew they could both feel it. Not just his pleasure, but also his love.

Because he could feel theirs. Clearer than ever before, he *knew* they loved him just as much as he loved them. The kind of love that couldn't change its mind. The kind that would last forever.

CHAPTER THIRTEEN

RED

They spent the rest of the night proving their love to each other. Eventually, the trio fell asleep, but Dom still woke early the next morning. When his eyes opened, the first thing he saw was Rayna's hair spilling in front of his face. A pale arm rested across her shoulder. That belonged to Shift, and the man's hand twitched subtly in his sleep, looking as if he was once again clutching his sword.

Dom leaned closer to move Shift's hand to Rayna's arm. Hopefully, that would change his dreams from memories of war to thoughts of their fiancée. Just the word made Dom smile, even if it was only spoken in his mind. Then, before he climbed out of bed, the King kissed his sleeping mate's back. Neither she nor Shift stirred, proving just how much fun they had the night before.

But they'd said yes. Dom got the impression that Shift hadn't believed he was truly a part of this relationship until he saw the ring. Or more accurately, when Rayna finally said she loved him. She wasn't the kind of woman to voice her feelings. She showed them instead. Her love was a smile of support or stepping in to help. Rayna had never been the kind to swoon or gush. She was too decisive for that, but evidently Shift needed more.

Dom could do that. If Shift needed someone to say it, then he

96

would, and Rayna would follow. She wasn't *scared* of admitting it, she simply didn't think like that. Clearly, Shift did, so Dom would talk to her later. After all, if this marriage was going to be a happy one, the three of them would have to learn how to work together as well in peace as they did in war.

And speaking of war, Dom had one more fight ahead of him. Once he was dressed, he sent a thought to Ilija, asking the Colonel to call the noble council together. It was late enough that they should all be awake, and the King needed them in the council room in half an hour. He didn't want to give the nobles enough time to cause problems or prepare for what was coming. No, this was going to be a surprise attack.

Before he left, Dom wrote a note for Shift and Rayna, letting them know where he was and that they had the morning to relax and spend time together. Then, he headed down to the kitchens to steal a mug of coffee from the head cook. She always gave him a splash of thick cream, and that was a luxury he'd picked up from Sal. With his cup cradled in his hands, Dom made his way into his office early, hoping to beat everyone else.

He didn't. Vanica, of all people, was waiting for him. Dom's sister had claimed the plushest chair in the room, and she was leaned back with her eyes closed, resting. Still, the moment he walked in, her lips curled into a smile, proving that resting was not the same as sleeping.

"Ilsa keeping you up still?" Dom asked.

"Nava, actually," Vanica admitted. "She wants to go to the Iliri Academy with the other kids."

"So send her," Dom said. "She's in the age group they're taking this year, isn't she?"

"Ilija wants her to wait until next year," Vanica admitted, finally opening her eyes. "He's hoping for a chance to get to know her before sending her away for months at a time."

"Ah." Dom pushed his cup across his desk toward her. "Need a sip?"

Vanica waved it away. "Unless I want Ilsa up all night, no. She's still breastfeeding, Dom, and one sip is just a tease. I'd want a whole cup."

"Right." So Dom took a sip instead. "Can I get *anything* for you?"

"Ilija's already taking care of it," she promised. "But I want to know what we're here to talk about. What is it that has you and my husband sneaking around like thieves?"

Dom found himself smiling and unable to stop it. "I'm getting married, and the council's not going to like it."

"Rayna said yes?"

He nodded. "And Shift. Kayden, I mean." Then he groaned. "He prefers Shift. Said that's the name his pack calls him."

"Yeah..." Vanica said, dragging out the word. "You're right, they won't like that."

"Don't care," Dom promised. "I'm the King, and this is a nation of many cultures. Two of them take multiple mates. And if I marry him, that makes Sal my sister-in-law. With Jarl and Nya? It's a good political move, but it's also what I want."

Vanica nodded once. "And Shift's place?"

"Royal Consort," Dom said.

She tilted her head slightly in a way that proved she thought that was a good title. "He'll be assumed to be *your* Consort, you know."

"Mhm. And like I told Sal and Shift, if having people think that we're fucking means our citizens can openly show their own love? Then I don't care what they say about me."

A chuckle proved that Ilija had heard the last part. A second later, the man rounded the corner, walking into the room with a tray of sweet pastries for his wife. "A little pick-me-up for you," he said, offering them to Vanica. "And Dom's right. What are they going to say, that he's not man enough? I think the Terran War proved otherwise. That he's less of a man? Well, that just gives women more rights, doesn't it? That it's gross? Doesn't make him any less the King."

Vanica accepted the plate. "That Salryc Luxx put him on the throne," she countered. "And now she has her brother in a position to run the human part of this nation."

"Mm, but the only people who know Sal had anything to do with Dom's succession aren't about to complain," Ilija told her. "And I think we'll leave that out of the debates."

"Does Cillian know?" she asked.

"Nope," Dom said. "He knows I pardoned her for Eriwald and any actions she performed as a soldier for an enemy nation before becoming our ally and co-ruler. I told him Eriwald and Bysno were in talks with the Emperor behind our backs. They were, and my grandfather was too, but I left that part off. Most of the nobles think that King Jensen was assassinated because he stopped the talks so Terric tried to remove him."

"But Sal's still pardoned regardless?" Vanica asked.

"I think she's proven herself," Dom said, "so yes. Her pardon covers anything that might come up. It's pretty broad, but only clears her of actions before she was named the Sergeant at Arms of Anglia. Sal says that's all she needs."

"Good," Vanica said, then paused.

It took a few more seconds before Dom heard the feet in the hall. Ilija moved silently, but the other nobles hadn't been trained by two assassins and a grauori. The sound of their fancy shoes on the stone tiles gave them away long before the first man walked into the council chamber. It was Cillian, but Lord Piet was with him. Linella's slippers were quieter, but not silent either. While they were still claiming their chairs, Bjan Arvo and Otso Aulis arrived. Dom waited for the group to sit before he gestured for Ilija to close the door.

"I'm getting married," Dom said to start the meeting.

Bjan Arvo narrowed his eyes. "To Rayna Mel?" he asked. "Sire, she's common."

"She's anything but," Dom assured him, "and we all know that I can give her a title easily. She more than earned one in the war. Not only did she save my life in Myrosica, but she's also an elite soldier, a Verdant Shield, and a military hero. I could grant her land out west, make her Lady Mel..." He tipped his head toward Linella. "Or Lord, as the case may be. And that would take no more than a few days."

"Fair enough," Bjan admitted.

Dom took a pointed sip of his coffee, his eyes moving to Lord Aulis. "Are you opposed, Otso?"

"I'm pretty sure it wouldn't matter, sire. You've already shown that you can make her my equal."

"Good," Dom said, "because I'm also marrying Kayden Savis. He will become the Royal Consort."

That made the entire room erupt into chaos. Aulis and Arvo both began talking over each other. Cillian had questions, but they were drowned out by the other two lords. Linella Piet tried once, huffed in annoyance, and then flopped back into her chair and crossed her arms beneath her breasts. Vanica and Ilija, however, smiled.

It was that more than Dom's silence which finally made the room go quiet. In fact, Lord Aulis paused in the middle of a word with his mouth partly open. It looked as if he'd just figured something out.

"You *knew* about this?" he demanded, glaring at Vanica.

"I got here before you, but I'm not surprised," she admitted. "I know my brother well, after all."

"You," Bjan spat, pointing at Ilija. "Were you involved in this?"

"I was," Ilija told him. "I actually commissioned the Consort's ring. And I mean Shift's, not Rayna's."

"You can't have a man as a Consort," Bjan barked. "What will people think of you?"

"That I won the war?" Dom offered. "Or maybe that I'm embracing the culture of our fellow citizens, the iliri and grauori?"

"No," Bjan said, shaking his head to make the point. "I cannot condone this corruption of our traditions. Marriage is a contract between a man and a woman to produce heirs."

Linella Piet scoffed loudly. "Maybe it used to be, but that doesn't make it right. Marriage for most Anglians isn't just about love and growth. It's a way to join families together, and the King is suggesting a very blatant bond between Anglia's humans and our iliri. Am I right, sire?"

"You are, Lord Piet," he said, the praise clear in his tone. "I see that your late husband wasn't the astute one in your family."

"No, sire, he wasn't," she agreed. "I also think that this move isn't completely a political one, though."

"It's not," Dom agreed. "I want to marry for love, and I can't think of a single reason I shouldn't."

"Alliances?" Cillian Tor suggested. "Because a marriage to another nation's elite is an easy way to gain an advantage, and marrying not just one Anglian, but two of them does close that option."

"Ah, but we already have their loyalty," Dom pointed out. "Thanks to the Kaisae. The only nations who aren't a recognized ally are Gallicor, Namisa, and Terric."

"But," Ilija added, "the new Emperor is living happily in Arhhawen now. Doesn't hurt that he occasionally sends letters back to his aides claiming that he's traveling, learning more about the modern world so he can lead better. That counts as proof of life, and so long as he's alive, he can't be replaced."

Vanica chuckled. "Sal thought of everything, didn't she?"

"No, actually," Dom said. "That was Narnx's idea. Sal didn't realize Terran law states that the Emperor is a lifelong position, no different than the King is here. The only way for Narnx to be overthrown is to kill him and present his corpse as proof. Since he currently has no children, he has no heir, and thus another Emperor could be chosen."

"But I dare someone to get to him in Arhhawen," Cillian mumbled under his breath.

Otso Aulis lifted a finger off the arm of his chair, signaling that he had a point to make. "Does this mean Terric will be a part of the Alliance talks?"

"For the new Conventions of War, yes," Dom said. "Narnx wants to make sure that Terrans are included so this can't happen again."

"Good. Will your marriage to this *man* influence that?" Lord Aulis asked.

"No," Dom admitted. "Again, that's Sal."

"But," Ilija said, "Dom's marriage to Shift will make him family to Sal, and *that* will make him - and the humans of Anglia - more powerful on the world stage. It will give him ties to Viraenova, the Conglomerate, and Terric through Narnx. It's a wise political move."

Bjan was still shaking his head. "I cannot condone a marriage between our King and a man."

"Never mind the mess it will make if his Queen gives birth to the iliri's bastard," Lord Aulis added.

Dom slammed his hand down on his desk. "That won't happen."

"You can't guarantee it won't," Bjan told him. "Accidental pregnancies happen all the time."

"Rayna can't have kids," Dom insisted.

"With you, maybe," Bjan countered.

"With anyone," Dom growled. "She was surgically sterilized! Not that it's any of your business, but Rayna chose not to have kids, and she made sure it wouldn't happen by accident. She didn't want to be pregnant in battle, and she's never wanted kids of her own, so she made sure she couldn't."

"What?" Lord Aulis gasped. "They can do that?"

"Why can't we do that here?" Lord Piet wanted to know.

Dom nodded at her. "Because in Anglia, we used to treat women like our property, not people capable of making their own decisions. In the Conglomerate, it's an easy surgery for family planning. I've been told most Conglomerate women prefer to use birth control because the surgery is not reversible, but Rayna's already had it done. She will not have any children, regardless of the father. That's why Jarl's my heir."

"And he's having children with a grauori!" Lord Aulis pointed out. "So does that mean his heir will be the next Orassae? Are you so willing to give up all human control of Anglia?"

"His *heir*," Dom said, "will be whoever rules as a human. If Nya's children don't identify as such, then they wouldn't be in the line of succession."

"That's not good enough," Lord Aulis said. "We need it in law."

"And the next King - or Queen - could just change it," Bjan whined. "If Jarl intends to legitimize those children, then there's no way to prevent our country from being given away right before our eyes!"

"Then maybe we should just let the iliri and grauori choose our next leader," Dom snapped. "If you have a problem with my line, we can find another. Or *they* can! I think the iliri have already proven that they'll step up to protect our segment of this nation, and the grauori fought for us when no one else would. They won't care about anything except who can work with them and rule this country fairly!" He thumped his fist down one more time. "Anglia is a nation of three species, so fine. If you're so worried about who will rule us, then let's just change it so that we can always have a good, rational, and loyal human, huh? That's what you want, right?"

"It's not a bad idea," Cillian said, glancing at the others.

"And you think the grauori and iliri would pick a strong leader for us?" Lord Aulis asked the King. "What if they don't? What if they work together to keep us weak? You've just made it clear that your *husband* is an iliri, your wife can't produce an heir, and your heir is having children with a beast. You're stripping away our power."

"Nya's a grauori," Ilija corrected. "Not a beast."

"Whatever!" Aulis snapped. "That's just one generation, and humans are already being pushed out of control. I don't mind sharing with them, but that's a very different thing from giving all of our rights away! The human kingdom deserves to have a *human* making the decisions for it."

Dom stood, leaning over his desk as his mind spun, desperately trying to find a way to make this all work. "Anglia is a nation of three species. Three species that are growing closer every day. The lines between human, iliri, and grauori are disappearing. In two generations, how will we tell? Am I human enough for you, Otso? Or am I too iliri? Is that why you were so interested in what Marcu was offering? Or did you simply think that I had no idea you were involved in that?"

And all eyes in the room turned to look at the one man who'd escaped that scandal unscathed.

CHAPTER FOURTEEN

CYAN

*L*ord Aulis lifted his multiple chins and glared back at the King. "I was more than happy to let Marcu tell me his plans because that was the best way to protect your crown, sire."

"Please," Linella grumbled. "That's not at all what I heard."

"And what would you have heard in your knitting circle?" Lord Aulis asked snidely.

Linella smiled at him sweetly. Too sweetly. "Why, I heard that you wanted to make sure that you had a foot on both sides of the line. That way if Marcu's coup worked, you'd keep your lands and title. You'd stay exactly where you are now. But if it failed, then you could claim that you were trying to stop him. That you had *no idea* he was serious and not just complaining."

"Treason?" Vanica asked, looking at her brother.

Dom shook his head. "I think that's politics, but it's also why I keep him on the council. I mean, it's not like he can truly start a rebellion without me knowing. He touches too many people in a day."

"I had the best intentions," Lord Aulis snapped. "I was trying to get proof of Lord Piet's - "

"Marcu's," Linella corrected, making it clear that she now wore the title of Lord Piet and didn't want it used that way.

"Fine," Lord Aulis grumbled. "The *former* Lord Piet's plot."

Dom turned his attention on Linella. "What do you think, Lord Piet? Should I ask one of the iliri to read him again and make sure? I have a feeling the Ahnor would be willing to check that he really is still loyal."

"Or the Kaisae," Linella suggested. "Or any of Ryali's ladies, truth be told. They *are* good friends to have."

"I vote for Linaeryx," Cillian said. "Granted, she might rip your throat out if she thinks you're a threat to her freedom."

"Fine," Lord Aulis said, "I'll support your marriage, sire."

"I thought you might," Dom told him. "What about you, Lord Arvo?"

Bjan sighed. "It's going to happen whether I like it or not, but I think it's a mistake. I think this new government you're trying to make is quickly becoming a mess."

"But he has a point," Linella said. "If the Orassae and Kaisae - whoever holds those titles at the time - pick our next heir, it does solve a lot of problems. We all know that relationships form from proximity, and each King - or Queen - will be working closely with the other two species, so why not choose an heir from the people of our species who've proven they're just and noble?"

"Not necessarily born noble," Ilija added. "But those who act with the integrity that we like to claim comes with that word."

"I like it," Vanica said, "because our own father proved just how easy it is to work around the limits of marriage and lines of succession. Now that women are allowed to rule their lands? It makes sense. And if an heir is chosen by the triad, then they'll have time to learn from the previous ruler, ensuring more consistency than Anglia has ever had before."

"Plus the right to choose our leaders," Linella said. "Because you can't all tell me that you were thrilled with the idea of the late Lord Bysno sitting on the throne. The man would've run Anglia into poverty!"

Dom looked at Lord Aulis. "Should I assume you're opposed to voting for our next King as well?"

"Will this apply for all noble positions?" the man asked.

"Nope," Dom said. "But I think the potential leaders should be chosen from all the nobles and highest officers in the military, not just the ones related to my family. If we include officers in the options, then we won't need to ennoble every war hero; we just have to make sure they're on the list."

Bjan sighed. "Sire, will this work in reverse? Will we, as humans, have the right to pick the candidates for the next Orassae and Kaisae?"

"The possibilities are a lot more limited," Dom said, "but if they agree to that, will you agree to this?"

"It would make the government less confusing," Bjan admitted.

Dom turned his eyes on Lord Aulis. "And you?"

"If the iliri and grauori are bound by the same rules, and the leaders are chosen to represent their own species first - or at least equally - then I'll agree, but you'll have to write that in as an amendment to the constitution."

"Which means a unanimous vote of the noble council," Bjan clarified, glancing at Ilija to make it clear who that comment was for.

Ilija tipped his head in appreciation. "Maybe you should write the first draft, Lord Arvo? Then we can take it to the other leaders. I recommend having the entire sitting triad select the most obvious candidates, and each species choose their representative from those. It will limit the chances for corruption."

"I can do that," Bjan agreed. "And once this is codified into our laws, then I'll have no problem with your wedding, sire."

"I can agree to that," Lord Aulis said. "But I won't vote for it until the other species are held to the same terms."

"Then get me the amendment by tomorrow morning," Dom told them. "Because I *am* getting married. I don't care if this council won't recognize it. We already have our allies coming, and I want to do this while they're all here."

"You can't," Linella hissed. "Sire, a state wedding takes years to plan."

"You have weeks," Dom told them. "I promised Rayna one week

longer than it takes to make her dress, and she'll want her friends and family here - which means our allies."

Vanica looked over at Linella. "We can make this happen."

"We have to," Linella breathed. "But I have no idea how we'll fit the ceremonies in among the Alliance meetings."

"It's also going to be a cross-cultural wedding," Dom told them. "Sal's working on a ceremony that respects Shift's iliri traditions. I'll want that included in the vows." Then he turned to Cillian. "Rayna wants you to officiate it, and Shift agreed. Would you consider it?"

"I'd be honored," Cillian told him. "And I speak enough Iliran to muddle through whatever words will be said for Shift. I also think the Kaisae will help me if I need it."

Dom chuckled once. "She's going to be one of Rayna's maids. Tyr will be another - and yes, I'm well aware he's a man. She's asked that Pig give her away. I'm going to suggest that Ran do the same for Shift."

"And you?" Vanica asked. "Who will give you to your spouses?"

Dom shook his head. "Doesn't work that way and you know it. I'm the one doing the marrying, so they're coming into my family, and both have agreed to take the last name of Jens. I thought we could borrow Nava and Valri for the flower girls, though?"

"Nava would be thrilled," Vanica assured him. "But who is standing up with you?"

"Ilija will be my best man. Shift said he'll have Arctic as the representative of his pack. We're going to try to make this close to a typical Anglian wedding without slighting any iliri traditions."

"Be that as it may," Cillian pointed out, "what about the national celebration? The populace needs to be told."

Finally, Dom claimed his chair and relaxed. They'd finally accepted that this was going to happen. All that was left now was the planning, and he'd been thinking about this much too hard. Dom had ideas. Hopefully, at least some of them would help with the cultural divide that started all of this.

"Did you know," he said, looking at every person in the room, "that we're having interspecies tensions because of cultural confusion? The best example is an iliri man who was jailed because he abused his wife.

He bit her inside their own home." He paused, giving them all time to think about that.

Cillian was already shaking his head. Ilija was smirking. Vanica pressed her fingers to her lips, but none of them gave away the point of his comment, so Dom lifted a brow at the others.

"Do any of you see a problem with that?"

"You said domestic abuse was a crime," Lord Aulis grumbled.

"I did," Dom agreed, "but you're making the same mistake. Iliri bite. Iliri men typically mate with a woman who has more iliri ancestry than he does. Men breed up, they say. Amongst themselves, they call it the iliri male curse. They physically cannot be attracted to a woman who isn't iliri enough."

"Which means she'd bite back," Bjan realized. "So the man was accused of a crime when he was merely doing something inherent to his species?"

"Exactly," Dom said. "His human neighbor didn't understand that, though. And to prevent this, I've agreed to make a new police force. We'll call them Peacekeepers. Each town will get a triad assigned to make sure that one species' laws are not harming another."

"And for the towns that are mostly human?" Lord Aulis asked.

Dom sighed heavily. "Peacekeepers are a triad, Otso. One human, one grauori, and one iliri. They will work together, explaining how their own species does things. We humans have been in charge long enough that our traditions are seen as 'normal,' and I promise the grauori and humans understand them - or at least know of them."

"And who will oversee it?" Bjan asked.

"We intend to have the Dorton triad - or Arhhawen, if they prefer to keep their office there - work like the commanding officers over all the others. Sal has chosen Ryali to represent the iliri. I would like to suggest Corporal Henrik Aben."

"Henrik is a good choice," Linella agreed, "and he works well with Ryali. If anything, she defers to him."

"He also isn't intimidated by the nobility," Cillian added. "My wife said that he can be a bit crass at times, but I think that will work for this position."

Ilija grunted. "He's a corporal? That's not an impressive rank."

"It should be a civilian position," Lord Aulis interjected.

Dom gestured to him, but his attention was on Ilija. "What he said. Granted, I think Henrik has earned a promotion, and giving him one before shifting him to the commanding human Peacekeeper, or whatever title we give them, would be a good idea."

"Then I'll promote him," Ilija said. "If everyone agrees he's the best choice, that is?" Around the room, they all nodded, giving Ilija the authority. "So, major?"

"Major's good," Dom agreed. "And we'll need to pick twenty-one other soldiers to assign to every town in Anglia. Sal intended to ask Rragri to bring a collection of grauori with her."

"With... her?" Bjan asked.

Dom lifted a hand, begging him to wait. "So, I think we'll need some kind of adjustment period, because we'll need the triads to work well together. It won't help any of our citizens if they spend more time fighting each other instead of solving cultural confusion."

"Agreed," Ilija said. "I think we should match them together in Arhhawen, though. Send our choice of men there and let Sal sort it out? She doesn't have a wedding to plan for, and it's one less thing to distract our human allies when they show up."

"And Viraenova will be impressed that we're even trying," Dom realized, nodding to show he agreed before looking over to Bjan. "Rragri was invited to Dorton for Nya's birth. The Kernor - Tyr - pointed out that grauori and iliri healing can't do much about birthing complications, but human surgery can. Combined, we're hoping that if Jarl's kids are too big for a grauori to birth, then we can still have a pair of healthy babies."

"And what kind of babies?" Lord Aulis asked.

Dom shrugged. "Don't care. They'll be Anglians, and I'm pretty sure they won't be the last cross-species offspring. I mean, just look at the iliri if you don't believe me."

"And where will we keep a pack of grauori?" Bjan asked.

"Rragri and her mates can have Sal's old rooms," Dom told him. "Her pack can take another one of the larger suites, because they will gladly share the space. The guards traveling with her can stay either in our barracks where they have friends, or in Arhhawen where they will probably feel more comfortable. And no, I have no idea when or if this is happening. I'm afraid that I was a little distracted yesterday."

"With his proposal," Ilija clarified. "For the very big wedding we're about to throw."

"Which," Dom said, "I'm going to need a budget for, Otso."

Lord Aulis sighed heavily. "I'll get that for you by tomorrow."

"Thank you, and if no one has anything else...?" Dom waited long enough for someone to speak up, but no one did. "Then I believe we're done here."

Linella immediately leaned toward Vanica. "I think we should go back to your rooms so you can feed the baby and we can start planning this."

"Someone has to," Vanica agreed, "because my brother seems to think that weddings just happen. Dom, tell Rayna to join us when she's free?"

"Why?" Dom asked. "She needs to get fitted for a dress!"

Cillian laughed at that. "Trust me, sire, there's a lot more to getting married than just a dress. Ladies, I'm sure my wife would be willing to help as well."

"We're going to need all the help we can get," Linella told him, "so please. Ria would be most welcome with this."

Cillian chuckled. "And this is why we need women in power. Let me know if I can do anything?"

"Oh, trust me," Vanica assured him, "everyone is going to get a list. This is a royal wedding. One being held in the middle of an international Alliance meeting. We will be judged, and we do not have *nearly* enough time to plan it. *Everyone* is going to have to help if we don't want Anglia to end up looking bad." She looked at her brother. "Especially you."

"I'm all in," Dom promised. "Clueless, evidently, but if you tell me, I'll make it happen."

"Step one," Linella said, "send Rayna to Vanica's room. Step two, get yourself and your future husband fitted for matching suits or uniforms of some kind. Step three? Get us that iliri wedding ceremony."

"Step four," Ilija said, "pick twenty-one soldiers to become Peacekeepers."

Dom groaned. "I think war was easier."

"But not nearly as much fun," Ilija assured him. "It'll be worth it, Dom. Trust me."

"Yeah." Dom grinned. "I can't believe I'm getting married."

CHAPTER FIFTEEN

BLACK

"*D*ava!" A small fist banged on Sal's bedroom door, pulling her from sleep. "Amma Sal? I'm supposed to go to school today, and you're all still sleeping."

Lasryn, Sal realized. Across the bed from her, Kolt groaned and shoved a pillow over his head. From behind her, Jase buried his face into her neck to smother his groggy chuckle. Thankfully, Gage had the presence of mind to answer the boy.

"We're up!" he bellowed at the door. "Brew some coffee, Las."

"I'm supposed to go to school," Las yelled back. "Rhyx and Raast are leaving soon, and I want to go with my sisters!"

"Brew the coffee!" This time, it was Kolt. "Because you're not going to school until I have some."

All of them heard the boy growl under his breath, but it didn't have the result he hoped for. Sal turned her face into the pillow to laugh. Gage sighed. Blaz chuckled. Still, they were all awake now, and Kolt was waving Zep and Tyr off the bed so he could get out.

"This," Tyr said, "is why I didn't want kids."

"Sucks to be you," Kolt told him. "Because you have six now."

"Four with fur," Zep muttered as he headed toward the closet. "You going in black, Kolt?"

"And white," Kolt decided. "Toss me that white shirt?"

Zep's hand landed on the material, then he paused. "Isn't this Blaec's?"

Kolt's head snapped up. "Fuck."

"Wear it," Sal told him. "It has the crossed swords on the chest, and Las wants a reason to brag."

But everyone was looking at the closet. "How much stuff in there is his?" Gage asked.

It was Jase who answered. "The stuff from Syhar was sent here and put away. We did na look at it, so we do na know."

Zep nodded slowly. "You want me to go through it, Sal?"

She stared at the white shirt in Zep's hands for a little too long. "He's gone."

"That doesn't answer the question," Blaz told her, scooting closer to her on the bed. "Sal, it's ok to need time. It took me over two years. You haven't even had one. There's nothing wrong with wanting to keep it."

Slowly, she looked over at Kolt. "I want to remember it differently."

He nodded, able to feel exactly what she meant. "Then I'll wear it. We're the same size. Pretty sure his stuff will fit Blaz as well."

"Or would that hurt more?" Blaz asked.

"No," Sal breathed, honestly thinking about it. "He's been dead a while. Now he's finally gone, and he died both times to save me. I mean, he was already dead the second time, but it feels more permanent. That doesn't mean I want to forget him, but I also don't want to pretend like he's more important to me than any of you."

"He was a good man," Gage reminded her.

Sal nodded. "He was. Blaec was an amazing commander, a wonderful tactician, and a ferocious soldier. He was also a good friend. And yes, I loved him, but that doesn't mean I should've. I loved him because of what he represented to me."

"Freedom," Jase said softly.

"Yeah," she admitted. "And power, I think. I came from a world where I was the lowest of the low, and here he was, part iliri, and the entire world respected him. I know I needed him, and I don't regret most of our time together, but..."

When she let the sentence trail off, Blaz reached for her hand. "We won't judge you, Sal. We're *all* here to help."

"That," she said, looking up to meet his eyes. "He was a good man, but the wrong one for me. The right one for the iliri, though. I needed him, but I also needed that time to realize that I didn't love him for him. I loved him for what he made me. I loved him because I wanted to *be* him."

"And now you're even better," Blaz assured her.

"Yeah." She huffed out a laugh, looking over at Zep. "Did you know that when I started dreaming of him, it was different?"

"How?" he asked.

"We became friends," she said. "Not lovers. He helped me, but more than that, I learned how to stop loving him as a mate, and start loving him as my commanding officer and just a friend, and yet he still tore himself apart to keep me from shattering. Does that mean I wasn't fair to him?"

Jase leaned closer to her ear. "It means he was finally fair ta ya, kitten. He owed ya, and he paid his debts. Do na blame yerself fer his choices. They were na yers ta make."

"That's why I want Kolt to wear the shirt," she said, sounding a little more confident. "I want to be able to see things that remind me of Blaec, but think of them without the pain he left me with."

Kolt held out his hand, and Zep passed over the shirt. While everyone watched, he pulled it on, then paired it with a pair of black pants that fit just a little too tight. The whole thing looked good in a way Blaec never would've. It wasn't professional. It wasn't respectable. When Kolt shoved his fingers through his hair, styling it haphazardly, Sal found herself smiling.

"Thank you, babe."

"Blaec never looked this good, huh?" But there was a hint of worry in his heart, palpable in their bond.

Sal just shook her head, still smiling. "No, he didn't, and Las will make sure everyone knows his dava is the Taunor of All Anglia."

"Technically, his amma is the Kaisae, which I think trumps Taunor," Kolt pointed out.

"And he still likes you more," Sal said. "Ok, someone get me something green to wear?"

"And black," Zep said, reaching for the other side of the closest. "How about with a bit of silver?"

And he pulled out a shirt she'd never seen before, but that wasn't shocking. The guys had started buying her things when she was still a recruit. They hadn't stopped since. New pieces simply appeared with her things. It was their way - all of the Blades - of showing her that she was important to them.

While they all got dressed, Jase moved beside Kolt. "Ya are na going alone, are ya?" he asked.

Kolt lifted a brow. "Peacetime, brother. I should be safe enough, I think."

"I did na mean that. I meant because it will na be easy ta let yer kid walk away after so long without him. Did ya want company?"

Kolt clasped his shoulder. "Hwa's going with the girls. I think the pair of us should be enough."

"I would," Zep offered, "but I need to get Valri back to her amma."

"I'll go," Blaz offered.

Sal shook her head. "I need you to show me the stables and help me figure out what else we need to do."

He dropped his head with a sigh. "Yeah, I can do that."

"Las likes you well enough," Kolt assured him. "He's just overwhelmed. I did tell him last night that you might teach him how to ride if he keeps his grades up, though."

"Definitely," Blaz promised.

Tyr groaned. "Fine! I'll go. And if you father-types get all gushy, I'm giving you shit."

"He's kinda your kid too," Kolt reminded him.

"Not my fuck trophy, though," Tyr teased. "That's all you, man. I know how to pull out."

"Uh-huh." Kolt grinned. "Only because you've never experienced estrus. Trust me, the mind shuts off and the dick takes over. So... Coffee?"

"Lots," Sal said, heading for the door.

Thankfully, Las had actually put on a pot to brew. He'd also set out sugar, cream, and cups for all of them. That was almost enough to distract from the stack of luggage beside the main door. Two different saddlebags had been conscripted, a leather bag, and an old, blue, military-style duffle bag. In other words, the boy was taking pretty much everything he owned.

"Where'd you get the saddlebags?" Sal asked.

Las's ears began to turn pink. "They were in the hall. I figured no one was using them, and they look better than a pillowcase."

"Mhm," Sal agreed. "Well, the black ones are mine, so you know. The greyer set?"

"Mine," Jase said as he reached for a cup. "Leather's a bit faded. Gage's are redder."

"Oxblood," Gage corrected. "Looks better on Cookie."

Jase nodded to show he'd heard. "Ya will get a set of yer own when yer horse is old enough. So decide if ya like a certain color more, or if ya wanna make yer horse look good. Ok?"

"So I can use them?" Las asked.

"Ya can use 'em," Jase agreed. "But there is a condition."

Las winced. "What's that?"

Jase pointed at the bookshelf. "See the green one? Ya need ta take that ta Molis. And when he growls at ya, ya will growl back."

"To Molis?" Zep asked. "I drop my eyes to him."

"Ta Molis," Jase said again. "He is an ilus. Lasryn is the Kaisae's son. It will na be easy, but ya need ta learn ta hold yer eyes up."

"Yes, Dava," Las promised before looking at his father. "So, can we go now?"

Kolt held up a finger and his eyes lost focus. After a few seconds, he smiled. "Hwa says he and the girls will meet us at the main entrance. Just one problem. I'm not carrying all of that."

"Maybe just the black saddlebags?" Las begged.

"If you want to take all of it, then you need to figure out how to carry it."

"Dad!" Las whined, then glanced over at Sal. "I mean Dava."

"Either works," Kolt assured him. "But we aren't royalty, and there's no one to carry our things. That's the first rule of being a Black Blade. You make sure that you're not a burden to the others."

Tyr tipped his cup back and swallowed the last of his coffee, then set it on the table. "Well, I can carry some saddlebags, because the second rule is that we all help each other. C'mon, Las. Load me up like a mule."

"Or a dog," Sal teased.

Tyr lifted his middle finger toward her. "You're just jealous that I have two loves."

"I have six," Sal countered. "Plus the kids. Keep trying, Tyr."

But he glanced back with a grin that proved he wasn't upset at all. "The difference is that I just need two. My girl and my family. I'll make sure the daddies don't get lost along the way."

Thank you, Sal told him, sending it to his mind alone.

Tyr nodded once. *Believe it or not, I like the kid. I also know that Las is more likely to accept that if he doesn't realize it. Seems to be an iliri thing, huh?*

I dunno, should we talk about you trying to resist being my mate? Sal countered.

Only because I didn't want to be your next mistake. Just didn't realize that it was already too late. You're stuck with me now. So go pet horses or something, Sal.

In answer, she lifted her cup at him, and watched while Tyr and Kolt loaded themselves up with Las's things. "Have fun at school," Sal told the boy.

"I will, Amma. I've never been able to go before." And Las slung the largest pack over his small shoulder.

The four remaining men were quiet until the others were not only out of their suite, but most likely far enough away that Las wouldn't hear them. Then, Gage turned to lean his hip against the kitchen counter.

"So, it's going to be weird not having him in the house, huh?"

"Still a suite," Zep pointed out.

"It's our house," Blaz said, siding with Gage.

They all looked at Sal. "Home," she told them. "Doesn't matter where it is, but rather who it's with. And yeah, I've kinda gotten used to having Las around. Guess this means we need to steal Valri more often?"

Zep shook his head. "No way Ryali will let that happen. Sucks though, because you're a good amma, Sal."

She ducked her head. "I'm trying. I don't have a clue what I'm doing, but I'm trying to treat them the way I'd hope a parent would've treated me."

"The way Ran does," Gage said. "A little respect, a lot of pushing, and plenty of praise and support when it's needed. He's a good example."

Jase leaned over to see him. "Did ya get the chance ta know both of yer parents?"

"I did," Gage said. "Well, I was a little older than Las when my amma was conscripted, and I was about seventeen when they arrested and conscripted my dava, but I still got to know them."

Blaz grumbled under his breath. "Do any of you have families left? I mean, I know about Inessi, but is she the only parent the Black Blades have?"

"Kolt's wife's mother," Sal pointed out.

Blaz shook his head. "Nimae's a wonderful lady, but she's not exactly a maternal figure to the pack. I mean, what happened to Shift's parents, or Ghost's? Arctic?"

"The war," Sal said.

Jase was nodding. "When I was a boy, they would send soldiers inta Guttertown ta pick up as many iliri as they could catch. Ever' night there would be a child wailing in the street because both parents were gone. Someone would take it in and raise it, but the next night it would happen again. Humans did na care about us back then, Blaz. They thought it was better fer us ta die so ya did na have ta."

"That's so much bullshit," Blaz mumbled.

"Yeh," Jase agreed, "but that does na make it less true. And now, it is why we do na have many old iliri. Na even the crossbreds."

"They used to send us out to catch arrows," Gage told him. "Send a unit of iliri onto the field of battle and figure out which way the arrows came from. Get a good count of how many soldiers were in the initial charge. Sacrifice a few of us to make the CFC's military strategy look that much better, because they didn't even count our deaths until Ran started."

"Never again," Blaz swore.

"If anyone tries," Sal promised, "all of Anglia will do something about it, and I'm going to make that very clear in this Alliance meeting we're about to have."

"Should help if you're considered a sentient species legally, right?"

She shrugged. "Hard to tell. I mean, there will always be a bad guy. My goal is just to make sure that it's never Anglia."

Blaz lifted his coffee cup. "I'll drink to that."

"And I," Zep said, "need to wake up my daughter, because it seems she can sleep through anything."

Jase chuckled. "It's a benefit of a peaceful life, big brother. She has na known a need ta sleep lightly. Do na change it."

"No, but I will make sure she gets back to Ryali before my ex tears my throat out."

CHAPTER SIXTEEN

YELLOW

*H*wa, Rhyx, and Raast were waiting in the main foyer of Arhhawen, and the girls had almost as much stuff packed as Lasryn. Kolt groaned, knowing this meant he'd be carrying a little more, but he wasn't actually upset. He just didn't want the kids to learn that their parents would solve everything for them. They were at that age where they were too easy to spoil.

"Tyr, wanna help Hwa with their things?" Kolt asked.

But Tyr didn't groan. He just moved Las's saddlebags to one side and scooped up the two largest bags to hang from his other, shouldering most of the burden. Kolt didn't want to admit it, but Tyr had ended up a good addition to Sal's harem. The man was so different from the iliri he lived with, but he didn't seem to care about it. He never judged them for acting overly iliri, and laughed when they picked on him for being too human. He also loved Sal, which was the most important thing. Enough that he'd tried to do the exact same thing as all the rest of her mates. He'd put her happiness before his.

"Hey," Las said, making his way over to Rhyx. "If we put the saddlebags on you two, then I can carry your shoulder bags, and it should be easier."

"Yeah," Raast agreed, "and can you carry my brushes?" She pointed at a smaller bag before her.

Because while Rhyx was more than willing to get filthy and ignore it, Raast had always been a little more gentle and a lot more concerned about her appearance. Thankfully, the kids' plan worked out, and when they all left the main city, the adults were only carrying a few bags each.

"How's Roo taking the girls leaving?" Kolt asked when they turned for the path that led up to the school.

Hwa flashed him a tongue filled smile. *She is busy with the new pups, she says, but she's also been hugging them more.*

"She says it's because of hormones," Rhyx added. "At least Dava Hwa admits we're just growing up too fast."

"It's not fair," Lasryn told them. "You'll be full-grown by the time you're my age."

"And having pups of our own when we're Jarl's age," Raast pointed out. "Which means you get to play longer."

"So what grade will they put you in?" Tyr asked.

Rhyx looked up at him. "Next week is testing. Our scores will determine our classes."

Because most grauori and iliri children have never been given a formal education, Hwa explained, *we have to start somewhere. That's why Inessi wanted to limit the first class of students. Next year, there will be more classes offered, until university-level courses are held on the lower levels, and the younger students will be taught on the higher levels.*

"Why the lower for university?" Kolt asked.

Hwa cocked his head to the side. *Because they will not be required to stay and will not have a curfew. Having them climb the stairwells past those of us who hear this well? It will give the younger ones ideas.* Then he looked at his girls. *Which neither of you will act on.*

"We want to learn," Raast assured him.

Rhyx just harrumphed at that. "I want to make friends," she said.

"Well, I was told that you get to come home to Arhhawen on the weekends, right?" Kolt asked.

"Yeah," Raast agreed. "And we can have visitors after our classes on school days."

"Well," Kolt went on, "if you have friends who don't have anywhere else to go, remember that we have room, ok? No one should be forced to feel alone. Not even the brerror."

"No more brerror, Dava," Rhyx said. "Sal accepts them, so everyone else does too. She says that none of us chose how we were born or raised, so she will never hold it against us."

"Sounds like her," Kolt agreed. "She's always believed that good intentions matter more than bad histories."

Thankfully, it wasn't a long walk, because the kids' luggage started getting heavy about halfway there. None of them complained, but Lasryn started walking a little slower. Hwa's tongue hung a little further from his mouth, and Kolt knew he was breathing harder, but he blamed the elevation and thinner air. Tyr just kept going like some kind of machine until they finally reached the front steps of the school.

"Want us to help you check-in?" Kolt asked his son.

Las gave him a warning look. "Being the Taunor's son is cool and all, but I don't want to get babied in front of them, ok?"

"Ok," Kolt said, sliding one of the bags off his shoulder. "You three going to be able to manage all of this, or did you want Tyr to help, since he won't treat you like a child?"

Las looked like he was about to refuse, but Rhyx nodded. "We need the help. Do ya mind, Dava Tyr?"

"Not at all," Tyr promised. While he picked up the things Hwa and Kolt had carried, he thought to them, *Wait here, and I'll give you a full report when I get back. And Kolt, this is why I'm the cool dava.*

The problem was that Kolt couldn't say anything back. Tyr had a valid point. It also worked out, since his carefree attitude meant the kids would feel comfortable confiding in him. And the truth was that having so many parents actually made it easier. The kids didn't mind, and there was always someone they felt like they could talk to. Today, that was Tyr. Tomorrow, it could be Hwa. Eventually, Kolt knew his son would come to him, just like he had last night.

Because this was what a family should be. Standing beside Hwa, the two fathers watched their children walk into the building without looking back. It was harder for them than the kids, and harder for Kolt than Hwa. Hwa had at least spent more than just the last few months with his girls. Kolt hadn't seen Las for so long. The boy had to think he was a stranger, but he never acted like it, and yet here Kolt was, sending him away again.

They will be fine, Hwa promised. *The professors are all family of some kind. Inessi has promised to let us know if there are any problems.*

It's not that, Kolt thought back. *The problem is that I miss him. I feel like his childhood is slipping through my fingers and there's nothing I can do to stop it.*

There isn't, Hwa agreed. *Because you were busy fighting for him to have a better adulthood. He knows that, even if he doesn't completely understand it.*

Kolt reached down to let his fingers brush the back of Hwa's neck. *I know. I really do, and yet I can't stop thinking that the last time I saw him before I left for Terric, he was five. Now he's seven, almost eight. He was a baby and now he's a young man. How much more will he grow before the semester is over?*

Does that mean you won't see him every weekend? Hwa countered.

No...

Or that you don't want him to have his own friends, potentially grow his own pack, or maybe even find his future mate?

Kolt held up his hand. *I think he's already met his mate, but I'm not sure.*

That had the grauori's complete attention. *What do you mean?*

He says he's meant for Valri. I mean, that does explain why he's been so good with her. She's like a year and a half old, but Las has always included her. Ever since she arrived here, actually. And he says she smells good. Like hope. The problem is that I'm not sure if he's mimicking us with Sal, or if he knows something we don't.

You know Ashir Doyin is working on some test to identify Kaisae gene carriers, right? Hwa told him.

Kolt turned to see his brother. *Jase mentioned something about that. What kind of test is it?*

Blood, I think, like humans do in their hospitals. He said it's based on research from the lab below Arhhawen, and that the genetics don't work the way he'd expected. If onsyc males carry the Kaisae gene, and Kaisaes have two copies, then what are the females with one? The carriers. Are they more dominant? Do they even exist? Because we rarely see Kaisaes born from non-Kaisaes.

They have to exist, right? Kolt asked. *Otherwise, how would we get more Kaisaes?*

From a Kaisae and an onsyc breeding together. That is how it works with grauori. A regular female cannot have an Orassae pup. Only an Orassae female can. The difference is that we still have enough women that we separate the potential leaders from those who have been chosen to step up.

Yeah, Kolt said, *which means Valri couldn't be a Kaisae, right? Ryali isn't one, so there's no way it's possible?*

Shouldn't be, Hwa agreed, *but what do I know? Before I met Sal, your human sciences were little more than magic to us. But it shouldn't hurt to test her, right?*

If her amma agrees, Kolt said. *Because Lasryn has a prophecy. He will stand to the left of a Kaisae who will rule in peace. Nimae rarely sees the future, but when she does, her visions are clear and easy to understand. Not like Blaec's.*

Hwa's head tilted. *I thought all the prophecies were done. That ayati was destroyed and our fates were once again in our own hands. How could she see that far into the future?*

Unless she didn't, Kolt thought. *Lasryn met Valri before ayati broke. Nimae was there. A prophet can only see what happens in their own lifetime. What if her vision has already happened? Could she have meant Las standing to Sal's left?*

Or could Lyzzi have already picked Las as her mate? Hwa offered instead. *We know she is a Kaisae, and we know Nimae has met her. They aren't that far apart in age, and it's possible they wouldn't tell us.*

No, Kolt said, *Las told me he's meant for Valri. He was very clear about it, but also confused. Enough so that he said all the right things but didn't know what they meant. I believe he's drawn to her, Hwa. I really do, I just don't know if ayati breaking could've changed his future.*

Or if Valri is a Kaisae, Hwa finished for him. *Talk to Joevar or Zep about it. They can convince Ryali to have her tested. Then we'll know.*

Yeah, Kolt agreed, *and it will give me something else to think about when Las's room is too quiet and he's not around to watch all day long. I can also ask Nimae what she's seen. Maybe there's something else to it.*

Maybe, Hwa said just as the main doors opened again, and Tyr came trotting down the steps.

"They're checked in," he announced. "All three of them are on the floor Inessi is watching, and the girls are being roomed together. Lasryn was paired with a human boy, but they seem to have hit it off. Kid's dad was a soldier, and yeah, he recognized the tattoo on my neck."

"And your arm?" Kolt teased.

Tyr just grinned. "I may have shown the dog off a bit. Just so Las has a little more reason to brag. I'm just helping the kids out, Kolt."

"Right." But Kolt couldn't quite bring himself to leave. "So they're going to be ok?"

Tyr grabbed his shoulder and turned Kolt down the trail. "They're fine. Right about now, those three feel like they're all grown up and important, and you both need to let them have it. We have eyes all over that school, and there's nothing they can do that we haven't done ourselves."

"That's what I'm afraid of," Kolt said.

Hwa was nodding. *I ran away from my pack to mate Aroora,* he reminded Tyr. *I would rather my girls didn't try the same.*

"Pretty sure they would talk to Sal first," Tyr told him. "Because unlike all of us, they know they have an entire pack behind them. Guys, this is what you fought for. This is the future we wanted for our kids, so *let them have it.*"

"Yeah, but that's my boy," Kolt whispered.

Tyr patted Kolt's back. "And he's a good kid who wants to make his sire proud. Think of this as his first mission: learning how to be a real iliri."

"Not helping," Kolt said.

But it was a lie. Tyr had both Kolt and Hwa marching back down the trail toward Arhhawen. His words made Kolt proud of his son. The best part was that for all Tyr's bluster, the man had just proven that he cared about the kids. He said he didn't want any, but that hadn't stopped him from accepting the ones that came with his mates.

"You're a good dava, Tyr," Kolt said.

Tyr just groaned. "Bullshit. I'm pulling all of this out of my ass. I'm also not a dava. I'm going to be their dad, because I'm fucking human, remember?"

Or is it because that will let you know when they're talking to you? Hwa teased.

"Aren't you supposed to be on my side, Hwa?"

"Which means he's right," Kolt said. "Tyr, I always thought Zep was full of shit, but I think you've got him beat."

"Fuck yeah, I do," Tyr agreed.

CHAPTER SEVENTEEN

CYAN

*W*hile Kolt took his son off to school, Zep went to wake up Valri, but the little girl wasn't sleeping. She had her brother's grauori toy and was galloping it across the bed. Clearly, she'd been awake for a while. Probably long enough to hear everyone talking in the other room.

"Why didn't you come tell Las goodbye?" Zep asked.

She looked up at him. "He's just at school," she said with the kind of logic only a child could have. "And he said he'd still tell me stories."

Zep nodded, unsure what else he could do. "Well, you ready to go back home to your amma?"

"Uh-huh!" Valri agreed.

"You ok if Amma Sal comes with us?"

This time, she just nodded, her little red curls bouncing with her enthusiasm.

"Ok." Zep held out his hand. "Let's make sure she missed you lots."

Valri's answering giggle was the most beautiful thing he'd ever heard. Zep had honestly never expected to have a child of his own. After all, he hadn't really wanted to carry on his family's name, and few iliri women were interested in breeding with a human. But the moment he'd seen her, Zep had fallen in love harder than he ever had before. Considering how much he cared for Sal, that said a lot, but she understood.

This was his *daughter*. His little girl. She was the most perfect thing he'd ever seen, with her mismatched skin, hair, and eyes. It made her look a little wild, but in the most iliri way possible, as if Zep's dark skin had been diluted somehow. She wasn't just paler than him; she was a slightly different shade. More vibrant than any human he'd ever met, and that was her iliri ancestry.

So were the sharp teeth in her smile. Milk teeth, Ryali called them, and Valri's were strong enough to bite through anything. Combined with her vertical pupils, there was no denying that she wasn't human, but to Zep, that only made her more beautiful. Granted, he'd say the same if she was dark-skinned with dull human teeth. The fact that he'd helped make her was really all that mattered.

When she tottered past, she caught his first two fingers, pulling him along behind her. Zep followed like a needy puppy. Yes, he knew he was a sucker for her big blue eyes, but he also didn't care. Joevar was an amazing father to her, and Jase had jumped in to help teach her all about being iliri. That meant Zep was allowed to spoil her to his heart's content, and Ryali didn't even mind. In fact, she said it was cute.

"Amma?" Valri asked when they reached the main room. "Dava said I need to go back to my amma now."

Blaz laughed at that. "Is there a trick to keeping track of which amma and dava the kids mean?" he asked.

Gage tapped his nose. "Children make no effort to hide their emotions, so we can usually smell what they mean. In this case, she wants Sal to go with her to Ryali's."

"Yeah," Blaz said. "I'm a little handicapped in that area. So, is there a way for *me* to know when the kids might want me around?"

"They'll look at you," Zep said, smiling down at his little girl. "At her age, she has no need to drop her eyes unless the adult becomes aggressive, so she'll look right at you when she's talking about you."

"Well, that helps," Blaz admitted, "and I'll beat the crap out of anyone who tries to intimidate your kid, Zep."

"Only if I can't get to them first," Zep promised.

Sal rolled her eyes at him, but paused when she passed Blaz. "You want me to come back here, or were we going to meet in the stables?" she asked.

"Stables," he decided. "And I'll probably be with Tilso for the rest of the day after that. Arianna wants to bring the mares up soon, so we're rushing this a bit."

"It's been three months," Sal reminded him.

"Yeah," Blaz agreed. "Three months after a massive war, with a barn that started as a warehouse, and which hadn't been used in a few centuries. That we have stalls at all is a bit of a miracle, and only because the iliri here started early. If Arhhawen is going to be known for our horses, then we're going to need to make this perfect."

"We have the land for it," Zep pointed out. "And we can always take another warehouse if we need to."

"Straw, hay, and burning lanterns?" Blaz countered. "Never mind that the mares won't cycle if they're kept in the dark. No, we're going to need actual light. Kolt says he can probably fetch rock, which means others could as well, so I'm thinking about expanding outside."

Zep just lifted a hand. "Sal will fill me in later. I have a little girl whose amma is probably wondering where she is, and if I don't get her home soon, Ryali *will* scream in my head about it."

"Go," Blaz told him. "And I'll see you next time, kiddo."

Valri just waved at him with her whole arm. "Bye, Dava. Love you."

Zep had to bite his lips together to keep from laughing at the look on Blaz's face. Four little words and Valri had wrapped the man around her finger. Never before had Zep understood when someone was described as melting, but Blaz just had. If he'd "awwed" out loud, it wouldn't have surprised anyone.

Sal flicked her eyes over to make sure Zep had seen the man's reaction, but like him, she didn't say a thing until they were in the hall. Then she reached down to hold Valri's other hand, putting the child between them as they walked deeper into the underground city.

"You're ok sharing her with the guys, right?" Sal asked.

"Yep," Zep said. "You're ok sharing her with Ryali, right?" he countered.

Sal smiled at him. "You know, I didn't want to like her as much as I do. I thought maybe you'd still... I dunno."

"Have a thing for her?" he asked. "No, Sal. She's the mother of my child - well, amma - so I care about her, but the same way I care about Shaden. She's a sister. Even back then, I had a thing for you."

"Yeah," Sal said. "And you two made a pretty little girl."

"Uh-huh!" Valri agreed.

Together, they wound through the "streets" of Arhhawen. When Zep had first arrived, he'd thought of them as halls, but streets really was a better term for how the iliri used them. On the upper levels, the space was wide and straight, giving the iliri room to socialize outside their homes. Lights ran across the ceiling, powered by whatever was down in the basement. It wasn't the ship, though. That was even further down. This was something that had been made after humans landed on Ogun, meant to run the lab that had created the first iliri. Now, it powered their home.

It was also the only reason the air inside was breathable. Otherwise, the smoke and soot from the lanterns would've smothered them all. Sure, there was good ventilation - the first humans had planned for that as well - but they'd created this space as a bunker. It was a fail-safe made in case the world wasn't hospitable.

And now, at least a dozen iliri were trying to figure out how it worked so they could replace all of the lanterns and torches in Arhhawen. It felt like progress was going to come quickly. Someone had mentioned using the ventilation from the basement to cool the upper levels, and Tensa had explained how fetchers could trade the air to keep it cooler, which was what they'd done in Guttertown. In other words, Tyr was right. The age of iliri technology was just beginning, and Zep was lucky enough to live in it.

It seemed that each time he ventured into the city, Zep noticed something else. The best part, though, was that Valri took it all for granted. The underground aspect of this place worked well for the iliri, who instinctually wanted to live in dens the same way the grauori did.

The humans could take it for a while, but eventually, they all had to spend a day outside in the open air. Oddly, that somehow made the community feel a little less isolated, though, because their iliri friends usually went with them.

And soon, they'd have horses outside to care for, culls to sell, and other industries that required more time on the hills outside the city. That would prevent Arhhawen from becoming xenophobic like Viraenova had been. Some days, it felt like Sal had planned for everything, but the truth was that she'd done little more than accept the advice of those with good ideas, and this was the result.

But just as they turned down the street to Ryali's place, Kolt brushed Zep's mind. *Hey, man? I got a question.*

Ok? Zep replied.

There any way you can ask Ryali about having Ashir run a test on Valri?

That was enough to make Zep's feet stop. Sal and his daughter both paused as well, turning to look up at him. Zep lifted a finger to show he needed a second and then turned his eyes to the ground.

What kind of test, and why?

For Kaisae gene carriers, Kolt explained. *We think it's a blood test, so not that big of a deal, but Las is saying some stuff, and it all comes back to Valri being special, so I figured we might as well start trying to convince Ryali now.*

Is this because my last name is Zepyr?

It is, Kolt said. *Zep, Las has a prophecy that he'll stand to the left of a peaceful Kaisae. Last night, he said he's meant for her. Valri, I mean. I figure that either means your daughter's a mix-bred Kaisae, or my boy is confused about what he's feeling. If it's the latter, then she shouldn't be spending the night in his room anymore, you know?*

He's seven, Zep shot back. *He sees his dad is mated to a Kaisae, and the rest of the iliri make that sound like a big deal, so he's pretending.*

It took a little too long for Kolt to respond. When he did, his thoughts sounded serious. *Then explain to me how his kauvwae had a prophecy that wasn't completed before the end of ayati? Either she saw Las and Valri before the final battle, or she was seeing things no one else can, and she's a damned good prophet, man. Not strong like Blaec, but deadly accurate and clear.*

Zep glanced over at Sal, pulling her into the link. *Kolt thinks Valri could be a Kaisae, and he says that crazy professor from Syhar could have a test to find out now, before she hits puberty.*

Then we should test her, Sal said, making the answer simple. *If she's not, then we can make it clear that there's nothing wrong with it. If she is, then we can prepare her for what that will mean for her future.*

He also thinks Lasryn might be meant for her.

Sal's face broke into a smile, and she looked down at their daughter. *They'd be perfect together, so I'm hoping he's right, but I honestly have no idea what age a male could feel that.* Then she knelt to look Valri in the eyes. "Hey, what do you think about your brother Las?"

Valri smiled, but it was the shy kind. "He's my favorite brother. He protects me."

"Yeah," Sal said. "That's what a good ilus does, huh?" *Yeah, it won't hurt to test,* she finished in her mind.

But, Kolt said, *Zep's going to have to convince Ryali.*

Or I can, Sal told them. *C'mon, Zep. I'll help with this one.*

Closing the link, Sal tilted her head for them to all keep walking, and when they reached Ryali's door, she was the one who knocked. A moment later, Joevar opened it.

The man was only wearing a pair of loose pants, and his eyes looked heavy, like he'd only just woken up after a very long night. The smell from their apartment gave Sal an idea why, but she had no intention of saying anything. Still, the moment he saw Sal, he smiled, pulling the door open wider for them all to come in. This wasn't the kind of handoff where the parents were polite while the child was around. Joevar and Ryali always made Zep feel like he was truly welcome. Like somehow they'd managed to blend their families so that there wasn't any resentment at all.

"How'd the date go?" he asked Joe.

The man reached up to scrub at his face. "I think that's more a question for her. All I can say is that I'm glad we don't have any windows so the sun doesn't wake me up."

"Long night?" Zep teased.

Joe flashed him a smile as he bent, holding his arms out for Valri. "Hey, beautiful. How did you like spending the night with Amma Sal and Dava Zep?"

Valri threw herself at his chest. "It was fun, but I missed you too, Dava."

"Aww, baby. Same." Joe stood, hauling her up with him. "You have breakfast yet? Your amma's making eggs and deer." And he jerked his head, indicating that Sal and Zep should follow.

Ryali's home wasn't as big as Sal's, but she didn't need as much space. The couple had three bedrooms, one large living area, two bathrooms, and a small storage area beside the kitchen. That was where Ryali was, rummaging inside for something, but the moment she heard them, she was right back out, stealing Valri from Joe's arms.

"Oh, I missed ya." And she kissed Valri's face repeatedly.

"Hey?" Sal said, taking a stool at the side. "Would you and Valri do something for me?"

"Anything," Ryali promised.

"Professor Doyin is making a test to find Kaisaes and Kaisae gene carriers," Sal explained. "I want to see if maybe Valri got the gene from her sire."

"Will it hurt her?" Ryali asked.

Sal shrugged. "It's a prick for a bit of blood. The subject came up today, and I'm curious about her. I just think you should test too, so she'll see it's ok if her amma's doing it."

"Then I will," Ryali promised. "What do I need ta do?"

Sal waved her down. "I'll have Ashir come by this weekend and find you. Just a prick of a finger, and then he puts a drop of blood into a vial and does things with it in his lab. Makes graphs somehow. I don't understand half of it, but he's excited about the ability to identify more bloodlines that could create future Kaisaes so the iliri don't become inbred."

"Nice," Joe said. "I was kinda wondering if the Emperor had killed everyone but you and Lyzzi - but if there's more?"

"Then eventually some will be born," Sal assured him. "And maybe some will even be crossbreds, so we'll stop thinking of purity of ancestry as something to strive towards, and start worrying more about just being happy."

"Then yeh," Ryali said, "I will do it. If ya will na make her mate a certain man if she is a carrier."

"I would never do that," Sal promised. "Valri deserves the right to decide her own future. It's kinda what we spent so long fighting for, and I'm not about to change that now. Not when we've actually won."

"Yer a good Kaisae," Ryali told her. "Now, did ya both want breakfast? Zep is sniffin' like he has na ate."

"I'd love some," Sal said. "How do I help?"

Joevar just pointed to the main room. "You get out of the kitchen. Trust me, you don't want to get in her way, and she says that soldiers have no idea how to make things taste good."

"Because ya do na!" Ryali said as she put Valri down. "Baby, go play with yer davas, ok?"

Joe and Zep shared a look, and both of them smiled. "This," Zep told him, "is why I always wanted to be iliri. You're a good dava, Joe."

The man's face turned a little darker. "Thanks, man. Gotta be honest, I like having a daughter to spoil. She's a good kid, and I'm in love with her mother."

"I had a feeling it'd work out that way," Zep said. "One of the last things I was sure of, man."

CHAPTER EIGHTEEN

BLUE

The smell of bacon was making Sal's mouth water, but she wasn't brave enough to interrupt Ryali while she was cooking. Instead, she decided to talk to Joevar about the Peacekeepers, because that needed to be settled as well. So, when they all found a spot to sit and Valri started pulling out her toys, Sal decided it was as good of a time as any.

"Joe, how would you feel about Ryali going back to work?" she asked, easing into it.

He gave her a suspicious look. "That's some kind of test or something? Trick question?"

"No..." Sal said.

Joe leaned back in his chair with a smile. "Sal, she can do whatever she wants. I'm still on active duty with the Dogs, so it's only fair."

"And if her job took her away for weeks at a time?" Sal asked.

Joe shrugged. "Then I might ask you for a little more help with Valri. You know, when I can't take her with me. Why? What are you thinking?"

"The Peacekeepers," Sal said.

Joe blew that off. "I knew you wanted to do that for a while, Sal.

Yeah, if she's into it, then that's her decision. I'll even offer some combat training if you'd like, but I think Ryek would be better at it."

"How's he doing anyway?" Zep asked. "Haven't seen him around."

Joe chuckled. "Um, he dated some girl right after he got here; she dumped him for being too human, so he sulked for a bit. Last I heard, he was working in the basement with the iliri technicians, since Pig says there's no need for us to worry about regular training. We all kinda have part-time jobs now, instead."

"And yours?" Sal asked.

Joe pointed at Valri. "I'm a stay-at-home dava. Was kinda hoping to get in on the horse thing when the herd arrives. Told Pig we should offer up our mares to the breeding string and make it a group effort. I mean, most of the Dogs know how to clean a stall, you know."

"That's actually not a bad idea," Sal agreed. "And maybe a few of you can help the kids learn how to ride?"

"We'll need calmer horses for that," Joe told her. "Most of our stock are battle-trained, and yours are worse." Then he paused. "So, are you going to train the Peacekeepers to ride?"

"We should," Zep told Sal.

She nodded. "Yeah, but I'm not sure we'll have enough time before we send them out. Still, they'll either need horses to ride or a carriage to haul them to their assignment."

"Where are you assigning Ryali?" Joe asked.

"Here or Dorton," Sal assured him. "I actually want her to be the lead iliri representative. I'm not even sure what title we're going to give her, but she'll be the iliri who all the others go to if they aren't sure. Like the general of the division."

"So, she won't be going anywhere?" Joe asked carefully.

Sal lifted a hand, holding back his hope. "She might. As an example, if they need help in Eriwald, Ryali's triad would go there to clear things up. I want the three of them to make the ultimate decisions, answering only to myself, Dom, and Rragri."

"I can hear ya," Ryali called from the kitchen.

"Good," Sal told her. "Because your next job is to ask the human representative if he's interested."

"Who's she going to work with?" Joe asked.

Sal couldn't help but smile. "I'm waiting to hear for sure, but Dom and I both think Henrik's a good choice. He has to run it by the noble council, though."

"My sadava?" Ryali asked.

"The very same," Sal assured her. "Speaking of that, lemme see if Dom's had a chance to talk to them." And she switched to her mind. *Dom?*

Good timing, the King replied. *I'm about three steps from my door, and I was just about to reach out to you. I'm guessing you aren't busy?*

I'm not, Sal told him. *Just sitting here with Ryali and Joe, talking about Peacekeepers.*

Well, tell her Henrik's been approved, and he's being promoted to a major. I think she's the perfect person to tell him.

Ok, gimme a sec, Sal begged before looking up. "He says Henrik's been approved," she repeated. "So, if you'd like to go into Dorton and ask him, Ryali, that would be perfect."

"Yeh," she agreed, coming around the corner to peek her head into the room. "We can talk ta him t'day. I want Valri ta go too, though. Is that ok?"

"That's fine," Sal assured her. "Take Joe with you."

"It is na a short walk," Ryali reminded them.

"So we'll ride," Joe said. "Sounds like you'll need to learn anyway, and I can carry Valri with me. We have a quiet horse somewhere, don't we?" he asked, looking back to Zep.

"Take Arden," Sal suggested. "She's tolerant enough, and I think Ryali can handle her."

"Not a bad choice, actually," Zep told Joe. "Sal's mare's wonderfully gentle when she wants to be. Blaec picked her because he knew Sal didn't have a clue how to ride."

"He did?" she asked.

Zep nodded. "He had a feeling you'd figure that test out, and he'd been eyeing her for a bit as his own backup mount, but he couldn't get over her flashy color. He guessed that you wouldn't mind - or he saw it. One never knew with him."

"And she's older now," Sal said. "Calmer. She'll also follow your horse without a problem, so Ryali won't need to worry about anything but hanging on."

"You mind if I use her later to teach Ryali to ride?" Joe asked. "Just the basics, mind you."

"Sure," Sal said.

Joe nodded. "Then I think we'll plan to drop in on Henrik at lunch."

"Make sure you tell him the job comes with a promotion to major," Sal added. "And I'm pretty sure the pay will adjust to go with it."

"Can do," Joe agreed, proving this was where he felt comfortable. "Weapons?"

Zep waved them both down. "I'll handle those. For all the Peacekeepers, I think. We'll want them to have the best stuff, and there's a resinsmith in Dorton who has some talent, but not enough contracts. I'd like to steal Pig and talk to him, if you're ok with that, Sal?"

"All you," she agreed. "We're also going to need a command structure for this. Joe, feel free to toss out any ideas, because I'm not sure I know how to make it happen. We want this to be a side promotion from the military - that way all of our Peacekeepers are empowered, but also civilians. We don't want to cause the same problem the CFC did, where Peacekeepers are feared because they were above - or beside - the law. The important thing is for them to be the ones the citizens of all species can go to for advice."

"So we'll ask the iliri," Joe offered. "Ryali will, I mean. A few are still nervous about so many humans here in Arhhawen, but your mates are helping to convince them that it's ok."

"We are?" Zep asked.

"Not you," Joe explained. "You're iliri, and everyone here knows it. I'm talking more about Tyr and Blaz. They're very different, but both respect the iliri, and they're seen as safe. Mainly because the people honestly believe that Sal would roll them for hurting anyone. The Dogs and Dark Heart are helpful too. I mean, we're nothing special, and yet we still want to be here, and we don't care about the growling, snapping, and harems. If anything, we're embracing the iliri way of life, and that's giving them a little pride."

"Will you tell me if there's a problem?" Sal begged.

Joe nodded at her. "Of course. So will the others. The truth is that we kinda like what you're doing. I mean, I honestly thought that iliri were meek and quiet people. Well, back in the CFC, every one I'd met kept his eyes down and his mouth shut - or hers. I was in my teens before I heard one growl, and I thought I'd imagined it for a few years."

"And now?" Sal asked.

He smiled. "Um, I think that freedom is good for their pride. The Dogs all talked about it, and we make a point of dropping our eyes and showing respect where we can. I mean, we can't always let them push us around, and a few have tried, but we're doing our best to show everyone what it means to be our equals. Shit, we're still trying to figure it out ourselves, I think, but we're getting there. The kids are easier. Valri doesn't know a time when humans weren't safe to be around."

"Good," Zep said, looking over at where his daughter was playing quietly. "Even Las is like that. He was so young when he left the Conglomerate that all he knows is Anglia, really. The trick is going to be mixing our species together, you know?"

"More humans will move to Arhhawen," Sal assured them. "And over time, plenty of iliri will move throughout Anglia for jobs. There's also all the land out west. Now that the grauori are willing to live beside us, it's safe to build out there, which means Anglia's going to need a better network of roads, mail, and everything that goes with it."

"Thus the horses," Joe said, proving he was keeping up. "Makes sense, and if Arhhawen horses are the best, well, the city will become a very comfortable place to live, supporting itself with iliri herds."

"That's the idea," Sal told him. "I mean, we want to make sure we have warhorses raised and trained as well, but hopefully they'll just be for parades. If we can do this right, there should never be another war."

"There will *always* be another war," Joe told her. "There always is. The trick is going to be shutting it down before the entire continent is caught up in it like this one."

"Yeah," Sal groaned. "But that doesn't mean I won't do everything in my power to stop it first."

But Dom had clearly waited long enough. *Sal?* he asked, interrupting.

She looked away, making it clear she was talking to someone else. *Yeah?*

So, did you find that ceremony you were talking about? he asked. *I'm going to need it for my wedding, and sounds like that's going to happen pretty fast.*

I think I have something better, she assured him. *So, when's the date?*

Still working on that, but Ray's going to ask you to be her bridesmaid. And Tyr, it sounds like. So, um, yeah. Any way you can come by Dorton in the next few days to help plan this?

Tomorrow, she promised him. *Today I need to clear my schedule.*

Tomorrow works. And we should start getting the first allies showing up within the week. Maybe I should push this back? Deal with the treaties first?

Which meant the King was getting nervous. Not cold feet, just second-guessing himself about the timing. Sal could understand that, but she was also enough of a friend to give him a little push.

No, we need the celebration to help the culture problems, remember. While we're all dealing with politics, the rest of Anglia will be throwing parties for you. So I think we should include our allies in the excitement. If nothing else, it will show them that three species can and do work together, and that there's no problem with recognizing us all as equal to humans.

Right, he agreed, but it sounded more like he was reminding himself than agreeing with her. *So, a month of nation-wide celebration isn't too much?*

No, Sal said. *And once Rragri gets here, I think we'll include her in this. Something to take her mind off Nya's condition. Oh! Speaking of that, can you send Dalyr Trant and his unit to her den with a carriage to haul Nya back? She trusts him.*

And only him, Dom said, proving he understood. *Yeah, I'll get them moving out either tonight or tomorrow morning. I'll also send my most comfortable carriage for her. No need to jostle around my grand-nephews or -nieces, right?*

Right, Sal said, knowing he just needed a weak excuse to help out. After he got over the initial shock of the cross-species pregnancy, Dom had actually started to get excited about the upcoming babies. *And Rragri's bringing a group of grauori for the Peacekeepers as well, so we should have that all settled before the CFC gets here.*

And Myrosica, Dom said. *Because they will probably be the last to arrive. Some summer celebration they have every year is just ending. But yeah. I'm not really worried about Tseri seeing us trying to fix this. I am about the rest of them.*

Me too, Sal assured him. *Now go start planning your wedding. I'm working on the rest of this so you don't have to.* She closed the link and looked up. "Sounds like Dom's wedding is actually going to happen."

"The nobles are ok with him marrying both of them?" Zep asked.

Joe's head twitched in surprise. "Both?"

"Yep," Sal said, raising her voice so Ryali would hear. "Dom asked both Rayna and Shift to marry him in an Anglian human ceremony. That means he's going to be our brother-in-law."

Once again, Ryali hurried over to look into the room. "The King will be Valri's uncle?"

"Yep," Sal said. "Welcome to a whole new world, Ryali. And if you have any ideas to make Shift's bond with Dominik fit into our traditions, then please let me know. The King wants to make sure the iliri are represented with respect."

"I do na know, but I like that," Ryali said. "And the food is done. It is na as good as Tensa's..."

"Yes, it is," Joe told them. "It's just as good as Tensa's, but she won't believe me."

"Because ya are too human ta know how things should taste," Ryali shot back. "And ya just like ta say nice things."

Joe pushed himself from his chair and headed right to her, hooking an arm around her back. "I do, and you're going to have to deal with it.

But I like your cooking too. Believe it or not, I don't like my food burned."

When he leaned in to kiss her, Sal wasn't the only one smiling at the cute couple. Zep was too, and somehow that made it even better.

CHAPTER NINETEEN

PINK

*A*fter breakfast, Zep and Sal headed out to do their own thing. Ryali knew the Kaisae was still a busy woman, and while Sal tried to say it was nothing compared to what she did during the war, she still worked every day keeping Arhhawen running smoothly. That was why Ryali wanted to get her visit to Henrik just right.

Well, she also missed seeing the older man, and she couldn't wait to tell him that they'd be working together again. Ryali was very excited about that part. Riding the horse? Not so much. Valri, however, didn't agree. The idea of riding with Dava Joe had the girl squealing in glee as they headed down to the stables.

But Joe had planned ahead. When the three of them walked into the barn, two horses were tacked up and standing tied for them. One was Sal's polka-dotted mare. The other was a dark brown horse with white up to his knees in the back and around his ankles in the front. Ryali wasn't sure what his color was called, as he was darker than a lot of others she'd seen, but not quite as dark as the black ones. The problem was that both of them were *huge.*

"Ok," Joe said, walking up to the mostly white mare first. "Have you ever ridden at all, Ryali?"

"I have na ridden one," she admitted. "I sat on a horse once but we rode here in a wagon or walked."

He nodded, then walked over to stand beside her, comparing their legs. "So, your stirrups will be just a bit longer than Sal's, I'm guessing. Let me fix those, and then we'll get you up on Arden's back. Make sure Valri doesn't get under their feet?"

"Valri," she hissed, calling her daughter back to her. "Ya wait fer yer amma before ya touch them, ok?"

"Ok, Amma."

"It'll just be a minute, sweetheart," Joe said, reassuring the child before he turned back to his mate. "They don't hurt people, Ryali, and these two are pros. You'll be fine."

"What if she falls?"

He tossed a smile at her as he moved to the other side of Sal's horse. "First, it means I'm not doing a good job as a dava, and second, we'll have a lot bigger problems. Unfortunately, I don't have a helm her size or I'd let her wear it."

"A helm?"

Joe nodded. "Keeps our heads safe. Also helps when we're knocked off the horses and hit the ground. I'll have to talk to Blaz about getting some made up for the kids if we're going to teach them to ride. Doesn't hurt to be careful, right?"

"It does na," Ryali agreed. "So could we na just walk?"

He did something with the saddle that made the leather snap, then walked back around where she could see him. "If you're going to be the head Peacekeeper for Anglia, you *will* need to learn how to ride, my love. Today is a good time to start, and I will not let you fall. I swear it."

"But what if the horse gets scared?" she asked.

He tried not to, but a grin broke out on his lips. "She's trained. I've been riding around with the Blades long enough to know that if I yell at Arden to halt, she'll stop. That horse also doesn't get scared of much. She's carried Sal through everything in this war, and this was the horse she learned on. There isn't a better animal in Anglia for you to ride, ok?"

"Amma, she knows ya are scared," Valri said. "She wants ya ta pet her."

Joe just canted his head to the side, using Valri's ability to speak to the animals to prove his point. "And that's the other thing. If your horse is scared, I have a feeling Valri will let us know, ok? Now, come pet Arden?"

"I do na know how," Ryali whispered.

Joe just took her hand and led her closer, over to the horse's head. Once there, he reached up to rub the spot on the front of its face, right between the eyes. Ryali did the same, and Joe let her, pausing only to check that Valri was standing in a safe place. Ryali knew she would be. The animals were always her friends, but that didn't mean they'd be nice to the child's amma. And the fact that this thing could lift its head so high Ryali couldn't reach it was intimidating.

"They like us," Joe whispered into Ryali's ear. "We give them food, scratch the spots they can't reach, and don't ask for much back. Arden's a good horse, baby. I wouldn't put you on her if I didn't trust her completely, ok?"

That made her smile. "Are ya taking care of me, Joe?"

"I'm trying, but I think you're pretty good at taking care of yourself. Now let me help you up, and then I'll get Valri on Dandy with me, ok? All you'll need to do is follow and get used to how she moves."

"Ok," Ryali finally agreed.

Joe untied the mare and moved her into the center of the alley. There, he told the horse to stand and moved over by the stirrup. Bit by bit, without rushing her, he explained to Ryali how to get from the ground onto the horse's back, and then he all but heaved her up there. Once Ryali's leg was across the saddle, she froze, convinced the horse was about to take off.

"She's just balancing," Joe assured her. "Now, put your feet in the stirrups, and hold onto that piece at the front of your saddle."

"Will she just stay here?" Ryali asked.

A chuckle from behind them proved they weren't alone. "She will," a man said, and Ryali twisted to see Tilso heading toward her. "But I'll hold her if it makes you feel better?"

"Yeh," Ryali almost begged. "I do na know how ta do this."

"Well, you're doing it," Tilso assured her. "Go ahead and get mounted, Joe. I'll pass Valri up when you're settled."

"Thanks, man," Joe said. "Valri, go over by Dava Tilso, ok?"

"Ok!" the girl agreed.

"You want to pet her?" Tilso asked, bending down as he offered to pick Valri up.

She immediately grabbed his neck and wrapped her legs around his waist. With one hand on Arden's reins, Tilso wrapped his other around Valri's back and twisted so she could reach Arden's neck. Ryali found herself relaxing when her daughter began to pet the spotted neck. The horse leaned into it as if she honestly enjoyed the child's touch, and somehow that made her feel less like a monster.

"She knows ya are scared, Amma," Valri said. "Pet her!"

So Ryali tried, leaning forward just enough to run her hand down the base of the horse's neck to where the saddle started. Over and over, Ryali petted the horse, realizing that it was calming her more than anything else. Plus, Joe was right. If there was a problem, Valri could talk to the beast, so this would be ok. If Sal, Zep, Tilso, and Joe all thought it was ok, then it would be ok. She could do this.

"Ok," Joe said as he turned his own horse to move beside them. "Pass her up, Tilso?"

"Stand," Tilso told Arden before he moved to give Valri to her dava.

Joe settled the little girl on the saddle before him then set her hands on the reins. Ryali was about to panic, but Joe grabbed a spot below, which meant that Valri didn't actually have control of the horse, but she'd feel like she did. Then, once they were all three in place, Tilso led them up the aisle and toward a massive door at the end.

"Loud noise," he warned before sliding one side open. "Let me know when you're back, and I'll open it so you don't have to get down. I'll probably be in here all day."

"Thanks, man," Joe said before riding through the opening.

And Ryali's horse followed. Each step made her sway in the saddle, but she knew the basics of what she was supposed to do. She'd sat on one before, but feeling it move was completely different. Joe would take care of her, though. He had her best interests in mind, and he wouldn't let her get hurt. Then again...

After only a few steps, Ryali realized that this was actually kinda fun. Oh, that didn't mean she wasn't scared, but it was ok. The polka-dotted mare really was as calm and predictable as they'd promised, and while the movement of her back was new, it wasn't meant to throw Ryali off. It was just what happened when she sat on a horse's back. The legs moved. The muscles stretched. By the time the group made it around the Arhhawen courtyard, aiming for the road down to Dorton, Ryali was actually smiling.

"Now come up beside me," Joe said, slowing his own horse to make that easier. "You doing ok?"

"It is na as bad as I thought," Ryali admitted.

"It's really not," he promised. "And Valri's a natural. You talking to Dandy, kiddo?"

"Uh-huh!" she agreed. "I like Dandy."

"Me too," he told her, making it sound like some big secret. "He's my buddy. Now, can you ask Arden to be careful with your amma?"

"She says Amma wiggles, and she doesn't wanna lose her."

Joe grinned. "Good, and will you ask Dandy to be patient so we don't leave them behind?"

Valri scrunched up her face for a moment, and then Joe's gelding dropped his head and snorted loudly. Immediately, the big brown horse began to walk slower, and Ryali's horse matched him. When Joe let go of the reins, she knew this would be ok. He was a good horseman, and Valri could talk to them, so Ryali would survive this trip.

"So," Joe said, "I guess we need to find you a horse of your own, huh?"

"One like this?" she asked.

He shrugged without letting go of Valri. "Maybe you wanna use Dandy? I mean, he's battle-trained, but I'll teach you how to use all that stuff. That way if things ever go bad - and I sure hope they won't - then you'll at least have an escape plan, right?"

"Ya would let me use yer horse?" she asked.

"Ryali, I would let you have everything I own. Kinda what I meant when I said I'd be your mate. I will help you when you're scared and come to you when I am. And yeah, I get scared too, so there's nothing wrong with it. I just figure that's what a partnership is, and it's kinda what I always imagined it would be like to get married, and this isn't much different, right?"

"We do na have ceremonies like humans do," she pointed out.

"Yeah, expensive and horrible things where everyone stares at the bride and groom. Bad time to mention that I get really shy talking in front of a lot of people? I'm ok with no ceremony. Promise."

"And yer a good dava," Ryali said as she reached down to pet the horse again. "Do ya regret na having yer own children?"

"Nope," Joe said as he hugged Valri to prove his point. "Kinda like the one I have. I mean, if we have more, I'm ok with that too. But you may get annoyed with me. That's one of the things that would scare me."

"More babies?"

"No," he promised. "You being pregnant. I mean, what if something goes wrong, or what if I don't do something right? Never mind when you go into labor!" He groaned, leaning his head back when he did it. "Yeah, that would scare me to death. Thinking about all the pain you're going through?"

"It is na bad," she promised. "And our healers make it easy. I just..." She rearranged the reins in her hands. "I know ya said it was ok, so I may have tried. That is why I have na wanted ta leave the house lately. I know ya can na smell it, but last night was the last night."

"Which... Oh!" Joe's head snapped over to her with a massive grin on his face. "When will we know?"

"A few weeks," she mumbled.

"That's all?" he asked. "It takes human women longer to be sure."

"We have healers!" Ryali told him. "I told Zep I wanted ta try, but I did na wanna get yer hopes up if it did na work. That is why I said we should let Valri spend the night with them, and since ya wanted a date..."

"I'm so ok with this," he promised as he moved his horse close enough so he could grab her hand. "And if it doesn't work, that will suck, but we'll just try again and again until it does."

"Do ya wanna have a girl or a boy?" Ryali asked.

"I don't care at all," Joe promised. "I just want to have a very big and very happy family with you, Ryali. If that's our friends, then I'm fine with it. If we have a hundred kids, I'm ok with that too. Besides, I kinda like being a dava."

"Uh-huh!" Valri agreed.

"But trust me," he continued, "waiting is going to suck. And next time - because there will be a next time - you should warn me ahead of time so I can be ready." He winked at her and moved his horse back into place.

But Ryali couldn't stop smiling. This was her ahnor. He was completely human, but he was still perfect. Somehow, Joe managed to make her feel like every single thing she did was the right one.

"I love ya, Joevar," she said softly.

"I love you too, Ryali," he told her. "And you too, Valri."

"Love ya back!" the girl said.

And that was when Ryali realized she was actually enjoying this ride. She wasn't scared anymore, and she was sitting on the horse better with every step. Joe wasn't mad about Ryali trying to have another child. The sun was shining and the weather was beautiful. In other words, it was turning out to be a perfect day.

CHAPTER TWENTY

YELLOW

On horseback, it took less than an hour to make it into Dorton. Joe didn't know exactly where they were going, but Ryali said she did. The trick was to find the right street. After that, Joe's mate directed them through a few turns, until they were on the edge of town in a very quiet and modest neighborhood. There, she pointed at a bright yellow house tucked between a blue and a brown one.

"Ok," Joe said when they stopped at the edge of the street. "Just sit there for a moment, Ryali. Arden, stand!"

Then he dismounted, being careful not to jostle Valri out of place. But the moment his feet were on the ground, he caught his little girl around the waist and pulled her onto his hip. The child was growing fast, and he swore she was heavier than she'd been last month. Enough that he had to hike her up a bit to keep her from slipping to the ground. Only then did he move to Ryali's side.

"The trick," he explained as he grabbed Arden's reins, "is to stand on the stirrup on this side, swing your leg over, and then brace yourself on your hands. When both of your feet are free, just slide all the way down to the ground. It's a bit further than you expect."

Ryali nodded to show she understood, and then tried it. The surprising part was that she didn't have a single problem. Joe knew she'd never done anything at all like this, and yet she made it down to the ground without squealing or slipping at all. He hadn't been nearly as graceful his first time.

"You ok?" he asked, just to make sure.

"I did it," Ryali said.

"Yes, you did," he agreed. "Now, Valri? Sweetie, I'm going to tie these horses up, then can you ask them to stay here?"

He didn't give her a chance to answer before he offered her to her amma. The request was mostly to make Valri feel like she was helping. Even if she got the idea across, horses weren't known to have a lot of patience, and he still wanted to secure them. Thankfully, Henrik had a tree right at the edge of his yard, and both animals had been taught to stand when needed. Joe led them over, looped their reins around, and ordered them to stand one more time.

Then he offered his arm to Ryali and headed to the main door of the cottage. He had a feeling this was something he knew better than she would. Neighborhoods like this were common for humans in the CFC, and Ryali had grown up in Guttertown. Joe had only ever been *there* once, and he'd been surrounded by the Blades and other Anglians when it had happened. The houses had been a lot closer together, the doors thicker, and the yards non-existent. Not the kind of place where a stranger might knock on the door.

So when he walked up to the front and rapped his knuckles on the wood, Ryali gave him a worried look. Joe just smiled at her reassuringly. Eventually, he heard the latch flick open, and the hinges creaked a second later. Slowly, a crack appeared with a woman looking through the gap at him.

"Can I help you?" she asked.

"Is Henrik home today, or is he on duty at the Palace?"

Her eyes moved to the side and landed on Ryali. Recognition lit up the woman's face. "Ilus Ryali! Henrik's home. Come in, all of you. I didn't know we'd be seeing guests today." Then she called back over her shoulder, "Henrik! Ryali's here!"

"Ry!" the man bellowed, and his feet pounded as he hurried into the front room.

"Sadava," Ryali breathed. "Ya have na visited in so long!"

"Since before the army got home," he agreed. "I thought you'd like some time to see your pack again. And you brought my little blossom with you. Hello, Valri."

"Gara!" Valri squealed, reaching out for him.

Without hesitation, the older man snagged her, hauling her against his own chest to kiss at Valri's cheek. "You got so big!"

"And she speaks Glish better than me," Ryali told him. "But I think that is because of my mate. Henrik, I want ya ta meet him. This is Joevar, my ahnor."

"Joe," Henrik greeted him. "I've heard so much about you."

"And I about you," Joe agreed. "Hopefully, you'll stop hiding away from Arhhawen now and come visit." He looked at the man's wife. "Both of you."

"Oh, I don't know if we'd be welcome," the woman said.

"My wife, Aleida," Henrik introduced. "Honey, this is the soldier with the Anglian army I told you about. The one Ryali talked to in her mind."

"A pleasure," she said demurely.

"The same," Joe assured her. "I've heard so much about both of you that I feel like you're family. And rumor has it there's a dog?"

"Rufus," Henrik agreed. "He's in the yard right now. I found out the hard way that they make iliri nervous."

"More so the other way around," Joe told him. "Dogs are usually on the menu for them. Um, but I hope it's not rude that we invited ourselves over."

"Why would it be rude?" Ryali asked.

"Human thing," Joe explained. "One of those foolish customs we have."

"Never," Henrik assured them both, gesturing for them to come deeper inside his home. "I'm curious what brought you all the way down here, though."

"Two things," Joe said. "First, I convinced Ryali to ride a horse. Second, well, we actually have something to discuss with you."

"We?" Henrik paused at a hall, then continued on toward the back.

"It's a nice day, so no reason we can't all sit outside. Aleida? Would you bring some drinks for my friends?"

"Yes, dear," she said, breaking off to head to what was most likely the kitchen.

Joe wanted to tell her not to bother, and that they were willing to help, but he knew Henrik thought of Ryali as the regent. She was above his rank, and in Anglia, that seemed to matter a lot. Ryali, on the other hand, would never understand such things. To her, this man was simply family. Joe could see both sides of it, but he had a funny feeling that these two would make a great pair for the Peacekeepers Sal was planning. The perfect example of how two very different cultures could learn to work together.

But once Joe stepped into the back yard, he had to rethink his opinion of Henrik. This wasn't a fenced-off chunk of land like he'd expected. It was a garden, complete with landscaping, manicured grass, and a simple fountain in the middle. And there, lying along the far side, was the dog he'd heard so much about.

"Bird dog?" Joe asked.

"Supposedly," Henrik said. "But he doesn't have the instinct for it. Got him as an older puppy, and he's tolerated all of my kids and now Valri."

"What's he say?" Joe asked the child.

"We smell new and he wants to say hi," Valri told him.

"Well, tell him to come say hi," Joe said. "I like dogs. Had one when I was your age, you know."

"Yeah?"

"Mhm," Joe said. "C'mere, pup!"

That was all Rufus needed. The dog raced over to the person who'd shown an interest, wiggling like he'd been left alone for years. Joe knew he hadn't, but it proved just how good-natured the animal was, so he ruffled the dog's ears as a reward, and Valri tried to mimic him. Oddly, she never once buried her fingers in his hair like most children.

"You're good with him, huh?" Joe asked.

"Gara Rik taught me how," she said. "Amma's scared of Rufus though."

"She's not scared," Joe told her. "She's worried the dog might bite you because your amma can't hear them. She can only worry about what *could* happen."

"Oh."

Henrik moved to kneel on his other side. "You're good with her. Got a few kids of your own?"

"Just her," Joe said. "I'm making this up as I go, but I've been around the iliri enough to have an idea of how they think. It really is a bit different from us, and yet not really."

"So, not just how they were raised?" Henrik asked.

"No, and they even have different emotions." Joe patted the dog one more time and stood. "In combat, we linked our minds together in a meld. Um, it allowed us to share senses. A good way to see behind your own back, you know?"

"I've heard," Henrik assured him.

"Well," Joe went on, "I was with the Devil Dogs. That means we rode with the Blades, so I spent quite a bit of time linked to some pretty pure iliri, including Sal. I could feel her and Jase kill. After that, I've never doubted that there are inherent differences between us. Not better or worse, just different. They see different colors, smell *everything,* and don't feel things like hate or guilt. The grauori are different again, but not quite as..."

"Aggressive," Ryali finished for him. "We were made ta kill, and humans did a good job of it. They wanted guard dogs, but did na know that grauori were as smart as them. Smarter, I think, because humans could na imagine us talkin' in our heads."

"Good point," Joe said.

Henrik waved to a table. "Let's sit. Valri, honey? There's a ball over there in the grass. If you throw it, Rufus will go get it and bring it back. He loves that game."

"Ok!" she agreed, hurrying over the way he'd pointed.

Joe watched, unable to keep from smiling when she hurled the ball as hard as she could halfway across the lawn. And, just like Henrik had said, Rufus hurried to get it. When he raced back toward Valri, Ryali tensed, but Joe caught her hand and squeezed, assuring her that it would be ok. Immediately, she relaxed enough to sit down at the small stone picnic table between the two men.

"So," Henrik said, "what did you want to discuss? In Dorton for something?"

"Ta see ya," Ryali said.

Joe slid his thumb across the back of her hand. "Sal's orders," he clarified. "We're actually here on business. Well, she is. I'm just tagging along because I wanted to meet you."

"And because I have na ridden a horse before," Ryali reminded him.

"Yeah, that too," Joe agreed.

"Ok?" Henrik said. "But why? What does the Kaisae need? I'm not on active duty anymore. Not with all the soldiers back from the war. Those of us who could be placed on a pension were, and I'm on that list. Most of us who remained behind during the war are, truth be told."

"So you wanted to retire?" Joe asked.

Henrik just shook his head. "Not at all, but I understand. Too many soldiers on the payroll, not enough money to just keep paying without raising our taxes. I mean, I have to retire eventually, right?"

"Na yet," Ryali told him. "Ya know how I helped the King when he was at war?"

"Hard to forget it," Henrik said.

Ryali bobbed her head, clearly building up her confidence. "They want ya ta join the Peacekeepers. Ta help me figure out how ta make humans and iliri work t'gether."

Henrik immediately looked over at Joe. "You?"

"Sal and Dom," he clarified. "I really am just here to visit. This is all Ryali."

"It is na," she scoffed. "Sal told ya about his offer. That he's gonna be a major, and we are gonna be the ones in charge."

"Whoa, wait," Henrik said, holding up his hand. "This just went from a will you help sort of thing to here's your dream. Major?"

"Sounds like Dom wants to make sure you're promoted," Joe explained. "Partly for helping out with Marcu Piet, if I know the man - and I do. Partly because he knows very well that a promotion means you get paid what you're worth, and it will give you more respect with the rest of the human Peacekeepers. The iliri will respect you for your actions, and the grauori tend to accept you until you screw up. Thankfully, they're pretty easy to get along with if you can understand them."

"I have a link," Henrik assured him, "so yeah, I can understand them just fine."

"Good," Joe said. "Because they want you and Ryali to help build this thing. Rragri's coming to Dorton for her daughter, but she's bringing along a few grauori to make triads. One human, one iliri, and one grauori. Each city will have a triad assigned to make decisions, and your group will be the top officers directing them all. Any questions, any problems, or any need for guidance, and they come to you. Well, mentally."

"You're serious?" Henrik asked, looking to Ryali for confirmation.

"Yeh," she said. "They need us ta make sure that Anglia works, so we all can learn ta be happy t'gether. Ya proved yerself when ya helped me, and Dom said that if I can work with ya, then ya have a good record, so he wants ya ta be the top human. So will ya do it? I do na think I can do this without ya."

"Ry, this is a big deal for me. I mean, it's a *real* big deal."

"About as much as freedom to an iliri?" Joe asked.

Henrik just smiled. "Pretty close, although I don't think there's much that could top that. Yes, Ry, I'll do it. I'd be honored to help any way I can."

"Then ya will be the top human Peacekeeper," she said, "but ya are still my sadava."

"Always," he promised.

CHAPTER TWENTY-ONE

CYAN

*D*om. Sal's voice was gentle in his mind. *C'mon, Dom, you should be awake by now, and I know you'd shut me out if you were with your mates. I forgot to tell you something last night, and I want to make sure I don't forget again.*

Sal? Dom asked, pulling himself awake. *It's still morning.*

And most people are awake by now, she teased. *Ryali talked to Henrik yesterday. They told me when they got back, but I was... distracted.*

Fucking, he clarified. *Which I was up doing until late last night with my two fiancées, so I should be sleeping.*

Henrik is a Peacekeeper, she said, stronger this time. *That means you need to find me twenty-one more, and preferably before the allies get here in about four days. Less, if they're moving quickly.*

I'm up!

No, you're not, Sal said. *Wake up Rayna and tell her to help you pick some human Peacekeepers. C'mon, Dom. We need to get this going before the allies arrive. It was your idea, remember?*

What the fuck was I thinking? he asked as he rolled onto his side. But the view before him was enough to make him wake up. *I'm good, Sal,* he said, closing the link before he leaked into it.

157

Because Rayna lay sprawled on her stomach with the sheets pulled low down her ass. Dom could see the two symbols inked onto her back. Marks she was very proud of, and which she'd definitely earned. There between her shoulders was the first one, a snarling dog. Beneath that was the second, a silver shield with a green triad woven together in the center.

The problem was that they were alone in the bed. Just him and Rayna, so where was Shift? While Dom's eyes ran over his woman's body, he forced himself awake enough to listen to the sounds in his suite. Finally, he heard it. Just a single splash that proved Shift was in the bath. Considering the positions they'd been in last night, he had probably needed a hot soak to ease his muscles, because Dom knew that as soon as he moved, he'd be feeling it.

And yet Rayna never did. She always managed to best both of her men in every single thing she did. That was part of what Dom loved about her. Rayna was never ashamed of herself. She didn't hold back to spare someone's feelings. If she was good at it, then she didn't hide it, but she was also willing to help anyone learn who showed an interest. She'd made him a better rider, fighter, and even a decent tactician. In fact, the truth was that the woman lying beside him in bed was the reason he was a king he could be proud of.

Sal had started the process, but Rayna had definitely finished it. And if she wanted another man in their bed, then that was exactly what she'd get. The fact that Dom enjoyed Shift's company didn't hurt at all. It was probably due to his iliri ancestry and some instinctual need for a pack, but he didn't care. It worked for them. Fuck, it worked for all of Anglia, and soon he'd be able to tell the world.

Another splash came from the bathing room. This one louder. Dom leaned over to kiss Rayna's spine, loving how she made a soft little sound when his lips touched her skin, then he rolled from the bed. Sure enough, Shift was done with his bath. He glanced over when Dom walked in, jerked his chin up in a greeting, then grabbed his toothbrush.

Dom headed straight for the toilet to relieve himself. "You hurt as bad as I do?" he asked.

Shift grunted in agreement. "She's going to be the death of us."

Dom laughed, but it was the lazy kind. "It'd be a good way to go."

"Yeah it would," Shift said. "And the water's still warm in the tub, if you want it."

"Sounds like a plan. She's still in bed, but I'm not convinced she's sleeping," Dom told him. "Sal woke me this morning. She said we need to pick a group of humans to work as Peacekeepers. You two willing to help?"

Shift stuck his toothbrush in his mouth and murmured something similar to, "Mhm."

"They're supposed to work with the iliri, and sounds like most of those will be from Tensa's former waitresses." Dom finished and headed to the bath, stepping right into the water. "I'm going to guess that means they'll be a little shy in some ways and very lethal in others?"

Shift popped his toothbrush from his mouth, spit into the basin, and then glanced back. "Not necessarily. Some of those girls had normal jobs before they were recognized as iliri. Others worked their way up. All of them are deadly, but not all have the accent or the habit of running from humans. Kaliryc, as an example. She worked for one of the Glish newspapers."

"You knew her?" Dom asked.

Shift lifted a shoulder in a weak shrug. "When Sal was assigned here, we were in Prin. Most of us ate at Tensa's when we could. She worked there. So did a few of the others. Linaeryx came later, when Ryali was home with Valri, it sounds like. The problem is that there aren't twenty-one former waitresses." Then he paused. "Dom, how typical do you want these Peacekeepers to be?"

"I don't fucking care," Dom said. "I just need people who can have empathy for others, make good decisions, and who know the culture of their species but can work with the others. Why?"

"The brerror," Shift said. "There are a few who might shock your humans, though."

"Such as?"

"Well, I know a woman who's really a man, but is a pretty skilled shifter. She's a beautiful woman, but a very unique-looking man."

"Wait." Dom sat up in the tub. "Like, all the parts are female?"

"Externally," Shift explained. "Shifting is only moving pieces around and adding color. That's why Sal could never become a horse or a flower. She's always going to look like an iliri body. Maybe human. Taller, shorter - but she will always weigh about the same. She can't add mass, just redistribute it."

"And what's the downside of *your* skill?"

Shift leaned over the sink. "I can't restart life, and serious injuries require me to work with others to get enough power for it to happen. I'm a very weak healer. Mostly because I'm barely iliri. With Raast, Risk, and now Blaz, I'm kinda useless."

"Not to me," Dom told him. "And Risk's healing hurts like a bitch, so I'll gladly take yours. Besides, it's a lot better than no skill."

"Good point," Shift agreed, proving he wasn't honestly upset about his ability. "But being less iliri does seem to weaken the skills. Kolt thinks that more use will strengthen them, and everything I've seen supports that. I mean, I can heal faster than other iliri since I've done it so much, and I'm much better than I used to be. But as to how it works? I'm not entirely sure. I just... feel it."

"What's it feel like?"

"Like a flaw. I put my hands on someone, and I can feel this smooth surface almost. Like the pieces inside - these are good, and these are good, but not at that one spot. So I try to smooth it out. I can feel the life force like a pool, or a fountain. It's hard to describe. My goal is to move the life to the bad spot, and let the body work itself out."

"So, is all healing just levels of the same thing?" Dom asked.

Shift shook his head. "No, not at all. Every healer I've talked to does it a little differently." Then he chuckled. "Kinda like sex, I suppose? We all stick it in, wiggle it around, and then add our own flair."

"I will never think of healing the same," Dom teased, sinking a little lower in the water. "But I was mostly asking because I don't know if it matters for these Peacekeepers, you know? Do we need strong skills? Do we need a healer with each group?"

"No," Shift told him, "because if you have a healer, then that's all the triad will do in town. Coughs, broken bones, or such. They'll stop being Peacekeepers and start being an emergency service."

But Dom was starting to smile. "But imagine if each town hired a healer. Iliri or grauori, it wouldn't matter. It'd still be a non-human living and working there who'd be respected in some way. One more step to bridging the gap between us, right?"

"And a good way for a lot of these iliri refugees to get a decently paying job," Shift agreed. "I'll bring it up with Sal. Isn't she coming to Dorton today?"

"Yeah, to talk to Rayna about wedding plans," Dom said. "I was hoping to send the Peacekeepers back with her. Not sure if that will happen, but it's the plan."

"Her and Rayna?" Shift paused to rinse his mouth, then turned to look at Dom. "Just accept now that the pair will vanish, and we'll be left to ourselves for the rest of the day. You're talking about two women, tailors begging for their business, and the need for a couple of *perfect* dresses. I know my sister has a slight addiction to fancy clothes. I'm willing to bet that Ray's just as bad if you let her."

"Dresses and tailors will come later, but she deserves to be spoiled," Dom said, "How long has Rayna been stuck in a uniform? And I don't give a shit what she wants to wear to our wedding. If that's pants, then fine. If it's a skirt so short some of the noble ladies faint, then perfect. If it's the most amazing gown the world has ever seen? Well, you'd better help me get her out of it on our wedding night."

"I'm in for that," Shift agreed. "What about you? What are you wearing?"

Dom lifted a brow. "Think we should complement each other?"

"And her," Shift said. "Not identical, of course, but we should definitely look like the three of us belong together. I'm also rooting for something a bit more flattering than a military uniform."

"Court attire?" Dom offered.

Shift shook his head. "I'm thinking more like what you wore to Parliament in the CFC. It flatters your build."

"And it reflects where you came from," Dom pointed out. "I can work with that. The big question is what colors Rayna will want."

The answer came from the doorway. "A silver dress," she told them. "White and green accents."

"Silver?" Dom asked, a bit surprised at the nearly traditional color choice.

"Well, it's close to grey, for the Dogs. White for the Shields. Green for Anglia. If the rest of the world wants to see that as national pride, then I'll let them, but to me, it's my heritage. My family."

"I'm wearing green," Shift declared. "Black and silver accents."

"I am *not* wearing green," Dom said. "Everything I wear is green. I always end up in green. Maybe I can pull off white?"

"I don't care so long as you're there," Rayna said. "Now both of you get out. I need the facilities."

Dom didn't budge. "And if we don't?"

She just pointed at the door. "If you want to keep your balls, get out."

Shift grabbed a towel from the rack and passed it to Dom. He barely had it in his hand before the soon-to-be Consort was hurrying out. Dom pretended to take his time, but he didn't exactly dawdle either. He also closed the door behind him as he left. Almost immediately, he heard Rayna rip out an impressive fart. The two men looked at each other, but neither of them dared to laugh.

But that was ok. This was what married life was supposed to be like: pretending that his woman didn't do anything that wasn't perfect. Somehow, it made it all feel a little more... real.

"I never thought I'd say this," Dom said as he flopped down onto the bed, "but I'm so ready to be married. I could honestly spend the rest of my life with the two of you."

Shift dropped down beside him, lying at an angle across the mattress. "Me too, Dom. Me too."

CHAPTER TWENTY-TWO

BLUE

*R*ayna refused to be distracted by the two naked men on the bed. Instead, she tossed clothes at both of them and reminded them that Sal was waiting for humans to pair with iliri. Granted, she stole a good, long look while she could, but she knew they needed to get moving. Peace might be easier for them, but it was just a normal day for the rest of the country. There was work to be done.

It was late morning when the three of them reached the barracks. Shift grabbed the door first, holding it open for her and Dom to step through. Inside, it was dark enough to make Rayna pause, but she couldn't miss the mass of bodies. There were too many men still on the payroll, and most had signed up for the war. Their term was a guarantee of two years, but it hadn't taken that long to defeat Terric - not with Sal's help - so they still had almost half a year left to go.

And Anglia had no idea what to do with *all* of them, although Rayna had a feeling they'd figure it out. So, before Dom could say anything, she marched forward, stepped up on one of the benches, and right up onto the table in the middle of the common area.

"Listen up, men!" she bellowed, using her command voice. "Gather 'round."

Someone else yelled, "And let the King through with Shift."

Soldiers moved out of the way. Dom headed over, but he didn't climb up beside her. He and Shift claimed a seat on the top of the table, clearly giving her complete control of this. That was why she loved them. They weren't trying to make her feel special. These two men both believed that she was just as capable as anyone else, and when she took charge, they let her. Not once had either of them made her feel like some cute thing playing at being a soldier. They treated her like their equal.

She smiled at them and waved for the rest of the Anglians to get close enough so she wouldn't need to ruin her voice for this. It didn't take long, and just like in the field, anyone who couldn't hear would get it repeated through the link for them. When the crowd finally stilled, she decided to just lay it all out there.

"We've all lived with the iliri and grauori, right? We know them, and I think most of us have friends from the other species. Now that we're back to being split again, we're starting to see some cracks in this grand plan. Civilians are confused. They don't understand that iliri and grauori are just a bit different. They can't understand why a woman would draw blood on her husband unless there was a bigger problem. They're terrified of the furry beasts roaming through their towns and can barely understand them because they didn't get a link. We need to fix this, and fast.

"Because the allied nations are coming to sign a new version of the Conventions of War," she continued. "If we want our other citizens to be included and recognized as sentient and sovereign species, then we *have* to prove this works. Are you all willing to help?"

The soldiers roared back their agreement. The words were different for each one, but there was no mistaking the intent. Almost everyone in here had been spared at least a wound - if not their very lives - by someone not human. Never mind the link. That, more than anything else, had brought the species together.

After a few moments, Rayna lifted her hand to calm them down. "Ok, our first step is going to be making a new police force. They will be called the Peacekeepers, and each city will get a triad made from one human, one iliri, and one grauori."

"Claimed or born?" someone at the back called out.

Shift answered before she could. "I think it has to be born," he said. "At least to start, because these first triads will be judged by how they look. Each species will want to see someone like *them* included, and I know what it's like to have humans represent me. Once we all learn that our species are more diverse than they initially appear? Then we can take claimed members."

"I'm out," a man grumbled.

Dom jerked his chin at him. "Why's that?"

"I'm a quarter nuvani, sire." He reached up to push his lip higher, exposing multiple canines. "I'm too human to be iliri and too iliri to be human. Sucks, because I want to help."

"We still can," someone else said, and this time the voice was female.

Dom chuckled and began shaking his head. "Come closer, Brisa. We can't see you back there."

People moved, giving the shorter woman space to weave between them until she stood before the King. "Sire," she greeted him, dipping her head to show respect.

"So how can you help?" he asked. When she paused for a little too long, he reached out to clasp her arm. "It's ok. Clearly you have something in mind, and I have a feeling it's a good idea."

She lowered her voice. "You once told me something in confidence..."

He waved her off. "I'm not worried about that. We talked often. What are you thinking?"

Brisa's eyes jumped up to Rayna, who then realized this conversation had happened in bed. Most of the men knew Brisa had previously been a sex worker, but not everyone knew she'd been in the King's bed. Still, she'd more than proven herself as a soldier. That meant she was probably worried about Rayna being jealous.

"We're good," she told the girl.

With a nod, Brisa sucked in a deep breath, as if her confidence had returned full force. "You said that the problem with combining the kingdoms would be policing them. That each noble would use their guards to keep their advantage, and you assumed the grauori would do the same on land they still controlled, right?"

"I did," Dom agreed.

"So what if we..." And she gestured behind her at the other soldiers. "Those of us who are still contracted, I mean. What if we're assigned to local police forces - supplemental, or something? Tell the nobles that their guards can focus on the palaces and keeps, and we'll manage the rest of the cities? The Kaisae does the same thing in Arhhawen, except she uses the Devil Dogs and Dark Heart to remind the iliri that their *friends* aren't always the same. You're already paying us, and right now, we're doing nothing."

"Yeah," someone else agreed. "Send us out to create a guard for the Peacekeepers. Human cities get us. Iliri cities get Sal's people, and grauori dens would get maargra."

"Yes!" Brisa said. "And *we* know that the maargra will be fair. Just like we know that the Kaisae is as much ours as she is the iliri's. But if we look human enough - and not even completely human - the claimed members will still have a way to help. Make the Peacekeepers our bosses."

Rayna knelt beside Dom. "It's a good idea, and I think Sal will go for it. I'm willing to bet Rragri will as well, but I don't know her like I do Sal. I also think Brisa needs to be a Peacekeeper."

"Me?" the girl asked.

Rayna nodded. "You're a damned good soldier. Exactly the kind of person I want to represent my species."

"But..."

Rayna lifted a hand, knowing that Brisa expected her to be petty. "I wasn't born in Anglia. I've been a soldier for a very long time, and I'm not ashamed of what I did before I became the Consort. You shouldn't be either. Brisa, we need women like you to prove that we can be more than wives and whores, right?" And she looked at the men. "Right? Sal's not the only woman who can hold her own, and I think the rest of Anglia needs to see it. Fuck, I think most of you men *like* it."

"But they aren't going to listen to me," Brisa said. "I mean, these guys know I'm a good soldier, but civilians?"

"We got your back, Brisa," someone said.

Rayna just lifted a brow, making it clear that proved her point. "What do you think, Dom?"

"I think I'm biased," he admitted. "Brisa's my friend, and I'm not sure I can be impartial."

"Well, I can," Shift said. "And anyone Sal respects works for me. Brisa's in. Now we need twenty more Peacekeepers and a plan for how to position our soldiers as city police."

"Ilus?" a man called out. "I'm willing to write up a plan, if you can give me until tomorrow?"

"That's Consort," Dom told them. "Guys..." He pulled himself to his feet and moved to stand beside Rayna. "It hasn't been formally announced yet, but I think you should be the first to know. I asked Rayna and Shift to marry me. I know that's not done, but it's not a secret in the ranks. Rayna will become the Queen of Anglia, and Shift? I'm naming him the Consort of Anglia."

"You claiming to be a human now?" Brisa asked, her eyes on Shift.

He shook his head. "I *am* iliri, and I'm proud of that. Just like you're all proud of your own ancestry. Rayna's my mate. She'll be Dom's wife. He's my closest friend. We have three species, but we're all living side by side. Why can't we blur the lines a little?"

"Or a lot," one of the men said. "We already have a noble council. Why not a council of species? Make laws that apply to all of us instead of dividing us by how we were born?"

"That's a good idea," Rayna said, pointing at him. "How?"

The guy's face turned red, and he looked at the people on either side of him as if seeking support, but they were all nodding. After a few seconds, he gave in. "Well, Sal - I mean, the Kaisae. She and Dom work good together. And Rragri's nothing like we expected. I served with her from Issevi to Terric City. She listened to us when we said humans could or couldn't do something. She's just as fair. Why can't the three of them work together to make rules that are good for *all* Anglians? We're not three kingdoms, sire. We're one fucking country with a bunch of different people. We need to accept that and stop trying to split it all up."

"Yeah!" someone else said. "Anglia is a triad, but we're also a whole. I mean, what if I want to have a mate instead of a wife? What if our lady soldiers don't want to get married? Iliri don't have to, so why should the women who fought beside them?"

Again, the soldiers began to murmur their assent. It wasn't as loud this time, but it was just as emphatic. The best part was that they had a point. Rayna lifted her hands, silencing them again as she stole back their focus.

"Sal's coming to Dorton today. She's going to be helping me with wedding planning, but I like what you're talking about. I'll have Dom run it past her, and when Rragri gets here - "

"The Orassae's coming?" someone asked.

Rayna nodded. "She's bringing grauori for the Peacekeepers, and Nya. Seems we humans can do a few things our friends can't. They want to make sure she has the best medical care, so they're coming to have access to *our* doctors. I think it's the perfect time to show them some human ingenuity while we're at it. I'll talk to them about it, but I need you all to do something for me. We have twenty-one cities to cover. Five of those are grauori dens. We're going to have a few iliri towns on the western side of the mountain, and we'll need Peacekeepers for that as well. Make me a list. Get me a structure. Give me *names* of the soldiers willing to volunteer for this, and I'll convince them that we can make it work."

"And I," Dom said, "will start working with the council to change the constitution. The idea of a single nation is what we've been talking about, but it's going to take some time. Probably years. This is the first step, people." He pointed at Brisa. "I want to see you in my office after dinner. Take the time to get your ideas in order, but I like where you're going. I want to make sure I'm on the same page."

"Yes, sire," she agreed.

The King grinned. "Still just Dom. Besides, I like that it makes all those noble pricks lose their minds when my soldiers call me that."

"Yes, *Dom*," she said, a smile touching her lips. Then she breathed, "Laetus, sire."

Rayna felt her eyes stinging at the woman's words. They weren't even for her, but they said so much. An iliri phrase for a human ruler. That, more than anything else, proved that all of this could actually work. The lines between the species were dissolving, and faster than any of them had expected. Faster than even Sal had dared to hope.

So bring on the allied nations. Maybe Anglia wasn't perfect, but they were closer than anyone else.

CHAPTER TWENTY-THREE

ORANGE

That evening, Sal headed down to Dorton, choosing Gage to go with her. Jase had no interest in dealing with the Anglian nobles, and while they all missed seeing Shift, they could talk to him at any time. That made the distance seem less important. Never mind that Zep had passed out on the couch, Kolt wanted to head up to the school to see Lasryn, and the rest deserved a little time to themselves.

It was still weird. They'd spent so much time following her around that she hadn't yet decided if she liked having more space or hated it. The one thing she didn't do was worry that they were tired of her. Even now, as she rode through the gates of the Dorton Palace, she could feel her men like a warm embrace in her chest. If she had to name the overall feeling, the best word would be trust.

She trusted them. They trusted her. Their love had become strong enough to weather anything, even a war, and while she was still learning about Tyr, Blaz, and Gage, it felt comfortable. Relaxed, even. Most of all, this new life felt *good*.

The guard saluted as he waved her and the Cinnor in. Gage pressed his fist to his heart in return, letting the man know he'd been seen. Sal caught the man's smile, but she didn't want to call him out on it.

Technically, that was a breach of protocol, but it was one she liked. She definitely did not want to discourage it.

After living here for a few months, she knew her way around. There was no need for someone to show her where to put her horse, so she aimed for the back of the building, toward the stables. As they came alongside the main pastures, Sal noticed people in one of the fields. Two of them, actually. The man on the horse had his arms straight out to his sides, and the person on the ground was lunging it the exact same way Tilso did.

Evidently, Gage noticed too. "Is that Arianna?" he asked.

"I think so," Sal said. "Sun's behind her, but I don't know of any other women who work in the stables right now. Who's she training?"

"Guess we'll see," Gage said as he squeezed his horse forward.

Sal followed, and the pair trotted to the front of the barn. There, they dismounted and kept going, leading their horses on a loose rein. Scorch was looking around, able to smell new mares, but Cookie didn't seem to care at all. The sound of the horses' feet on the hard-packed aisle was loud enough to bring three grooms, and each of them offered to tend to their horses. Two of them offered their laetus.

"We'll be staying a few hours," Sal told them, "and they were walked most of the way. You can just throw them in a stall."

"Yes, Kaisae," the man with her horse said. "Grain?"

"Just water," Gage told him. "They'll be fed in Arhhawen."

The groom nodded and took the horses, leaving Sal and Gage to make their way out the back of the barn, right where the rider was having a lesson. That was definitely Arianna, and the man on the horse was a soldier, but it was the animal itself that caught Sal's attention. She knew that gelding.

"Is that *the* bay?" she asked, walking forward.

Arianna turned, flashing a smile. "We call him Scout. It's good to see you again, Sal."

Then, without warning to the rider, she dropped the lunge line and hurried over, leaving the man on the horse to deal with his own mount. Sal laughed when he scrambled to pick up his reins, grumbling curses under his breath that most humans wouldn't hear. Still, he got the horse stopped just as Arianna reached the paddock fence and leaned over to hug Sal.

"We're planning to bring up the herd in the next few days," she said, tilting her head to include the man on the horse. "Niran's offered to help."

"Niran?" Sal asked, recognizing the name as one of the men who'd helped Ryali. That was all she needed to duck under one of the rails and hurry over. "Corporal Niran!" she yelled.

"Yes, sir!" he responded automatically.

Then he saw her. Awe took over his face as the man quickly dismounted, swinging his legs over the saddle like he'd done it a million times. When his feet were on the ground, he immediately saluted, thumping his fist against his heart.

"At ease," Sal told him, offering her hand when she got close enough. "It's a pleasure to finally meet you."

His eyes flicked from her hand to her face. "An honor," he said, clearly meaning the touch.

But when his skin met Sal's hand, the only visions that came across were of Arianna. The woman's smile, her silky blonde hair, so unusual in a human. There was even the man's perception of her scent, and the emotion that came with it was happiness. In other words, Niran had a crush, and he didn't seem to be hiding it at all.

"Does she know?" Sal asked.

He sucked in a little breath before realizing Arianna couldn't hear. "No, sir. Or maybe. I never really can tell with her. She's been focused on the horses, though. Making sure everything's ready for her to move from here to there." He paused to swallow loudly. "Kaisae, I want to go with her. To Arhhawen, I mean. The King already knows, but I'm not sure I qualify since I was raised as a human. I don't even know all the iliri customs yet."

"Niran, if you feel iliri, then you are iliri," Sal promised. "Doesn't matter how old you were when that started or how much you know."

"But my ancestors were nuvani, not true iliri."

"Nuvani are nothing more than iliri who embrace their human side," she countered, gesturing for him to walk with her back toward the fence. "I feel bad for taking another of Dom's soldiers, but only a little bit." And she held up her fingers almost touching. "Very small. Thank you for helping Ryali."

"The Regent - er, I guess she's just an ilus now that you're back, huh? Well, she's an impressive woman. I heard that she took the Devil Dog as her mate?"

"She did," Sal agreed. "I'm also making her the leader of our new Peacekeepers. She and Henrik will head a triad based out of Dorton. I'm hoping they will become advisors to us as leaders, as well as the final authority on cross-species cultural differences."

"She'll be good at it, and Henrik deserves the promotion, Kaisae."

"It's just Sal," she assured him. "But why haven't I met you before now?"

He gestured to Arianna. "I kinda got drafted. I wanted to learn how to ride, Ryali introduced us, and now Arianna has me helping with the iliri horses, since she says I'm the closest thing she has to a brother here." And he slanted his head to the side as he dropped his voice. "Which isn't really the term I was hoping for."

"For us," Sal explained, "a brother is family. There's no problem with going from a brother to a lover. In fact, I think all of my mates wore that title at one time or another. It just means that we feel safe with you, and Tilso's sister learned most of her iliri culture from the Blades. Well, from talking to Ahn and his mates, but still. Now tell me how you ended up riding the bay?" She changed the subject, knowing they were close enough that Arianna might hear.

"Scout?" he asked. "Valri, actually. She said he wanted to be scratched, so I was petting him when we all realized she wasn't simply making a guess. She was actually talking to the horse. I guess it's not a typical iliri ability, because her mother seemed pretty shocked, but she also said it sounded like the right skill for the Dernor's child. Anyway, Arianna said the horse seemed to like me, and that he's gentle enough to learn on, so she's had me using him. I hope that's ok?"

"That's perfect," Sal said. "Did you know this horse saved my life?"

"Really?"

Sal nodded, reaching over to pet the gelding's neck. "It was my first mission. Blaec warned me not to take the dun, and that ended up being the one was closest to the door, so it would've been easiest to grab. He said to take the bay. I ended up riding this guy bareback across the foothills of the Siahies - which are a lot steeper than the Ahnian Ridge - and he not only kept his feet under him but also kept pushing himself until we made it to safety."

"Until Zep saved her ass, she means," Gage corrected. "Because the way I heard that story, the poor bay was giving it all he had, but there wasn't much left, and she had a few guys bearing down on her. Zep lanced one, slashed another, and gave Sal the chance to make it behind the line. Blaec was worried this guy was going to founder from being run so hard, but he recovered nicely. Figured we'd use him for the kids."

"He's been great for me," Niran admitted. "Cinnor, right?"

"Yep," Gage said, "but I prefer Razor or Gage. Especially to family."

"Uh..." Niran looked at Arianna for help.

"Ryali named you a friend," she explained. "I figure you're kinda like a brother. They take that sort of thing seriously."

Gage pulled in a deep breath, but his eyes were on Arianna. "Is that really what you're going with? Brother?"

"I can't smell like you," she pointed out.

Niran just groaned and hung his head. "And I'm not used to having blatant iliri around. Yeah, um... sirs? You should probably know that the soldiers suggested a few alterations to your Peacekeeper plan, and um, Dom's supposed to be meeting with one of the guys right about now. I think Rayna's being assaulted by noblewomen who all want *their* tailor to be the one making the Queen's wedding dress."

"So they told you?" Sal asked.

Niran wobbled his head from side to side. "They told the soldiers, but it was in confidence."

Arianna scoffed. "He walked into the barracks and announced it. That's not in confidence."

"In Anglia, it is," Niran said. "We all knew they shared a bed, but the King's been good to us, so if keeping our mouths shut helps him out? Then yeah, we're not saying a thing. Same applies to the Kaisae."

Sal clasped his shoulder. "Thank you, but I don't keep many secrets. I'll also have them get a room ready for you on the Blades' street. I figure between Arianna, Ryali, and your work with the stable, that will mean you're living beside friends. Now, which room is Dom in?"

"He said his office," Niran told her.

"I know the one," Sal assured him. "Oh, and Niran?"

"Yes, Kaisae?"

"Do you like horses?"

"Yes, sir," he assured her. "Never got to see a Blade in the saddle, but I've heard stories, and I've always wanted to ride like that."

"Then you're hired," she told him. "I want you helping the Tilsos keep the horses in shape, and if they think you work well enough, have Ahn train you on foaling and the basic care. That way he and Arianna aren't the only ones trying to do everything."

The man's face lit up in the biggest grin Sal had ever seen, and he looked back at Arianna as if to make sure it wasn't a joke. "You think I can do this?" he asked.

"You'll probably be working nights," she warned him.

"Have been for a while," he countered. "Seems to bother us crossbreds less. Maybe because we can see in the dark? I dunno, but I was the night guard for the iliri Regent. I think I'm ok with this."

"Good," Arianna said, "because that's my shift." Then she pointed toward the barn. "Tack down your horse, soldier."

"Yes, sir," he said, but the smile didn't leave, not even as he led Scout away.

You know he's interested, don't you? Sal asked.

Arianna pressed her hand over her lips to keep from smiling. *Ryali told me. I just wanted to get my brother's opinion first. I'm kind of a bad judge of men, but he's... nice.*

Cute, Gage corrected, proving he'd been included in the conversation. *Did Ryali also mention that living as an iliri means that your kids get to be Tilsos? Plus, we don't judge you for changing your mind about your mate. No marriage means no divorce. Just keep that in mind.*

Means it's ok to go for it, Sal told her. *And I like him. His thoughts are honest. He'd be a good addition to the family.*

"Thank you," Arianna whispered, taking a step back. "And um... you're supposed to be talking to someone besides me, right? So I'm gonna..."

Kiss him, Gage suggested. *The man stinks of desire. When you're ready, just kiss him.*

Soon, she said, but her cheeks were turning pink. "I have a horse to check on."

And with that, Arianna Tilso spun for the barn, walking just a bit too fast. She also smelled like excitement and fear mixed together. Another name for that was anticipation.

Sal caught Gage's hand and led him toward the back entrance of the Palace. "Our pack's growing fast," she pointed out.

"Our pack is also growing well," he said. "I honestly like every member of it, and that's not an easy thing to do. Now let's go add a couple more."

"Some royal ones," Sal agreed.

CHAPTER TWENTY-FOUR

GOLD

*T*he King's office was the same place where Sal had promoted Ilija, and where she'd faced down the noble council after Dom had been attacked by Terric. In their time away, it hadn't changed much. Someone had cleared away the loose papers - probably Cillian when he served as Regent. Everything else was exactly how she remembered it, including the sweet smell of humans and the man behind the heavy wood desk.

Sal knocked as she entered. Gage followed silently behind her. Dom paused to wave her in, then immediately gestured to an Anglian soldier standing at ease. The woman turned and immediately stiffened. Sal recognized her. Even worse, the last time they'd talked, it had been about Tyr, and Gage had been there to see it all.

"Sal," Dom said, "You know Brisa. Well, she has a pretty good idea for the Peacekeepers." Then he tipped his head at Sal as if hinting that the woman should lay it all out. Clearly, he hadn't heard about the blowup between Sal and Brisa that Tyr had caused.

"Kaisae," Brisa said before swallowing back her nerves. "Um, our larger cities are policed by the house guards."

"The ones paid for and ordered around by the local lord," Sal said, proving she understood. "I actually knew that. It's ok, Brisa, keep going. Sounds like this might be important."

"Did you know that they enforce the laws as their provincial lord demands? Often that means ignoring ones he doesn't care about, Kaisae. Like you said when you first came to Anglia, our country is antiquated and backwards. My time in Unav made me see what a true democracy is, and the police are independent from the local government. I mean, they're all bound to the same laws, but a civilian policeman can arrest a sitting mayor. A noble guard cannot do the same with the lord he's sworn to."

"That's a problem," Gage said.

Brisa nodded at him. "Yes, sir, it is." Then she paused. "I'm sorry, sir, is it Taunor?"

"Cinnor," Gage corrected. "I'm the fourth. Kolt is Taunor, or third. Tyr is now the sixth. Relax. You can just call me Gage."

"Yes, sir," Brisa agreed, then winced. "Gage!"

Gage just laughed, waving for Sal to take the chair before the King's desk. "So, how do you propose we fix this problem, Brisa? I'm assuming you have a plan?"

"I do," Brisa said. She shifted slightly, then cleared her throat as if about to present her case again, but Sal waved her off.

"Brisa, I'm tired of military protocol," she told her. "Would you grab a chair, pull it over, and pretend for just a moment that you and I are friends, or at least friendly?"

"See?" Dom said. "The kinging gets old fast."

"It really does," Sal agreed.

But Brisa had relaxed a bit. It only took a moment for her to get comfortable, and then she started again. "Sal, when Dom asked who would be interested in the position of Peacekeeper, someone asked if they had to be born into the species or if claimed members counted."

"Like Zep," Sal said, proving she understood.

"Yes, sir. Shift said he thought we should start with born members, so the representation is easily seen, and add in claimed members once everyone feels like they're truly represented."

"Once the species feel more at home," Dom clarified. "Because I'm sure there are quite a few iliri who wouldn't want Tyr representing them."

"No, I agree," Sal said, gesturing for the woman to keep going.

"Well," Brisa said, "a lot of us want to help. Some of the guys I served with are a little nuvani. Never mind that one unit who claims to be grauori. Add in the policing problem, and I think I have an idea that might make it easier. See, start with a triad calling the shots, sir, and give them a group of mixed-species soldiers - whether that's crossbred members or groups made up of multiple species. Basically, a way to include the people who aren't perfectly what their species should be, you know? Assign them to carry out the triad's orders. That would give the Peacekeepers power and let the community get to know various examples of what it means to be Anglian. Sure, there's the problem of the military working inside our own borders like that, but I figured you already had some kind of idea for handling it."

"A side promotion," Sal explained. "Those who are chosen will keep their rank and pay schedule, but they'll be assigned to an equivalent civil service role. So police instead of soldiers."

"Well, that would give the Peacekeepers their own command structure which bypasses all local politics - and prejudices," Brisa said. "They wouldn't answer to the lord, but rather to their own triad. And *they* would go straight to the one you have overseeing them all. Ryali's, I think it is. This way, when there's a problem, you'll have sufficient - and loyal - police to counteract any riots or to extract prisoners from a lord's jail. People who ultimately answer to the rulers of each species. Hopefully ones who are willing to educate about our new citizens' habits as well as enforce the laws."

"One unit per triad?" Sal asked.

Brisa shrugged. "I would think that's a good place to start. More, if it ends up working out. We're all sitting around, waiting out our contracts, so why not use us? I mean, there's quite a few of us who are going to need the work, in all honesty. Especially us women. The truth is that it's still easier for men to get a job, and sexism is a very real thing. Anyway, I thought the duty might be a nice step in the adjustment from the intensity of war into life as a civilian again, sir."

"Still Sal," she teased. "You were doing so good for a bit there."

Brisa ducked her head to laugh. "Habits. Sorry. Sal, the truth is that we all signed up because we want a job where we can help and be respected for it. *We're* the ones who get that it doesn't matter what you look like on the outside. Combined arms, right? We all make each other better, so use us to erase these lines. Let *us* prove that I, a human woman, can work just as well with an iliri man or a rafrezzi grauori. We fucking fought for the right to be free, and this shit ain't right. If we can't be free at home..." She clamped her mouth shut when she realized what she'd just said.

Sal waved the woman down. "I agree with you completely, and I love your vehemence. Dom, please tell me she's on the shortlist?"

"Definitely," Dom said. "I want Brisa in a triad, and we're in the process of finding more. Brisa said something else I found interesting, though. We're going to be expanding out west, now that Rragri's ok with it. I want to set up a relay system to get civilians across the mountains. Believe it or not, grauori aren't the only dangers over there. Bears, avalanches, and more. There are plenty of reasons to have an escort."

"And it makes use of the men still serving," Sal agreed. "I like it. I'd suggest letting them volunteer for each position and keep a selection here for the Palace Guard. The Verdant Shields aren't enough to protect the capital on their own."

"So you're ok with this?" Dom asked. "Sending out soldiers to enforce the laws?"

"Not exactly," Sal told him. "I'm ok with knowing that just because a man learned how to kill, it doesn't mean that's all he's good for. The ones serving the Peacekeepers will be Enforcers, or something similar. Inter-species policemen, not military." She groaned. "We'll have to find some fitting names. But the point is that our men learned how to make judgment calls in the field. They can use force when they have to, and hold back when they shouldn't. I believe they'll hold each other to the highest standard, letting us know if there's a problem with a unit or if one person is abusing his power. I also think we just brought home a few thousand men and women who no longer have jobs waiting for them. Tens of thousands, if we're honest about it. They need work, and we need to expand our national infrastructure."

"So do your iliri," Dom pointed out.

Sal smiled. "Well, I have a few thoughts about that as well. Once living in predominantly human cities is safe for us - or at least we feel safe doing it - then I think our innate abilities might be very useful. I mean, the mail would travel a lot faster if you used iliri and grauori fetchers."

"Nice," Brisa breathed. "Being able to see the benefit will also make a lot of the older generation more accepting. Healers, especially."

"But," Gage said, "that's going to take time. The Blades aren't the average iliri. We spent years learning how to live among humans. The refugees? They've seen horrors that most of you can't imagine. They won't want to live in the middle of a species who used to terrorize them."

"Someone has to do it first," Brisa said. "I mean no offense to the iliri, but we didn't do it. We may not understand, but how can we learn to accept the iliri if you're all hiding away in Arhhawen? Most of us learned to accept the other species by getting to know them."

"You're right," Gage assured her, "but it's hard to ask someone to move far away from their pack and take that risk."

"So incentivize it," Brisa said. "Offer free relocation for a whole pack if they have enough of the skills you need to set up these ability-based jobs. Don't make them live alone, but don't let them get too comfortable in Arhhawen either."

Sal leaned back with an amused huff. "That's honestly not a bad idea. You know, I think we should pair you with Linaeryx."

Gage groaned. "Not even nice, Sal."

"Brisa won't be scared of her," she pointed out. "And Linaeryx will work better with a human woman than a man."

"I do know how to drop my eyes," Brisa promised, glancing over to Sal before lowering her gaze to the ground to make her point. "And I heard about the Regent's ladies in waiting. Rumor has it they're a force to be reckoned with."

"They're a little feral," Gage admitted. "Linaeryx is the most temperamental of the group. She tends to bite first and ask later."

"Then maybe you can find us a mild-mannered grauori to balance us out?" Brisa joked. "I can hold my own though. Being a former whore was a bit rough for my first few months in the military. Until the elites stepped in, I mean."

"And you more than proved your worth, Brisa," Sal said, leaning over to clasp the woman's forearm. "I like where you're going with this, so I'm leaving Gage here with you and Dom to work out the kinks."

"Uh-huh," Gage said, turning to look at the King. "She's leaving me here so she can have girl time with your fiancée and giggle about what they've been up to."

"I know," Dom said, flicking his hand to shoo Sal out. "Go play. Don't worry, we'll do all the hard work."

"Oh," Gage groaned. "You're a braver man than me."

"And she knows I'm joking," Dom promised. "Seriously, Sal, have fun. Make sure Ray gets everything she wants?"

"That," Sal assured him, "I will definitely do." Then she turned to Brisa. "I think we're going to match up triads in Arhhawen. With the allied nations coming, the Palace is going to be insane. Can you organize getting all the candidates together and let me know when you'll be ready?"

"Me?" She looked over at Gage as if seeking help. "Are you sure, Sal? I mean, after what happened with Tyr, I figured you wouldn't want me in your home."

Sal leaned over to meet Brisa's eyes, resting her hand on the woman's shoulder. "That wasn't your mistake," she whispered. "I was hurt, not mad - and none of it was your fault. Not once have I ever blamed you for my mate's bad decisions. All you did was try to take care of him, ok? You and me? I'd like us to be friends."

Brisa reached up to press her hand over Sal's. "That would be an honor, Kaisae. He told me he was trying to chase you off, you know. That he was in a position where he couldn't win either way. I had no idea that it was so much more complicated than that. I just thought I was helping a friend."

Sal paused, feeling Brisa's memories through the contact, but all she could smell was respect. "Did you know he was doing that to protect me? Not himself, but *me*. Tyr thought that leaving me - and smelling like another woman to prove he was serious - would make me get pissed at him, have a tantrum, and then get over him before we were close enough for it to *really* hurt? It's how humans react, I've been told. He just didn't stop to think that iliri don't change our minds."

Brisa carefully eased herself to her feet and turned to face Sal, her hands closing on the Kaisae's shoulders. "Sometimes, it's easier to pretend that we don't care than it is to show the world what could break us. You, Sal, are Tyr's weakness. I can only guess the same is true for all of your mates, but more so for him. It's hard to find love when you're used to being used. Even harder to believe it's real."

"Trust me, I know," Sal said, offering the woman a weak smile. "Il bax genause, Brisa. Thank you for always being where you were needed most."

"Thank you, Kaisae. You matter too."

"Now go *play*," Gage said. "You're making me all sniffly, sweetie. I'm supposed to be a predator, remember?"

"Love you too, Gage," she laughed, deciding he had a point.

So, pausing only long enough to kiss the side of his neck, she decided to make her exit. After all, they still had a wedding to plan, and Sal had a funny feeling that Shift would rather be helping Dom and Gage with this than helping Rayna with flowers and dresses.

CHAPTER TWENTY-FIVE

BLUE

*W*hen she got there, the King's suite was in chaos. Sal could hear it even before she knocked on the door, and the wood opened a lot faster than she expected. Shift was on the other side, smelling annoyed. Sal canted her head, about to ask why, when he pulled her inside and closed the door.

"If you can get these women out of here and make them leave her alone," he begged, "I will do anything you ask."

"Go help Dom," Sal told him. "Gage is there, and they're working on the Peacekeepers. I got this."

He leaned closer. "It's Lady Arvo, Sal. She brought swatches. Even Linella can't get her to stop, and Ray's about to lose it."

"I got this," Sal assured him again. "Now get out of here while you can."

"Thanks," he breathed before doing just that.

Then, from the other room, Rayna called out, "Shift? Who was that?"

"He's needed with the King," Sal said as she walked the rest of the way in. "I came to make sure you get this right."

Thank you, Rayna thought. *These women want me to wear*

something that resembles a strategy pavilion, and Lady Arvo thinks that pink is my color. Pink!

Just play along, Sal warned her as she surveyed the insanity before her.

At least five different noblewomen had carried up bags of ideas. Lady Arvo had cloth. Lady Aulis had trim. Two others Sal didn't recognize had color palettes, and the last was Linella Piet with a small handful of flowers. She looked as confused as Sal felt, which gave her a little credit in Sal's mind.

"None of this is right," Sal said. "There's going to be an iliri portion of this wedding, so we'll have to decide that before we can pick the colors or styles. Rayna, I have a tailor I'm taking you to this weekend. She made my dress for the Spring Ball when I was here for it last time."

From the far side of the room, Ria Tor chuckled. "She's in high demand, Kaisae."

"She'll take the order," Sal promised, turning to look at the women making Rayna crazy. "If you all don't mind, I need a moment with the Consort."

"Yes, Kaisae," Lady Aulis and Lady Arvo said, quickly putting their things away.

Sal barely caught Lady Aulis nudging one of the girls beside her. "It's time to go. We'll come back later."

At that, both of the younger women began packing, which meant they were probably someone's daughters. Sal didn't even care whose; she just wanted them all gone. Well, most of them. Ria Tor was a friend, and Ryali had good things to say about Linella, even if Sal barely knew the woman herself.

"Lord Piet?" Sal asked. "Can I borrow you for a moment? There's a few things the council will need to consider, and I'd love to go over them with you now so I don't have to make a trip back."

"Of course, Kaisae," Linella agreed.

Ria didn't budge, but the others all hurried out. A few random growls made them do it even faster, and the smell of anger was fading quickly, which meant that Rayna could finally see the humor in all of this. Then, when the four of them were *finally* alone in the room, Sal let out a heavy groan and flopped down into the closest chair.

"Who were the younger ones?" she asked.

"Bysno and Eriwald," Ria said. "They're desperately trying to get back in favor since their husbands just barely kept their lands after the fiasco while you were gone."

"The one orchestrated by my late husband," Linella said. "And it's ok to say his name, Ria. Ryali killing him was actually a relief."

"So..." Sal said, "Bysno and Eriwald got to keep their titles?"

"No verifiable proof to strip them," Linella admitted. "Marcu's documents were addressed to them, but it wouldn't hold up. They could easily say they had no idea and would've refused. It was enough to condemn Marcu, but not them. Still, Ryali's ladies made it very clear that all they would need was a single touch to prove it."

"Then why has no one read them?" Sal asked.

Linella smiled slyly. "Because legally, they didn't actually do anything wrong. They may have planned to, but it's not a crime until they attempt it. The fact that they know that we know? It's a powerful motivator."

"So," Ria said, picking up the story, "Those two lords have become the most agreeable men you can imagine. It actually works in our favor. I mean, Lord Eriwald hates *you* for killing his father, but he can't prove it."

"And I've been pardoned," Sal pointed out. "Long before I was a Kaisae."

"Exactly," Linella said. "But I've made it *very* clear to them that the sitting king has the right to remove their titles on a whim, and that it's a good thing we haven't told him about it."

"They told me instead," Rayna said. "I, of course, told him, so he knows, but he's playing politics. Said that it upsets the populace too much to change leadership that often. He thinks both boys can be trained, but I'm not convinced Eriwald is redeemable."

"If he's not, Dom will handle it," Sal said, dismissing the problem. "And I seriously doubt that they could kill him now. He's not the same pampered boy who rode off to war."

"He's really not," Ria agreed. "This King makes the last look weak and indecisive. He's safe, but Eriwald is probably going to be replaced in a few more years if he doesn't change. Although I'm sure this isn't what you came to talk about."

"Nope," Sal agreed. "I actually came to tell my best friend congratulations on her wedding."

"I don't want to get married anymore," Rayna groaned. "Not gonna do it and you can't make me."

"You have to," Sal said.

"Why? I've been jumping on his dick since Myrosica, and that's working just fine."

Linella sucked in a shocked breath.

"Sorry," Rayna said, glancing over.

Linella just waved her down. "You're fine, I'm just not used to anyone talking that way."

"Which is another reason you have to do this, Ray," Sal said. "You are about to become the icon for all Anglian women. The strong one who makes it clear that you don't care if the men like it or not - and that you can kick their asses in your sleep. Never mind that the iliri and grauori need you to be their hero, so you kinda wanna do this, right?"

"Only because it means I get an iliri boy-toy," Rayna grumbled, leaning a little to watch Linella's reaction.

"I was expecting it this time," she promised. "And I've now learned how to say 'shit' without blushing, so it's working."

"Fine!" Rayna said, sitting back up with a smile that made it clear she was just having a mock-tantrum. "The truth is that I do want to get married. I really want to rub it in a few people's faces, and I love my guys so much, but *that*? All the insanity that goes with it? Why can't we just make a decision and run with it?"

"Which is exactly what we're going to do," Sal said.

"Well, my first decision," Rayna announced, "is that the Kaisae is my maid of honor. I also want Tyr to stand up for me, though. Is there any way to make that happen?"

"We'll find one," Ria promised. "He's your brother, isn't he?"

"Close enough," Rayna said. "And I really wanted to invite Kesh."

Sal's brows rose up toward her ears. "Your ex?"

"My friend," Rayna clarified. "Look, we split on good terms, and yeah, we hooked up a few times after, but he's a good soldier and a better friend. I really want him to be here for this."

Sal lifted a finger. "I heard he's coming in with Viraenova. Want me to see how far out they are?"

"Please?" Rayna begged. "Fuck, Dom even likes the guy, so I mean, if that doesn't make it ok, I'm not sure what will."

Sal nodded, but she was already reaching for Tseri. It took a bit, but the woman responded with surprise. *Sal?*

Kaeen, Sal greeted her. *I heard you're coming to Arhhawen to attend this Alliance meeting we're about to have.*

I am, Tseri assured her. *We're about two days out.*

Two? Which meant they needed to get the horses moved tomorrow and prepare some rooms for visitors. *Well, then I'm glad I got in touch with you. Are you by chance bringing your Conglomerate ambassadors with you? Specifically Kesh?*

You mean my Taunor? she asked. *Yes, Kesh and Lightning Brigade are with us. My three mates have been the only thing keeping me sane since my daughter's death.*

I'm very glad you've got them to lean on, Sal told her. *But I was hoping you could pass a message to Kesh for me. Let him know that Rayna and Dom are getting married? Well, and Shift. Rayna really wanted him to be there.*

Then we will all be there, Tseri promised. *The truth is that I need something happy in my life. Please give her my best wishes. Whatever is appropriate for a human.*

I will, Sal promised. *Ride well, and if you have any problems in Anglia, let me know?*

Your country has been very welcoming, Tseri assured her. *Expect us the day after tomorrow, around lunch. I have thirty riders. A small party.*

And I will have the best rooms for your entire pack, Sal promised, releasing the link. "Kesh is coming," she told Rayna. "And Tseri offers congratulations in the best way for a human."

"I like her," Rayna said, letting out a relieved sigh. "And we know the 112th is coming with the CFC, so I think that's everyone. What else is there?"

"Linella? You brought flowers?" Sal asked, having seen them.

"The King said this would be happening within the month. These are the seasonal blooms that will be easy to get," Linella explained. "We can force a bouquet in a hothouse if we have more time, but I didn't think the Consort - "

"Rayna," she broke in.

"Rayna," Linella corrected. "I didn't think you cared about a specific flower too much. I was just wondering if you had a color palette in mind."

"Green, silver, and white," Rayna said. "Well, grey, but silver will be the right shade of it."

"Anglia, Dogs, and Shields?" Sal asked.

Rayna just snapped and pointed at her. "Nailed it."

"So, you're wearing a silver dress?" Sal asked.

Rayna rolled her eyes playfully. "Of course!"

Linella nodded. "And we can have blue flower pins, maybe forget-me-nots, to hold on your veil. When you remove it - because I think you should remove your own veil - you'll have greenery underneath, in your hair. Ferns, maybe?"

"Are they easy to get?" Rayna asked Linella.

"This time of year, yes," Linella agreed. "And you'll be expected to have a bouquet. You want to stick to those colors or add a splash of something else?"

Ria lifted a finger. "What about azaleas? White ones are easy enough to come by, and I'm sure we can have a few painted to be silver."

"I like the silver," Rayna said, "but I'm not as concerned about the flower. Just pick something that will hold up so I'm not spending the entire ceremony terrified I'm going to ruin it."

"Gardenias," Ria said, picking up a book from her lap to make a note. "And you already have a tailor, so all we really need now is a menu."

"That's it?" Rayna asked.

Linella gestured to Sal. "Well, except for the iliri portion of the ceremony."

"And Cillian is honored that you'd ask him to officiate," Ria added. "So you know the ceremony will be respectful to both species. The men will need to get their clothes ordered, but there's no reason we can't make this happen."

"Where?" Rayna asked.

Both women looked at her like she'd lost her mind. "The throne room, of course," Ria said. "It's where all the nobles get married if they can."

Rayna's eyes hit Sal, pleading for help. "I wanted an outdoor wedding, and I want commoners to at least see the event."

"There's a large pasture on the east side of the stable," Sal said, nodding at Ria to show she should be making notes. "It has a large, clear pond, and it should be empty of horses with plenty of time to clean it up and set up seating. We can open an adjoining pasture to commoners, which will let them see the ceremony but not interrupt. Nobles will be seated in the King's section, but remember that we will have our allies here as well. Plus, you'll need to split the seating arrangement into three sections instead of two."

"Mine won't have anyone," Rayna pointed out.

Sal flicked her ears forward and tilted her head. "Like Pig and the Dogs? Or do you mean like Tseri and her envoy? Rragri?"

"Jarl and Nya will be on the King's side," Ria pointed out. "You don't think Rragri would want to be with them?"

"I don't," Sal said. "I think Rragri and her pack will make it clear that Rayna has her full support as a dominant female leader. Dom's side will be full of nobility, and Shift's side will have the Blades at the very least. Let me know how many chairs, and we'll make sure they're packed."

"Thank you," Rayna breathed. "That's been my biggest worry, that I don't have any family."

"You do," Sal told her. "The food should be divided by species, with plenty of dishes from each nation attending the convention. That means there's less need to pick a special menu, and more reason to make sure everyone is respected. The only question left is if you want a cake."

"No," Rayna said. "I want mead and a toast. I don't trust Shift to not smear it across my face." But she was smiling again.

"See," Sal said, "this is easy. The hardest part is going to be what comes after."

"One more thing," Linella said. "There's a crown."

"No crowns," Rayna told her. "I'd never keep it on my head."

"Every Queen has a crown." Linella sounded like she wouldn't budge. "I have the keys to the royal treasury, and they're all laid out in there. We will find one that you don't hate, and I was thinking that you might help me choose something for the new Consort."

"Shift's getting a crown?" Rayna asked.

Linella ducked her head. "I just thought that if he's marrying the King, then we should make sure he's recognized. I haven't asked anyone else, but if we just do it, they won't be able to stop us, and it will give the man that much more respect by the people. It's a symbol, Rayna. A sign that you've been chosen, and I honestly believe that an iliri wearing a human crown makes a powerful statement."

"Then we'll wear crowns," Rayna decided. "Mostly because I know how much that little resin circlet matters to the iliri. One with jewels? It's a bigger step than any of us imagined."

But something the soldier in Dom's office said was tickling the back of Sal's mind. "Blurring the lines," she breathed. "Maybe we had it wrong. Maybe we need to worry more about erasing them?"

"I'm not letting them replace you, Sal," Rayna warned.

"No," Sal said, proving that wasn't what she meant. "I just mean that if we keep dividing ourselves between the species, then everyone else will. *That* was what Blaec was trying to tell me. We need to stop being humans, iliri, and grauori, and start being *Anglians*. This is the first step, isn't it?"

"The second," Rayna told her. "I think you were the first. But Dom mentioned something about having all three leaders choose the next heirs. You need to talk to him about it before you leave tonight."

"Then I will," Sal promised.

"So is that the third step?" Linella asked. "Combining our three governments into one? Because that will be the final one, won't it?"

"It should," Sal agreed. "Three species, so three steps. The problem is that I honestly don't know, but at least we're going the right way."

"That we are," Rayna told her. "And tomorrow I'm going to be very, very excited about getting married, but right now?"

"Overwhelmed?" Sal asked.

Rayna nodded. "Why couldn't I have picked a *nice* man?"

"You did," Sal teased. "Not his fault most people call him sire. He's still pretty nice."

"And all yours, Rayna," Linella said. "That man is madly in love with you. Well, both of them are."

"Every woman's dream," Ria said. "And a huge step forward for women's rights."

Sal chuckled. "And I bet you just thought this was about getting married, huh?"

"Nope," Rayna said. "I learned a while back that it's *never* that simple. Ayati, you know?"

"Yeah," Sal agreed, but she didn't point out that ayati was gone. Today wasn't the day for that.

CHAPTER TWENTY-SIX

YELLOW

"It's too quiet without the pups," Perin said as he flopped down onto the couch beside Tilso. "I kinda liked having the kids around."

Risk, sitting across from them in his chair, looked up from the book he was reading. "Roo's their dam, and they do need time with her. We can't have them *all* the time, you know."

"I know," Perin groaned, "but c'mon. It's not like *we're* going to have our own kids. I mean, don't get me wrong. I love that the pack shares the kids. I do! I just..."

"Want a family?" Tilso asked as he moved closer to snuggle against Perin's broad chest.

The man turned to make room for him, then pulled Tilso even closer. "I would be an amazing dad," Perin whispered in his ear. "Just imagine some guy trying to flirt with my daughter?"

"Son," Risk corrected. "Iliri women do the chasing. The boys are the ones who need a dava to stand up for them."

"Yeah, well, I'd give the little bitch a talking to," Perin said, changing gears quickly. "Sit her down, make it clear that she needs to have my boy back by midnight or I'll hunt her down. See? I'd be great at this."

"You're so human," Tilso teased.

Perin just shrugged. "I'm good with it, and you two seem to like it well enough."

"We just like putting you in the middle," Risk said without lifting his eyes from his book.

Tilso laughed. "Uh, that's you, baby."

"Pretty sure that's all of us," Perin pointed out. "But honestly, I miss the boys." With a sigh, he looked over at the spare room they had. The door was open and the crib inside was visible. "Would you two raise a human child?" he finally asked.

"Why?" Tilso wanted to know.

"Well..." Perin snuck in a kiss against his neck before leaning back. "I heard Keeya gave a child up for adoption, which means there's probably a few other human girls who do the same, right? I mean, is there, like..."

"A system?" Risk supplied, guessing where he was going. "I don't think so. They didn't talk about those things here, and iliri tend to raise the children in the pack, so if the mother isn't able to handle it, the others step in to help. Thinking about starting one or something?"

"I dunno," Perin said.

Tilso turned to face him. That put his chest against Perin's, leaving the arm of the couch to hold them both up. "Having trouble retiring?"

"Maybe," Perin agreed. "Mostly it's not knowing what to do when I wake up, and the kids helped. Well, and I kinda like being a dad with you two."

"I love you," Tilso told him, stretching just a bit more to steal a quick kiss. "With or without kids."

Perin's hands slowly slid up Tilso's waist until they got to his ribs. Then, a mischievous grin took over his face, and Perin grabbed, pressing his fingers right into the gaps, not quite tickling, but making it clear that he could. All he'd need to do was wiggle a bit.

"Don't mock me because you have your horse babies," he joked.

"Don't!" Tilso begged.

Perin's fingers tightened a bit more. "But you squirm so nicely."

"I'll share my horse babies," Tilso swore.

"Do it," Risk said.

Yet before Perin's fingers could torment him, a thought brushed Tilso's mind, and one that he would be a fool to ignore. *Sal?* he asked, pulling himself from Perin's arms. His lovers looked at him in confusion, but Tilso just held up a hand, begging them to wait.

I heard from Tseri earlier, Sal told him. *She says they're two days out, which means the CFC won't be far behind, and I'd rather not be moving our herd into the stable with a dozen other people milling through the barn and paddocks. Can you see if your sister can make the transfer tomorrow?*

I can, he promised. *You know how many Viraenovans?*

She said thirty riders, but I think part of that is Lightning Brigade. Please tell me we'll have the space ready?

We will have the space ready, Tilso promised, even as he ran through the number of unfinished stalls and gates that still needed to be hung on the paddocks just outside. *How's our brother?*

Shift? She pushed a bit of amusement across the link. *He's happy about the marriage, annoyed with the nobles, and helping Dom with the Peacekeepers. He's good, Tilso. This life suits him in a way the military never did.*

Good. Tell him we'd better get an invitation to the wedding, and yes, I'll arrange everything else with Arianna.

Oh! Sal thought. *You should know that an Anglian soldier named Niran is interested in her. He's part iliri - well, nuvani - and will be moving to Arhhawen with the horses, he says. Make sure Arianna knows that we consider her iliri?*

You might, Sal, but Mom doesn't. Tilso sighed, then looked up at his mates and smiled to let them know it wasn't a problem. *And if Arianna is moving with the horses, that means my mother will be coming too, huh?*

Or... Sal offered, *I could always ask Dom if he'd welcome her into court. I have a feeling Lord Piet would be more than happy to include her.*

Perfect! Tilso said. *I love her, and she needs someone to take care of her, but she does not understand iliri at all. I think she'd be miserable here.*

Then I'll do that. I'm heading to talk to Shift right now, Sal said. *Linella and Ria are with me. I have a feeling I can call in a favor to make this happen, but I'll let you know tomorrow? Probably won't be back until late tonight.*

Thank you, Sal, Tilso said. *And I'll have everything ready for Viraenova. Tseri will be jealous of us. Promise.*

I know. Let me know if there's a problem, ok?

Will do, he replied, but she was already backing out of the link. "That was Sal," he said, because both Risk and Perin were clearly waiting. "I need to get the horses moved in tomorrow, and Viraenova will be here the day after. Sounds like Lightning Brigade is coming with them."

"So Kesh did it, huh?" Perin asked. "Got himself in bed with an iliri."

Risk scoffed. "You did, so don't sound so shocked." He smiled as he closed his book and set it beside him. "You said you needed something to do, right, Perin?"

"How do we help?" Perin asked obediently.

Tilso blew out a heavy breath. "We need to bed down the stalls. All of them. Tomorrow, we'll need to hang gates on the paddocks."

"We can do that tonight," Risk said. "Most of us can see in the dark. I'll get some Blades to help me. Ghost definitely will."

"Baeli," Perin added. "I'll ask her. You ask Ghost. We'll grab anyone else who knows about fencing and spreading straw. Doesn't take much skill to carry around the bales of bedding, either." Perin slipped off the couch but paused to give Tilso one more kiss on the neck. "Talk to your sister. Risk and I will get a labor force going."

"Thank you," Tilso breathed, looking between the two men. "I love you both, you know that?"

"I do," Risk promised.

"Kinda have to," Perin teased as he reached over for Risk's hand. "We'll be in the stable."

Tilso watched them leave, trying to run through a list in his mind of all the things that still had to be done. He'd hoped for a few more days. The barn was close to being finished, but close wasn't the same as complete. Still, Sal was right. If Viraenova was only a few days away, then the other allies would be as well, and barn space would be at a premium in Dorton. Tseri wouldn't judge the iliri for still working on their home. She knew it was under renovation. That didn't mean she'd want her own mounts kept in less than ideal circumstances. They were her ride home, after all.

So, once his mates were gone, Tilso reached out for his sister. *Arianna?* he asked.

Hey, little brother, she replied. *I saw Sal today.*

She hinted at that, he said. *She also told me that Viraenova is going to be here sooner than we expected. Is there any way we can move the herd tomorrow?*

I'll need more hands!

How many? he asked.

Well, I can ask Niran, because he already said he wanted to help, but I'm not sure if he's on a shift tomorrow. Um...

How many? Tilso asked again. *Gimme a number, Arianna.*

Ten, she tossed out. *I don't know, but we have twenty mares and a few geldings. With ten people, we should be able to manage.*

Ok, so does that include you?

Sure, she said. *And Niran will make two. Who else can we get? Think you can send some riders down?*

I have a better idea. Hang on. And he immediately switched to another mind. *Ricown?*

Yeah?

Is there any way I can get a few Shields to help move the Blades' horses tomorrow? We need to get them out of your way if the allies are coming, and sounds like we're running behind.

Tomorrow? Ricown asked. *Sure. You want all of us? I think Ilija might be busy with Dom's wedding plans, but the rest of us should be free.*

As many as you can get, Tilso told him. *Arianna and Niran are all I have so far, and she said she's got more than twenty horses.*

Ricown just laughed in his mind. *Tilso, we have an entire barracks full of soldiers who know enough to pony a horse from here to there. Offer them a meal at Tensa's, and I'm sure we'll get plenty of hands. So, should we plan for lunchtime?*

Perfect, Tilso said. *I'll have the Blades move our warhorses and the hitch teams out of the way, get the last stalls finished, and we should have all the paddocks ready by then.*

But I'm gonna call in a favor for this.

Anything, Tilso promised.

Make sure the Shields get a special price when we start shopping for remounts. Fuck, any price, because I know firsthand that your horses put ours to shame.

I'll train them myself, Tilso promised. *Was already in the plans, Rico, so yeah, I can promise that. Sal wanted all of the leadership's guards mounted on the best animals Anglia has ever seen, and we're going to breed them.*

Then I'll start finding helpers. Tell Arianna to link to me when she's got a plan. If she handles the horses, I'll handle the soldiers, deal?

Deal, Tilso agreed before letting go of that link and finding his sister's mind again. *Arianna, I got help for you.*

How many? she asked.

As many as you need. Ricown said most of the Shields will help. Ilija's booked, but the rest will be there, and he's headed to the barracks to ask some of the veterans to help pony the herd.

Silence hung in his mind for a long time. Just as Tilso was about to ask if that was ok, Arianna finally said, *And just like that, we have help?*

We have friends in high places now, Ari.

Ahn, that's the King's Guard. That's not just high places. It's the highest! I mean, Sal talked to me today, and that was shocking enough, although I remember you talking about her when she was a new recruit. But when the King smiles at me? Or the Sergeant at Arms?

Ilija, Tilso corrected. *And the man was just a soldier until he talked back to Sal. Dom was just a bastard's kid until she put him on the throne. Yeah, they're leading the country, but believe it or not, they're just people, and pretty amazing ones.*

That's the part that feels unreal, Arianna admitted. *These people running the country are willing to drop what they're doing to help us move horses?*

The very same horses Ricown just asked for a chance to buy? Yeah, Ari. Dad's stock is the best this country's ever seen. That we've been able to find so many of them and bring them with us?

What about Mom? She asked after the mention of their late father.

Sal's going to get her set up in court. The human court. She's asking Lord Piet if she'll help.

Our mother's going to be a real lady?

Yeah, Tilso said. *Which means she won't be all up in our lives all the time. Also means you're allowed to flirt with that soldier Sal told me about. What's his name?*

Niran, Arianna said. *You know, he's part iliri.*

I was told.

Yeah, but did you know that iliri custom is to name the children after the mother? Which means my kids would be Tilsos? Think that would get Mom off your back?

Sure wouldn't hurt, he said. *But I'm less worried about that than you being happy. Well... I mean... Perin said he wants kids, so if you decide to have an entire herd of them, you pretty much have free babysitting.*

No. Just no, Ahn. I'm having one or two, and that's it. Now, I'll still take you up on the babysitting, though, because I plan to spend the rest of my life on a horse. You know, since Mom can't complain about it anymore.

Tilso chuckled. *You know, she's really going to fit in well at court. Her ideas are about as outdated as theirs.*

Only because her grandparents were Anglian, Arianna said. *Mom mentioned that they were so strict about what a woman could do.*

When?!

When we came here. We had a big fight around Myrosica about how she wanted her kids to live in a modern age and such, and how she was so proud of us. Then in the next breath, she was telling me that I should find a nice husband so I wouldn't need to spend the rest of my life in a barn.

She just doesn't get it, Tilso said. *She hated living on the farm, so she can't imagine that we don't.*

But she loved Dad, Arianna said. *I think she likes that we're carrying on his work. She just doesn't know how to fit her upbringing together with Conglomerate modern life and the iliri culture. Things are changing too fast for her.*

Not fast enough for me, he said.

Me either, she agreed. *But the truth is that I like it. Thanks for getting me this job.*

That, he told her, *was Blaec. We weren't the only ones trying to chase down Dad's herd. He started first.*

Kinda feels like it was meant to be, huh? she asked.

Yeah, Tilso agreed. *Almost like fate.*

CHAPTER TWENTY-SEVEN

SILVER

Geo was cleaning the plates when Baeli got a message that she was needed in the stables, so dinner would need to wait. He'd been looking forward to an evening alone with his mate, but he understood. And while he tried not to let his disappointment show, her sense of smell was better than his.

"Go eat at Tensa's," she said as she pulled on her shirt. "I'll probably be busy for a few hours."

"Not why I'm disappointed," he told her, catching her around the waist to steal a real kiss. "I'm just thinking that I'm going to miss you. Unless you need a few more hands?"

She smiled up at him. "No, we'll be fine."

"You'll tell me if you aren't? I know how to care for horses, you know."

"I love you, Tane, but we're good. Go eat something and talk to your pack. If I need some hands, I promise I'll call you first, but it sounds like Risk and Perin already have a small army headed that way."

"Ok." He kissed her again. "And tell me when you get to a stopping point and I'll bring dinner down, ok?"

"You," she whispered against his lips, "are perfect."

"Only for you." And he turned her toward the door, sending her out with a swat on her tight little ass.

Baeli flashed him one last grin before she left, but he loved it. She was so different from her brother, and yet so similar at the same time. The Blades had embraced her easily. Thankfully, according to her, they also didn't make her feel like she was his replacement. She was just family, and having the pack accept her as such felt good for both of them.

For the first month, she'd asked for every story about her brother that she could. Quite a few were things that even Geo hadn't heard. So many of the men had served with Blaec before Sal joined. They'd been through some rough patches, some good times, and a whole lot of war. They also didn't hide his mistakes.

The time since his death had eased the pain of it a little, erasing the haze of nostalgia from his memory. Blaec had been a good commander. He'd been a great man. He'd been a pretty decent friend for the most part, too. Still, like everyone else, he made mistakes. The problem was that everything had been riding on his shoulders, so when something went wrong in his life, it was never allowed to be minor.

But he'd helped make all of this possible. At least that was what Geo got from Blaec's books. The man had written down every vision he had, recording them into a pair of heavy journals that had been given to Sal. When they'd made it back to Arhhawen, she'd passed them to Baeli. Geo had peeked at them a few times, but he'd never been brave enough to read them from cover to cover.

Mostly because the visions he *had* read were intimidating. Most prophets could see a sliver of the possibilities. They were given enough knowledge to make a prediction, but nothing else. Blaec had been different. He'd seen it all. If his actions affected things in the chain, he could follow it until the end, and meeting Sal had spread eternity out before him. It was like he'd been a part of ayati, and Geo wasn't convinced that so much knowledge hadn't wounded his mind toward the end.

It would've broken most people. Then again, the last entry in the last book could be proof that Blaec hadn't been as strong as he pretended. It didn't read like a prophecy. More like an idea, or maybe a lesson Blaec had learned. Possibly a summary?

Patterns don't appear from nothing. They're made. Decades of fighting and losing have an effect. What would happen if we won? What if we could live our lives in color?

That was it. No explanation. No list of options where the best and worst were marked out. Just that one last entry, almost as if he couldn't stop himself from writing it down. Geo could almost imagine the man in his last days, leaning over the book by lamplight while Sal was across the camp in a tent with Jase and Zep. He wondered if Blaec had been strong enough to cry, mourning his own death, or if the man had tried to ignore that too.

At least it hadn't been in vain. Even if Blaec could've been insane at the end - or verging on it - he'd still been a good man. He'd given his life so that everyone else could live theirs in color, hadn't he? Or could that have been all he meant? For so long, the Black Blades had only known love, death, and pain. Now, they experienced the entire spectrum of emotions. They had not only the time for it, but also the freedom.

And the responsibilities that came with it. Geo sighed, knowing that his musing wouldn't help Baeli finish any sooner, and he was honestly hungry. Spending most of the day in bed with her tended to have that effect. Since cooking an entire meal just for himself was pointless, he decided to do exactly what she'd suggested. He found a set of clean clothes, pulled on his boots, and headed for Tensa's.

It was still early. Just after when most people ate dinner, actually, so there were plenty of open tables in the diner, and the smells of fresh food were very tempting. Geo was headed for a table on the far side when he noticed someone sitting alone. It was the black that caught his eye, since pale hair and skin didn't stand out in Arhhawen. Turning a bit, he found Narnx hovering over a cup of coffee and a blank journal.

"Want some company?" Geo asked.

Narnx looked up with a smile. "I'd love some. Where's your mate?"

Geo smiled, well aware that Narnx paid just a little too much attention to Baeli. "In the stables. Sounds like they're finishing up tonight so the horses can show up tomorrow. Why aren't you at the school?"

Narnx huffed, the sound a mix between amusement and scorn. "I am *not* living with a bunch of children who think I'm the enemy. I have no interest in waking up with my skin stained brown or my hair dyed pink. They absolutely hate me, and the parents aren't much better."

"So they know you're still the Emperor, huh?"

Narnx nodded. "And they haven't yet learned why I'm keeping the title. They will, though. I plan to cover that in the first week."

"Good call." Geo leaned back to flag over one of the waitresses.

She was new, not one of the women he recognized, but she clearly knew who they were. "Ilus," the woman said with awe in her voice.

"Can you get me a plate of whatever's easiest?" Geo asked. "I'm not picky. And a cup of coffee to go with it?"

"And you, ilus?" She asked Narnx.

He waved her off. "I'm good."

"Eat with me," Geo said. "Unless you already finished?"

Narnx looked up at the girl. "I can't read the menu. Do you have beef? Pork?"

"Boar," the waitress assured him. "Yellow or white cheese?"

"Yellow," Narnx and Geo said together, making the woman smile.

"And another coffee?" Narnx asked.

"Yes, sir," she breathed. "Of course."

"Just Narnx," he assured her. "I'm done with being a sir. I'm just Narnx."

The girl nodded, but backed away without responding. Narnx sighed, turning his attention to spinning his almost empty cup between his hands. The scent of sorrow leaked from him.

"It's because you're in black," Geo said. "They all treat us like that. To most of the iliri, we're heroes."

"You, maybe," Narnx said. "I'm just the traitor whose father killed someone that they know. Everyone has a story like that. Fuck, even Sal."

"Your sire did that," Geo corrected, "and you're not responsible for him. Shit, Narnx, did you know I used to get the same thing? Soon as someone heard I'm a friender, they backed away slowly, refusing to even look at me."

"Really?"

Geo nodded. "Yep. Frienders can't be trusted, you know. All it takes is a touch and I can make you believe we've known each other forever. I could convince you to tell me your deepest secrets, jump in bed with me - "

"Not onsyc," Narnx pointed out.

Geo chuckled. "My skill doesn't care, but I knew that. Not with the way you've been watching Baeli."

Narnx's head immediately shot up, and he met Geo's eyes. "I didn't mean to."

"Sure you did." Geo chuckled. "I don't blame you, either. She's kinda hot. No. She's definitely hot. You meant for her?"

"No," Narnx assured him. "At least, not like that."

"Then like what?" Geo asked. "I'm not upset, man. Just curious."

"I had a vision before ayati broke. I haven't seen it since, so I'm not sure if it's still possible, but she was in it."

"Naked?" Geo asked.

Narnx sighed. "Um, pregnant."

"Yours?"

"Partly? See, I always saw her standing beside a window, looking out at the southern range. I was lying in bed, and I could describe the entire room. Well, it's the room I have now. I told Sal I needed a room with a window, and she understood. The view's the exact same, and Baeli was looking out the window, talking to me about what to name the baby. She hoped Sal wouldn't be upset if she named him Blaec. When she turned, I could see that she was close. Fucking huge, man, and so beautiful. And um, right about the time Anglia made it into Escea, it changed. I started to realize there was someone else standing in the doorway. The one from the main room to the bedroom. I'm pretty sure he was wearing black, so I think it's you."

"I'm cool with that. Like the name, too. Baeli's kids will all bear the last name of Doll, so it works."

"Yeah." Narnx paused when the waitress headed their way, waiting until she'd put a plate down before both of them and handed them each a new cup of coffee. He thanked the woman, then waited a little longer until she was out of the way, then said, "I didn't choose the vision."

"Trust me," Geo assured him, "I know how that works, and I'm cool with it. Would rather have you around than some idiot who barely understands what we went through, you know?"

"But I'm the man who abducted Sal in Syhar - don't you know that?"

"I do," Geo said. "I also know that you used chloroform instead of something that would kill her. I heard you convinced the rest to let Blaec live. That you gave Kolt not only Blaec's sword, but also Sal's daggers, and that you risked everything to help them get out. You didn't choose your sire, Narnx. You did, however, choose to help. Isn't that enough?"

"Yeah," Narnx said, "but who wants to mate *the Emperor?*"

"Um, probably the same woman who wanted to mate a friender, and one of the strongest I know of." He canted his head. "Or the woman who's only known as her brother's lost sister. She didn't know him, Narnx. Sal forgave you. Sal made you a *brother*, and that says more than you know. She's running Hax out of Arhhawen, you know."

"She is not," Narnx countered.

"Oh, she's making it uncomfortable enough that he wants to leave," Geo promised. "And that bitch of his? Fuck, but they're the perfect match. Seems even iliri have speciest fools. Sal hopes that living in the middle of nowhere will do them some good, and neither seems to have a problem with grauori, so they shouldn't mess things up on that side of the mountain."

"Least there's that." Then Narnx paused. "Wait, so you're ok with the fact that I honestly believe Baeli will one day be my mate?"

Geo laughed, but softly. "Man, she's not going to become your mate if you don't talk to her. I'm only confused by one thing."

"Ok?"

"Your vision was after the Terran war. You saw something past ayati. How?"

Narnx just shrugged. "No idea. I don't even know if it's valid anymore, and I haven't had it again since. I can tell you that the trees were a bit taller, so it'll be a few years."

"She's not ready for kids yet," Geo said. "so it works out. Baeli wants to prove herself to the pack first. I keep telling her she doesn't have to, but she thinks she does. Kinda like you do. I get it. I felt the same way when I first became a Blade, so yeah. But I'm not about to get in your way, and I think Baeli's feeling too intimidated to make the first move. I do know that she thinks you're attractive. Well, she said cute."

"I'm not cute," Narnx said.

Geo shrugged a little too innocently. "She said you look like a pale version of Arctic. She also pointed out that black is a good color for you. *And* we've talked a few times about how hard it was to do what you did up in Terric. Pretending to be the enemy, risking your own life, and all of that? But yeah, she definitely said you're cute."

"Do I even want to know how this came up?" he asked.

"Well," Geo said, dragging the word out, "I noticed you checking her out when you caught up with us on the road. I, um, may have brought it up. I mean, Sal looked from you to her and smiled, which means she knew something, and I've gotten used to paying attention. Kept us alive, you know."

"Sal knows," Narnx admitted. "Baeli was the thing that kept me going. My own hope, I suppose. Like some promise that if I could push just a bit more then I'd end up with a perfect ending."

"Won't happen unless you talk to her. Granted..." Geo was enjoying this just a little too much. "She's going to be working in the stables for most of the night, if I know my mate. If you want to help me carry her dinner down, I'll introduce you properly."

"And you're honestly ok with this?" Narnx asked.

"Look, just because you were raised around humans doesn't mean the rest of us were. I know she'll have more mates. Personally, I'm completely ok with sharing a bed with the Emperor of Terric. I mean, *this* version. No offense, but I would've gutted your sire."

"Me too," Narnx agreed. "I honestly thought about it when he killed Blaec, but Sal... She was trying to die, Geo. I've never seen anything like it. I was terrified that she would will herself to death, but then Kolt was there, watching over her, and I just... I had this idea to get them out. And it worked!"

"And here we are because of it," Geo said. "The truth is that most of my friends have mates of their own now, and, well, it's kinda just me and Baeli. I don't really have a lot of guys to hang out with. So, yeah. I kinda like the idea. And if you saw it, well, maybe that means ayati isn't all gone, right?"

"I don't know," Narnx said honestly, "but, um, if you ever want someone to hang out with, I'm usually up at the school, and I'm only teaching two classes. I can sneak out between them."

"And probably wouldn't mind another Blade showing up to make it clear you're accepted, huh?"

"Not at all," Narnx agreed.

Geo nodded at him. "It's a date. And hanging out with me also means..."

"Hanging out with Baeli," Narnx finished for him. "Damn, but you're a good ahnor."

Geo had to duck his head because he could feel his face getting warmer. "Fuck, man. I'm human enough to blush, ok?"

"I'll keep it in mind," Narnx said. "So you know, I can't. I can barely cry."

"So more iliri than Arctic?"

"No idea," Narnx said, "and no one was brave enough to ask Makiel. Not even me. How much is Baeli?"

"More than three quarters," Geo said. "Sounds like a perfect match, huh? Man, I hope the kid ends up being yours."

"I honestly don't care," Narnx said. "I just want the feeling that comes with it."

CHAPTER TWENTY-EIGHT

YELLOW

The next day was all about the horses. Arianna told Tilso they were moving toward Arhhawen. Tilso told everyone else. Sal had gotten in late the night before, which meant she was still asleep when the Blades were all called to come help. Still, she managed to not only wake herself up, but also get all of her mates moving.

As a group, they headed down to the highest basement level. From there, they followed a hall toward the back on the south side. Eventually, they reached a massive set of doors that had been thrown open for all the people coming in to help. It wasn't just the Black Blades, either. The Devil Dogs were there, and some of Dark Heart - since Perin wasn't the only member who'd retired as soon as the war ended.

Then there were the family members. All of the wives and kids who'd been smuggled out of the CFC had eventually ended up in Arhhawen with their husbands. Some were there to help. A few had kids old enough to pitch in. Since the Dogs had declared themselves to be iliri, it was technically legal, but it hadn't been at the time. Still, that meant the entire warehouse-turned-barn was packed.

"Listen up!" Tilso yelled as he climbed up on the front of a stall to be seen. "Arianna is about half an hour out. I need everyone to collect the spare horses for each unit and move them into an assigned paddock. Unit leaders, see myself or Baeli to be told which one. The horses left in here - which may be needed for traveling over the next few weeks - need to be moved toward the inner door. I need a few of you to clean the stalls they're pulled out of, and we're going to block off forty stalls for our diplomatic visitors, just so we have plenty of extra room. Everything else will be saved for the bred mares coming in."

"If you aren't sure where to put a horse," Baeli said, raising her voice, "ask anyone in black. That will keep Tilso and me from being overwhelmed with the chatter."

"Yes, sir!" the group agreed, and then they started moving.

The result was chaos, but the kind that worked. Dogs slipped between Blades to move horses outside. Blades wove between Dark Heart to clean stalls. Sal was in the midst of them, doing the exact same dirty work as everyone else. At one point, Jase was beside her. A few minutes later, it was Tyr. Zep ended up helping Tilso and Baeli manage it all, and then, just when they thought they were done, another voice rang out.

"I just saw the herd moving up the hill," Keeya called out from the door that led outside. "Looks like the horses are feeling frisky."

Pig thrust his arm to the side. "Then you get out of the way so they don't knock you over!"

While Keeya was obviously pregnant, she'd never been the kind of person to sit around and be pampered. Rolling her eyes in protest made enough people laugh to prove that Sal wasn't the only one who saw, but Keeya did move. Far enough to be out of the way, but still close enough to offer a hand if it was needed. Sal had a feeling it wouldn't be. Not even if it really was.

Then Arianna arrived, sitting on a dark black horse with spots across its hips, and she had a pair of horses connected to her by leads. Behind that was Niran on the bay, with another gelding being led close behind. And after him came not only the Verdant Shields, but at least ten other soldiers in green.

"We got your horses," Vanja called out. "The mares aren't happy about the climb. Got a few kickers."

Baeli took over. "Mares on the left-side alley. Geldings on the right. We'll give them all a few hours to calm down and then turn them out. Don't need anyone getting kicked and losing a foal. Guys, take a horse and get it stalled. If you aren't sure of the gender, ask or check the underside."

Sal was heading forward when she saw Tilso take the horse from Niran. He paused long enough for the man to dismount, and then offered his hand. Niran took it with a look of confusion.

"Ahn Tilso," he said, introducing himself. "Arianna's younger brother."

"Niran Kyrixx. She's been teaching me how to ride. I have two geldings. Evidently, the one I'm riding is special."

"This way," Tilso said. "And yeah, I know the bay."

Sal moved up for the next horse. Dag passed her a lead and Blaz reached around her to grab the second one the man held. "Where do you want our own horses, Sal?" Dag asked.

"You can put them with the geldings," Blaz told him. "We're going to have extra room there. Believe it or not, we got just over a hundred stalls finished last night."

"Fuck me," Dag breathed. "Nice! Guess you're gonna need it though." And then he was moving out of the way so the next rider could dismount.

At first, it looked like everything was going to be just fine, but horses didn't work like that. Just as the helpers found a nice routine, a crimson red horse squealed and threw itself against the halter. The rider holding it almost lost his seat. The horse managed to rear straight up, pulling hard and giving the soldier no other option but to let go.

The moment the lead was free, the mare bolted, heading back out to the open air just behind her. Pig screamed for Keeya to get out of the way, but she wasn't even close. Baeli cursed under her breath. Tilso moved to check the rider, making sure his palm hadn't been burned by the speed of the rope slipping through it. Blaz just started walking.

Zep met him from the other side of the barn. They didn't run, not even when the mare flagged her tail high in the air and whinnied for her friends to join her. They just casually followed her, making the entire barn stop.

"Let's put the rest away," Sal called out. "They'll catch her, and if her whole herd's in here, she'll come back."

Slowly, the horses began to move again. The Anglian who'd let go was apologizing profusely when Sal slipped past him, but Tilso said it was ok. Part of working with horses, and expected. It made Sal appreciate her Stablemaster a little more.

Outside, the day was bright. Large clouds were forming on the far side of the mountains, just visible from where Sal was standing, but they were moving away. A few puffy ones on this side cast shadows across the hillside, but the breeze was gentle. Sal knew that would help keep the horse calm. An oncoming storm would've sent her into a panic. This? It was just a highly bred mare showing off a bit.

Up ahead, Zep held his hands open as he mumbled nonsense to the mare. Blaz had hopped over the fences to get around behind her. The lush grass was tempting enough to make her drop her head to grab a bite, but she didn't stop for long. The only problem was that the poor thing didn't stand a chance. While Zep kept her attention, angling her closer to the paddocks, Blaz hurried to get the gate. Then, just as Blaz released the latch, Zep yelled, "Ha!" and the mare spun, bolting straight through the opening.

And that was it. She was caught. Sure, she had a small pen to run off her excitement, but she wouldn't go far.

"Nice work, guys," Sal called to them.

Zep tossed a smile over at Blaz. "Almost like you've been doing this a while, huh?"

"Not as long as you have," Blaz said as he secured the gate. "You think we should try to get that halter off her?"

"Nah," Zep said. "Let her step on the lead a few times and she'll get her head back on straight. I just hope she's in foal to something nice and calm."

"Probably not," Sal said as she reached them. "She's nice, though."

"One of the Tilso finds?" Blaz asked, having heard all about their horses.

Zep just nodded. "I think Arianna picked her, but I'm not sure. Believe it or not, while Sal was up in Anglia the first time, Blaec was buying horses. When Tilso said his sister was willing to travel to get the best stock, well, she pretty much got an open budget. Most of us pooled our spare cash - which was quite a bit - and told her to pay what they were worth."

"Which is how we got the second string of mounts?" Sal asked.

Zep wobbled his head. "Tilso was involved with that, too." Then he paused. "Huh. I guess I need to start calling him Ahn or that's going to get confusing."

"Tilso works," Arianna said as she walked over. "Came to make sure you caught her."

"Yup," Zep said. "Believe it or not, we're not all horse idiots."

Arianna rolled her eyes. "Believe it or not, I know that. I also know that Carmine's not exactly easy, but she'll make great babies for us."

"Us," Blaz said, grinning at Zep.

"Oh, she's family," Zep assured him. "Arianna's been in on our retirement plan from the start."

"Wait..." Blaz said. "Blaec came up with this idea about the time Sal went to Anglia?"

"Mhm," Zep said, looking a little smug.

"So he knew we'd win?"

Zep just shrugged. "No one really knows what he did and didn't know, but we're talking about Blaec. I think he would've done this if there was the slimmest chance. Good horses are hard to find now. So many were killed in the war, and what's left are mostly farming stock and crap that was overlooked the first ten times the armies were buying. These?"

"Rank and spread across the northeastern Conglomerate," Arianna said. "My dad liked the polka dots, so he started breeding military horses with them. Said it was his thing. We had to sell everything when he was killed, but Ahn made a deal with one of the military buyers to get hired on at Stonewater Stables. They had him cleaning barns for a couple of years."

"Where he was once nice to a new elite soldier," Sal finished. "When he stood up for me, Blaec wanted to thank him somehow. Gage looked up his employment history, and realized that the Tilso family started the lines that almost all of our horses trace back to. He decided that Ahn would make the perfect Stablemaster."

"And my brother hired me for the night shift," Arianna finished.

Blaz just groaned. "We could never figure out where the Blades were finding these amazing horses." And he gestured to the mare. "Rais checked every known military breeder, and got nothing, but the Blades kept showing up on something new. Like Sal's mare!"

"Because he bent the rules," Zep said. "Nothing said we couldn't buy our horses ourselves. The only catch was if we wanted to use official unit funds for it. That's allowed if we're in the field, but not at our home base where we had our resupply. So, we bent the rules to get an advantage."

"So, are we going to sell to other nations?" Blaz asked. "I mean, when the foals are born and we select the culls we're not keeping?"

"Yup," Zep said.

"And they won't come cheap," Arianna added. "The CFC paid my father pennies for what these horses are worth. When he died, my mother couldn't even afford to keep the farm. So, yeah. If the CFC wants horses this nice? They can pay enough that my new family won't have to worry about it."

Blaz just offered his hand. "I think we're going to get along *very* well. Nice to finally meet you, Miss Tilso."

She smiled at the honorific commonly used with civilian experts. "Thank you, sir," she replied. "Now, let me show you what we've got. And I really hope you're going to let us train up some help for foaling season."

"Anyone you think will work," Sal assured her. "And stall cleaners, because I think someone else can do that for a bit."

"Oh, yeah," Arianna agreed.

Blaz just laughed under his breath. "I kinda like cleaning stalls."

"Hired!" Arianna teased.

Zep shook his head. "Trust me, you want him to help you break out the young stock. Believe it or not, this fool can ride. Better than you, even. Fuck, better than me, and I hate saying it."

"As good," Blaz told him. "How about we go with that, because I've seen you in battle."

"I'll take it," Zep said, slapping Blaz across the shoulder as the group headed back toward the barn. "And today is the first day of our new dream. Iliri horses."

Arianna nodded. "The next step is buying one of those fancy things the nuvani ride. Preferably a bigger one."

Sal just smiled. "I might know someone willing to make that deal."

CHAPTER TWENTY-NINE

CYAN

When the whole thing was done, Sal invited everyone who helped up to have lunch at Tensa's. The men from Dorton readily agreed. They were all a little dusty from the straw, the horses, and the chaos in the barns, but no one cared. Not even when the entire group walked into Tensa's and began pushing tables together.

Lyzzi was one of the waitresses who came over to take orders, but Sal just waved her over. "Just bring a little of everything for everyone? Some of these guys have never tried iliri cooking."

"And some of us miss it," Ricown said from a few seats down. "I'm going to have to start visiting more often."

"You're *always* welcome to drop by," Sal told him.

"Yeah?" He flashed her a grin. "Have a couple of empty rooms we can steal for tonight?"

"Planning to stay?" she asked.

He nodded. "Thought I might have a few drinks with some old friends, and I do *not* want to ride down that mountain drunk. If you don't, I'm sure we can beg space on some couches."

Zep answered before she could. "Guys, we have a whole wing open. There's always room for the Shields in Arhhawen. And if the rest of you want to crash, we'll put you up in exchange for the help."

"Thank you, Dernor," one of the men in green said just as Narnx claimed the seat next to Geo.

"Hey, Emperor?" Vanja asked. "Got a question for you."

Narnx groaned.

Geo leaned over to see down the table. "He fucking hates the title, ok? Lay off."

"No shit?" Vanja asked. "Dude, you worked your ass off for that. Figured it would be a thing of pride."

"In case you forgot," Narnx said, "the Emperor of Terric killed a lot of good people. *My* people. So yeah, I kinda hate that title."

"Point," Vanja admitted. "Sorry, man. Let me try that again. Hey, Narnx, I have a question for ya?"

Narnx just jerked his chin that way, knowing the man was going to ask anyway, but he looked like he didn't really want to know.

"That big tower," Vanja said. "Is that where all the metal went?"

Narnx groaned and let his head flop onto the table. "Maybe? Makiel didn't really keep records of how much he pulled out of the ships. He just had it hauled back and smelted."

Geo patted his back in sympathy. "So what is it, anyway?"

"And why did it hum?" Sal asked.

"*That* monstrosity," Narnx told them, "was supposed to be a call to the gods." He leaned back and gestured for them all to wait. "Makiel wasn't exactly the most stable man. Mentally, I mean. Back when I was a boy, he seemed like he was fine, but something happened. The more people who followed him, the more strange he became."

"Men aren't meant to hold Kaisae powers," Sal said, wondering if that was it. "You think it broke his mind?"

"Fuck," Danku groaned. "Isn't that some reverse sexism there, Sal?"

"It's not," Narnx said. "Kaisae powers come from Kaisaes. It's no different than saying that women can't piss standing up. They aren't made for it. Oh, I'm sure they could, but it wouldn't be the same, you know? Kaisaes aren't women, either, so don't get that confused."

"We know that," Ricown assured him.

"I don't think you do," Narnx said. "Kaisaes are a female gender with brains that are formed differently. And yeah, Makiel cut a few open to see. The dominant female type of iliri has an extra lobe in there." He shuddered as if remembering. "And that was how the extermination started. Makiel wanted to know why iliri could do these things. Keep in mind that he never called himself one. And the more iliri he killed, the more jobs opened up in Terric. It used to be a very poor country. But when we pushed into Unav, we stole art, equipment, and resources. Then we sold it, making our country even more wealthy. The economy improved, the people believed that this man was the answer to their problems, and he got more powerful."

"Weren't you a kid back then?" one of the Anglians asked.

"About six," Narnx said, "but I remember it. And I don't mean he gained political power. I mean he could heal himself. He could move things. Miracles, they said. And when people pushed back against his right to control them, he trotted out his abilities and told them he was meant to rule. Divine right, he called it, saying it was written into the Terran founding documents. I mean, it is, but the line says that man will not impose on the divine right of another to live in liberty or something. I don't remember it now."

"So he was gaining abilities," Sal said.

"Yep," Narnx agreed. "And the more he gained, the less stable he was. His wife began to hire men to help him plan battles, and she pushed him to take more land. The truth is that there was nothing more nefarious to the entire war than plain, simple greed. The iliri just got caught in the middle. Makiel wanted to be respected, his wife wanted to be wealthy, and the populace wanted to have security. Somehow, they realized that blaming the iliri was easy, and it just went from there. Escea kept iliri slaves. The CFC was highly segregated. Unav was divided, with the humans living there upset because they were in the minority. Everyone thought *their* problems were someone else's fault, and pointing at our differences was an easy answer. Add in the idea of divine right?"

"A perfect storm," Gage said softly.

"He could na have picked a better time, either," Jase said. "Iliri were na free until a few decades before he was born. In the CFC, we were property, and they would na have wanted ta lose us. When we got free, we were hated fer it."

"Yeah," Narnx agreed. "But as to the original question? That tower was his way of calling in help. Deep in that ship we were excavating was a map to the origins of humans." He looked down the table. "You humans came from the stars, but not the way Makiel believed. He thought you were made from them. Most of us think you traveled from somewhere else. Another world. Either way, that tower sends an ancient pulse of sound waves that are supposed to travel far. Radio waves, I think they're called. All it does is repeat the same thing over and over. Dot-dot-dot, dash-dash-dash, dot-dot-dot. Then it pauses and does it again."

"Why that pattern?" Dag asked.

Narnx shrugged. "It was in the records. Said that if communications failed and assistance was needed, then that was the code to let the United Nations know. I'm not sure what they were united in or for, but that's what the directions said. Evidently, they had something to do with the trip, because that's their symbol on the end of Sal's daggers. And when Makiel couldn't make the ship send the signal - because he'd already stripped too much out of it - he ordered the backup system to be created beside his Palace. That way his ancestors from the stars would know where to find him."

"The man was nuts," Tebio muttered.

Narnx nodded his head. "*I* think so. And the more detached he got from reality, the harder the Empress pushed to get her way. Sending iliri heads as trophies was her idea. Then again, so was sending her only son to Anglia to defeat the antiquated government here." He looked over at Sal and smiled. "He didn't see you coming."

"Narnx?" Baeli asked, leaning back so she could see him. "What was it like for you? Being an iliri in the middle of all that?"

He blew out a heavy breath. "Hard," he admitted. "I honestly didn't know the man was my father until I met Sal. I was raised to think I was their 'help.' Most iliri were dead by then, so I was pretty much all alone - the beast they took in and trained to prove their greatness. Dozens of times I thought about giving up, but something always happened to change my mind. Then I met Sal, and I knew I could finally do something to change it." He licked at his lips. "I'm sorry I couldn't save your brother."

She dropped her head. "I never knew him. I knew about him, and I knew I wanted to be as strong as him, but that was all. From the stories I've heard, you did everything you could."

"I should've done more," Narnx said. "I just thought I had more time."

"But I made a bad decision," Sal explained. "I got angry and lashed out. Blaec kept telling me that I had to do something. I don't even remember what now, but I had the chance to strip Makiel's abilities and so I took it. I made him as mute as any normal human, but Blaec was killed for it."

"Yeah," Ricown said, "but just think about how much worse it would've been if you didn't. If the Emperor could've seen us coming? If he'd still been able to heal himself? The war would've gone on forever, Sal, and a lot more people would've died. You made the right call, and Blaec knew it."

"Yeah," she agreed, "but that whole thing about the good of the many outweighing the risk to the few? It doesn't make it hurt less."

Tyr reached across his mates to grab her hand. "That's what we're for, Sal."

"And he planned for this," Zep reminded her. "Blaec came up with the idea for the horses. He sent you to Anglia! When he did it, he even made sure that you had the right man at your left."

"But all of you did the same," Sal countered. "Jase taught me to be strong. He showed me what it means to really be an iliri. Zep, you? How many hours did you spend helping me with one thing or another? Even Tyr had my back when I needed it. Each one of you did something to get me here. Blaec doesn't get all the credit for this. Every single person who fought that war did his or her part."

"Well said," Caein told her. "But we can't forget the woman who made it all possible."

"The one who almost outran an arrow," Ricown added.

"And who faced down Ilija in the barracks," Zain said. "That, right there, changed Anglia's military forever."

One of the Anglians nodded. "The woman who taught us how to survive it all. Kaisae, the men we were when you took over? We never would've made it through the fighting in Unav, let alone anything else. I don't think even the grauori could've kept us alive."

Sal chuckled at the truth of that. "Well, make sure you tell that to the allied representatives that are coming."

"The 112th Mounted should be with them," Blaz said. "We - I mean they - always got those assignments. Mostly because we know how to ride pretty."

"And because we took almost everyone else?" Sal teased.

"There is that," Blaz admitted. "The truth is that Anglia is just a better country. I mean, I get why they stayed. Sucks knowing I won't be able to see my relatives as much, but I can live with it."

"What about you?" Zep asked Tyr.

He shrugged. "Dogs are here. My girl's here. And if I get hard up, I got you guys. Figure the rest doesn't really matter, right? Blue or green, it's really more about what we do with the people around us than the flag we're flying."

"Well said," Vanja agreed. "And just in time for the food. Guys, if you haven't had Tensa's cooking, you don't know what you're missing."

A hearty laugh sounded from behind him. "I did na expect a human ta say such things," Tensa teased as she set a platter down before him. "But ya eat so much that the little Kaisae could na carry it all. Now, what about drinks? Do ya wanna try the colors?"

"I want orange," Vanja said. "Don't care what it tastes like, but I could use a little joy on my tongue."

The woman who fed all of Arhhawen reached out to rub his shoulder. "Then that is what ya will have. Fer the rest?"

Ricown pointed down the table at the men in green. "Most of them won't know. Good men, though, ilus. They all fought for you."

Tensa smiled at one of them. "Ya are with the 257th, yeh?"

"I am, ilus."

"I remember ya from the trip here. I think ya will like pink." Then she shook her head. "Na, I will bring ya a pitcher of each. Does this mean the horses are here?"

"They are," Sal said. "And be ready. Viraenova should be here tomorrow."

"Oh! Then I get ta show off," Tensa said before clapping her hands. "Faster, Lyzzi. They are na gonna eat if it is na in fronta them."

"I'm trying," Lyzzi snapped, a rumble audible in the words.

Tensa turned to glare at the girl. "Ya are na *the* Kaisae. Just *a* Kaisae. Do na growl at me."

"No, ilus," Lyzzi said softly. "But I *am* trying."

"That's the right tone, Kaisae. Now I will help ya." And while Lyzzi held the tray, the owner of the place moved to offer each of them a plate.

"Don't worry," Caein told Lyzzi, "she was meaner to us the first time."

"Because ya were humans in a place where humans did na come," Tensa pointed out.

Caein shrugged. "We were Anglians trying to help our people. You just didn't know it yet."

"But I do now, so ya get the best we got in the kitchen." And she smiled at him wide enough to show all of her sharp teeth.

The best part was that no one even noticed except Sal. Being iliri was no longer seen as strange or lesser. They were just Anglians here, and it felt like a dream come true.

CHAPTER THIRTY

RED

The rest of the day was spent getting everything ready to host their first international visitors. Arctic and Shade got an entire street of suites decked out in Anglian green and Sal's black, then stocked it with everything a nuvani guest could want. Ghost, Baeli, Blaz, and Zep made sure the horses were turned out in groups that would work together. Arianna was told she didn't need to help, so Tilso's sister finally got the chance to spend time with her brother and his mates.

Sal and her men, however, were stuck with the worst parts: the paperwork. Records had to be kept to keep the finances balanced. Gage handled that. Talking points for the Alliance meeting needed to be finalized. Jase, Sal, and Tyr worked on that. Kolt helped, but since it was the weekend, much of his time was spent with his son. When the first Viraenovans were sighted coming up the trail toward the city, they were ready.

Dozens of pale gold horses walked lazily into the courtyard. Mixed among them were ten larger, darker mounts, and the men riding them wore a combination of the blue, gold, and silver of Lightning Brigade. Gone was the formal presentation the Viraenovans had made in

Myrosica, replaced with the casual order of veterans after an exhausting war.

She saw Exton and his mate, along with a few other faces that she couldn't quite put names to. It seemed that the Viraenovan guard was made up of people she actually knew - most likely those who'd volunteered so they could see old friends again. Then, sitting at the front of it all, Sal found the woman she was looking for.

"Kaeen!" she greeted, hurrying over to take the horse's reins.

Tseri beamed at her. "Kaisae! Your home is amazing." While Sal held her mount, Tseri Janoyc, the leader of Viraenova, dismounted and stepped in to hug her friend. "It is good to see you again."

"You too," Sal agreed. "And your mates. Syed. Daest. I hope you're doing well."

Like the obedient males they were, the pair dropped their eyes in respect. "Thank you, Kaisae," Syed breathed.

"Still Sal to both of you," she reminded them, "and in Arhhawen, we behave like iliri. No need to put on a show for people who won't care anyway."

Daest hopped off his horse, dropped his reins, and grinned just before he scooped Sal up in a hug. "Then I will say it is wonderful to see you again."

Syed laughed, but he wasn't far behind. "My brother has bragged often that he knows the Kaisae of All Anglia and the Iliri. I think he's showing off."

Sal turned to him and hugged Syed as well. "And now you can do the same." Then she dropped her voice. "How's Tseri doing?"

Syed canted his head slightly, and his eyes flicked over Sal to where his mate was greeting Jase. "She hurts for the loss of her daughter, but she's strong enough to heal. Ylexa has helped, and I think that she will become the heir apparent, as humans call it."

"Ylexa?" Sal asked. "I thought she and Tseri..."

Daest leaned closer. "It seems that Ylexa learned to manage her temper while she was with Anglia's army. That is why she is acting as Kaeen while we are here, staying in Viraenova to manage everything during our absence. She helped a lot after we lost Ynta, proving just how devoted she is as a leader. While Tseri grieved, Ylexa kept the nation moving and organized the memorial. It is Reko we are worried about."

Syed nodded. "We think he should stay with you. He needs family and pack. He needs someone who can understand what it feels like to have his mate ripped from his mind, and who knows the conflict that comes with knowing she died to save him."

"Me," Sal said softly, knowing that was what they meant. "Is he ready to leave Viraenova?"

"His things at home are packed and could be easily fetched, so yes," Daest said. "I just do not know if he will ask, so we're asking for him."

"Well, he's welcome, and I think my brothers can help." She glanced back to see who was close. *Geo? Can you find Reko and get him out of this mess? He's still in mourning, and it sounds bad.*

Oh yeah, Geo promised. *I'll drag him into Tensa's while you get them settled. He probably wouldn't mind seeing the Shields, either.*

Good, Sal said, nodding to let Tseri's mates know it was handled. Then she turned back to the Kaeen, "I see you brought Lightning Brigade with you."

From a few feet away, Kesh chuckled, clearly having heard. "We thought it would make the CFC feel better."

"And for the next few days, he is not my Taunor," Tseri added.

Sal chuckled. "I think we can make that happen. So the arrangement is working out ok?"

The man moved between Syed and Daest. "International relations, Sal. I'm just making sure we understand our neighboring country. And yeah, it's working out pretty fucking good."

Jase snorted in amusement. "Is that what ya call it?"

"Legally, yeah," Kesh said. "It's also why I thought it made sense for Viraenova to stay in Arhhawen. Fewer politicians demanding reports or accidentally catching me in the wrong room." Then he paused. "Um, we brought something else for you."

"I heard about Reko," Sal said, subtly flicking a finger to where Geo was leading the man inside.

"Something else," Tseri said, shooing Kesh away. "Although I hope you know that Reko is still my family, and always will be. I just know that he is taking this hard, and I cannot seem to help. I am not disowning him. Your brother will always be my son."

"Which makes us family as well," Sal pointed out. "How convenient."

Tseri smiled. "It is one reason I did not oppose my daughter mating him, but no, that is not why. I truly respect him, and..." She paused, a small sigh slipping out. "He needs family as much as you do, Sal. Iliri are not meant to be without a pack. Mine will always claim him."

"So will mine," Sal promised, just as Kesh and another man from Lightning Brigade approached.

Each one held the hand of a small girl. Each girl had ears on the top of her head and her fingers tightly gripping the fingers of the soldier escorting her. It took Sal a moment, but then she realized who she was looking at.

"The twins?" she asked.

Tseri nodded. "When you went to the Conglomerate, I offered to take them back to Viraenova, to get them further from the war. The Unavi Rebels refused until you made it clear I was your friend. Then they begged us to protect them, but they are iliri, not nuvani. They belong here, with people who can understand what they lived through."

Sal let out a heavy breath. "They'll need parents. Someone to adopt them."

"Sal?" Risk asked, proving he was among the crowd around them. "Um..."

"Me!" Perin said, pushing closer. "I mean us."

Tseri bit her lips together, but it wasn't enough to stop her laughter. "You both want to adopt the girls?"

"All three of us," Risk said, pulling Tilso forward. "I mean, you do, don't you, Ahn?"

The Stablemaster just nodded. "We were talking about adopting only a few nights ago," he admitted.

"And if the humans change their minds?" Tseri asked Risk.

"I'm not going to," Perin promised.

Tseri gave him a look that said she knew better. "Humans do not bond like iliri."

"Kaeen, I've been chasing Risk for years. I'm not going anywhere."

"What about you?" Tseri asked Tilso.

The man lifted his chin. "I'm iliri. I've been a Black Blade as long as Sal, or almost. I may not have an ability, but I promise you that we're as stable as any other iliri family you can find. Perin is also iliri now, and he defected before Risk accepted him as a mate. We really are committed to this."

"And we want a family," Risk added.

"They're good davas," Sal added. "They've helped Roo with both litters. The rest of us are lucky if we can pry the boys away from them. They would be perfect."

Tseri squatted down before the children and spoke in Iliran. "Would you like your own davas?" she asked.

The one holding Kesh's hand nodded. The other, who looked like a mirror image of the first, shrugged. That made the first one look over, but neither said a word. Still, Sal knew they were talking, even if it was only in their minds.

"They're six?" Sal asked.

"About that," Tseri said. "No one knew their birthdate. They just knew that their amma sent them to a relative in Issevi. He was killed, so the neighbor tried to keep them safe, but when we began pushing Terric east, more soldiers flooded in, and they were handed to a friend of the neighbor, taken to a farm, and ended up with one of the Rebels."

"Sounds like they moved around a lot," Sal said, looking at the girls to prove she was talking to them. The one holding Kesh's hand nodded, but she didn't say anything, so Sal switched languages. "Do you speak Iliran or Glish?"

"Iliran," the first said.

"Glish some," the second offered, but she also used Iliran.

So Sal bent to be on their level. "See those three men there? They want to be your davas. They speak both languages, and you'd have a home where you'd never have to move again."

"Not ever?" the shy one asked.

"Never," Perin promised, coming closer to squat down before them. Like the others, he spoke Iliran. "I always wanted a little girl of my own so I could get her dresses and toys. What are your names, sweeties?"

"Nissa," the braver girl said.

"Nylla," the shy one whispered.

"I'm Perin, and that man with the gold hair? That's Celyn, my mate. Most of us call him Risk, though. And the other man beside him? That's Ahn. We'd love to have you stay with us, and we have some toys for you to play with."

"Toys?" Nissa asked. "Do you have kids?"

Perin shook his head. "Our pack does, so we have toys for them, but we can't have our own. We just love the ones we can. Wanna come see? We can bring someone with us if it makes you feel better?"

Nylla let go of the soldier's hand and took the few steps to stand before Perin, tugging at her lower lip. "We do not belong."

"Oh, honey, yes you do," Perin promised.

Risk moved beside him. "You mean you haven't had a place to stay for long, huh?"

Nissa let go of Kesh to move before her sister. "We just stay for a bit. Then soldiers come."

"Not anymore," Risk promised. "They can't get you again. This time, you get to stay as long as *you* want to, ok?"

"Yeah?" Nissa asked.

Risk nodded at her and offered his hand. "Let me show you."

The moment Nissa grabbed his fingers, Nylla stepped into Perin, lifting her arms in the universal symbol of a child wanting to be held. Perin scooped her up and stood, then gestured for Risk to take care of Nissa. Tilso was smiling at them both, but his eyes were glassy and he kept pressing a hand over his lips.

"They're my friends," Kesh told the girls. "You're safe with them." And to Risk, he added, "Their caretaker couldn't come, so my men have been watching them the whole way here. I'm sure they're tired of being passed around, but they might act out because of it."

"We'll have Raast check them out, while she's here for the weekend," Risk promised. Then he looked at Sal. "Thank you, sister.

We..." He glanced away. "We'll share them with you. Perin just didn't think. He's been wanting his own kids so badly."

"You're fine," Sal promised. "I think they need the attention you three can give, and I can't promise that. Go, show them their new home and make sure they have all the toys. Besides, we have Lyzzi, and I'm more than happy to count her as my daughter."

He nodded, but it took a moment before he could finally turn away, and Sal understood. Her brothers knew she couldn't have kids, and yet everyone else around her was growing their own families. They all expected it to hurt, but it didn't. Not really. She was happy for them.

She was also a realist. All of the children in the pack were hers in a way the others couldn't quite understand. Kolt had Las and Zep had Valri. Jase had taken Lyzzi under his wing, and she often called Sal her amma. So the truth was that Sal already *had* her family, and a bigger one than most ever got. Risk, Perin, and Tilso? They'd never get another chance like this.

So it worked, but there was also a part of Sal that was jealous. A very small part, and she *knew* this was for the best, but if Perin hadn't spoken up so fast, she would've offered her own home to those girls. She could understand them in a way Perin couldn't, but no. She wouldn't do that.

A hand gently clasped her shoulder and a feeling of comfort began to swell in Sal's chest. She looked back to see Tyr smiling at her. "You're a good Kaisae," he said.

"You are," Tseri agreed.

"I'm just tired of seeing the destruction of war," Sal told them both.

"Bullshit," Tyr said. "Letting them raise those girls was the right call, but that doesn't mean you need to like it."

"No," Sal agreed, "but this is a happy day. Our friends are here, our home is almost done, and we have places for all these horses." She pushed a smile onto her lips and gestured at the main doors. "Please, Kaeen, come in and be welcome. I'd like you to feel like you're at home."

Tseri turned with a smile on her lips, but then paused when she noticed the inscription on the doors. "Who wrote that?" she asked.

"Our human friends," Sal said. "Anglia wanted us to know that we're not just tolerated. They put those words there to show that *this* is our home."

"Then I think we will be very welcome. Sal, I'd like to talk to you about our border, and who we're going to let cross it. As you know, we've never allowed humans inside Viraenova before."

"Until Kesh," Tyr added.

"Until his unit," Tseri agreed. "But I think it's time that we learn from you, and I'd love a little advice."

Sal gestured to the stairs. "My office is this way. Can someone tell Shaden her friends are here? Tyr? Would you make sure the nuvani are settled? Jase?"

"Nah," he told her. "Ya do na need my help, and I wanna show Tseri's three mates where they will be staying. I think we need ta make a little change, cuz Kesh will wanna be near his men."

"You got this," Gage told her.

Tseri chuckled. "You want to go play with my boys, huh?"

"Oh yeah," Gage agreed. "But I'm only a thought away, Sal, and your liquor cabinet is full. Stick to the mead?"

Tseri laughed. "Where's the fun in that, Cinnor? I intend to make all of our men chase after us, because for once in my life - and possibly Sal's - we don't need to be respectable."

"I have rum too," Sal fake-whispered before jogging toward the stairs, and yes, Tseri was right behind her.

CHAPTER THIRTY-ONE

SILVER

*R*icown was sitting with his unit-mates, nursing a very strong cup of coffee. The men around him were quiet, all of them feeling the pain of their hangovers. It had been a fun night, and Ilija assured them that they deserved the time off. Dom, Shift, and Rayna could protect each other, and they were spending most of their time planning their upcoming wedding, so guards weren't needed.

But the iliri knew how to have fun. The Shields had a few drinks with their old friends from the war, then a few with new friends they met while doing so. Somewhere along the way, Rico had switched from mead to brandy, and now he was regretting that decision. Granted, he also had a pocket filled with guilders, and he vaguely remembered someone betting him he couldn't hit something with a new bow, but the parts after that were a bit blurry.

Of course, Vanja had started it. He'd figured out that Ricown had a skill, and he'd been using it all along. Like so many of the Blades, his was a mutated ability, but unlike theirs, not a strong one. Still, it worked. Ricown could see further than anyone else, even Sal. He could also hit whatever he looked at, but he had to focus. He had to use his ability. Vanja had named him a "bullseye" because of it. Evidently a cross between fetching and a lookout was a pretty specific skill set.

Still, when a purebred iliri man walked into the diner with Geo, everyone noticed - and not just Ricown. For a moment, he thought it was Hax, but this man's posture was completely different. Broken, almost.

"That's Reko Wyra," Tebio said. "Sal's brother."

"Guess that means Viraenova's here," Caein added.

"Yeah," Ricown said, "but something's wrong."

"Maybe that his mate died in the Terric City battle?" Vanja offered. "I mean, you know how long it took Sal to get over that."

Ricown pushed back his chair. "I'm gonna go talk to them. You guys stay here."

"Why you?" Dag asked.

Ricown lifted a brow and just looked at him. "Because unlike you, I'm a bit more iliri. He's been with Viraenova. Thought I'd see if he needs company or wants to be alone. Stay *here*."

Before they could say anything else, he stood and headed over. Geo noticed, jerking his chin up with a welcoming smile, which said enough. The pair wasn't trying to hide. Still, Ricown wanted to be sure.

You want company or to be alone? he asked Geo.

Pretty sure he could use something to take his mind off things. Just don't mention his mate for a bit? I'm telling him about Anglia and Arhhawen, and what it's been like after the war.

Ricown made it to the table in time to catch the last bit of that as Geo said, "And all the Terran conscripts who surrendered repaid her by fixing the place up. Man, it's huge!"

"And still getting bigger," Ricown said as he grabbed a chair. "You mind, Reko?"

"Please," Reko said, gesturing for him to sit and join them.

"How bad was the trip?" Ricown asked.

Reko groaned. "Tseri's hovering over me like a mother hen. I get it, though. I'm the last of her family, so to speak, but still. I just..." He sighed. "Sorry."

"No," Ricown said. "No apologies needed. Coming from the CFC where you were all but ignored, I bet the last few months have been overwhelming."

"To put it lightly," Reko agreed. "I..." He paused as Lyzzi came over to take their order.

"What can I get you?" she asked, looking at Reko. "If you've never had Tensa's cooking, I'm happy to offer suggestions."

"This," Geo said, "is Sal's brother. Not packmate, Lyzzi. Her real brother."

But Reko was staring at her with his mouth open. It was a look Ricown completely understood, so he added, "They were both born in the same lab and didn't know it until last summer. They were also the first two purebred iliri to make it into the Conglomerate elites, if I'm not mistaken."

"You're not," Geo said. "Reko was accepted with Azure Silence a few months before the Blades took Sal. Hax didn't get into Dark Heart for almost a year after that."

"So you're not a Blade?" Lyzzi asked.

Reko slowly shook his head, but he still couldn't speak.

"He is and isn't," Geo said, answering for him. "Lyzzi, go get us all some coffee and a couple samplers?"

Ricown groaned. "No food."

"Yes food," Geo told him. "It's the best way to get over your hangover, and the more meat, the better. Trust me, man. I've perfected this. Three of them, Lyz'."

"Ok," the girl agreed before hurrying away.

Geo immediately leaned over the table to look at Reko. "We know she's a Kaisae. Seems she came from Terric as an infant, her mother was killed on the Namisa-Terric border, and two onsyc humans raised her. When we were headed home, they had her packed up and waiting, because she was growing up and they thought she'd do better with her own kind."

"It's not that," Reko said. "Although being a Kaisae makes sense. She smells...."

"Amazing?" Ricown finished for him, his suspicions confirmed. "But like what?"

"Like Conglomerate resin," Reko said. "And like horses, I think? But Viraenovan horses."

"Not like hope?" Geo asked.

Reko shook his head. "Not like Sal does. I mean, there's a hint of it, but no. That's not what I'm getting. It's..."

"Something else," Ricown said. "Reko, what's your happiest memory?"

"Being accepted into the elites and given - " He looked up. "Oh shit."

"Shit?" Geo asked.

"She's like, what? Twelve?"

"Thirteen," Geo answered. "Why?"

Ricown leaned closer. "Because he thinks she smells like his happiest memory, man. Sal's brother is meant for her adopted daughter. Reko just caught her scent, Geo, and he can only describe it as his happiest memory, not the hope everyone else smells."

"Fuck," Geo breathed, looking at Reko. "Really?"

"I... I can't be meant for her," Reko insisted.

"Why not?" Ricown asked.

"She's a child!" he hissed.

Ricown shrugged. "The girl I'm meant for is younger. I knew it before she could walk on her own."

That caught Geo's attention. "You're meant for someone?"

"Have been for a while," Ricown told him, "but unlike you crossbreds, I'm human enough to suck it up and deal."

"Who?" Geo asked.

Ricown ignored him. "She won't know, and she won't be able to tell unless you act on it. And no, it doesn't mean anything about Ynta."

"How'd you know that's what I was thinking?" Reko asked.

"Because there's clearly one thing that runs in your family, Reko, and that's mourning hard. I was with Sal after she lost Blaec. I know how much that hurt, and you look the exact same way." He lifted a hand. "And I'm not saying it's wrong. I'm just saying that I understand. I'm sure the timing on *this* is the worst it could be, right?"

But Reko shook his head. "It's not. I..." He huffed out a sigh. "Don't judge me, and I wouldn't say this anywhere around Tseri, but, yeah. I think that's been one of my problems. I'll always be known as the Kaeen's daughter's mate. Nuvani are different from iliri. They aren't pure, but they feel so close. It's why it works for me, since I'm pure."

"But are you ready to move on yet?" Geo asked.

Reko just shrugged. "I'm pretty sure this is the kind of thing I'll never be ready for. Ynta's gone. She died so I could live, and her last thought was this concept that the world needed me more."

"Because you're a purebred," Geo groaned. "The Viraenovans damned near idolize Sal, and you're just as pure."

"But I'm not going to be able to - " One more time, the man stopped with his thought half finished.

"Breed more?" Ricown guessed. "Because if you're meant for Lyzzi, your kids won't be crossbreds. They also won't be nuvani."

"She is *thirteen!*" he reminded them. "I am not breeding with a child."

"She won't be thirteen forever," Ricown reminded him. "The hard part is knowing that you're about to be the most loyal man ever. For a few years, in fact. But don't worry, you can still jack off."

"Didn't need to know that," Geo grumbled. "No, what *I* need to know is who you're supposed to be meant for, Rico."

"Don't worry about it," he said.

"I'm worried," Geo countered. "C'mon, what's it going to hurt?"

"You're going to laugh," Ricown said. "Probably both of you, but I didn't pick. I just... She was a cute little baby, and I held her. She reached up, grabbed my finger, and that was it."

"You're bound to a baby?" Reko asked.

"Not anymore," Ricown assured him, "but trust me, it doesn't get any less creepy. Lucky for me, she'll be mature in a couple more years."

"A grauori?" Geo guessed. Then he paused. "Oh fuck. Roo's girls?"

"Just Rhyx," Ricown told him. "I'm fine with Raast, but not her sister. I turn stupid when I get around her. And yeah, I think it's just as weird as you do."

"No," Geo said, "that actually makes a whole lot of sense. She wanted to be iliri, remember?" He waited for both of them to nod, even though Reko looked a bit confused as he did so. "Man, when we defected to Anglia, Rhyx shaved her body, left her mane to mimic iliri hair, and was adamant that she was an iliri, not a grauori." When both Ricown and Reko continued to stare at him like they had no idea what he was talking about, Geo sighed. "It affects the women too, just differently."

"Really?" Ricown asked.

Geo was nodding. "Sal and Kolt? You can't tell me you didn't notice her go weird about him. She pushed him in without asking the others and - "

"I thought that was because she was mourning," Ricown said.

Geo lifted a brow. "Rumor has it that she thought he smelled like hope. She didn't know that was the scent, but Jase could smell it through her, being cessivi and all. Kolt told Ghost, Ghost told me, and yeah. I figure it means that while the women aren't as stupid about it as we guys, they're still feeling something, right? And what would a kid do? Try to be what she thought he wanted."

"Iliri," Ricown said, finally understanding. "But I wasn't around her that much. Fuck, I'm still not if I can help it."

"Help what?" Lyzzi asked, appearing almost silently at their table.

Reko sat up straight and whipped his head around to Ricown for help. Instead, it was Geo who answered. "Just talking about women, Lyz. Have a feeling Baeli's going to be looking at a new mate soon."

"Who?" she breathed.

Geo shook his head. "I'm not telling, but when you see them together, don't make it weird, ok? I'm not sure *he* would take it well."

She just nodded, moving to set the plates down before them. "I'll tell the other girls to be casual about it too."

"Thank you," he breathed.

She grinned at him and then moved to put the plate in front of Reko. For a moment, she paused. "I didn't get your name."

"Reko Wyra," he said softly.

Her white eyes landed on his while her teeth clamped down on her lower lip. That was bad enough, but when the teenaged Kaisae flicked both of her ears forward and locked them on him, Ricown wanted to blush for the guy. There was no doubt that she was checking him out. Thankfully, she was also trying to be professional.

"Stop flirting, Lyz," Geo teased. "Reko lost his mate in the war. He's not ready for that."

"I'm so sorry," she breathed.

He nodded, but his eyes were locked on hers. "I am too. She jumped in front of an arrow to save my life. A very good woman, and I did not deserve it."

"It's hard to say what we deserve," Lyzzi told him. "That doesn't make it hurt any less, but they say that ayati made things work out the way they're supposed to. Maybe saving you was what she was supposed to do? Maybe you are more important than you know, but you just haven't gotten the chance to realize it yet?"

"I like that," he breathed.

"I think you're important, Reko."

"Lyzzi!" Geo snarled.

"What?" she asked, jumping back from the table. "He is! There aren't many purebred iliri left, and everyone knows it. Sal can't have kids, and Hax mated with that *bitch* from Escea. But Tseri brought the twin girls here. They're going to stay, so maybe..."

"Maybe," Ricown said, cutting her off, "a man wants to be worth more than merely the children he can produce."

"I was *going to say*," Lyzzi went on, "that it means we aren't the last ones in the world. Maybe Reko's going to help find more or something. Or maybe he'll help Viraenova leave their home. I mean, with them traveling around now, that means there's almost as many iliri countries as human ones, right? Or it could be something else, Reko. You can't tell the future, and all the prophets are mute."

"Actually," he said, "I think you nailed it. Tseri's my amma in many ways, and I'm staying here. That means she'll have to come visit, right? And our two countries together? Viraenova and Anglia?"

"That," Geo said, "is called a dream come true."

Lyzzi gently clasped Reko's shoulder. Thankfully, her hand landed on the cloth. "I am sorry about your mate. Maybe some dessert would help? Tensa has chocolate pie."

"I'd love some," he promised.

She nodded her head quickly and skipped away. Her feet seemed a little lighter, but she wasn't the only one. Reko had the hint of a smile on his lips as well.

"Ynta would've hated her," he said.

"Ynta hated anyone who got your attention, though, didn't she?" Geo asked.

"Yeah," Reko agreed. "And she still wanted me to live. I'm starting to think it might be time to start living again, or at least remembering how."

Geo leaned closer and bumped his shoulder. "Women have that effect on us, but I agree with you. I'm also glad you're staying. Sal will be too."

"You don't think she'd mind?"

"Not at all," Geo promised. "It seems she has this thing about wanting a really big family. And you know, Kolt can always fetch your things."

"Kinda why I packed them," Reko admitted. "I just didn't expect to find a mate."

"A future mate," Ricown reminded him. "And we can suffer together. Five years isn't *that* long, is it?"

"Not anymore," Reko said. "Not when we know we'll still be alive."

CHAPTER THIRTY-TWO

WHITE

*T*hat night, Arhhawen celebrated. Tseri and Sal didn't spend much time actually working, but they did catch up on all the important things - like their mates, their friends, and the kids. It was different spending time with their allies in peacetime, but in a good way. Gone was the serious side, replaced with a lot of laughter and music.

Because one of the many people Tseri had brought with her was a nuvani singer. The man had a voice like perfection, and he was thrilled to get the chance to sing before the Kaisae. When some of the former slaves offered to play instruments for him, he accepted. The result was a mixture of all their cultures. Conglomerate music with iliri cadence and a nuvani song.

At some point, Kesh carried over a bottle of green liquid and sat beside Sal. "I heard this is a drink for you," he said. "It's not Unavi absinthe, but it's close, and the nuvani make it."

"You drink it?" Sal asked.

He nodded. "I get tired of all the mead, and I'm not a rum man. Not a whole lot of whiskey or beer in Viraenova, sadly."

"I'll have to send some back with you," Sal promised. "I'm assuming you're staying there?"

"I'd like to, and Tseri seems inclined to keep me around. The only question will be whether or not the CFC will keep me posted with her. They already tried to swap out Lightning Brigade for Azure Silence once."

"Tseri had a fit?" Sal asked.

Kesh nodded. "Said something about a certain assassination attempt on the Kaisae and their history of treating her son poorly. The best part, though, was that Raj helped. He and Rais pulled up some old records from back when you were in Azure, and the trial that followed."

"He's trying," Sal said.

"He's a good soldier," Kesh assured her. "Human as they get, though, but he's got that officer of his who keeps him in line. But expect the Conglomerate to be pretty upset about Ran."

"Because he defected?"

Kesh nodded as he poured them both a glass. "Yep. He also wanted me to take over running the elite units, and I used to think that sounded like a great idea. General Kesh, you know? Well, I pulled a Blaec Doll and passed it up so Lightning Brigade could be the Viraenovan ambassadors. Suggested Rais as an alternative, and he took it."

"Rais is a general?" Sal gasped.

Kesh grinned at her. "The man deserves it, too. His unit lost the least amount of men in that war. Except for Blaz, who was one of those 'dark iliri.'"

"Is that what you're saying?"

"It's what Rais said. Pointed out that Blaz had been healing them for months, but they didn't realize it. And to replace him, Rais took this iliri woman I worked with in the northern camp. When we bailed to rescue you, I asked a crossbred who was acting as their kaisae, and they all pointed at her. A girl named Vecys. Well, Rais recruited her after we talked on the way home. So the poor thing got a quick lesson on a horse, and she should be coming up this way."

"What about the Vanguard?" Sal asked.

Kesh shook his head. "No way will they let an iliri unit into Anglia right now. The 43rd is being promoted to an elite group, though. That man you saved, Odi? He suggested the name of Ardent Sky. Said it reminded him of something - and yes, he meant your horse. The rest of the unit loved the idea of being named after an equine war hero."

"But how are the iliri?" Sal asked. "The ones who stayed?"

Kesh wobbled his head from side to side. "They're better, but not there yet. Those of us who served beside you are helping, though. Guttertown is gone. The empty houses are being torn down to make room for more businesses. The iliri who stayed in Prin all moved to regular neighborhoods, but they're sticking close together." He lifted his hand. "I know, it's a pack thing."

"It really is," Sal assured him. "And the ones from Merriton?"

"Most are here," Kesh pointed out. "The few that stayed are free, and Ninsa Ardiel has either hired or sponsored most of them. Seems she's spreading her fortune out, and her 'kids' are taking over when she's gone. They call her something. Um, Kauvwae?"

"Grandmother," Sal translated for him. "Ok, that's kinda sweet."

"No one else would call Ninsa 'sweet,' Sal. That woman is as sly as they come, and she used the fall of Merriton to get even more military contracts."

"Which she then hired iliri companies to help fill?" Sal guessed.

Kesh grinned. "Exactly. Let me guess, you touched her, right?"

"Once is all it takes," Sal said. "But she's one of the good ones, and I think she'll help make the CFC a better place for both species."

"Well, I can tell you that Murah is now a recognized civilian assistant with the 112th. Rais refused to make him a citizen, but Parliament keeps trying. His point is that until the... man? Do grauori call themselves that?"

"Male," Sal supplied. "Man is used for those who walk on two legs."

"Well, either way, until Murah is recognized as equal to a human, Rais says the grauori will not swear any oaths. And when asked, Murah says he's a nomadic grauori. According to him, that's what brerror means. Beholden to no one and bound to no land."

"Close enough," Sal agreed. "But what about your men? How's Lightning Brigade handling their time in Viraenova?"

"They love it," he said. "I mean, we get stared at a lot, and growled at plenty, but it's nothing like any place I've ever been before. Did you know that most Viraenovan homes are backwards? The people live in the basements and store goods on the first floor. Tseri's 'palace' is little more than a large house. The kind of thing you'd expect a merchant in Prin to own. And Ylexa? Well, she has a farm in the mountains. Basically lives in a cave. A really *nice* cave. Kinda like Arhhawen, but a lot smaller."

"I think it's instinctual," Sal explained. "Grauori live in dens. Literal holes dug out on the sides of cliffs. Most have been around long enough to be decorated and finished, but the kind of place a human would walk past and never even notice."

Kesh nodded. "Can't say I'm shocked. It makes sense. The weather wouldn't be a problem, and no visible towns to be raided by humans who assume they're barbarians. I've also seen a few of them climb now. Their feet make a lot more sense. So, how are your humans dealing with life underground?"

Sal just pointed up at the lighting. "That's not fire, and it works really well. It's called neon, and works by heating gasses in glass or resin tubes. Came with the place, but we have people learning how to make more. Granted, windows are a problem, but the summer heat isn't."

"It doesn't get hot in Anglia," Kesh teased.

"Ran doesn't agree," Sal told him.

"Yeah, speaking of him, where is he?"

Sal leaned a bit to point through the crowd. "He's sitting at a table with Jase's amma."

"So he's..." Kesh paused when he saw the man. "Is she holding his hand?"

"Looks like," Sal said. "I caught him bringing her flowers the other day. Had to explain to Inessi why he'd do that, and I've never seen Ran blush before, but it did happen."

Kesh chuckled at that. "Yeah, I can only imagine. He ever tell you about his girlfriend? The iliri one?"

"Some," Sal said. "She left him, he chased her down, only to find that she'd been killed and buried before he got there."

"He's not so sure she was buried, Sal. When you were in Anglia, he was trying to find records on where Lamarck Labs got their breeding specimens. Seems the graves where she was buried? There was nothing in them." Kesh paused, his eyes scanning her face. "He thought you might be her kid. Said you look like the spitting image of her, but he has never been able to find anything to prove it."

Sal felt her breath rush out and her lungs freeze. That explained why he had the documents about her. No, even before that, why he'd taken an interest in her. If she looked like his mate, of course he'd pay attention to her and want to keep her safe. The problem was that there weren't any records left. Escea had stolen iliri where they could, selling plenty into the CFC as slaves. The Conglomerate wasn't any better. There was no way to know the names behind the serial numbers assigned to the iliri at Lamarck labs.

"What if I am?" Sal asked.

"I think the bigger question is what if you're not," Kesh countered. "Sal, there are no records left from back then, and the people who worked there didn't *talk* to the iliri they were testing. They treated them like livestock. Everyone was assigned an identifying tag. Haven't you ever wondered where you got your last name?"

"Not really," she admitted. "It's just my name."

"It's not. This is one thing I did learn. The first letter shows if you have the gene they were looking for. It's an L for located or W for withheld. The next one is for the paternal allele. Y for the boys or a letter assigned to the paternal kaisae line for the girls. A 'U' in your case. And the last two are for the maternal lines. As a female, both of yours are Xs, but for the guys, it's the mother and the paternal kaisae gene carrier."

"What does that mean?" she asked.

"That neither Reko Wyra nor Hax Wyvr are Kaisae gene carriers," Kesh explained. "But both their fathers and mothers were. No females were born at that lab who didn't have two Kaisae genes. The scientist I talked to said he thinks it may be non-viable to have a single gene in a female."

"A malformed brain," Sal mumbled, remembering what Narnx had said. "But some survive. We have records of non-Kaisaes having Kaisae children!"

"Maybe it's just rare," Kesh said. "Either way, I've had people looking since we got back, and I know Ran's going to ask me, so I figured I should tell you. I don't know, maybe it's something the two of you need to work out. Maybe it's not?"

"But it's worth knowing that he's looking," Sal agreed. "Thank you." Then she paused. "Wait. Can you lie to him?"

"What?"

Sal pulled in a breath, her mind spinning. "What if you told him I'm her daughter? What would it hurt?"

Kesh shook his head. "I'm not going to do that, because you don't deserve to live a lie. I couldn't find it, and I do want to keep looking, but I'm not sure there's anything left to be found."

"But what would it hurt?" Sal asked. "If it makes him feel better to get a little closure?"

"Then what if you're not and that comes up later?" Kesh asked. "Sal, I'm going to tell him I couldn't find it. I'm also going to tell him that if you look just like her, then maybe you're her daughter, or her sister's daughter. Or maybe you're not related at all. Either way, he's your father now, and there's no going back on that. The two of you *belong* together. Doesn't matter that he's human and you're not. Doesn't matter that we do or do not know your ancestry. All that matters is that he was there for you when you needed someone, and that you'll be there for him when he does, ok?"

She nodded. "I just... He didn't even tell me he was looking!"

"Because I'm not sure he knew which answer he wanted," Kesh said gently. "Is it better to know she was tortured and all but raped? To wonder if she loved the man who sired you? Or is it easier to think that she died? Sometimes, Sal, there's not a good answer."

"That's what Blaec said."

"And he was right." Kesh reached over to rub her arm. "And that's why I followed you all the way to the Emperor's Palace. Not just because I wanted to make sure things could get better, but because there wasn't any better option. The war sucked. There's no way around that."

"But it wasn't all bad," Sal said, looking up to meet his dark, human eyes. "I made some pretty good friends along the way."

"Me too, Sal. I also lost some. The most important thing, though?" He tilted his head to smile at her. "I found a whole lot of hope, and it came in a short white package that I count among my friends."

"Thank you," she mumbled, not sure what else to say.

Kesh simply grabbed his glass and leaned back into his chair. "Goes both ways. Without you, I never would've met her, and I think I've finally found the woman I was meant to be with."

"Interesting choice of words," Sal pointed out.

He shrugged. "I always thought Rayna and I would end up together because we couldn't find anything better, but we both did. I dunno. I guess that iliri phrase just fits, you know?"

"I do, and did you know they're getting married?"

"I was told that."

Sal took a drink as she tried to judge his reaction. "So you're completely ok with your ex getting married?"

Kesh leaned his head back and smiled. "I'm honestly happy for her. I love her, don't get me wrong, but I never loved her the right way. Rayna and I were friends who were amazing together in bed, but that was it. We both knew it. The whole time we were together, we were seeing other people, and neither of us cared. It always felt like we fit together just right, but the colors on our puzzle pieces didn't line up."

"Like you belonged somewhere else?" Sal asked.

"I dunno, maybe? All I can say is that when I met Dom? My first thought wasn't that I was jealous. It was that she'd finally found the place she belonged. She found her missing piece, you know? I'm so happy for her."

"Then I'll let you tell her about Tseri yourself," Sal said. "Because they're having the wedding while all the allies are here, and she really wanted you to come."

"And I'm going to be there. Tseri said we'll make it a political thing if we have to."

"What is a political thing?" Tseri asked as she stumbled over. "Taunor, I'm drunk. They have brandy here."

Kesh pulled her over, hauling her into his lap like she was just some ordinary woman, not the leader of an elusive country. "Do I need to have Syed and Daest help me carry you to our room?"

"Oh, yes," Tseri giggled. "That sounds like a wonderful idea."

Kesh glanced over at Sal. "Sorry. Gotta go." And then he scooped up the Kaeen into his arms and marched straight for the stairs.

Sal giggled as she scanned the crowd, not surprised at all to see both Syed and Daest break off from what they were doing to follow. This was not at all how she'd expected her first diplomatic visitors to act, but it was perfect. The humans could have their stuffy ceremonies and political maneuvering. Arhhawen would simply be a home. The kind of place where those inside it could finally relax.

After all, traditions had to start somewhere, and this seemed like a good one to have.

CHAPTER THIRTY-THREE

PURPLE

That night, Sal stumbled up to her room late. Jase and Zep had already gone to bed. Gage and Tyr were with her, but Kolt and Blaz had left a few minutes before to make sure Las was tucked in bed. It was the boy's last night before he had to go back to school in the morning. Sal was pretty sure he should've been in his dorm already, but Inessi said that it was a special circumstance, since he was the Kaisae's family, and that he could walk up with Narnx in the morning.

So, when Sal found her suite dark, she was surprised. Tyr clasped her hand, silently asking for a little guidance through the obstacle course of their main room. When Gage locked the door behind them, another opened. Kolt stepped out with a finger to his lips.

Las is out cold, he explained, telling all of them. *I think Jase and Zep are as well.*

I think, Tyr said, *that we have another room for just this reason. Anyone wanna help me see how many of us can fit on that little bed?*

It's a full-size bed, Gage pointed out.

Blaz opened the door to the bedroom, proving he was in the conversation as well. *It's a full-size bed for a normal person. Sal has a*

247

few more men to fit in hers. Your Ahnor and Dernor are drunk, and I doubt they would appreciate being woken up by any of us.

"Mm," she murmured as she reached him, sliding her hands across his bare chest. *So does this mean you were in bed as well?*

I was debating it, but no. I was in the bath thinking about a very beautiful woman.

His hands closed on her waist and he steered toward her right, backing her into the larger of their smaller rooms. Sal let him, reaching up to wrap her arms around his neck. He kissed her without stopping. It started soft, like always, but his teeth closed on the full part of her lower lip when she tried to pull back.

No, he thought. *You do not get away from me that easily.*

Who said I wanted to? she teased.

Do it, Gage thought as he slipped behind her, wrapping his arms around Sal's waist. *Stop playing nice, Blaz. Not a single one of us care.*

Blaz smiled against her lips, but there was a hint of darkness with it. *Throw her on the bed, Gage.*

Those arms tensed, lifting her feet off the ground, and Gage turned while carrying her. He took two steps before he obeyed Blaz's order, tossing her onto the soft mattress diagonally - the wrong way - with her head near the foot of the bed. Kolt followed, grabbing her hands to pin them as he leaned over her, and Tyr moved to the other side of the bed, by her hips. Those, he didn't hold down. Instead, he began slowly, sensually removing her pants.

"I'm not going to be quiet," Sal warned.

Blaz smiled and pointedly closed the door. "Las knows and if Jase or Zep wake up, then they can play too. Tyr, her boots."

"Got 'em," Gage said.

Blaz just dropped into one of the chairs in the corner. "I said *Tyr.*"

Then he flicked the striker and lit the lamp beside him, turning it down until the light was dim and seductive, making it easy for Sal to see him watching her. His dark eyes glistened and a smile curled one side of his mouth higher, proving that *this* was what he truly wanted.

"Just going to watch?" Sal asked as she tugged her foot from her boot, helping Tyr out.

"Gage," Blaz said, "stick your dick in her mouth."

"Gladly," Gage agreed.

"Fuck," Tyr breathed as his hands moved back up to her pants. "That's hot."

"The sucking?" Kolt asked. "Or do you mean the orders?"

"The orders," Tyr confirmed.

And while he eased her pants off, Gage pulled his own open. The moment his dick was free, he grabbed it, slowly stroking it while he walked around the foot of the bed to her face. Sal's feet were at one side, angled slightly toward the pillows. That put her head on the edge near Blaz, angled perfectly so that Gage wouldn't obstruct his view. The moment his dick was close enough, she stretched, reaching for it, but Kolt still held her down.

"Link us," Blaz told her. "Not just cessivi, Sal. I want it all."

She quickly opened their minds, adding one more layer of sensation to the experience. Blaz's need hit her first, followed closely by the arousal of her other mates. She couldn't help but moan, yet the moment her mouth parted, Gage moved in, pressing his swollen head lightly to her lips. Opening just a bit more, she took him into her mouth. Although when he reached down towards the mattress for support, his hand landed on her wrist, pinning it down.

"Kolt," Blaz said, his voice calm and deep, "Let Gage have her hands, and you open her shirt. Slowly."

Tyr had her legs free and bare. Unable to help himself, he leaned across the side of the bed to kiss the inside of her ankle, then her calf, making his way higher. While his mouth moved up her leg, he crawled higher, pressing one knee onto the mattress, making Sal's body lean into his weight.

"Blaz?" he asked, looking up.

"Not yet," Blaz said. "You can kiss, but that's all."

Tyr grunted, reaching down to give himself a squeeze, but it didn't relieve the pressure. Sal could feel his need, and it made her swallow Gage a little deeper. She wanted to use her hands, though. To stroke him with one and fondle him with the other, but she couldn't. Gage now held them both, and she was completely at his mercy. Here to please them all.

Kolt was taking his time about opening her shirt. His knuckles skimmed across her skin as he moved from one button to another, tantalizing her. As he slipped each one through its opening, she felt the fabric sag and more cool air on her chest, making her nipples harder than they'd ever been before. The cloth shifting over them was almost torment, and the only release she had was to lap at the shaft in her mouth, teasing Gage a bit before she swallowed his length again.

"Touch her," Blaz said as the last button came free. Then, "No. Her stomach. Don't rush, Kolt. I want her to beg."

Fingertips traced the swirls across her belly. They moved higher, close enough to make her breasts feel heavy, but never enough to relieve the ache. Then a hand began to do the same on the inside of her thigh. Tyr sucked at the tattoo of Kolt's name and licked the sensitive skin just above it, but she wasn't ready to beg. Not yet - until Kolt's mouth found her breast.

The heat of it felt so good, and his tongue flicked across the hardened tip. Sal moaned around Gage's dick, and he pushed in just a bit more before withdrawing, taking over so she didn't need to think. Next, a hand slid across her chest to close on her other nipple. That was Tyr, and he pinched the aching pebble hard enough to make her gasp.

"Suck her, Tyr," Blaz ordered.

Immediately, the man's tongue flicked over her clit, sending sparks of pleasure through her body. Sal pressed into it, begging for more with her body, asking without even forming the words in her mind. Yet when she looked up, Blaz appeared as calm as ever, as if he was simply taking in the show. Across the distance, their eyes met - and he smiled.

"On your side, Sal. If you want someone inside you, then I want to see." A flick of his hand gestured for one of the men to move.

Sal let Gage fall from her lips only long enough for her to roll onto her side, facing Blaz. Then she reached for Gage's shaft again, this time with her hand. He caught her wrist, guiding her palm to his hip instead of his erection. Behind her, the mattress shifted with someone else's weight. Kolt's, and he was crawling his way across the bed behind her.

Gage once again pushed himself between her lips, then withdrew partway, thrusting slowly, setting the pace, and tormenting her. Each time she tried to take over, he paused. Blaz might be giving the orders, but Gage was in control of his own part. She wasn't pleasing him this time. He was using her to please himself, and she had never felt so turned on in her life.

A hand grabbed her topmost leg. Another, belonging to a different man, held the lower one down. Tyr and Kolt, but which was which? So much contact, and so many sensations against her body made it hard to be sure. All Sal knew was that she wanted this. Wanted them to have their way with her, and having Blaz watch it all made it even more sensual.

But she couldn't focus with what Tyr was doing to her. He sucked, flicked, licked, and teased her, always pausing just when it started to feel good. Her hips bucked, thrusting out of instinct, and he pulled his head back - which was when Kolt pressed in, his dick slipping into her body from behind. When her back arched, feeling her body stretch around him, he took the chance to hook her leg over his hip, spreading her open just a bit more to give Blaz a better view.

"Tyr," Blaz said, "don't stop. I want you to eat her until she screams. Kolt, take your time."

Cloth shifted and men kept moving, filling her, thrusting into her body from both sides, but it was too slow. She wanted more, needed them to stop thinking and start feeling. Sal was pushing them toward wild abandon, and Tyr broke first.

The sound of cloth proved he was fumbling, and his ache throbbed in her mind. Kneeling between Sal's legs, Tyr opened his pants with one hand to grab himself. His body was positioned awkwardly, but he didn't care. Her upper leg was hooked on Kolt, Tyr's arm was braced across her lower, and the man was on his knees. That was how he managed to stroke himself, squeezing hard enough that the intensity made Kolt gasp.

"Fuck," Gage groaned, proving he felt it too. "She comes first, man."

"She always comes first," Blaz told them. "Now fuck her deeper. All of you." His voice had turned hard and gravelly.

Gage caught the back of her head, using the grip to pump into her mouth, but the angle gave her a perfect view of Blaz. Even while she sucked Gage with everything she had, she could see her fifth mate reach into his pants with one hand, the other pushing the waistband lower. Low enough that he had to lift his ass from the chair. A drop glistened on the head of his dick, and Blaz ran his palm across it before sliding his fist down the shaft.

The whole time, he watched her suck Gage, his eyes flicking back to where Kolt fucked her and Tyr teased her clit. Blaz's hand moved in time with Kolt's thrusts, joining them in his own way. Four men, one woman, and she could feel them all. A rush of desire proved something had changed, but she didn't care what. The hands, mouths, and dicks on her body, their need, and her own were too much. The only thing that mattered was how very good this felt.

Tyr and Kolt were working in tandem, not caring how close their bodies were. That Gage kept her from looking somehow made it better. Naughty, almost, since the sensations were starting to blur together. All she could go by were Blaz's eyes, but they said enough. He was hungry, and she was the thing he needed to survive. Seeing her worshipped was what gave him pleasure.

Kolt could feel it too. Faster, deeper, he used his hand on her leg for balance. His eyes were closed as he lost himself in the feel of her body, and Gage was growling softly with each thrust into her mouth. So close. They were all ready to explode, but Blaz's calm held them back, building the pressure to impossible levels.

Then, while he sucked hard at her clit, the tip of his tongue flicking across it inside his mouth, Tyr reached up her body for her breast with one hand. Every inch of her was being touched, and her men didn't care by who. Tyr wasn't worried about the proximity of his face to Kolt's dick. He just wanted to make her feel good, to give her everything she'd given him. Kolt just wanted to get her there first. Gage had his head thrown back, struggling not to lose control as her tongue pressed against the underside of his swollen, straining dick. And watching it all, Blaz felt in control.

"Harder," he ordered. "Fuck her. I want her to roar."

As one, they obeyed, pounding into her in time with Blaz's fist on his own dick and Tyr pumping his. It was hard, unforgiving, and so damned good. Savage. Feral. Beautiful. Sal grasped at Gage, clutching his hip just below that line of muscles to pull him deeper, and she swallowed every single inch. He took the hint, fucking her mouth the way Kolt fucked her pussy, and she stopped thinking.

It didn't matter who was where, just that they were together, and they worked. There was no shame. No fear or judgment. This was all she'd ever dreamed of and more. Her men, her body, and all of them liked it. Sal's hips jerked, pushing back into each of Kolt's thrusts, and Tyr rode her, refusing to let go. Not a single one of them worried about the other men because it didn't matter. They were cessivi. They could all feel this, so they wanted to feel it together, and each mind in their link made it that much better.

So good that Sal didn't stand a chance. She didn't roar - only because she couldn't around Gage's shaft - but she moaned against it as her climax hit. Her back arched hard, pushing her breasts toward Blaz, and her core tightened, shuddering with the intensity of her release. Then she had to swallow, because Gage was right there with her. And Kolt, who buried himself deep inside her to spill out his orgasm with hard throbs. Both Tyr and Blaz managed to groan, their voices synchronized, but her eyes were closed. Still, she knew they'd finished as well, the five of them finding their orgasm together.

Slowly, Gage extracted himself from her mouth. Kolt withdrew and eased her onto her back. Tyr stayed, rolling with her until his head was pillowed on that spot between her hip and thigh, but he laughed. The first one was soft, but the second a little louder.

"What?" Kolt asked.

"I damned near sucked your dick," Tyr managed to get out.

Kolt huffed at that, but then he laughed too. "Yeah, um, sorry. Never learned those stupid rules you humans follow."

"Like being disgusted by guys?" Tyr asked.

Sal sat up to see Kolt's reaction. "Maybe?" he said. "I mean, I like women. Well, mostly Sal, but she's a woman. I just..."

"It's stupid to worry about such things," Gage said for him. "If you're trying to stay away from everyone else's dicks, then you're not focused on her, and we all lose out. If you don't worry about it, then it's just one more orgasm in the mix. If neither of you care, then what's the harm?"

"Figured you wouldn't mind," Blaz said, "since you seemed obsessed with Sal's dick. Just thought that being close to Kolt's wouldn't bother you too much."

"Sal's isn't the same!" Tyr said. "Hers. That makes it a girl dick. I mean, that kinda means it's different, doesn't it?"

Blaz tugged his pants back up. "Trying to tell me that Sal doesn't own your dick? Because I think all of the ones in this room are hers, so technically girl dicks. That means your argument is mostly invalid."

"Huh," Tyr said. "Ok, I can go with that, and the truth is that I don't really care about it, but I have one rule."

"What's that?" Blaz asked.

"Only dick going in my ass will be hers. Mainly because she's got a tiny one, and I'm not really into that."

"Not *really* into it?" Gage asked.

Tyr just grinned. "I mean, it's all about the end goal, right? I'm down for a finger or something - preferably hers - but I'm not about to start being picky *now*."

"I'd rather fuck Sal," Kolt assured him. "Kinda meant for her, but I'm pretty sure everyone in this room agrees with me."

Tyr shrugged. "I'm so ok with that, man." Then he paused. "Nah, I'm just ok with this. All of this, even if it means some balls swinging in my face."

Blaz groaned. "Do you have to make *everything* into a joke?"

"Yeah," Tyr said, "kinda my thing, but if you ever want to take charge again, I'm in, Blaz. You wanna order someone around? Then I will play all day long - or night."

"Me too," Sal agreed. "The only downside is that Jase and Zep weren't here."

"Oh?" A voice asked from the door. It was Zep. "They screwed you so good that you missed us linking in?"

Sal turned to see both her Ahnor and her Dernor standing just inside the room, leaning against the wall. Clearly, their desire had blended perfectly with everyone else's, because she hadn't realized they were there.

"I was a little distracted," she admitted.

But Jase flicked a finger in the direction of the bed. "Ya did na honestly think that I coulda slept through that, did ya?"

"I heard you were drunk," Sal said in her defense.

"Na that drunk," Jase promised, pushing himself away from the wall to head toward her. "And next time ya wanna do that, ya should wake me."

Kolt scoffed. "For Blaz to order you around? Don't see that happening."

"Or ya, since I know ya wanna," Jase said. "Because I agree with Tyr. Sometimes it is nice ta na have ta make the decisions."

Kolt smiled. "Take turns, Blaz?"

"Oh, yeah," Blaz agreed. "I'm good with this plan."

Sal let her eyes close and smiled. "Every. Single. Night. I'm so ok with that."

And then Jase slipped his arms under her back and knees, lifting her against his chest. "Yer in the wrong bed, kitten. Ya can lannar in here, but ya sleep in our bed."

"Make love?" Tyr asked. "Is that what that one means?"

"It is," Zep agreed, "and I'm not carrying your ass to bed."

Kolt chuckled. "I will."

"I'm up!" Tyr promised. "And I'm definitely sleeping on the edge tonight so Kolt can't get any ideas."

"Yeah," Gage said as he followed Sal toward their bed. "Bad time to mention that he's not the only one who doesn't care? I think the three of us who were born iliri were taught that *this* is completely and totally normal."

"Man, I think the three of us who were born human are starting to see why," Tyr assured him. "It's always better when we share."

"He just had to think it through," Kolt said. "Takes humans a little longer, Gage, but they'll get there."

"I think they already are," Gage agreed.

CHAPTER THIRTY-FOUR

BLUE

For the next few days, everyone found a comfortable routine. The kids went back to school, the Blades started working with their horses, and the Verdant Shields returned to Dorton. Then, halfway through the week, Rragri arrived at the King's Palace. Sal wasn't there because her date with Rayna for more wedding planning got canceled. She offered to come anyway, but Rayna promised that she had plenty of help - too much, actually - and the Palace was getting crowded.

Although Sal had a feeling Rayna just wanted to run interference for Jarl and Nya. Those two were just kids themselves, and between their parents, the King, and everyone else, things couldn't be easy. Sal could only imagine how terrified Nya was. After all, she was pregnant with children of an unknown species - or hybrids no one had seen before. Jarl, from what Sal had heard, was being asked if he was still capable of being the heir to the throne, since the populace wouldn't accept a man who slept with beasts.

Rayna would put an end to that, as much as she could. People would still talk, but Rayna had accepted the triad of species in Anglia even easier than Sal had. She'd know best how to deal with the fears and whispers. In Sal's opinion, the soon-to-be Queen was the best ally Jarl and Nya could ask for.

Even better, lookouts said that the Unavi delegation was almost there. One more day, two at the most, and the focus would shift to the upcoming Alliance talks. The main goal was to rewrite the Conventions of War to include all three known sentient species, but that wasn't as easy as it sounded. First, the grauori and iliri had to be recognized as sentient and sovereign creatures equal to humans. That would have implications on the laws of every nation on the continent.

After that would come the treaties and trade deals. Myrosica had already made it clear that they wanted an agreement of mutual military support with Anglia. Unav was once again in a position to negotiate with the Conglomerate. Who knew what Escea wanted, but their party was coming across Anglia from the west, and updates showed they should arrive in less than a week.

Myrosica and the Conglomerate should be there around the same time, so Sal needed to get her arguments in order. This wasn't the kind of thing she could simply make up as she went. For every point she made, someone would ask for proof or clarification. Probably the Conglomerate of Free Citizens. And depending upon who they sent to speak as the country's representatives, it could get ugly.

So Sal asked Tseri for help. No, it wasn't common to have the leader of another nation involved with negotiation planning, but both the Kaisae and Kaeen knew better. All it would take was one touch, and both of their secrets would be in the open. Sal had a slight advantage there, but only because her abilities as a genetic Kaisae gave her some ability to block surface reading. The same wasn't true for Jase, who could be read as easily as any other iliri.

They were just finishing up when Sal felt a request brush across her mind. She accepted, recognizing the feel of Jarl's thoughts.

Sal? he asked. *Are you busy?*

Just finishing some work with Tseri. How are you?

I wanted to tell you thank you, he said. *Nya's here and she's doing as well as my mother ever has. She's very pregnant, though. Bigger than any grauori I've ever seen, and she says she's miserable and can't sleep because she can't stand lying on her stomach like she's used to.*

Sounds like things I've heard humans complain about, Sal assured him. *And I'm sure if you ask your amma, she'll explain what it's like.*

I did, he promised. *Granted, that came with a lecture, but still. I'm just...* He paused for a moment, gathering his thoughts. *I just want to thank you for standing up for me. For explaining to Rragri that I'm not going to hurt the babies, you know? And to make sure Tyr knows that his idea was brilliant. One of the doctors said he's pulled enough arrows and bolts from grauori to feel confident that he can perform a surgical birth if the grauori healers are willing to help close the incision and repair any potential issues that arise in the process.*

So human and grauori medicine working together? Sal asked.

Yeah, Jarl said. *Kinda what it sounds like. I just hate that I can't see anything. The future, I mean. I keep hoping that I'll have a dream or a vision that will show me they're all ok. Nya and the babies.*

You're going to be a great dad, Sal told him, *and we'll make sure we do everything we can. Can you talk to the pups yet?*

Yeah! he said. *Nya has to help link me with them, but yes, I heard them. They don't speak like adults. It's more like they ponder sensations. Loud or warm, things like that, so I've been talking to them. Nya thinks it's silly, but my mother said that's what my dad did before I was born. I can't help but wonder if that's why I always liked him, you know? Because I knew the sound of his voice before I was born?*

I don't know, Sal told him, *but it sure can't hurt. You know I'm willing to come help, right? If Nya needs to be knocked out, or even if you just need some moral support, I'll be over there as fast as I can.*

I know. You've always been so good to us, Sal. I used to think that your request for me to take care of the iliri was just your way of making a kid feel better about having his life turned inside out, you know? But I've been thinking about that lately. Kinda a lot. I think you taught me something really important. That it's not always about what we can do now, but sometimes about what we'll be able to do later. That it's ok to value someone's potential more than their current state.

In many ways we're all potential, Sal agreed.

Yeah, Jarl replied, *but isn't the trick to know the difference between a dream and true potential? I mean, when I met you, I wanted to be a Black Blade so bad. Then you gave me that blade and I knew I had a choice, right? I could ignore everything else and embrace my iliri side and join your pack. But if I did, I would never be the king. I'd just be another iliri crossbred struggling for equality, and while that's not a bad thing, I have a lot more potential if I'm the king. Well, chancellor, since I don't want to be a king. It wasn't an easy choice to make, but you let me make it. You gave me both options, and a reason to choose each one, and then you trusted me to get it right.*

Because I believed in your character, Sal told him. *You'd always been fair to me, so I owed it to you to be fair back.*

Is that how you're raising the iliri kids? he asked.

I hope so, she said. *History says that the next generation won't have a strong Kaisae, but we don't want to lose everything we learned fighting against Terric. Not about our history, our freedom, or what it feels like to be the weak ones. I'm trying to build a culture where we're allowed to be strong and weak at the same time. Where we're judged on good decisions, not showing off. Granted, that's the kind of thing that's a lot easier to say than to do.*

But you can do it, he assured her. *Sal, if anyone can, it's going to be you. I think that's why you lived.*

No, Jarl. I survived because many people cared enough about me to risk their own lives. Not because I was powerful or a good fighter. I was brought back to life because I stopped doing what I thought I had to so I could listen to a man mourn. Because I didn't care that another was human. I am still here because I accepted that impossible things could happen. It might have been a longshot, but I dared to hope for them instead of simply giving up.

And because we still need you, he pointed out. *I mean, all of that's true, but we all need you, and that's the bit you forget. You, Salryc Luxx, Kaisae of All Anglia, are the person who makes everyone around you feel like they might actually mean something. Doesn't matter if that's the guy serving drinks to Parliament, the kid running messages in the Dorton Palace, or the ruler of a nation who locked themselves away for* centuries. *You treated us all the same: like we're people who have feelings.*

Sal looked down at her desk and smiled. *I think that's the nicest thing that anyone's ever said to me, Jarl.*

I mean it, Sal. You told me that you want me to take care of the iliri, and I'm going to do it. May not be the way you meant when you asked, because I know you weren't planning on coming back, but I still mean it, ok?

I have never doubted you, she promised.

Yeah. The thing is that I actually know that. Everyone else has. Even my dad and the King, but not you. And yeah, I know that Nya and I screwed up. We thought we had it all figured out, and now she's pregnant, and I just turned sixteen last month! I just wanted to tell you that you've kinda helped me through this. Everyone says that I'm going to screw up these kids' lives, but I'm not. I'm going to be a perfect dad, and I'm going to try to do the right thing with them. Kinda like you did the right thing with me.

Then trust Rayna, Sal told him. *She's on your side in this, and she'll fight for you if you need it. She'll also tell you bluntly when you fuck it up, but that's why she's my best friend. She won't lie to you, not even when you want her to.*

I know. Anyway, Nya's waking up again, and I want to make sure she's not going crazy. They have her on bed rest now. Said they're worried that walking around in this state might be more than her body can take, and she said the kids are heavy. Feels better when she walks on her hind legs, but then her back hurts, so she's ok with lying around. I'm trying to get her everything she wants. To spoil her a bit.

Go spoil her, Sal told him. *And if you need someone to listen, I'm always available. I'll make time for you, even if I'm busy.*

Thank you, Sal. I think I needed that talk.

He slipped out of her mind, but she was still smiling. Jarl sounded so excited and nervous, all at the same time. She had a feeling that was how most dads felt just before the kids were born. He knew everything was about to change, yet he couldn't imagine how.

But she honestly believed that he and Nya would make it work.

Rayna was convinced that their kids would be iliri, and if so, this would be even better. That one family would tie all three of the species together? Because they were public figures, it would set a precedent that the country couldn't ignore, yet would make their lives harder. Still, Jarl was a strong young man, and Nya would definitely be the next Orassae. They'd been raised to ignore the things they couldn't change and to face head-on the ones they could make better.

And if the babies were iliri, it would prove something else. The records Ashir Doyin had found all said that human-grauori breeding was impossible, and yet Nya was pregnant. The only viable mix, in the past, had been created in a lab. They'd cut out genes and spliced in others, picking the exact pieces the humans wanted in their new labor force.

The strange thing was that it had only worked with one woman's genes. Zep's distant ancestor, who was the first person to claim the name Zepyr. Did that mean that she could've crossed with a grauori male? Could one of her sons have impregnated a grauori female? Ignoring the fact that they'd - wrongly - assumed the grauori were stupid beasts, would it have been biologically feasible?

And if so, how many people in the world were like Jarl? Zep was one. She already knew that, but he'd never have another child. Thinking about it reminded her of something else. So, on impulse, Sal reached out for the professor who was trying to find the answers.

Professor Doyin? she thought.

Kaisae, he immediately replied.

I heard you were doing blood tests. Can you test me?

We already know you're a Kaisae, he said.

We do, she agreed, *but your tests should prove it, right? And if so, would it be able to find the gene in a man?*

It should, he said. *Although it sounds like every onsyc male should have it.*

Yeah, Sal agreed, *but I've been told that's a sliding scale. Some onsyc males are attracted to females, so it could be hard to know for sure. Considering how we iliri mate bond, that so many men are meant for a specific female, and all of that, I was just wondering if it would?*

It would, he promised. *I used onsyc males to test it initially.*

Then I want you to test me and all of my mates, Sal said. *And if the test comes out like we expect, I want you to test the King's family as well.*

Humans?!

Humans, she agreed. *Unless you can think of another reason why Jarl Vayu Valmere is expecting children with a grauori bitch?*

The professor was silent for a very long time. *No, Sal, I can't. You think the King's line carries the Kaisae gene?*

No, Sal said. *But I think the next king's will. I think Vanica has it, and I think there's a chance Jarl's kids might. If Nya has the same thing and it can be passed down? And if we can prove that Jarl's not the only one?*

Then you wouldn't be a rare thing anymore, Ashir realized. *I'll come down and draw blood for those tests tomorrow at lunch. If you're right, I'll make a point of riding to Dorton afterward. Kaisae, you know what this could mean?*

That we iliri aren't even close to being done, Sal told him.

Well, that, he agreed, *but something even bigger. It means we don't need to worry about purity. Not if humans carry Kaisae genes. It means, Sal, that we won't need three different species. We can hybridize between us until we're all just Anglians.*

Fuck, she breathed. *We could destroy the iliri ourselves. Because we want to!*

Because we could love whoever we wanted, and it sure explains an anomaly I'm seeing. Some iliri males seem to be drawn to completely human women. Njeri Zepyr didn't only pass the gene to her sons. She would've passed it to daughters as well.

CHAPTER THIRTY-FIVE

PURPLE

At the end of the week, Sal called all of the Black Blades' kids home for another attempt at a family dinner. This time, Risk, Perin, and Tilso would be bringing the twins. The girls were slowly starting to open up, and the hope was that seeing some more kids around would help. Lyzzi, Lasryn, Rhyx, and Raast went out of their way to include them.

The guys also decided to have the meal at Tensa's, because none of them were doing well with the concept of cooking. Blaz and Gage could make something edible, but that wasn't the same as good. Oddly, Arctic was good at it, but it wasn't fair to always make him handle things. Well, and Ryali.

So, on the last day of the week, the Blades were seated at a group of tables, digging into a delicious meal made by someone who knew what she was doing: Tensa. Risk's girls were still shy, but they'd started talking. Mostly because no one at the table cared which language they used - or even if they mixed them together.

It seemed that was part of their problem. Going from an iliri house to a human one and then back so many times had them unsure of how to communicate. Too many of their temporary guardians hadn't been able to use a link, but the Blades could, and now the two girls were a part of it. Then there was Sal. Even at their young age, they realized she would protect them, and that made all the difference.

Rhyx, Raast, and Lasryn were explaining to them that school wasn't the same thing as being sent away, and that their parents could come see them at any time, but the twins weren't sure about that. Nylla kept asking if that meant they'd have another amma, and Roo's girls couldn't make them understand. Las, however, could.

"Our kauvwae watches us."

"What's that?" Nissa asked.

"Grandmother," Rhyx translated. "Our Amma's amma."

"Kinda," Las said. "Inessi's actually the Ahnor's amma, but she adopted Sal too - and all of our pack. That means you two, because you're pack members now."

Nylla looked up at Perin. "Are you in the pack, Dava?"

"I am," he assured her. "I wasn't born in the pack, though. They took me in when I needed it. See Tyr over there? He actually has *two* packs. The one where he was raised, and this one. He couldn't choose, so he gets to have both."

"But why?" Nissa asked, her eyes landing on Tyr.

Tyr leaned over the table toward her. "Because I was scared. I didn't want to lose the people I used to know, but I wanted to live with the people I care about now, and that's ok."

"So..." Nissa chewed on her lip. "We can still be family with our amma?"

"Which amma?" Las asked. "Sounds like you've had a few, and that's ok."

"Our real amma," Nissa said.

"Their dam," Risk explained. "They remember her."

"Do you know your last name?" Sal asked. When both girls shook their heads, she tried again. "Do you remember your amma's name?"

"Kyrinae," Nylla whispered.

"Then why don't we make that your last name so you'll never have to forget her? You can be Nylla Kyrinae, and your sister will be Nissa Kyrinae. Then your davas won't need to pick which name you use?" Sal looked at the three men, belatedly hoping that was ok with them.

"I think it's perfect," Perin said. "And it shows just how much she matters to you, right?"

"It's a good name for them," Tilso said, and Risk nodded his agreement.

"And we can still stay with our davas?" Nissa asked.

"Forever," Risk promised. "If anyone tries to make you leave and you don't want to, everyone at this table will fight to protect you."

Perin pointed down the table, his finger aimed across the room. "And the ones at that table." Then he pointed behind Sal. "And the ones over there too. Probably more than that. See, those are our friends and even more of our family. I bet Tseri would help too."

"And Kesh?" Nylla asked.

"Definitely Kesh," Sal assured her. "Probably all of his pack too, although humans call it a unit."

"Lightning Brigade," Nissa said, proving they'd spent a bit of time with the men on the trip from Viraenova. "They let us ride the horses with them!"

"You know," Zep said, "Your dava, Tilso? He can teach you how to ride a horse on your own."

Tilso groaned. "Sal? I'm going to need a little loan."

"For what?" she asked.

He smiled over at the girls. "I think we need a couple of ponies - but good ones. Not the nasty kind that have horrible personalities. Short horses."

"Uh..." Sal leaned back in her chair. "Tseri?" she called, seeing the woman eating across the way.

"Yeah?" Tseri yelled back.

"You happen to have a couple of short but quality horses you'd want to sell? We need something the kids can get on, but not something too lazy so they'll never learn."

Tseri looked over at her mates and was silent for a moment. Syed was nodding, but Kesh just shrugged. Daest eventually grinned. That was when the Kaeen turned back.

"I'll trade you a nuvani warhorse for an iliri one. When we get back, I'll send up a couple of good saddle horses for the other kids, but we have a horse with us that would be perfect to start them on. A little mare, and she's trained for battle but a bit too lazy for us."

Tilso sighed. "I only have a couple of geldings I can send back with you right now," he said.

"A gelding is fine," Tseri assured him. "And we'll trade you the saddle horses for a pair of foals when they're weaned. Your choice."

"Throw in a larger warhorse mare," Tilso said, "and I'll give you a breeding quality colt as well."

"Done," Tseri said. "But I want one of the best colts you produce."

"Not a problem," Tilso assured her. "We have quite a few nice stallions, and we don't need all of them. I'd like to see the lines keep going. I'll even offer you the best of the lot if you get me a mare worthy of crossing to Sal's stallion."

Tseri nodded once. "It's a deal. And I expect to make many more trades in the future. I assume you want gold ones?"

"Color isn't as important as ability," Tilso assured her. "If you can get me both, that would be great, but I just like how your mounts are put together. They're sized just right for the iliri."

"That they are," Tseri assured him, pausing as the dining room door opened and a wave of noise flowed through.

That meant someone was in the main entrance of Arhhawen, and it sounded like a large crowd. Sal turned to look, only to find Ran standing there, surveying the tables. His eyes landed on her a moment later.

"Sal, you have some applicants here for the Peacekeeper positions. Thirty grauori and thirty humans. They say the King sent them."

She smiled. "Their timing is perfect. Ryali? Can you call the other girls? And Gage, tell the Peacekeeper candidates we've picked to meet us at the entrance."

"Joe," Ryali said, "take care of Valri?"

"Always," he promised. "And pretty sure Zep will help."

Ryali pushed back her chair. "Henrik says he is with them. Ya do na have ta do this, Sal."

"I do," Sal assured her. "Mostly because I want to see what we're working with."

But they weren't the only ones getting up. Tseri and Kesh clearly intended to see what was going on, and Jase wouldn't leave her to manage this alone. Kolt, however, waved Tseri's other two mates over, inviting the men to join the Blades' dinner. The surprising thing was that Syed and Daest did.

In the large gathering area inside the main doors of Arhhawen, the space was filled with humans and grauori. Every shade of pale fur was visible, which meant that Rragri hadn't judged the candidates by their coat color. As for the humans, Sal was impressed to see that they weren't all soldiers. The entire group, however, looked a little confused.

"Welcome to Arhhawen," Sal told them, pausing for everyone to turn and find her. "Henrik?"

"Here, Kaisae," the man said, hurrying toward the front.

Sal walked toward him with her hand out. "Congratulations on the promotion, Major. You're a good man and an even better friend to the iliri. The King, Orassae, and I were unanimous in choosing you to represent humans in this endeavor."

His cheeks began to flush where they were visible above his beard. "Thank you, sir. I'm honored to have been chosen."

"The rest of you," Sal told them, "were all picked as examples of your species who can think fairly and who are sympathetic to the differences of Anglia's other two species. Our goal is to divide you up into groups of three: one human, one iliri, and one grauori. Each triad will be assigned to a city in Anglia - no, not only the human cities - where you will help mitigate cultural confusion between our species. As we've seen firsthand, laws designed for humans often do no justice to the iliri or grauori, and vice versa. While our country grows closer together, our people will as well. That's going to cause even more confusion when citizens who are part grauori and iliri, or part iliri and human, end up being judged by a standard that doesn't truly apply. Your jobs, should you choose to continue with this process, will be to find that middle ground that is fair, follows the legal structure of Anglia, and can educate the community you'll be assigned to."

"How will we enforce this?" someone asked. "It's all well and good to say that something's wrong, but what power will we have?"

"You will be the ones who decide which jurisdiction a crime will be tried under. Anglian Peacekeepers will be a part of both the police force and the judicial system. Neither a guard nor a judge, but the organizers of both. The police will arrest individuals, and you will determine if they should be fined, released, or tried in a court of Anglian law - and which one. Because we all know that iliri and grauori do not obey all human laws."

"The example given to me," Henrik said, "was that of an iliri man biting his mate and being accused of domestic violence. By human law, the charge is true, but by iliri custom, it's not a crime. In the future, the same thing will happen with grauori who live among humans, humans who live here in Arhhawen with the iliri, and even iliri who have moved into grauori dens. This is how we learn, but each society deserves an expert. Someone to ask when they aren't sure if it's really wrong, or just new and different. That is what we Peacekeepers are going to do."

Sal gestured to him. "And this is why Major Henrik Aben has been selected to be the final authority for human Peacekeepers. I have chosen Ryali Lyas to represent the iliri. She will work with him and one of the grauori."

Kaisae? a young male thought as he slunk forward. *The Orassae sent me to work with them. She said that, from the stories she's heard, I might suffice. My name is Gawyrr.*

He was an aufrio male, but his points were the darkest Sal had ever seen. Charcoal was a good way to describe the color. It was too reflective to truly be black, but not by much. From the shape of his body, she had a feeling he was younger, barely mature. In other words, Rragri had found someone who would be in this position for a very long time.

"Welcome, Gawyrr. Are you linked with Ryali and Henrik yet?"

"Henrik, yah," Gawyrr said, glancing over to Ryali. "But I have na yet touched yer sister. Ilus?"

"Gerus," Ryali said, walking over to offer her hand.

Gawyrr stood and shook like a human, but it worked. Skin to skin, the connection formed, allowing him to find her mind in the jumble of the mental hubs they now used. The male smiled, his tongue leaning to the side while he looked her in the eyes. His were almost blue, hers a shade darker but still icy pale. Neither seemed offended.

"Rragri is my amma's mate's sister," he explained. "I also stayed here during the war, tasked ta organize the maargra between packs."

"Ya are na grey," Ryali pointed out.

He whuffed as he lowered himself back to his haunches. "I am na gold or white," he countered. "Ya are na white."

"I am na," Ryali agreed. "I am rafrezzi."

"And me?" Henrik asked. "Is there a color for humans?"

"Ya are confused between aufrio on yer head," Gawyrr said, "and rafrezzi on yer face, but ya have almost as much fur as I do."

"That I do, my friend," Henrik agreed. "I think he'll do well with us, Kaisae."

"Good," Sal said, "but you'll get a few more days to be sure of it." Then she raised her voice to address them all. "Tonight, I want everyone to get to know each other. Tomorrow, your leaders here - Henrik, Ryali, and Gawyrr - will begin to organize each triad. We will have a few sample scenarios for you to decide. That will help us determine if you really are a good fit and willing to accept the cultural differences of all Anglians. We hope to assign you to cities by the end of the week, and send you out before it snows in the passes."

Jase gestured behind them to the doors that led to Tensa's. "Ya can start here. Find a place ta sit and talk. Order food and drinks. Ask questions. While ya meet yer coworkers, we will make sure there are rooms fer all of ya."

"I have space for Henrik and Gawyrr," Ryali said.

"And that precious little girl of yours?" Henrik asked. "We aren't going to put her out, are we?"

"Na," Ryali assured him. "Her sire does na get ta see her enough, so she can stay with him t'night. I think we have too much ta talk about, and she would na know ta ask anything but why."

"Why is a good question," Gawyrr pointed out. "But ya do na look old enough ta have pups."

"Ya do na either," Ryali countered.

"I'm old enough that both of you could be my pups," Henrik teased.

But Sal couldn't help but notice that Raast and Rhyx were standing beside the door staring. Not at all the grauori in the area, but just at one. Rhyx kept looking back at her sister, who seemed completely entranced. From the sparkle in Raast's eyes, it seemed that Gawyrr was clearly a very handsome male.

Even worse, the young male noticed. He glanced at the girl once, made a point of shaking out his mane, and stood just a little too perfectly. Then he glanced back to see if she'd noticed. The problem was that Raast had, and for a split second, their eyes met. Gawyrr's immediately dropped to the ground, but his lips curled into a grauori smile.

Ryali? she warned. *My pups have a crush. Let me know if they get in the way?*

Do na shame them fer growing up, Ryali told her. *I will na let them make fools of themselves, but ya will na stop them from being girls either. Fair?*

Very fair, Sal agreed. *Thank you, sister.*

Always, Kaisae.

CHAPTER THIRTY-SIX

ORANGE

*W*ell over a week after Rayna accepted Dom's proposal, Sal finally got the chance to take her shopping for a dress. Ryali, Henrik, and Gawyrr had taken over everything with the Peacekeepers, which meant Sal had plenty of time to do whatever she wanted. Unfortunately, the Unavi ambassadors arrived that morning, which meant both she and Tseri needed to make an official appearance to welcome them to Anglia for Sal, and to the Alliance meeting for Tseri.

But they escaped as soon as they could, thanks to Rayna. She apologized profusely, saying today was the only time available to get all three women measured for their dresses. The excuse got them out, but was also how Tseri ended up with Rayna and Sal at the tailor's shop, helping to pick out the perfect wedding dress.

"Silver?" Tseri asked.

"And white and green," Rayna said. "Silver for the Dogs that got me here. White is for the Shields who accepted me without question. Green, of course, is for Anglia and the life I hope to have here."

"Sounds like you already have the iliri included in your ceremony," Tseri told her. "So how are you going to celebrate Dom's humanity?"

"Huh," Rayna breathed. "I honestly hadn't thought about it like that. I just..."

"Got enamored with the way we do things, thinking it sounds better than the way you always have?" Tseri finished for her. "I hear humans use rings, are you getting Dom one?"

"Shift and I are doing that together," Rayna assured her. "Don't tell him, but it's special. Um, Shift was given a piece of a broken machine. It's not much, but the jeweler said it's real gold. We were going to set that in a white resin band so that it's two rings in one. Mine and Shift's."

"That's perfect," Sal said. "Love and strength?"

"Because becoming the King wasn't easy for him, Sal. He never wanted this, but he refused to give up even when it would've been easier. And he fought to include everyone in his idea of the future. I dunno, it just feels like he deserves to have someone acknowledge that he's a strong and fair king."

Sal nodded. "So how are you and Shift showing your bond?"

Rayna pulled back her shirt to show the stippling of scars along her neck. "I want my dress to leave my shoulders bare," she said. "And in the ceremony, I will be calling Dom my husband and Shift my Dernor. We thought it was a good balance."

"It is, actually," Tseri agreed. "But I suggest you have Shift give you a necklace or another ring. Something the people will see him bestow. An item they can relate to."

"A dagger," Sal said. "Ray, I know where to get another steel dagger for you to give to Shift."

Her mouth fell open in shock. "Are you serious? It's not one of yours, is it?"

"No," Sal assured her. "Marnia snuck a crate out from Fort Landing with her. We have twenty-four of them in there." Sal paused to roll her eyes. "She gave one to Nyurin."

"But we can't give out two steel daggers," Rayna said. "That would cause too much talk, and everyone would assume they were yours. So if I give Shift a dagger, then what would he give me?"

"Shift should give you the dagger," Tseri said. "It will make it clear that you are the fighter in the family. Shift is a healer and a Black Blade. What would symbolize that to a human?"

"The crown," Sal said. "Rayna, you need to give it to him and ask him to rule *with* you. Make it clear that he's not a trinket to show off, but an integral part of the Anglian leadership."

"He already knows he'll have to wear a crown," Rayna said.

Sal slowly nodded. "He does. That doesn't mean he knows how you *feel* about it. That you honestly *need* his help. That Dom *values* his opinion. Make it clear that he is an equal part of your relationship."

"Gifts are only things, and things can be lost," Tseri said. "Words are what matter. Feelings, too. Those are the things that iliri and nuvani treasure above all else."

"Then it's perfect," Rayna said just as the tailor came back into the main area of the shop.

"Consort?" she asked, cradling a bolt of cloth. "Silver is not an easy color to find, but I have a bolt of a shimmering grey."

Rayna sighed at the sight of the fabric. "I think that's close enough," she assured the tailor. "My idea is to have white and green accents somehow."

"How obvious?" the woman asked.

"Obvious," Rayna said. "I want my gown to drip with the colors."

And the tailor smiled. "How do you feel about crystals sewn into the cloth? Using the grey base, we can add accents down the body, shifting from white to green around the thigh, and increasing the quantity so it looks like you're wearing gems."

Sal was nodding encouragement, but Rayna shook her head. "That's... I can't."

"You're about to be the Queen of Anglia," Sal reminded her. "You certainly can if you like the idea. Besides, if Dom can't afford to buy it, I will."

"You would?" Rayna asked.

"No," Tseri said. "*I* will. Don't humans have a custom about something being given? Well, I'm buying your dress, so get what you want."

"My lady..." the tailor said.

"Kaeen," Tseri corrected. "That's the Viraenovan equivalent of a king. I assure you, ma'am, that I can afford it."

"Probably better than I could," Sal added. "So, Ray? Is this what you want?"

"With a dipped neckline," Rayna said, tracing the shape across her chest to make it clear what she meant. "And since it's summer, I want short sleeves, but the kind that aren't on the shoulder. I want my neck and shoulders bare. Um..."

"The skirt," the tailor reminded her.

Rayna nodded to show she'd heard. "I kinda want a slit up the leg, but I also want something full, and those don't look good together. What do you two think?"

"Full," Tseri said. "Smooth down the front and trailing in the back."

"You don't need to show off your legs in your wedding dress," Sal added. "You've already caught the guys, so no need to flaunt it to the rest, right?"

"Right," Rayna agreed. "Sal, help? I'm overwhelmed."

Sal reached up to rub Rayna's shoulder, but she turned her attention to the tailor. "Make it as form-fitting as you did for the iliri, something to prove that the body under it isn't bound and trussed up. Rayna worked for every muscle she has, so she deserves to show them off. She'll need a matching garter, preferably with a loop to hold a dagger. Not a sheath, just a loop. And make sure the fasteners along the back of this dress are torture to get out of. She'll have two men assisting, and we won't want the wedding night to finish too fast."

The tailor grinned. "Lucky woman, but I can work with that. I have some pearl toggles that are tiny and beautiful. I also think we should add in a matching comb, decorated with the crystals."

"And crystals on the veil?" Rayna asked.

"I can do that," the woman promised. "Now, shoes? I have a cobbler who can work with the design I give him."

"Boots," Rayna said. "I have ugly feet, but I want a heel."

"Green with white lace over it?" Sal suggested.

"Ankle high," Tseri said. "Trust me, Ray, you do not want to wait for your men to get those off."

Rayna gasped. "Underthings!"

The tailor just laughed. "I already have that planned for you, Consort. I was told that you are not shy or..."

"She's not a virgin," Sal finished, helping the woman out.

"Yes, that." The tailor cleared her throat, proving that while she might understand everything they were talking about, that didn't mean she was comfortable saying it. "Well, many of the working girls have bustiers and lingerie meant to entice. I may have purchased a set so I could make a pattern from it that's more appropriate. Something beautiful, supportive, and seductive. Lady Tor suggested it, along with a.... soldier? A woman wearing a uniform."

"Brisa," Sal realized. "Formerly a whore?"

"Yes, Kaisae," the tailor agreed, sounding almost ashamed of it.

"She's our friend," Sal assured her, "and a war hero."

"Ah, I understand." Again, the woman cleared her throat. "But I thought that might be more accommodating of your Conglomerate background?"

"It is," Rayna agreed. "Where I'm from, women are neither possessions nor ashamed of our desires. We are just as strong as men in many ways. There's not a single thing wrong with enjoying the men I'm going to spend the rest of my life with."

"I hope you teach that to the rest of this country," the tailor said. "I've always thought it was unfair, so we spoke about such things in whispers and blamed the excitement of the weddings. It shouldn't be shameful when we're the ones carrying the resulting babies."

"Even if we can't," Rayna told her, "we deserve to enjoy our relationships. Don't worry, I'm going to make it very clear that women gained our equality beside the men in the Terran War."

"She saved the King's life," Tseri added. "In Myrosica. The Consort fought off an elite unit of Terran forces beside myself and the Kaisae."

"Some of the guys helped," Rayna said, glancing over at Sal.

"They did," she agreed, refusing to mention that Zep had given his life that day. "And you deserve to have the best wedding because of it. So, besides the dress, what else do you need?"

"Lord Piet and Lady Tor are handling the flowers," Rayna said.

"Cillian is taking care of the location. Sal, you have everything for the iliri portion of the ceremony?"

"Inessi has an idea. She just has to find the right words now," Sal assured her.

"And my only jewelry will be the rings. So, I don't know." Rayna turned to the tailor. "What am I forgetting?"

"Nothing, Consort. Weddings are much easier when you have a staff to handle the organizing. The only other typical Anglian ceremony is your ladies' night."

"What's that?" Sal asked.

"Traditionally, the men have a party for the bachelor. That same night, the women gather with the bride-to-be and explain to her about what happens in the bedchamber. Since it sounds like you understand that already, I'm not sure."

"A party for the bride-to-be," Tseri decided.

"A wild one," Sal said. "Conglomerate style."

Rayna was nodding. "And we should invite all the girls. Brisa, Shaden, Baeli, Meia, Teya, and Keeya. Maybe Vanica, Linella, and Ria? Definitely Rragri, if she'll leave Nya's side."

"Keeya's heavily pregnant," Sal warned.

"So?" Rayna asked. "I'm sure one of you has a carriage somewhere, and I'll be too drunk to keep a leg on either side of my horse. She can laugh with us and make sure we aren't too foolish."

"And Roo," Sal suggested.

"Can the girls come?" Rayna asked.

"No," Sal said. "Not with alcohol and humans. Believe it or not, they are still kids."

"Kids who were born in battle and grew up saving our lives," Rayna reminded her. "Well, they're invited. Bring everyone, and tell them all to wear pants!" She paused, spinning back to the tailor. "Oh! How long will the dress take?"

"How fast does it need to be done?" the woman asked.

"Dom promised me a week longer than it'll take for you to make it."

The tailor smiled. "Well, for a royal wedding dress, I promise I'm not working on anything else. Can I have four days to sew on the crystals?"

"It won't be possible until the allies are here," Sal assured her. "So take six, and then another week after that to make the announcements?"

"He's already started," Rayna said.

"And Kesh and I are coming," Tseri promised. "I think *everyone* is coming to this. If you don't mind, Viraenova would like to sit in the section for your family, since the iliri will be there for Shift."

Rayna reached over and grabbed her hand. "Thank you, Kaeen."

"You are most welcome, Your Majesty."

"Yeah," Rayna breathed. "That's going to take a while to get used to."

"But you're the perfect woman for the job," Tseri assured her. "Now come. Let's look at the pubs and find one that can fit an entire party of drunk women with swords."

Rayna laughed, looking over at Sal. "You might have competition for the spot as my best friend."

"No I don't," Sal assured her. "We're iliri. We share just fine."

CHAPTER THIRTY-SEVEN

GOLD

he three of them found quite a few bars that were suitable, and it was entirely possible that they sampled a few drinks at each one. It was late when the Arhhawen party returned home, only to be met in the entry by one of the lookouts. The man said he'd seen the Conglomerate envoy stop to camp between Valmere and Dorton, merely a few hours away from the capital city.

So, the next morning, Sal woke early. She and her men dressed in their finest, saddled their horses, and headed down the mountain toward the King's Palace. Tseri would come later. They didn't need the CFC to know they were being watched, and it was unlikely they'd think about it otherwise.

Sal had no idea which Representatives would be attending the meeting. It wouldn't be all of them. Right now, few nations could risk sending their entire government on a trip that would take them away for months at a time. But, depending on who was there, this could either be very tense or wonderfully amiable. After all, Anglia had stolen quite a few of their best military units.

Never mind that they'd won the war. The CFC had a habit of overlooking such things when it suited them. Even worse, when Sal rode into the Palace courtyard, it was full and everything was decked out in blue and gold. The horses were being attended by grooms; some had been led away already, which meant the politicians were waiting inside.

"Kaisae?" one of the guardsmen said, speaking up. "If you'd like to leave your mounts there, we all know they'll stand. I can have them moved for you."

"Do you know who's here?" she asked him. The guard wasn't one she knew, but his uniform said he was a soldier.

"No, sir. I can tell you there's one woman and three men. They brought a few dozen assistants with them."

Gage clasped her shoulder before she could start cursing. "Sir, did you see if the King's smile was real or faked?"

"Somewhere in the middle," the soldier answered honestly. "Guarded is the best word I have. Dom - I mean the King - looked like he didn't quite trust them. Then again, it's the CFC."

"He has a point," Tyr said. "C'mon, Sal. We got this. Besides, what can they do, yell at us some more?"

"Not recognize my species as deserving of the same rights as a human," Sal countered.

"Then we don't trade with them," the soldier said. "I mean, that's the feelings of the men, sir. If they don't like all of Anglia, then they can't have part of it. Figure that after what Terric did to their country, they're going to need someone willing to sell lumber and such, you know? If Anglia doesn't, then won't Viraenova follow us?"

"And Unav," Gage reminded her. "Although they'll be desperate as well."

"Escea will," Sal pointed out.

Blaz huffed in amusement. "Um, correct me if I'm wrong, but doesn't Vilko outrank Jurij?"

Sal began to smile. "She does, and I don't think the CFC would know what to do with her style of politics."

"Exactly," Gage said. "We got this, Sal. Anglia is holding the CFC by the balls, and they'll agree to respect us. They kinda have to."

Kolt leaned over her shoulder. "So lift that pretty little chin of yours, put those ears back against your skull, and let's make a show of this. Remind them that you won this war, and fuck them if they don't like it."

So she did. Her mates fell in around her like a personal guard. Jase was at her left, keeping pace, Kolt beside her on the right. Zep and Gage were behind them, with Blaz and Tyr on their flank, just beside and behind them. Their swords had been left at home, but all of them carried some kind of weapon, and Sal had her daggers strapped on her belt once more.

That, more than anything else, made it easy. The weight was a reminder of everything she'd been through and why. Then there was the respect of her men. Technically, they were the King's soldiers, but as Sal approached the main entrance of the Dorton Palace, two guards stepped up to get the doors for her. They opened them wide and dropped their eyes.

In unison, the men whispered, "Laetus, Kaisae."

Because no matter what happened next, she'd already earned their respect, and they wanted her to know it. Just like the guard had felt comfortable enough to speak up about her horses. These men were doing what they could to support her without stepping out of line. Sal nodded at each of them as she walked inside, pausing in the open area just inside. Thankfully, Linella Piet was there and knew what Sal was looking for.

She pointed up the stairs. "They headed to his office," she said. "Rragri should show up since Nya's room is just down the hall."

"Thank you," Sal told her.

Her mates didn't say a thing, but they also didn't break their formation as they all headed up to the second floor. At the top, a pair of guards thumped their fists to their hearts. One of them flicked a finger to the left, directing Sal subtly. She caught his eye, smiled, and kept going straight to Dom's favorite place to host visitors.

Not his real office, but the formal one with the big chair and impressive desk. It was where she'd recently met with Brisa - and where none of the books or documents held any national secrets. The seating had been designed to appear casual, but Sal knew better. She'd been in Anglia long enough to figure out that this King had done it on purpose to gain the advantage. Relaxed people were more likely to let something slip, and none of them trusted the leaders of the Conglomerate.

She also didn't care that the door was closed when she got there. Without knocking, Sal turned the handle and entered, her men right behind her. Dom looked up with a smile, but the four people before him stood, turned, and bowed to her respectfully. Sal recognized every single one.

"Representative Anis," she said to the woman closest to her. "It's a pleasure to see you again."

"I hope so, Kaisae," the woman said, adding a smile with it. "You know Natyn Grenso from Lewes, but I'm not sure if you remember Kalt Sherin from Merriton or Lethanul Jakin from Alverton?"

"I do," Sal said. "We met at the Prin arena, and I'm sorry for the pain, Representative Sherin. My mate had only died a few weeks before."

"And now my city is in shambles," he told her. "I was told the iliri slaves rebelled after your assault failed?"

"That's right." She glanced back. "Relax, guys. You look amazing, but I'm sure that none of our guests would try to assault me on my ground."

"Or ever," Grenso assured her. "All of us were in the Parliament building when Toth made his last mistake."

Sal offered her hand over to him. "I'm glad to see you, Natyn. I wasn't sure you'd still have your seat after everything that happened."

He chuckled as he reached up to clasp her palm. "Haven't had elections yet, Sal. I see you picked up a few more men to stand behind you."

"Had to die to do it," she teased.

But their conversation wasn't as simple as the words they spoke. Through his touch, Grenso pushed a warning at her. The CFC was angry about the damage to Merriton and the loss of their units. They were pissed about her taking Ran Sturmgren. Almost as much as her restructuring of the Conglomerate's military to include mixed iliri and human units. Those, however, were working well, even if some humans didn't want to admit it.

"Well, I for one am glad you survived," Natyn said as he finally released her. "Please, join us, Kaisae. I hear the Orassae is in Dorton as well?"

"With her daughter," Dom explained. "Nya is not only pregnant, but overdue. We brought her here to make sure she had access to the best human doctors available."

"Not grauori healers?" Jakin asked.

Dom smiled. "In war, we called it combined arms. In peace, we call it working together. You see, grauori can heal the body from the inside. That doesn't do much to help the babies get out. Surgery can assist if they are too big to fit through the birth canal, and either a grauori or iliri healer can heal the incision. The healers can also sedate her for the procedure, which makes it easy since we're not sure how our chemicals work on their bodies yet."

"Which means we humans aren't completely useless," Anis pointed out.

"Kinda how I felt," Dom said. "So, Representatives, I'd normally offer a drink, but it's still early. I can call in coffee, if you'd prefer? I'm afraid your rooms are being finished right now since you're earlier than we expected."

"Oh?" Sherin asked. "And when did you think we'd get here?"

"Three months after you left Prin, of course," Dom said. "It is a long journey, but I'm guessing the weather was nice?"

Grenso ducked his head, pressing his fist to his lips. "Not much rain in the summer, sire."

It seemed that as a lookout himself, the man understood what Dom wasn't saying. He also wasn't about to enlighten the others. That in itself spoke volumes about the state of the CFC's iliri-human relations. That they hadn't kicked him out of his position left her hopeful, though.

"So," Sal said, claiming a seat beside Dom's desk to face the Citizens, "this makes you the third nation to arrive. The Unavi delegation has rooms on the third floor. The Kaeen of Viraenova will come to pay her respects later today. Her party is being hosted in Arhhawen, which is about an hour away by horse."

"Do we know if Escea is coming?" Jakin asked.

Sal nodded. "Their party is in western Anglia, heading this way. They've stopped at some of the grauori areas to camp. We expect them to be here shortly. I don't have an update on Myrosica, though."

"Two more days," Anis told her. "They just finished their summer celebration. Sounds like we're going to be able to start this meeting on time."

Sal chuckled. "That rarely happens, right?"

"Correct," Anis said. "One country is always delayed by weather or circumstance."

"I was wondering," Sherin said, "if you were interested in discussing trade deals while we wait for everyone to arrive?"

"We're not," Sal told him before Dom had a chance to answer. "I'm afraid Anglia's stance is that we will only trade with nations who support our entire country, and the vote at this Alliance meeting will prove that."

"And I would hate to negotiate in bad faith," Dom told them. "However, I would like to invite all of you to my wedding. It would only extend your stay a few days, but I completely understand if you can't."

"We can," Anis assured him. "Congratulations, sire. I assume that Rayna Mel is the lucky lady?"

"And Kayden Savis," Dom said. "You see, it's common in Anglia to have multiple partners. My wife has claimed an iliri mate, and I accept him as well. She will become Queen and he will take the title of Royal Consort, equal to her in all ways."

"The name sounds familiar," Jakin said softly, his words meant for Sherin.

Grenso looked over at him. "Call sign Shift. He's one of the Black Blades, which means that the King is about to become the Kaisae's brother-in-law. How do the grauori feel about this, sire? Left out?"

The door creaked as Rragri slipped inside. "Re do na," she told him. *Translate for me, Sal?*

"She says his heir is the sire of her grandpups," Sal told them, paraphrasing the thoughts Rragri was sending to her. "The grauori Raewar is pregnant by the heir to the human throne, which means that my brother's nephew and my cousin's daughter are having a child."

Jakin nodded. "I just have one question, and I wouldn't ask it of anyone else, but... Kaisae, is that confusing at all?"

Sal tapped her nose. "We can smell it, and the humans trust us. So no, not really. Families are made by the people we trust. Bloodlines matter little in that arrangement."

Sherin leaned over his knees toward her. "Well, since we're being blunt, can I do the same?"

"Please," Sal said.

He nodded once. "Sal... May I call you that?"

"Please," she said again.

"Sal, the four of us have every intention of voting yes to the recognition of iliri and grauori as equal species. With that said, there's a lot of pressure from the rest of my party to get some kind of reparations for the destruction you caused in Merriton."

"I didn't cause it," Sal pointed out. "Kalt, Terric flanked us. They were waiting in Alverton to come in from the backside. I had a noose around my neck, and Lightning Brigade pulled a miracle out of their ass to save us. *That* is what earned them the trust that got them into Viraenova - just so you're aware. The Terran leader of that assault was killed, but we were badly outnumbered and the city itself worked against us. You had traitors in there selling Conglomerate supplies across the border to Escean tribes."

"We heard," Sherin assured her.

"So Anglia pulled back."

Jase broke in. "I called a full retreat, and we had ta abandon the southern camp. Escean ships carried Terran soldiers inta the harbor, where my sister burned both them and herself ta make sure ya did na lose more of yer country."

"And we were forced to regroup at our safe house," Sal finished. "Representative Sherin, Merriton was freed by the slaves. They rebelled against their masters, killed the invaders, and chose to take advantage of the law your country voted to accept. I knew that would hurt your economy, which was why I did not want it to happen. I'm also not sorry it did."

"Ninsa Ardiel is putting Merriton back together," he assured her. "She's also a vocal supporter of my campaign. She told me in no uncertain terms that if I do not vote yes on the sentient and sovereign clause, I wouldn't see another krit."

"I knew I liked that woman," Sal said with a smile.

He nodded. "I do as well. The problem is that I can't keep my seat if I don't bring up the Anglian acquisition of Conglomerate units. I understand that you followed the technicality of the law, but not necessarily the spirit of it."

"Whose spirit?" Sal asked. "I promise you that Tseri pushed you to sign that before you could pick apart Dom's phrasing of the law."

"Viraenova?" he asked. "But Anglia and Viraenova didn't have an alliance back then."

"Not a legal one," Sal agreed, looking over at Rragri. "You see, we have *many* things in common. To start with, we both respected the Orassae. You assigned my brother as Tseri's translator - because you didn't have anyone else. The Conglomerate dismissed us, but Viraenova and Anglia didn't. Anglia, because I showed Dom how powerful his country really was. Viraenova because just like us, they're part iliri, and your nation has spent a very long time showing them exactly what you think of their species. They built walls. Dom tore them down. Who did you expect her to side with?"

"Does this mean we're already outplayed?" he asked.

Anis groaned. "Yes, Kalt, it does. Haven't you figured it out yet? Sal has the support of Viraenova and Unav. Dom has Myrosica. Who do we have? Escea? If we're *lucky?*"

"Actually," Tyr said, lifting his hand like a kid in school. "I hate to break it to you, but Sal kinda kicked the shit out of the Escean Warlords, took control of their nation, got them out of a bad deal, and then gave it back as soon as she could. Pretty sure they're going to be on her side too."

"Yeah," Sal said. "Is it a bad time to mention that the Emperor of Terric will be there?"

"He's dead!" Anis hissed.

"Wrong emperor," Sal told her. "When Makiel was killed, his son inherited. His iliri son. The one who doesn't even live in that country, but is still the legal ruler of it."

Dom leaned over his desk. "And Narnx is a Black Blade."

"I told you," Sal said. "Back when I was in Prin, I *told* you that I had someone positioned in Terric. I assured you that I'd get Star Fall put in a good place. That's because I went right for the top. I flipped the Emperor's own son by promising him the one thing no one else ever had."

"A place to belong," Grenso said. "You gave him hope."

"And that's the only thing that is going to change this world," Sal told them. "I honestly want the Conglomerate to change with us."

"We do too," Anis promised her. "That's why we all volunteered, because we thought you'd actually work with us. Just like when I asked for General Sturmgren to be your oversight while you managed our military. I knew, Sal. I'm the Representative of Fort Landing. I knew you were close with him. Believe it or not, a few of us have been on your side this whole time."

"Regardless of which party we're in," Jakin said as he turned to look at Blaz. "I also requested the 112th Mounted as our escort. Sir, your friends are probably in the stable complaining that their horses aren't being cared for properly."

Blaz grinned. "I actually doubt that."

"Go," Anis said. "Sal, I know he won't leave you, and we're just waiting for our rooms so we can bathe. Go see your friends and let us catch up with the King and Orassae."

Sal nodded. "Thank you. I think I judged the four of you wrong."

"Believe it or not," Sherin told her, "we aren't your enemies. Hopefully, we can prove that over the next few weeks."

CHAPTER THIRTY-EIGHT

YELLOW

*J*ust like they'd said, the men from the 112th Mounted were in the barn. Their horses had been stabled beside the King's, not in the area typically reserved for guests. And no, they weren't complaining. Instead, the men were looking over the facilities, pointing out a few things they didn't have back home. Sal and her mates walked up the alley to find Rais Tolan, the commanding officer, pointing up toward the ceiling.

"See something you like?" Sal called out.

The man turned with a smile on his face. "Well, hello, Kaisae!"

"How are you, Rais?" she asked, stepping up to give him a hug. "It's good to see you again."

"You too," he said as he pulled away and turned to Blaz. "And you? How is Anglia treating you?"

"Good," Blaz assured him. "How's the unit?"

Rais cleared his throat and gestured for someone to join him. A moment later, a sooty-haired woman stepped out of a stall to move closer. Sal didn't recognize her - nor did Blaz it seemed - but Rais seemed proud to introduce her.

"This," Rais said, "is your replacement. Corporal Zenya Vecys, the woman who held the northern camp together when Lightning Brigade headed out to save Sal in Merriton. She's staying in the CFC to be with her mate, so I'm taking advantage of it."

"Thank you," Sal told the woman, offering her hand. "You stepped up when we needed it the most."

"Major Kesh insisted, sir," Vecys told her, accepting her hand. "He needed a leader, so he asked a conscript who was in charge as the acting kaisae. He didn't even pretend we were beholden to the human command structure, just cut right through it."

"Which gave her the chance to shine," Rais explained. "And when I needed to fill a spot in my unit, well, she came to mind. Thankfully, she knew the basics of riding and we're teaching her the rest."

"Which is a lot more than I expected," Vecys admitted with a smile. "Although, is it allowed for me to offer laetus, Kaisae? Since I'm not of your pack or nation?"

"It is," Sal assured her, "although you are not expected to follow my orders."

Vecys shrugged. "I'm not sure ignoring them is possible, sir. Laetus, Kaisae. You made it possible for me to be here, and for that I thank you."

"Being the first does not mean I deserve all the credit," Sal told her. "It simply means I was one of many. Enough that they could no longer ignore us. The 112th are good men. Take care of them for me?"

"I will, sir," she promised.

"And we're going to take care of her," Rais added. "But I am curious about those doors in the ceiling, Sal. What's up there?"

"Hay," Sal told him. "It's wet enough in Anglia that we build in stone instead of wood. That means the building is strong enough to support multiple floors, and directly above the stable is the hay storage. Instead of carrying bales down here to hand them out, the flakes are dropped directly into the stall. There's also a silo out back for the grain, and each stall has a small door over the manger so the staff can wheel a cart down the aisle to feed."

"Nice," Rais said. "And did you hear about my promotion?"

He reached up to turn his collar toward her, showing off a single cluster pinned there. It wasn't a knot or paired bars. This was the insignia of a general, and Sal's eyes widened in respect.

"They let you operate in the field as a general?"

"Because it's peacetime, yeah. And I'm in charge of the elite units in Ran's place, so I argued that I needed to be *involved* in elite operations. The position was offered to Kesh first, but it seems he got this idea to work as an ambassador instead. Said he finally figured out why Blaec never cared about rank, because sometimes it keeps a unit from doing what they should."

"He and Viraenova are already here. Well, in Arhhawen. They'll be coming to Dorton later today." She paused to look around. "Where's Murah?"

"Gone," Rais told her. "He took off last night, saying he had people to see. I'm assuming he's visiting the grauori he knew before he came to help us, and that's fine. We're all linked into the hubs now."

"Good," Sal said. "I just wanted to make sure you're not mute. So, he's intending to go back with you, or will he be staying here?"

Celso chuckled, making Sal look up to see him leaning against another stall just a bit further down. "He's coming back with us. The mutt actually admitted that we're his pack, and that he wouldn't have one otherwise. I'm assuming that's a big deal for a grauori?"

"Yeh," Jase said. "Ya can na understand what it is like ta be alone in yer mind. As a linker, it would be harder, since his skill encourages him ta bring others t'gether."

"Makes sense," Lorenz agreed as the rest of the unit began to form up around them. "Hey, Blaz."

"Hey, man," Blaz said, stepping forward to clasp his hand.

But Lorenz pulled him into a back-thumping hug, destroying any chance Blaz had of acting proper. The others moved in for their chance, and quite a few of them were smiling. The men began to ask questions, some of them too fast for Sal to follow. Rais just ignored it, gesturing for Sal to head a little further up the hall with him.

"Hey, have you seen the Representatives yet?"

"I have," she assured him. "Anis, Grenso, Sherin, and Jakin."

"Yeah, and while you got the best of the lot, you need to know that they're going to want something back for all the soldiers who defected to Anglia."

"That's understandable, actually," Sal said. "An elite unit is a big investment, and we took three."

"You also gave us two new ones," he pointed out. "The Vanguard and the 43rd. You handled their training, showed them how to think outside the bounds of traditional strategy, and linked many of us to make us more efficient. Counter with that. Present it as the trade off."

"Good idea," she agreed. "Do you really think they'll vote for iliri and grauori recognition?"

"I do, but I think they're going to try to use their vote to get reparations for the lost men. Don't let them. Mostly, those four need it documented that they tried. It'll keep them from being voted out in the next election, and it'll give them talking points for when they're in Parliament again."

"I can do that," Sal promised. "But what about you? How are things in the CFC now that there's no war?"

"Busy," he joked. "We don't need to release troops because we lost so many. In fact, we're still recruiting. Numbers are almost at pre-war levels, though. The interesting thing is that a lot of our servicemen have been standing up for the 'scrubbers' in the ranks. I've convinced the other generals to keep the Conscript units, and we've actually had a few iliri volunteers."

"Really?" Sal asked.

Rais nodded. "The benefits are good, and most of the iliri who stayed still live in poverty. The military offers a good and steady paycheck, and those who sign up on their own get other benefits, like retirement."

"Wow," Sal breathed. "I never thought I'd see the day."

"Helps when a large portion of the population owe their lives to people who aren't human," he pointed out. "Sal, Anglia saved a *lot* of lives. No, that doesn't mean they love your kind, but it does make them a little more willing to not hate them. I think the CFC has reached a level of inter-species apathy, which is a step up."

"I'll take it," she decided. "And you know that we're still accepting immigrants, right? We always will."

"I do, and I've told a few about it, but Calyx was right. Things won't change unless we make it happen, and the continent is no longer under human control."

"That's been mentioned a few times," she assured him.

"Yeah, but I'm not sure you understand. A year ago, humans ruled the world. Now, there will be as many iliri leaders at this Alliance Meeting as human ones. Sal, you made that happen by standing up and daring them to pull you back down. Unav is following your lead. Viraenova has left their borders. This is a big fucking deal, and if you play it right, you could rule the world."

"No," she said, waving him off. "I do not *want* the iliri to rule the world. That would only swing the pendulum the other way. I want us to finally be equal. Not better, Rais. Just equal, even if we are different. I want the grauori to have just as many rights. I want us to bicker about policy and politics, not the number of teeth in our mouths or how many legs we use to walk. It's too easy to go too far, and Tyr keeps saying this is the Age of the Iliri, but that's wrong. This should be the Age of Equality. I don't need to subjugate you as a human to have my own rights as an iliri."

"And that's why I'm telling you this," he assured her. "You're not done, Sal. This, what we're doing right now at this Alliance Meeting? It's what's going to set the tone for the next generation. Get it right. That doesn't mean backing down, and you're right, it also doesn't mean crushing us. You still need to make it clear that you're not *our* bitch, ok?"

She reached up to clasp his bicep. "Thank you, Rais. Will you help me? I'm sure you'll be in the room as a guard."

"I will," he promised, "and yeah, if that's what you want. I'm not about to betray my own country, but I know that you're the pivotal leader in all of this. If I see something, I'll point it out. Benefits of the link, right?"

"And it's why I wanted you to have one," she told him. "I think you can walk this tightrope with me. Finding that place where we're working together without betraying the interests of our own nations."

"Always, Sal." He stepped closer and lowered his voice. "The 112th will *never* stand across the line from the Blades."

"We'll stand together on it." She looked up into his eyes. "And thank you for Blaz."

"Thank you for taking care of him. How's his depression?"

"Not bad, actually." The conversation had just changed topics easily and she let it. "When he starts to feel like he's a burden, we know and can reassure him. Being cessivi, he can feel it, and I think that makes all the difference. He knows we're not filling him full of empty words and platitudes. He can honestly feel that we need him and want him around."

"Think that's why he's always liked iliri?" Rais asked.

She could only shrug. "Or maybe it's because we're so likable?"

He laughed and stepped back. "That's nothing but the truth, Sal."

"Oh," she said, remembering one last thing. "Um, you're invited to the wedding, too. Dress uniforms will be acceptable."

"What wedding?" Rais asked.

Sal couldn't help but grin. "Dom, Rayna, and Shift's. The three of them are getting married in a pretty lavish state wedding."

"Fuck, really?" Rais's smile matched hers. "That's amazing! An openly accepted marriage with more than two people?"

"The noble council isn't thrilled about it," Sal admitted, "but Rragri and I think it's a good idea. That means they've been outvoted. It's happening. It's also one more step to tie our nation together. Dom becomes my brother-in-law. His heir will be the father of Rragri's grandchildren. Rragri has claimed me as her cousin. Human, iliri, and grauori, the lines are starting to blur."

"And Anglia is ok with this?"

"Mostly," she admitted. "We are having some cultural confusion, but I'm in the process of making Peacekeepers to handle that as well."

"Shit, Sal," he breathed. "You keep this up and Anglia won't have three kingdoms. You'll have one, and a Parliament to lead them."

"Council," Sal corrected. "We don't want to have our leadership turn over as fast as the CFC. Iliri and grauori choose our leaders based on dominance, not popularity. Dom has a good idea for how to do something similar with humans."

"Should I ask what?"

Sal paused, trying to figure out how to explain it. The idea made sense in her head, but if they wanted it to work, they'd need to be able to convey the concept to the populace, and this was her chance to test it out. Next, she'd end up telling the alliance, and that could sway how the other nations voted.

"Each species will have representation on the council," Sal began. "The candidates for those leaders will be chosen by the other two species, making it clear who they are capable of working with. So, when I am ready to step down, the human and grauori leaders will name five iliri Kaisaes - probably less, since there aren't many of us - as candidates. The iliri will then choose who they believe in the most. Same thing for the grauori. With humans, it's slightly different. We'll pick the names that are put on the ballot, and yeah, the citizens are going to get to vote."

"Does this apply to Jarl?" he asked. "I honestly like that kid, and I think he'll be an amazing king."

"Chancellor," Sal corrected. "He doesn't want Anglia to be a monarchy anymore, and he's where we plan to start. He's the current heir to the throne, but once we have all the pieces in place, he intends to be the one to announce it and allow a vote. To make it clear that he doesn't want to *inherit* power, but rather to be granted it by his people with the blessing of all our species."

"That," Rais said, "sounds like the right way to go."

CHAPTER THIRTY-NINE

WHITE

That afternoon, Dom couldn't take it anymore. Between the two women from Unav, the four from the CFC, and the nobles trying to convince him that including Shift in his marriage was a bad idea - which was really only coming from Lord Arvo and Lord Aulis - he needed a break. So, inspired by the whining lords who felt a triple marriage made him look like less of a man, Dom decided he needed to get out of the Palace.

A thought warned Shift to meet him at the stable. Another explained to Rayna that she would need to translate for Rragri while they were gone. One more warned Ilija that no, he was not taking a guard with him. The Sergeant at Arms needed to manage the chaos taking over their home. Even better, Shift knew exactly which tailor Rayna had chosen to make her dress.

So the pair headed there. Alone. Without the trappings of his office, hardly anyone recognized the King outside the Palace. The few who did were all soldiers stationed around the city, but they didn't give him away. A few nodded in greeting, but that was all. For Dom, that was the highest praise. The men didn't think he needed to be babysat anymore. They knew he could handle himself, and Shift was better than most of his bodyguards, so they were finally allowed a little privacy.

When they reached the tailor's shop, the pair tied their horses to the rail out front and walked in. A tiny ceramic bell on the door tinkled, announcing their arrival. A moment later, the tailor stepped out from the back.

"How can I help you today?" she asked, smiling at him blankly.

"Came to order a pair of suits," Dom told her.

"I'm afraid I'm booked for the next week," the woman said. "I have an order that is going to require all of my attention, but if you're not in a hurry, I'd be happy to help."

Dom walked up to the counter she stood behind and leaned over it casually. "Madam Clendsy, correct? Believe it or not, you've already planned for these. My soon-to-be husband and I want to make sure our attire matches our wife's."

The change in the woman's face was impressive. Her eyes went round and wide. Her lips parted and a breath rushed out. Mentioning his future husband made it clear that this was no ordinary wedding, giving away exactly who stood before her. The tailor stood a little straighter as the implications hit her, and her eyes jumped to the top of his head.

"Sire?" she asked.

"Dom," he assured her. "I'm not kinging right now, and my dernor doesn't always wear black."

"Yeah I do," Shift said. "At least a little."

"Oh my," the tailor breathed. "I'm so sorry I didn't recognize you!"

Dom just gestured to his worn brown pants and comfortable white shirt. "Think it might be the clothes?"

"Or the lack of a crown?" Shift teased.

"Probably the lack of an armed escort," Dom told her. "It's ok, Madam Clendsy. You're not required to know my face on sight. Especially when I've been gone for over a year."

"We kinda had to sneak out," Shift told her. "With all the allied diplomats showing up, the Palace is a madhouse."

"I can imagine," the woman said. "Sire, you know I can't tell you what she's wearing, right?"

"I know her colors are green, white, and silver," Dom assured her. "I believe that you can make sure our attire compliments hers without detracting from it."

"Oh, I'm not sure you'll be able to detract from what she has planned," the tailor said. "But yes, I can work with it. Do you have a style you prefer?"

Shift flopped his elbows down on the counter. "Nothing too foppish. I'm not a noble, and I won't pretend to be. I want to wear black somewhere in this, and Dom will want white in its place. I'm thinking well-fitted pants with a double-breasted coat."

"Cravats," Dom added. "Designed to match her veil or dress."

"Do you both want to wear the same color?" she asked.

Shift turned to look at Dom. "If you wear green, you'll stand out more, and you should as the King."

"No," Dom said. "You are not some add-on in this marriage. You're my best friend, Shift. I want the world to see you as my equal. Ray's the thing that binds us together, but we can't let human men think that means we're not on the same page." He looked over at the tailor. "What do you suggest?"

"I think you should both wear green," she told them. "Sire, you need to incorporate his black somewhere, and he should have your white, but in reverse. I can easily have buttons, belts, and boots made to work. I'm thinking black and white boots, but alternate the colors. So where yours will feature white with black accents, his will be the opposite."

"Two-toned boots?" Shift asked.

She nodded. "I've seen the style with horsemen. Usually it's a lighter leather paired with darker, but I think you can pull off the stark colors for your wedding."

"I actually like it," Shift said.

"And of *course* it's green," Dom said.

"But the weather won't be suitable for heavy coats," Madam Clendsy went on. "The Consort said this will be held within the month, and you'd both swelter in heavy layers. Since it appears neither of you care to prove your worth with cloth, what do you think about a vest instead of a jacket? Maybe a shirt similar to what the King is wearing now beneath it?"

Both men turned to look at each other. Dom tried to imagine what Shift would look like wearing that, and he thought it would be nice. The green wouldn't be overpowering with the paler shirt underneath. For a moment he contemplated putting Shift in a black shirt and him in a white, but that would make them look too dissimilar for his tastes.

"Maybe silver shirts for both of us?" he asked the tailor. "Since green and silver are the Anglian colors."

"With white cravats," she suggested. "I think I can trim the edges of his in black to keep it subtle, sire. Yours could be either green - which I think would look best - or white. Alternating leather colors, and you'd look like a matched set without being identical."

"I like it," Shift said. "No, I love the idea that I'm not going to be dressed up like some token crossbred to stand pretty. If I'm getting married, I want it to be something that feels good, and sweating my balls off wouldn't."

"Shift!" Dom hissed, flicking his eyes over to the woman.

"Sorry," Shift muttered.

She waved him down. "I promise that I've heard worse. From your Consort, I believe. That woman, so you both know, is amazing. She's going to be an exceptional Queen. Not necessarily an easy one, but once the people get over their shock of you both marrying each other, I think they'll see it too."

"Thank you," Dom said. "And I assume she arranged for you to bill the Palace for her dress?"

"Um..." Madam Clendsy looked between them. "Actually, her dress was paid for by the Kaeen of Viraenova. So that it would fill the spot of something given. She'll still need something borrowed, something broken, and something whole."

"Really?" Shift asked. "Dom, this entire wedding thing just got complicated. What the fuck would work for 'something broken?'"

Madam Clendsy pointed toward the front of the store, her finger aimed at a sign across the street. "That's the jeweler. I suggest you talk to him, because a necklace is the traditional item used to fill that role, but..." And she lowered her voice conspiratorially. "She specifically said she wanted her throat bare. Sounded like she had a reason, too. Try a bracelet."

"Actually," Dom said, knowing that Rayna wanted her scars to be the only thing adorning her neck, "I have a better idea. Madam Clendsy, we will be right back. I want to get this started, and I have a funny feeling you already know which fabrics we're going to need."

"Just need your measurements," she assured them.

"Perfect," Dom said. "Shift, let's see if this jeweler can make miracles."

And he headed toward the door, leaving Shift to hurry after him. Yet, the moment they were in the street, Shift grabbed Dom's arm and pulled him to a halt beside their horses.

"Dom," he said, "what are you doing?"

He grabbed both of Shift's arms and looked right into his face. "We are going to get our mate the last things on the traditional list. Something broken and something whole. I have a feeling that either the Devil Dogs or the Blades will handle something borrowed. Fuck, maybe even the Shields, I'm not sure."

"No," Shift said. "I mean all of this. You're just running around like this is the most important thing ever, and..." He paused to let out a sigh. "Iliri don't get married, Dom. I know it happens, and I've heard enough to understand, but a lot of these traditions? I don't understand them! I also don't really know where I fit in."

"Right beside me," Dom assured him. "Man, I love you like the brother I never had, ok? Like Ilija, but you don't blush when I'm crass, and you're always willing to talk shit with me. Ilija's great, but he's kinda a prude."

"He is," Shift agreed.

"But he's my brother-in-law, and you really are my best friend. I dunno, like the partner in crime kind of soulmate. I just feel like I don't have to hold back with you, and you don't give a shit if there's a crown on my head or a title before my name. You make me feel like you honestly respect me for more than the fact that my father fucked my mother, and I like it. So, as far as I care, you are the one man who will *never* need to bow before me."

"Only because Sal and Rragri are women?" Shift teased.

"Yeah, actually. And I think the positions of Kaisae and Orassae always will be. But look, this jeweler? I want him to make a sheath for that steel dagger you're going to give Ray. Something whole, right? And we're going to decorate it with pieces of all of our symbols. Like a puzzle. Devil Dogs, Lightning Brigade, Black Blades, Verdant Shields, the 112th Mounted. All of the people who've made Rayna the woman we fell in love with. She's made it clear *that's* what she wants to honor, so let's fucking honor it?"

"I can't afford all of this," Shift said.

"You're about to be my fucking *husband*," Dom said. "That means every single thing I own is yours, Kayden. My name is the least of it. The treasury, my Palace, our wife? It's all yours, man. I don't give a fuck that once, long ago, you were a poor iliri 'scrubber' living in some slum in a town that didn't want you. That's their loss. Here, in Anglia? You are a Black-fucking-Blade. You are the Kaisae's brother, a war hero, and a miraculous healer. Stop thinking about all the things you shouldn't be allowed to do, and help me show the rest of this world what happens when the boot is taken away from your neck. Help Anglia embrace your species as our pride and joy, because *that* is why I'm so fucking worried about this wedding."

"Can we arrange the puzzle pieces in a specific symbol?" Shift asked.

Dom's eyes narrowed at the change of subject. "Sure. I suppose you have something in mind?"

"Home," Shift told him, glancing away. "I want Rayna to know that the two of you are what finally made me feel like I have one."

Dom stepped into him and wrapped his dernor in a smothering hug. "Yeah, we can do that. If that's what it means to you..." Dom paused, feeling his throat tense. He had to step back and clear his throat, nodding to show he wasn't done. "You really think that?"

"Yeah," Shift said. "The Blades was the first home I ever knew, but being with you and Ray? It's... better."

"It really is," Dom agreed. "And yeah, I think home is the perfect symbol for this. I think the two of you are the only home I'll ever need. The rest of this mess just gets in the way."

Shift canted his head toward the jeweler's shop. "Then let's make our *wife* something she can actually use. Something a hell of a lot better than jewelry, because Rayna doesn't need anything else to make her beautiful."

"No, she doesn't," Dom agreed. "And I need to remember to have you added to the expense authorization list."

"I'll never use it," Shift told him.

"Don't care," Dom said. "I just want to make it very clear to the rest of the world that I really am marrying you as much as her. This thing between us? It's a commitment, and I know it. It's not simply convenient, Shift, and I'm not doing this so I can keep Ray. I'm marrying *you* because I want to. Because I kinda need every person in my country to understand that when I accepted Rayna having two mates, this is what that means. For me, nothing is changing. For Anglia, everything is."

"Then we'd better get it right," Shift said under his breath.

"I'm going to make sure of it," Dom swore. "And you're going to help me."

CHAPTER FORTY

PURPLE

When Dom snuck out of the Palace, Sal told her mates they could go back home. Tseri would be there soon enough, and the CFC Representatives were distracted with Rragri and the Unavi senators. She wasn't needed for the political side of things, but she did want to check over the Peacekeepers. Plus, with everyone arriving, that meant Dom's wedding would need to happen sooner rather than later, and Inessi hadn't yet found the right words to work in a human ceremony.

So when they approached the courtyard that protected the great entrance to Arhhawen, Jase decided to head up the hill toward the school. His amma should be done with classes soon - if she wasn't already - and he could help her look for exactly what Dom needed. Zep offered to go with him, but Jase waved him away. They weren't in danger anymore. Besides, the idea of a few minutes alone with his amma sounded nearly nostalgic.

So instead, Zep offered to put his horse up. There wasn't a place to keep a mount up there, but it was a short walk. After passing over the reins, Jase began to make the hike. In truth, it was nice. Within minutes, Arhhawen was far enough away that the sounds began to fade. All around him was nothing but the rustling of the trees and the small sounds of wild animals.

This was his idea of peace. Uninhabited land where iliri could roam without needing a reason. Yes, he loved the fact that their city felt like a den, but hunting was a part of him. Jase had grown up tracking dogs and guards in the streets. Now he had more options, but he didn't need them to survive. Life in Anglia was easy. Not necessarily simple, but that was ok. He liked having something to keep his mind engaged, and Sal was more than willing to put him to work.

Like this. She was sure there had to be some historical ceremony for the iliri. They'd been living among humans for thousands of years now. In all that time, their species would've picked up some of the customs just to fit in, if nothing else. It didn't matter that choosing a mate was a thing done between those involved with little to no ceremony. Humans would want a formal ritual to make it clear which groups belonged together. Since Jase knew more about the history of their species than anyone besides his own amma, Sal had asked him to help.

She didn't do that as much anymore. Partly because she finally understood that he'd always be there for her. Some of it was proof of how far she'd come since the first time he'd seen her. The meek and obedient slave was gone, replaced with a woman who made everyone around her take notice. *His* woman. Theirs, too, because his fellow mates had just as much of a claim to her as he did. Being the first mate didn't make him more important or mean that she loved him more. It simply gave him more responsibility to take care of her.

When he finally reached the school, Jase headed inside and up the closest set of stairs. From the sounds, classes were still in session. The calm and monotonous voice of Narnx was audible. On the next level, he heard Molis explaining that colors could be blended to create more complicated emotions, but the reader might not interpret them the same. Then, on the third floor, he found the dormitory wing. At the very end was a much larger suite that Inessi had claimed as her own.

Most of the teachers and professors walked back to Arhhawen every night and up to the academy every morning. Only Inessi and

Molis were living there right now, but soon there would be more. As the school shifted from teaching iliri children to including more complicated courses for adults to research, it was even possible that they'd need another building, but not yet.

When Jase reached Inessi's room, he rapped his knuckles on the door and stepped inside. He didn't actually expect his amma to be there, but the sound of movement proved he was wrong. The snarl that followed was clearly his amma's, although there was something else. Jase pulled in a long, deep breath to be sure, but there was no mistaking the smell of sex and the man she'd been with.

"Amma?" he asked.

"Jassant!" she hissed, coming out of her room a moment later. "Ya scared me."

Her hair was disheveled and her shirt was askew. Jase paused, tilting his head slightly to be sure, and listened to someone else scrambling in her room. He turned his eyes to Inessi.

"Ya know I can smell that, yeh?"

"It is none of yer business," she snapped just as the man she'd been sharing her bed with stepped around the corner.

Ran Sturmgren paused at the sight of Jase. "Is there a problem at the Palace?" he asked.

"Do ya think ya can fuck my amma like she is some human?" he snarled back. "Do ya na realize that I can smell it, and so can ever' child who comes in?"

"Oh?" Ran asked as he stepped closer, his eyes holding Jase's. "Do you think they don't understand the difference between lannar and rornnar?"

"Do ya?"

"I do, and I know it is not your place," Ran said, his voice as close as a human could get to a growl.

"Jassant," Inessi warned.

"This is na about ya," Jase told her.

"Then what is it about?" She demanded.

Jase smiled cruelly, his sharp teeth visible. "It is about seeing if this man is strong enough ta be more than a toy. Do I scare ya, Ran?

Because yer relationship with my cessivi is na the same as fuckin' my amma."

"No, it's not," Ran assured him, taking another step closer. "Sal is my daughter, and there is nothing you can do to change that. Inessi? Yeah, you can convince her I'm too much trouble. You can make me miserable for wanting to see her. You also know better, Jase. *You* showed me that no matter how feral you look on the outside, that mind of yours is always going. Being lethal is not the same as feral, and I won't fight you."

"I could kill ya," Jase warned him.

"You could," Ran agreed, "but you won't. It would hurt the two people you care about most. Jase, protecting someone isn't just about fighting for them. Sometimes, it's also about not fighting." And he took the last step, putting himself within Jase's reach. "It's not your decision who she chooses. It's mine whether or not to accept, and for the first time in many years, I've found a place where I feel I belong, but if you want me to go, I will."

"Ya will na!" Inessi told him.

Ran just lifted his hand, begging her to wait. "My dear, this is between your son and myself, and he deserves the chance to say what's on his mind."

"Ya will na hurt her," Jase warned.

"It's never that simple," Ran said, his voice gentle this time. "You know that. Sometimes our best intentions still hurt. I don't ever want to, but I will, and I hope that you'll help me fix my mistakes."

"Then ya can na leave her!"

Ran reached out to clasp Jase's shoulder. "I promise I don't want to. I care about your amma a lot. She's an amazing woman."

Without asking, Jase pulled Ran's collar away from his neck, exposing the bite marks that had pierced his skin. "I will na say this again," he breathed. "If ya hurt her, I will make ya pay. If ya break her heart, I will cut yer flesh from yer body and feed it ta ya. If ya treat her like she is yer pet, I will rip your throat out with my own teeth. Do ya un'erstand me?"

"I do," Ran assured him. "Do you honestly think I will do that?"

Jase shifted his eyes over to his mother for a moment, then back, pleased to see that Ran had shifted his gaze to Jase's cheek. "I do na," he assured him, "but she does na have anyone else ta speak up fer her, so I have ta."

"Trust me, Jase, I thought about it a long time before I allowed Inessi to lure me into her bed. First, because I do not want to betray Sal, and I wasn't sure how she'd feel about this, but also because I think of you as my son, too. Ahnor, I am iliri. I live in Arhhawen. I have no intention of seeing anyone treated like a pet again. I care about Inessi a lot, but if you aren't ok with this, then I will get my things and leave this room, never to come back."

"Do ya love her?" Jase asked.

Ran smiled and offered his hand. "That's something I'll tell her before you."

Jase grabbed the man's palm and sighed in relief. "Ya will do."

"So will you, and *very* well. Just know that you're not the only one looking out for her anymore, ok? I promise I know how to swing a sword."

"Are ya her mate?" Jase asked.

"Na yet," Inessi said, answering before Ran could. "I wanted ta talk ta ya before I took another."

Releasing Ran's hand, he turned to smile at her. "He is strong and fair, and he is na scared of me anymore. Ask him, Amma. When ya are ready, I think he would make a good ahnor. I also am na sure I could make him submit."

Inessi smiled, her eyes jumping up to find Ran's. "He is strong. He is also kind. Jase, he makes me happy."

"And ya deserve that," Jase said, "I just did na expect ya ta be in bed while the classes are still going."

"It's the best time to not get caught," Ran said around a chuckle. "Inessi, dear? Your hair's a mess, and your shirt is crooked."

"I do na intend to have it on long," she assured him. Then she changed not only the subject but her tone. "What do ya want, Jassant?"

"Sal needs the ceremony. She said many of the allies are here, and they will need ta practice the words, so she wants ta make sure we have them."

Ran held up a finger and turned for the far side of the room. "For Dom's wedding? I've been helping her look through the histories."

"Ya have?" Jase asked.

Ran chuckled. "It's the best way to improve my reading, and it's a lot harder to learn a second language at my age. Ah, here it is."

He pulled a pad of paper off the shelf, tore off the top sheet and carried it back. When he passed it over, Jase scanned the words and decided that they would work perfectly. This was a public announcement that two different packs were joining into one. From the accents on the symbols, it was old, at least a few hundred years, but it would work. His mother had also changed the words to have a masculine edge to them.

"Is that what she needs?" Inessi asked.

"It is," he assured her. "This will bind the King ta our brother before all of Anglia. It is the first step."

"For what?" Ran asked, "Because that sounds like Sal has a plan."

Jase nodded. "She does na want there ta be three kingdoms under one nation. She wants one. A whole one that does na care about what we are, just who." He glanced over at his mother. "She wants ta slowly erase the lines between the species."

"But then iliri will go extinct!" Ran said. "If there's no difference in the cultures, humans will cross with iliri until your species is gone."

Inessi was shaking her head. "But na our culture."

"And the King is his mate's ahnor," Jase told them. "The lines are na so clear anymore. When Nya has her pups? It will na happen fast, but it will happen, so we need ta make sure it happens right."

"What's right?" Ran asked.

Jase shrugged. "That is why she keeps talking ta Tseri, because they do na seem ta care that the nuvani are na pure, and they have found a way ta make it work."

"And don't have the grauori," Ran pointed out.

"Which is why we will na be nuvani," Jase agreed. "We will be

Anglians, whatever that ends up being. Her goal is ta see it happen b'fore she dies."

Ran huffed once. "Sounds like my little girl. Sal's always aimed for the stars."

"And she will make it happen," Jase promised. "There is a reason she is na just the Kaisae of All Iliri."

"But of all *Anglia*," he agreed. "Can I help?"

"Ya already are," Jase assured him. "That ya are willin' ta be my amma's ahnor? It helps, and it will na go unnoticed." Jase smiled and took a step back. "Ya can finish now. I have what I need."

"Asshole," Ran called after him.

Jase paused to squeeze his mother's hand, and tossed one last sharp smile at Ran. Then he was gone, easing the door closed behind him, but his steps were a little too light. Ran was a good dava. The best he knew of, and he hadn't even flinched when Jase had challenged him. That meant he didn't just love Inessi, he would die for her. It was the kind of relationship they both deserved.

He couldn't wait to tell Sal.

CHAPTER FORTY-ONE

GOLD

S al snapped awake, trying to identify the sound that had pulled her from sleep. Beside her, Jase and Tyr lay perfectly still, but she knew they were awake. All of them were.

A moment later, the tap came again. This time, she recognized it for someone knocking on the door to their suite, but lightly. Almost as if whoever had to wake them knew better than to pound on the wood. At the edge of the bed, Kolt sighed, but he started moving. In one step, he grabbed his pants from the floor. The second shoved one leg in. The third, the other. Before he left the bedroom, the Taunor had his ass covered and was quickly tying the laces that would close the front.

"What?" he asked, pulling open the front door a little too hard.

The man's voice came back almost too soft for even Sal to hear. "Someone's pounding on the gates of Arhhawen," he whimpered. "They're humans. We're not sure if we should unlock the doors."

Beside her, Tyr leaned forward and crawled until he reached the end of the bed. And while it gave her a great view of his ass, she had no idea what he was up to, until he flung a very large grey shirt toward her.

"Put this on," he said. "Pretty sure that's one of the lookouts on the night watch."

Because Arhhawen didn't need men to stand outside and risk their lives. There was no need for a gate to secure the grounds. Sal's home was built into a mountain and guarded by two massive doors that it would take an army to break down. An army strong enough and fast enough to do it before the people inside destroyed them. So anyone banging to get in would probably have a very good reason, and this man would've seen them.

Sal quickly pulled the shirt over her head and scrambled off the end of the bed. Her mates were also moving, each one aiming for some piece of clothing they could locate. Clean, dirty - right now it didn't matter. And while Tyr's shirt was the wrong color, it covered her enough that she didn't need to wait. Sal marched toward the door and stepped around Kolt with her hand out.

"Show me who," she ordered.

The iliri male had his eyes on the ground, but he clasped her hand without hesitation. A moment later a memory slid gracefully into her mind. It was a woman pounding on the doors, but she wasn't alone. Behind her were ten others. Some men, some women, but they were all dressed for battle instead of politics, and yet the woman's face was familiar. So was the cable wound through her hair.

"That's the Chieftain of Escea," Sal told him. "Her name is Vilko. Warlord Vilko if you want to be fancy, but I promise she won't care. Open the doors, invite her in, and apologize for waiting too long. I'll be down as soon as I have clothes."

"Yes, Kaisae," the lookout breathed before turning to run toward the stairs.

"Vilko?" Jase asked, clearly having heard. "I did na think she was coming ta Arhhawen."

"Makes sense," Zep pointed out. "She came from the west and we're closer than Dorton. Anyone know the time?"

"0300 hours," Kolt said as he lifted a pair of black pants, then tossed them in a lazy arc at Sal.

She caught them and pulled them on. "Which means they didn't want to wait another day and were too far into the foothills to stop. I need a shirt that fits my body."

"But you look good in mine," Tyr said.

"She looks better in her own," Blaz teased.

"You wouldn't say that if it was your shirt she was wearing."

"Probably not." Blaz flashed a smile at Tyr. "But it's not mine, is it?"

"Hey," Tyr said, "You can give her the next one. Or maybe we should make her alternate every time she's lounging around the suite? You know, just so I'm not the only one getting her out of her clothes and into mine."

Zep just sighed, pretending to ignore them and failing. "Black ok, Sal? I mean, you have more of those than anything else."

"I honestly don't care," she assured him.

So when he held one out, she grabbed it, swapping out Tyr's massive grey thing for one of the stretchy black shirts the Blades had started wearing near the end of the war. It took less than ten minutes for them all to get dressed. Maybe two more to get their boots on, and none of them bothered with weapons. Sal's daggers were once again hanging on her wall in a decorative display that Kolt knew well. He could fetch both in an instant. The men's swords were the same. The only one whose weapons couldn't be easily reached was Jase, because he'd stored his daggers in a glass box to show the words carved on each blade.

But they wouldn't need them. If this was Vilko, then she wasn't here to pick a fight. If she tried, she wouldn't get very far, since Sal wasn't the only one being pulled from her bed. The rules for Arhhawen were that if anyone needed access at night, both the Kaisae and the Raewar would be asked, and that meant Arctic's mates would be there as well. Even in peacetime, the iliri would be protected, and Shade was the best weapon on the continent.

Thankfully, it didn't take long to get from their room to the main entrance. The stairs ended at the side, along the main wall. Sal was in front, but all six of her men were right behind her, and there, in the middle of the open area, was Vilko, grinning at the Kaisae like she'd just found a long-lost friend.

"Sal!" Vilko said, striding over with her arms open for a hug.

Confused at the unexpected familiarity, Sal hugged back. "Do you know what time it is?" she asked.

"Not exactly," Vilko admitted, "but I had a feeling this place had better beds than the mountains out there."

"Up there," Sal told her. "Because you're kinda standing inside one."

"The whole place?" Vilko asked.

The answer came from across the room as Arctic reached the ground floor. "The whole place," he said. "It's a den, Chieftain. A very large, very nice, and very comfortable one."

"Ah, the Raewar," she said, turning to offer him her hand. "I was told good things about you. And I should assume that the woman scowling at me is the monster I've heard so much about?"

"My mate," Arctic said. "Her name is Shaden. The man beside her is Ghost, and he's the reason why so many of your warriors lost their courage."

"Amazing," Vilko said before turning to gesture at the small tribe with her. "And these are my men. Two are women, but they're still my men."

"I actually understand that," Sal assured her. "Just like Shade is one of mine. Are the rest outside?"

"Rest?" Vilko asked. "No, I only brought my main guards. This is a political meeting isn't it? I didn't want to scare the other countries away."

Blaz scrubbed at his face. "So you know, most of them brought more men than you."

"Most of them *need* more men than me," Vilko reminded him. "The only nation I'm worried about is Anglia, and I honestly believe it's the one I can trust most." She tipped her head at Sal. "Thank you for giving us back our country."

"I never wanted it in the first place," Sal assured her. "I also expected the fight to be a lot harder, to be honest." But at the same time, she thought to Gage, *Can you get some rooms for these people? Preferably not on the same street as Tseri.*

On it, Gage promised, but he didn't move. Then again, he didn't need to.

Vilko didn't even notice the exchange. "Sal," she said before pausing. "Is it rude to call you Sal instead of Kaisae?"

"I prefer it, actually," Sal told her.

"Good," Vilko said. "Makes me feel more like I'm talking to a friend than an enemy. The truth is that I'd been told to let you win."

"And who tells the Chieftain of Escea to do *anything?*" Sal asked.

"One of those slaves you hauled up here. People, I suppose, although I may slip a few more times. Not because I don't want the iliri to have freedom, but the word is a habit, you understand."

Maybe it was because Sal had just woken up, hadn't gotten a whole night of sleep, or lacked enough caffeine to function properly, but she felt like she couldn't keep up. Vilko wasn't her friend - or at least she never had been before. And yet, the woman acted as if they were. She'd been overly amiable about their challenge in Escea, too, all but throwing the fight so Sal could win. It didn't make sense, but she also didn't smell like lies.

"The words slaves, scrubbers, and beasts might get you growled at here," Sal warned. "I'm sure you can understand that many of us are a little bitter about being owned by humans for so long. We're not pets, after all."

"No," Vilko agreed. "You're solutions, which is what made you so valuable to us. It was an iliri slave who predicted that you would come. He told me if I believed in hope, then she would save us. Another slave, days later, mentioned that the Kaisae was supposed to smell like hope. Not to me, but it got back to me. Considering that we've known about your gifts for a long time, it didn't take much to realize that you were our answer to breaking the agreement with the Emperor without suffering the repercussions. My husband made that deal, and I thought it was a bad one back then."

"The husband who wore the title of Vilko before you?" Sal asked.

She nodded once. "The one that you killed so easily. Yes, the same man. No, I don't blame you. We were at war, right? I think using you made up for it. Letting you defeat me on the Chieftain's Plains was the only way for us to avoid the repercussions of that alliance. Since you broke the treaty, we can't be held responsible. Since you legally took control of our government, we were beholden to follow your directions. And most importantly, since you killed that disgusting old man, Escea is once again welcome at the alliance table. So..." She thrust out her hand. "Here's to alliances and friends. Two neighboring nations who I hear think a *lot* alike."

Sal knew Vilko meant the iliri and the Escean tribal mentality. Jurij had made Sal realize just how similar their cultures were. Both were based on the idea of strength and dominance, but iliri focused more on protection and Escea was centered around personal pride. Still, it meant fewer offenses when one of Vilko's men was growled at, or when one of the warriors stared down an iliri.

Then Arctic broke in. "Chieftain, should we assume that you and your men will be staying in Arhhawen for the duration of this Alliance Meeting?"

"Yes," Vilko said, "I believe we will. I'm willing to bet that Viraenova will be here as well, but *not* the Conglomerate, am I right?"

"You are," Arctic assured her.

"Let's just say that I'm not sure putting Escea and the Conglomerate too close together would be a wise idea. We kinda destroyed their borders and were well into the process of defeating their 'unbeatable' army before Anglia stopped us."

Arctic chuckled. "Well, I hope you'll mention that when it comes to reparations. It seems the CFC isn't happy with Anglia either."

"The CFC isn't happy with much," Vilko told them. "They want to stand on their stages and scream that they, and only they, can solve everything, but they forget that doing things differently does not mean we're doing them wrong. Escea is a warring nation. Our country's government was built on the idea of being ruled by the strongest among us. Are the iliri really that different? The rest of Anglia?"

"No," Shade said from where she stood on the stairs. "But that didn't give you the right to own people."

"We owned human slaves too, girl," Vilko told her.

"Doesn't make it better," Shade told her. "You are strong. That means your job is to fight for those who can't fight for themselves. It doesn't make you weak to have a cause; it makes you *just*."

Vilko smiled at her. "Shall I assume you'll be the next Kaisae?"

"No," Shade said. "I may be the most destructive iliri on the continent, but that doesn't mean I'm the strongest. I *want* to make people pay for what they've done. I'm too weak to accept that they can be taught. Sal isn't. Lyzzi won't be. That's why our leaders smell like hope, Vilko. It's because that's the strongest thing in the world."

Vilko looked back at Sal. "Tell me, Kaisae, do you think I can be taught?"

"I think you're begging for me to try," Sal realized.

The leader of Escea nodded. "I am, because your weapon over there is exactly right. We came to Arhhawen because I need to learn how to do something besides kill. I need to learn how to lead, and I think you're exactly the kind of person who can show me. After all, you are the only leader of Escea to ever defeat a continental power."

Arctic turned to look at her guardsmen quickly, his eyes scanning them. "Which is why you only brought the people you trust? Everyone here is from the province of Vilko, and I'm willing to bet they're not just your guards, but also your inner circle. You didn't want the other Warlords to see this as a weakness."

"Exactly, Raewar. And I intend for the Kaisae and the Kaeen to become my dear, close friends. Close enough that I can prove to Escea that sometimes it makes more sense to talk than to fight."

"Then you should include the Orassae and the Queen in that as well," Sal said. "Because the King's about to get married, and the woman he fell for is another one of us."

"Us," Vilko repeated. "The handful of women strong enough to rule when no one else wanted us to. I think that's the kind of crowd I'd like to be a part of."

"Me too," Sal agreed. "Enough that I'll help you on one condition."

"And that is?"

Sal smiled. "I need Escea to agree to recognize the iliri and grauori as sentient and sovereign species, equal to humans in all things."

"Then I will do that," Vilko promised. "And I'll only add one condition to it. That the friendship between us is honest. Sal, I'm fucking tired of war, and my nation can't afford to be isolated anymore. Escea needs a friend, and our best chance? Anglia."

"Then welcome to Arhhawen, my friend," Sal told her. "I think your rooms should be ready."

CHAPTER FORTY-TWO

BROWN

*A*fter that, Vilko honestly tried to be the friend she claimed. The woman was a bit strange, but also whimsical, determined, and more than willing to laugh. Oddly enough, Tseri adored her. When the allied leaders went to Dorton for the formal dinners and events, the Orassae became intrigued by her. Rayna felt she could become a kindred soul.

Even better, Vilko was more than willing to discuss the past. She wanted to learn from it, after all, and she was determined to make Escea into one of the strongest nations on the continent. Not by mimicking what other countries had done, but by improving on it the same way Sal had. She felt the right answers would be found only when they looked outside the proverbial box.

The Conglomerate representatives were initially wary of her, and for good reason. Escea had nearly decimated the CFC's army. Unav refused to be around the Chieftain alone, but Vilko made a point to apologize to both of the senators for her nation's part in the war. She explained that she'd been against working with Terric from the start, and how she hoped an alliance with Unav would build a bond between their two nations that would prevent anything like this from ever happening again.

Over the next week, the Unavi senators began to relax around her. They also fawned over Sal, making it clear where their political interest lay. Even Dom commented on it, pointing out that Sal seemed to be the new world leader, but he said it with pride. Unfortunately, Rragri didn't spend much time at the social activities, preferring to hover over Nya since the babies *still* weren't born.

Eventually, the Justices of Myrosica arrived, being the last nation to send representation. It had been expected, but the men still apologized for delaying such an important event. To celebrate it, Dom held another formal dinner at the Dorton Palace, then announced that the Alliance meeting and agreements for the new Conventions of War would start the following morning, with his own wedding to be held once the agreements had been completed.

Notices were sent out through the city of Dorton, and the amphitheater where the meeting would take place was open for the public to sit in and observe. The Conglomerate wasn't sure that would be a good idea, but Dom insisted that a free nation should not hide its activities behind closed doors. Unav agreed with him, and the matter was settled quickly.

So, on the morning of the first day of talks, the streets were crowded and the building was overflowing. Sal and Arctic would be there to represent the iliri of Anglia. Rragri had her Vargwar, Harrgra, to translate her thoughts into Glish. And Dom decided that Rayna would serve as his advisor, just to keep things even. Most of the allies were doing the same, including experts in their party to be consulted with as needed. Only the actual leaders would be allowed a seat at the table, but instead of guards waiting behind them, the floor would be filled with those who had the knowledge to make the process smoother.

Dom had also selected a venue outside the Palace. Each group made their way there on their own, giving the nations a chance to have a little pomp and ceremony. For Sal, that meant riding in with her pack around her - who would end up waiting in the stands with the other viewers. That the Black Blades included both humans and grauori didn't go unnoticed, and the Anglians cheered her loudly the whole way there.

The Devil Dogs and Dark Heart were also going, although they didn't ride with the main procession. Because of that, they offered to escort the kids. Roo's boys were cradled in the arms of Ryek and Meia. Rhyx and Raast trotted along beside their horses. Lasryn and Lyzzi shared the lazy Viraenovan warhorse given by Tseri, but the mare was led by Pig. Behind them came the rest of the people in Arhhawen who wanted to witness the event, including Kinetry, holding Valri on his horse before him.

When they finally reached the building, they were met by the grooms and stable help from Dorton. The Blades dismounted as one, all of them wearing their most formal uniforms to make a statement, and marched inside. Dom and his noble council came next, followed shortly after by Rragri and her own pack. From there, the other nations began to blur together, and the seating quickly filled.

Rragri caught Sal just before she headed down the stairs to the floor of the amphitheater. *The healer said that Nya's pups are ready. They could be born at any time.*

"That's great," Sal told her. "Isn't it?"

It is, Rragri agreed. *But she and Jarl want to wait until she experiences labor. They're worried that inducing birth early could harm these pups, since they're different. No one really knows what they will need.*

"If she needs help, both Blaz and Raast are willing to head over there."

Rragri nodded. *Thank you, Sal. I'm so worried about my daughter. Enough that I'm not sure what help I will be here today. Can you make sure I'm paying attention?*

"I'll try," Sal assured her. Then added in her mind, *And I'm sure that Dom and I won't care if Harrgra adds words to your thoughts, or words instead of your thoughts. He's your dernor. No one will know the difference between him speaking for you or speaking his own mind.*

Then I will also ask him to help, she decided. *Because we need them to accept us legally. If the human nations refuse to acknowledge our species as equal to theirs, then another war will happen.*

Then say that, Sal told her. *Let us make it clear that we will not suffer any more for human arrogance. All we want is the right to rule our own countries and for our people to live in freedom.*

Rragri nodded in agreement and turned for the stairs, but Sal cast one last look over the crowd. All around her, people were hugging and greeting old friends. Some of them had fought together, but not all. Kinetry was talking with the Viraenovan lookout, Exton, and his mate. A pair of grauori were sitting beside men from the 112th Mounted. Then there was a group of Anglian soldiers laughing with a trio of iliri wearing Unavi colors. It seemed this had become as much a reunion as a diplomatic ordeal.

Only a few feet away, she saw Pig. He hovered over Keeya, blocking her round belly from being bumped, but Sal didn't recognize the humans they were talking to. The man seemed angry, though. Whatever he was saying was hard enough to make spittle fly from his lips, and the woman - who appeared to be his wife - cowered behind him. Belatedly, Sal remembered that Keeya's parents were supposed to be here. Stretching her short legs, she made her way over, hoping to diffuse the situation, but Pig seemed to have it well underhand.

"*Mister* Tikva," he said, "you will *not* speak to her that way!"

"She is *my* daughter, and her loose morals have her pregnant with a bastard yet *again!*" The man hissed. "Although I'm sure she didn't tell you about that disgrace. My whore of a child will spread her legs for any man she finds, or so it seems."

"Dad, he's my mate," Keeya insisted.

"Mate? You make yourself sound like a beast," the woman - clearly her mother - gasped.

"Am I a beast?" Sal asked as she moved to stand beside Keeya. "Think before you answer that."

"Kaisae," the man breathed, but Sal ignored him.

"Keeya, are you ok? I wanted you to have the chance to see what you made possible, but you don't deserve to be harassed to do so."

"Sal, these are my parents. Can I introduce you to Farlim Tikva and Karine Tikva?"

"I hope it's a pleasure," Sal said, offering her hand to the man first. "You must be very proud of your daughter."

The man accepted her grip out of habit, but his eyes were narrowed in suspicion. "Proud? That she's with child and not married?"

"She has openly acknowledged Major Feofilakt Pigaris as her ahnor," Sal said. "They both also claim the nation of iliri, which means that's the equivalent to a human marriage. Although, I was referring to her actions, Mr. Tikva. Were you not aware that Keeya singlehandedly slayed Makiel Geirr, the former emperor of Terric, along with removing his entire line from succession? Sir, she *ended* the Terran War. Keeya Tikva is a hero."

"How?" her father demanded. "What could she have done that was so impressive? Unless she kept this *soldier* warm at night?"

Sal felt her ears flick back against her skull and she stepped closer. "Keeya is an elite soldier. She infiltrated the upper levels of the palace in Terric City, assassinated Makiel Geirr, his wife, and their son in her efforts to save the Sadava of the Iliri. Her husband, as you would call him, is not only my friend, but also my closest advisor." Then she leaned a little closer. "Let me make that even more clear. Your daughter, who you are so willing to disparage, is my sister, my friend, and the equivalent of a human noble. Their child will be raised beside the next Kaisae of Anglia, will learn to ride with my own sons and daughters, and will most likely hold the title of Kalargi after its father."

Pig glanced at her. *My official title is 'brother'?*

It's fitting, Sal pointed out.

I'll gladly take it, Pig assured her.

But Keeya's mom had just realized what Sal's words meant. "You're nobility?" she asked her daughter.

"The iliri don't really do those things, Mom," Keeya told her. "They also don't see anything wrong with a woman doing more than just getting married. Yeah, Dad, I'm pregnant again. Yes, Pig knows about the child you gave away to 'help me.' He also doesn't care. Iliri don't care about such things. He doesn't think I'm less because I can swing a sword and saddle a horse."

"I don't," Pig agreed. "Keeya is my mate, which means you have no control over her anymore. If you want to meet your grandchild one day, I suggest you change your thinking, and fast, because women rule in Arhhawen, Mr. Tikva. Your daughter made something of herself even when the rest of your country said it couldn't be done. She's just a woman, right? Well, so is the Kaisae. So is the Kaeen of Viraenova. So is the Orassae! And just like the King, I happen to like a woman willing to stand up for what she believes in."

Sal crossed her arms and smiled. "Did you know that when Keeya signed up for the military, they called her the little Sal? She's been compared to me more times than I can count."

"They did?" Keeya asked.

Pig chuckled. "Um, I may have started that, but Ilija thought it fit a little too well." He looked over at her father. "Yeah, the same Ilija you'd call Lord Valmere."

But Sal had a better idea for how to make their point. One thought was all it took and two more people headed over to prove Keeya's worth. The first arrived with a squeal of delight and hugs for both Sal and the girl. The second made Keeya's father blanch in awe.

"Sire," he breathed.

"Mr. Tikva," Dom said, pausing to smile at Keeya. "I honestly didn't expect to see you here," he told her.

Keeya rubbed at her belly. "I'm not an invalid, Dom, just pregnant."

"Keeya!" her father hissed, shocked that she'd talk to the King so casually.

Dom waved him down. "She's about to become family," he told the man. "And promise me you'll let Rayna play with the baby when it's here?"

"Of course!" Keeya promised. "I might even let you hold her."

"Her?" Dom asked. "So do you know, or are you guessing?"

"Healers can tell," Pig explained. "They say the child doesn't have a link, so it's not guaranteed, but they believe the baby is a girl. Like most humans, we have to wait until she gets here to be sure."

Rayna giggled. "Sounds like there's a little disappointment in the Pigaris household, huh?"

"No," Pig assured her. "I'd be just as thrilled either way. Naturally, we call it our Piglet."

"Oh, that's adorable," Rayna said. "I'm definitely using that."

The whole time, Keeya's parents stood silently, their eyes wide. Sal fought not to laugh, but she also understood. No one expected their child to talk so casually with the leaders of their country. Little did they realize just how close Keeya had become with all three of them.

"So," Sal said, looking at the Tikvas, "you know your King, Dom. The woman beside him is Rayna, his fiancée and soon to be Queen. Pig, here, was Rayna's commanding officer for many years. He leads the Devil Dogs."

"Like, *the* Devil Dogs?" Mrs. Tikva asked.

Pig nodded. "The same. Your daughter is one of my soldiers. We accepted her to replace the Queen when she became Dom's bodyguard and moved into the Verdant Shields."

"But I'm still a Dog," Rayna reminded him. "You can't get rid of me that easily. Guess that kinda makes Keeya my sister, huh?"

"I won't complain," Keeya teased.

"Good," Rayna said, "Because Lord Piet and Lady Tor wanted to know if you'd sit with them and explain what's going on." She looked up at Keeya's parents. "I'm sure they'd love to meet both of you."

"Both are women, Dad," Keeya told him. "So don't say anything stupid?"

"But we're common," her mother whispered, clearly unaware that Sal heard very well.

"I was a slave," Sal reminded her. "Where we start has no bearing on where we can end up. Be proud of your daughter. Very proud, because history is going to remember her name." Then she looked at Keeya. "If the trip back is too hard, you and Pig can stay in the Palace, ok? I have no doubt that Dom will find space for you, and it means less riding."

"I'll even offer a carriage," Dom said, but his words were for Pig.

"I'll take it," Pig said. "She's adamant that she's just fine, but I'm going to have a heart attack before my Piglet gets here."

Rayna just rolled her eyes. "She's the one doing the hard work, Pig. Now go sit, and please help Linella with the political stuff? She's linked now."

"Perfect," Pig said. "Mr. Tikva? Would you and your wife like to come with us?"

Sal watched as the group walked away, then sighed. "Thanks, Dom."

"Didn't do that for you, Sal. Finally, I can see what you tried to explain so long ago. We treat women like shit here, and I'm done with it. I figure that if we can liberate an entire species, then giving equal rights to a single gender should be easy, right?"

"It'll take longer," Rayna warned him.

Dom just laughed once. "Sounds like a challenge. After all, no one thought the iliri would be free within a year, and look at us?"

"Good point," Sal told him. "Now let's make that universal. I think it's time to get this meeting started."

"Then you can start it," Dom told her.

CHAPTER FORTY-THREE

GOLD

"*I* would like to call this meeting of the Continental Alliance of Nations to order," Sal said, standing at her place between Dom and Rragri. "This meeting was requested by the Parliament of the Conglomerate of Free Citizens, and seconded by Viraenova. Every known government on the northern continent of Ogun was invited. Most accepted, and are represented here. Namisa's government was still in the process of being reformed, but a temporary representative let us know that they would be proud to honor the agreements we make in their stead. Gallicor refused." She picked up the letter Gallicor had sent in response to their invitation, which Dom had brought. "They claim that, 'as a nomadic anarchy, it would be against our nation's policy to engage in politics of any sort.' They also go on to state 'we understand the need for an international agreement, but prefer to remain withdrawn from the process required to achieve such agreements. Gallicor understands that this does not absolve our people from the rules and regulations that will be decided in their absence.'"

Sal passed the letter to Dom, who handed it to Narnx as the representative of Terric. He scanned it quickly and passed it to Marin, who sat in as his advisor. From there, it moved down the line through Unav, to Escea, the Conglomerate, Viraenova, and finally to Myrosica.

"Now," Sal said, pitching her voice to carry, "are there any issues that need to be brought before the Alliance?"

Representative Anis stood. "There are, Kaisae. The Conglomerate of Free Citizens requests reparations for the acquisition of multiple units of elite trained soldiers, along with damages incurred while Anglia supposedly aided our nation."

Vilko shot to her feet. "Escea claims responsibility for that damage. Under the alliance negotiated by our former Chieftain, we were beholden to not only conquer the Conglomerate, but also to raid Fort Landing. We were unable to complete the task due to the Anglian armies. Reparations for the damage should be the responsibility of my country, Representative."

"And yet we cannot ask for reparations from a nation we had declared war upon," Anis pointed out.

Vilko smiled. "I know. That still doesn't make your allies responsible."

"And Anglia does not recognize any illegal acquisition of military units," Sal told her.

Justice Krex of Myrosica sighed. "Let us put the posturing aside," he said without standing. "Anis, you signed the law that allowed iliri to emigrate from your country. So did I. You were under no pressure, and Anglia didn't even call that vote. Viraenova did. The CFC is just upset that you pushed your men far enough that they stopped wanting to play. This isn't an international problem. It's a domestic one."

"And yet Anglia has left us understaffed and vulnerable. Escea has just admitted that they caused massive amounts of damage, and our military is currently under-qualified to protect our borders."

Tseri lifted her chin. "But there's no war, Representative. There's nothing to defend against."

One of the senators from Unav stood. "My country does not condone a strong military presence along our border. Especially not from a nation that has previously enslaved our citizens."

Grenso flicked a finger at her. "Senator? I'm afraid we have not been properly introduced. I'm Representative Grenso. May I get your name and the name of your fellow senator?"

"I am Telyra Dolrix, and my associate is Vinx Lymorae. We are the leaders of the Unavi Senate, which is comprised of five individuals chosen for each region. By Unavi traditions, we use our first names, Representative."

"Thank you, Senator Telyra," Grenso said.

Should we give the Conglomerate anything? Rragri asked. *We did take a lot of highly trained soldiers.*

Dom glanced over at her. *But Sal's right. We didn't steal them. We gave them a better option. I'm more worried about the precedent it would set to pay for the right of people to move.*

Dom has a point, Sal said, standing again. "Representatives of the Conglomerate?" she asked. "Do you honestly feel that a government is - or should be - responsible for the natural migration of the citizens? Do we honestly have the right to tell people where they can and cannot live?"

"We should," Sherin said, answering for the CFC. "That is why we have immigration policies."

Senator Vinx pushed to her feet. "I was under the impression that the CFC's policies were to prevent the escape of iliri, since your humans are typically allowed to relocate with minimal issues."

"Unless they are in the military," Tseri said, "often with sensitive information. You see, the Conglomerate hasn't yet realized that political secrets are no longer as easily secured. Their leadership does not have access to readers."

"Makes sense," Vinx said. "But do they not also allow humans a way to discharge from service? The iliri in their nation don't get that."

"Actually," Grenso said, "our laws have recently changed. Iliri volunteers are treated the same as humans. Our nation also has an iliri Representative in Parliament."

Tseri chuckled. "I wasn't sure you'd admit it on record, Representative Grenso."

"I'm proud of my species, Kaeen. And I'd like to ask if, for the sake of this discussion, your people would tolerate being referred to as iliri rather than nuvani?"

"We are iliri," she assured him. "Nuvani merely means the new iliri, referring to our crossbred ancestry. That makes most of the iliri 'nuvani' as well - with the exception of my son-in-law, the Kaisae, and a few others. It is merely a term to help clarify that we cannot boast the same diversity as our international brethren."

"So, does your argument mean that Viraenova would allow humans to enter your country now?" Jakin asked.

Tseri smiled. "It is under consideration. Our concern is not their species, but their habits. You see, Viraenova locked ourselves away from the rest of the world to escape slavery. Mainly by the Conglomerate. Currently, we have one of your elite units welcomed into our nation's capital to make sure that the inclusion of humans will not result in conquest by them."

"Which means you're being careful about it, correct?" Jakin pressed.

"We are," Tseri agreed.

"Then are you not restricting the movement of your people?"

"In," Tseri agreed, "not out. Plenty of nuvani have moved to Anglia over the years. The King himself is related to one, but distantly. Never have we trapped our people like livestock, hoarding them as a commodity. There's a difference between national security, Representatives, and ownership."

Justice Krex stood. "Kaisae, are you suggesting removal of the borders, or something different?"

"It is my opinion," Sal said, "that people should be allowed to live where they want. With that said, I understand the need for restrictions to limit criminals and dissenters from coming in to make things worse. I'm also not here to talk about immigration, because that is each country's own purview. I'm more concerned about emigration, because no one should be trapped in a country they feel restricts them."

"Is that why," Sherin asked, "Anglia took the Devil Dogs? Because they are not iliri. The entire unit is made up of humans. Dark Heart is the same. You claimed one of our best generals as well. Is that because you felt they were restricted by the Conglomerate?"

Dom pushed to his feet. "The Devil Dogs came to Anglia requesting asylum. Their situation is different because they were accused of treason for assisting iliri dissenters, Representatives. Because this unit was willing to help another escape persecution in your nation, they risked their lives. Yes, I accepted them, because Anglia wants more people like that."

"What about Dark Heart?" Anis asked.

Above, one man leaned over the railing, gesturing that he'd like to be addressed. It was Perin, and Sal pointed toward him. "Would you like to ask their commanding officer?"

So Anis turned to him. "Sir, your unit is human. What made you defect from the Conglomerate to join forces with Anglia?"

"Hate," Perin said. "Representative, I am not a politician, but a soldier, so forgive my lack of eloquence. The truth is that Dark Heart came up with the plan to defect on our own, without any of the Anglian leadership knowing about it until we were sworn in. You see, our unit is as close as family, and one of our members is a purebred. My first officer is married to an iliri woman. For her to be allowed to leave, but not him? I am mated to an iliri myself. Another member of my unit has a stepchild who claims iliri ancestry. You see, the lines between species is a blurred one, and it's hard to watch part of your family leave, knowing you cannot because of a war. We finished your war, Representative Anis. We just didn't come home to be accused of improper behavior with our allies."

"Then it seems," Anis said, "the Conglomerate is the only one losing here. We funded the education and training of these soldiers. We invested in the system that Anglia weakened by removing key figures. Anglia left us no choice but to accept their help, blackmailing our nation to get access to the people who could jump their country forward militarily."

"You're wrong." The words came out clear, in a male voice which had only a slight accent, but Rragri stood in her chair while her Vargwar delivered them. "Anglia's *military* advantage comes from my people. The strategic advantage came from the iliri. The Kaisae knew how to remake everything the Conglomerate has, and she'd already started with the Verdant Shields. These soldiers you're talking about? They left because they had no reason to stay. These people are not machines and they are not possessions. They are individuals who were drawn to the inclusion Anglia offers, rather than the elitism of the Conglomerate. We owe you nothing because they wanted out. We owe you nothing for securing your borders. In truth, the Conglomerate should be offering reparations to Anglia for every human, iliri, and grauori we lost assisting you."

Grenso calmly tapped the desk before him. "Then I suppose, by your reckoning, Orassae, that this is a wash? Our devastation was the price for your assistance?"

"No," Rragri said through her Vargwar. "Your devastation was the price of not stopping the Terran Empire sooner. The defections are the price of discrimination, which is why you lost these units. It is a price you only pay to yourself, both with the gains of your country's security, and the loss of your men. Anglia tried everything to help, even forming new elite units in the CFC to replace the ones who no longer wanted to be there."

Senator Telyra leaned back in her chair with a smug look. "That is a price you will keep paying as well, since Unav is also willing to accept defectors from your nation to rebuild the losses from our own. We do not care what species they are."

Tseri leaned over the table. "I think the Conglomerate has their answer. Viraenova feels that the loss is no fault of Anglia, and I would like to call a vote. Those who believe Anglia owes reparations to the Conglomerate of Free Citizens?"

Naturally, the Representatives all raised their hands, but no one else at the long table joined them.

"And those who feel the defection of Conglomerate soldiers within the accepted international law is allowed and means Anglia is not beholden to the country of origin?"

She lifted her hand, and a moment later others joined her. Everyone but the Representatives from the CFC. The Kaeen smiled. "Then it is settled. There is no debt, thus no need for reparations. The issue is dismissed."

Across the table, Grenso met Sal's eyes. *Well played, Kaisae. We had to get that in a legal record so it couldn't come up again. You and your friends made some very strong points. Hopefully, we can now set this behind us?*

So you knew you'd lose? Sal asked.

Three of us were hoping for it, he assured her. *Sherin could see both sides, and he's worried about the future of the CFC, so he dared to hope.*

Wrong hope, Sal pointed out.

Trust me, Kaisae, I know. I just hope you haven't used up all your political creativity, because next, the Unavi senators are going to ask for an expansion of their borders. Stuck between Terric and Escea on the eastern side, they suffered the worst in this war, but we're worried that granting their request will set a destructive precedent.

It would, Sal agreed. *Still, I think Narnx and Vilko can think on their toes. This time, it's their job to lay out their defense, but I should probably let you know that Escea is actively looking for allies in this new world of ours.*

Oh really? he asked. *Well, that is good to know. I hope you don't mind if I tell my associates?*

Not at all, Sal assured him. *That's actually why I mentioned it.*

Thank you, Sal, Grenso said, his mental voice filled with appreciation. *You are making this world of ours a better place, and I think everyone at this table knows it.*

I'm just doing my job, she assured him. *I'm leading my people. No one ever said that Kaisaes are only good for war.*

CHAPTER FORTY-FOUR

GREEN

*T*he next few hours were spent hashing out anything and everything. Mostly to get it on record, but a few minor grievances were handled. The best part, though, was when Narnx refused to accept sanctions against Terric for their part in the war. Clearly, the other nations now knew about his connection to Sal, and they'd expected him to have no loyalty at all to the place he'd been born. Instead, he'd argued that the ones responsible for the war were dead, and thus any penalties levied would only punish those who worked to stop the fighting.

So, after four hours at the negotiation table, no borders had moved. No governments were toppled. While everyone acknowledged that the Terran War had been horrendous, the ones responsible for it had paid their price and there was nothing else to do but move on. The only changes the alliance made were a few unpaid debts being acknowledged.

Myrosica claimed the Anglian government owed for medical aid. Dom agreed to pay the bill in full. Unav claimed Viraenova had been outfitted from the national armory and owed the country for the armor and weapons that were never returned. Tseri agreed to the cost. The last one was Vilko saying that Terric owed Escea exactly three crates of steel as per the treaty they'd signed with the former emperor. Narnx calmly told the Chieftain that she was welcome to collect it from the tower Makiel had created in the middle of Terric City, but that he had no idea how to section it to give her a fair share.

Then, with all the grievances aired, decided, and recorded, the first day of the Alliance Meeting came to a rather boring and inconclusive ending. Dom announced a formal dinner at the Dorton Palace the next evening, and the meeting was closed. Like most political situations, the entire thing was boring, but they'd gone through it to set the precedent for future generations. Now, they got a few days off to mingle with each other and prepare their positions for the big stuff: acknowledging iliri and grauori as equal persons, then correcting the conventions of war to accommodate modern warfare techniques. In truth, those two things were the real reason they were all here.

As the crowd began to file out of the building, the friends and family of the politicians made their way onto the floor. Among those were both Sal and Arctic's mates. Ghost greeted his ahnor with a smile and a slap on the back, which Sal saw even as her own mates surrounded her.

"You make it look like he worked hard," she teased, since Arctic had barely gotten the chance to say anything at all.

Ghost shrugged. "He had to sit there, stay out of your way, and not fall asleep. Not as easy as you think, Sal."

"I'll need him again next time, so he had to be here today," she explained. "I promise that I do not want to deal with definitions of torture with three species and have no one to find the parts I miss."

"I've been working on it," Arctic promised. "In truth, I'm also not offended at all to let you do the heavy lifting. I'm done being a soldier, Sal. I just want to retire with my family and worry about the boring little things."

"Like kids," Ghost fake-whispered.

Sal flicked an ear to Shade. "Any news?"

"I see the healer in a few more days," she said. "I'm just scared they'll say no, or that I can't have children."

"The pack has children," Sal reminded her.

"It's not the same," Shade told her. "I want theirs! I want to worry about decorating the nursery and changing diapers. I want..."

"To be normal," Arctic finished for her. "Not to be a weapon, a force of fear, or a strategist. Sal, the three of us aren't meant for war. We may be predators, but our dream is to learn new recipes, argue over the color of the curtains, and fret over our kids. We just want the mythical life that everyone else takes for granted and which we never thought was possible."

Blaz took a step closer. "Um, I may not be an expert in maternity, but I've been told I have a strong skill. If you want..."

Shade thrust her hand forward. "Please tell me I'm pregnant. I know I could still lose it, and that I shouldn't get my hopes up for months yet, but I just want to know if it worked."

"Here?" he asked.

"Yes!" Shade hissed. "I can't think about anything else. I've been second-guessing every possible symptom, even though it's too early to have any. I just want to know."

With dozens of people milling around them, the leaders of nations starting to make their way out, and her closest friends watching, Blaz gently took her hand and closed his eyes. It was so calm. Such a casual thing to do, but only a few moments later, Blaz sucked in a breath and his eyes went wide.

"You're pregnant," he assured her. "Shade, there's a glow of life in you that's impossible to miss."

"Twins?" Ghost asked.

Blaz shook his head. "I can't tell that yet. I can say that there's an alien life in her. I mean another life. Definitely a baby."

Shade pressed both of her hands to her mouth and turned her eyes to Arctic first, and then Ghost. She didn't say a thing, but her expression made it clear she was mentally speaking to her mates. Watching her, Sal couldn't help but smile - and feel a small pang of jealousy, but she pushed that away.

"I'm so happy for you, Shade," she said, stepping in to wrap her sister in a hug. "I knew you'd be able to have babies."

"But I burned myself nearly to death," Shade reminded her.

"All on the outside," Sal said gently. "And your baby won't care. You'll still be his or her amma."

"So will you," Shade promised. "You all saved my life when you found me, and I will never forget that. I want our baby to call you amma too, ok?"

"Thank you," Sal breathed. "And we're all here to help."

Shade looked over at Arctic again. "I think I'm going to be ok. He's been studying about the best way to raise them, and both of my mates knew their families. They know how to do this right."

"No one knows how to do it right," Sal countered. "Being a parent is about caring, trying, failing, and then learning from your mistakes. But so long as you have the caring part first, the rest will always work itself out in the end, ok?"

"Ok," Shade agreed. "Yeah. Ok." Then she laughed. "Sal, I'm finally going to be an amma."

"Yes, you most definitely are," Sal agreed as she turned to Ghost. "I'm happy for you."

He nodded. "I know there's still a risk, and that it's hard for us to breed, but... It's going to be worth it, right? Even if we lose this one?"

"No losing," Sal assured him. "We're healthier than ever before. We get plenty of iron, have less stress, and we no longer need to hide our skills. Your child is here, and we're going to keep it going until it's born. And you're going to be an amazing dava."

"Thank you," Ghost said before pulling away to wrap his arms around Shade.

Arctic stepped back to let him, but he caught Sal's eye and tilted his head to the side. Sal moved over with him. It wasn't outside of iliri hearing, but they got out of the way so everyone else could congratulate Shade.

"You ok?" Arctic asked.

"I'm happy for you," Sal told him.

He just lifted a brow. "That is not what I asked. Are you ok, Sal? I know this has to be hard for you, even if you won't admit it."

Sal paused, dropping her head to scratch at the tip of her ear. "Um," she tried, but wasn't quite sure how to answer his question. He deserved honesty, and she knew Arctic wouldn't judge her. The least she could do was admit what she was really feeling. "For the first time in my life," she finally said, "I have the chance to stop, relax, and simply live. I don't have any more excuses for why I don't want a family, and yet here I am, with a uterus full of scar tissue that will never carry a child."

"Blaz said he felt like he had to choose," Arctic said, reaching up to clasp her arm. "Do you resent him for that?"

"No!" she breathed. "Oh, no. Not at all. I honestly never wanted kids. I didn't want to bring someone into this world to suffer what I went through, but that's done. Iliri children can finally grow up free and safe. I said I couldn't get pregnant in the middle of battle, but the war's over. And there, near the end, I lost the choice. I never got the chance to *want* kids, Arctic. Now, seeing everyone starting families and settling down, I still don't have it. I just... I honestly don't know what I would've done if I could."

"What do you mean?" he asked.

"Would I wait? Would I start now like almost everyone else seems to be? Would I have one? More? Or would I never get the urge and simply be happy with the babies my pack has? I'm jealous because Shade got to choose, and my whole life, choices were something I wasn't good enough to get. I think it's that, more than anything else, that I regret."

"That makes sense," he told her. "It really does, Sal, and it's ok to mourn the loss of choice. I'm also here to listen anytime you need an ear, ok?"

"I know," She said, looking up at him with a smile. "I promise I do not begrudge you, Ghost, and Shade at all."

"You never would," he agreed. "But do you think your mates will? Do they regret losing the chance to have their own babies?"

Sal looked back at where the six men stood smiling around Shade and shook her head. "I think Blaz wishes it could've been an option, but not enough to call it regret. I think Jase found his paternal streak with Lyzzi. Zep has Valri, Kolt has Lasryn, and Tyr doesn't want kids.

Gage, though? I honestly don't know, and he hasn't leaked anything to me."

"Razor takes things as they come," Arctic explained. "He always has. He doesn't wish for something until he knows how he's going to make it happen - like you. I think he'll be wonderful with all the children of the pack and never think twice about it. I mean, the chances of you producing a child that one of them sired? One in six at best? For them, the baby would've been yours - biologically - not necessarily theirs. So it's not that different for them to accept the pack's kids as their own."

"Huh," Sal said as she thought about that.

Arctic was right. Iliri didn't have children easily. Most females had one, maybe three at most, although the more human they were, the easier it appeared to be. If Sal was lucky, that meant only half of her mates would ever sire a child with her, probably less. The others would simply accept those children as their own. So what was the difference between that and what they were doing now?

There wasn't one, except Sal's lack of ability to carry it herself. But if they could do it without resentment, then so could she. Besides, it *didn't* matter. She wouldn't love a baby more because it smelled like her, or had her ears, Kolt's smile, or Jase's eyes. It wouldn't matter if the baby was practical like Gage or a clown like Tyr. She couldn't predict if it would love horses the way Zep and Blaz did. Any child she had would need to be judged on who *it* was, not who'd made it.

So she wasn't really losing anything. She'd never had it to begin with, and now she'd found something else to take its place. She had a pack. She had so much love in her life. She also had plenty of children, and she intended to love them all.

"You aren't going to get annoyed with us when we try to steal time with your child, will you?" she asked.

Arctic shook his head. "No, Sal."

"Good, because I think I really needed this talk. I honestly hadn't thought about it in that way before. That the guys wouldn't ever have their own baby. I dunno, but that somehow makes it better. Makes this..."

"Fair?" he offered. "Kinda why I said it, because you've always needed to find that balance. And truth be told, I've always wondered if that's why Kaisaes never made it. Each one of you is so strong that there's nowhere left to improve. Your children would always be failures when measured up to the things you accomplished, and that, Sal, isn't fair. Ayati seeks a balance, right? This is balance, but you will always have a family, ok? We will have as many family dinners as you need, and send our children to you for date nights and babysitting. We do that because no matter what changes in our lives now that we're not having to fight for every single thing we get, we *are* still a family. And we love you."

Sal wrapped her arms around his neck and hugged. "I love you too, brother. Thank you for hearing the things I don't even think to say."

"Always," he whispered against the top of her head. "Sal, so long as you take care of everyone else, I intend to be the person who takes care of you. You're the best sister I could've asked for."

"You're going to be an amazing dava," she told him.

His lips broke into a smile. "I really am. Now, c'mon. Let's get out of here."

"Yeah," Sal agreed. "Because there's one more amma I need to check on, and I kinda feel like I can do that now."

CHAPTER FORTY-FIVE

PINK

*N*ya's room was one of the most lavish in the Palace, but it needed to be. The grauori bitch was curled on her side, lying on a bed with most of the blankets removed. When Sal walked into the room, the very pregnant mother looked miserable, but she still smiled in recognition. That made Jarl turn to look.

"Sal!" he said, surging to his feet. "I didn't expect you to come by."

"Had to make sure the Raewar's still in one piece," she teased. "How are you holding up?"

"I feel so bad," he said. "I mean... I can't do anything to make it better."

"You do," Nya told him. "You hold my paw and read to me. I can't do anything else, but you make me feel like I'm not alone."

Sal pointedly glanced around the room and then lowered her voice. "I bet you also keep Rragri at bay."

Nya groaned. "My amma is going to drive me insane. She worries about everything! I sneezed yesterday, and she wanted five different healers to look at me and make sure I wasn't dying."

"You're her only daughter," Sal reminded Nya. "I think she'd be bad with a normal pregnancy, but this? You're more than a month overdue, and the healers kept saying the pups weren't ready."

"Roo already had hers, even though you both got pregnant around the same time," Jarl told his mate. "Even Keeya's not that far from her due date. Months still, but she's human."

"And Keeya's allowed to walk around," Nya countered.

"Humans are built to carry their babies like this," Jarl reminded her. "You're meant to have multiple smaller babies, held tight to your body. The weight of the babies puts strain on your back and hips. You have to relax or you'll end up hurting yourself too bad to have an easy birth."

Nya groaned as she flopped her head over to look at Sal. "I never should've let him be in the room when the healers talked to me."

"Those are my babies too," Jarl reminded her.

"And you did this to me!" But Nya was grinning at him.

"You were there," Jarl teased back. "And I seem to remember you jumping on me a few times."

Sal giggled at them as she claimed a seat beside Jarl. "So any news? Rragri said something about them being ready?"

Nya nodded. "It seems they're formed enough to live on their own now. That means I could go into labor at any time."

"Are you scared?" Sal asked.

"Terrified," Jarl answered.

Nya whuffed in amusement. "I'm nervous, but not as much as my mate or my amma. This happened before, right? In Arhhawen, they bred iliri babies from grauori mothers. Inessi said the records show the dams raising their children, which means they survived."

"And they didn't have the options you do," Sal added. "The scientists thought they were simple animals because they didn't speak out loud. They had no idea about skills and abilities, so wouldn't have allowed them to mingle during birth. That means the grauori survived with nothing but human medicine."

"And I have more," Nya said. "See, Jarl? It's going to be ok."

"I'm still worried," he told her. "And Nya, you can't stop me. Look, we screwed up, ok? You're too young to have pups, and I'm not even legally an adult. We should've waited."

"Too late now," Sal told him. "Besides, how were any of us to know it was possible? All that matters now is making sure you do right by the kids."

"We've kinda been talking about that a lot," Jarl admitted. "I mean, a lot of it depends on what they are, you know? And I hate saying that about my own kids, but it's just the truth. If they run on four legs and will look like adults in two years? Well, then that's one set of options. If they're humans and completely helpless, that's another."

"And if they are iliri," Nya added, "that's a third. I think they will be iliri, though. I don't know if you'll still call them that, because of what we are, but the professor said Jarl must have the gene. He said that's why I got pregnant, because he's descended from the Zepyr line."

"Far back," Jarl added. "Zep and I aren't really related."

"But," Nya went on, "if combining humans to grauori made iliri, then isn't that what these are? And if they are, then what does that even mean?"

"It means," Sal told her, "that you two will bring the kingdoms together. I kinda feel like everyone is assuming they will be iliri, but it doesn't matter. These are your babies. They will be unique regardless of what they are, and I will help you however you need, ok?"

"Will you teach us how to raise an iliri?" Jarl asked. "Will you help us integrate them into a pack so they never have to be alone? Because if the babies are grauori, then Nya's sisters have sworn they will accept them."

"We'll do whatever we need to," Sal assured him. "If that's an iliri pack, then that's what we'll do. I don't know if anyone told you, but I have a little bit of pull in this country, so I can make things happen."

Jarl laughed. "Yeah. Thanks, Sal. Just kinda sucks, you know? I mean, we're not ready - or old enough - to have kids, and you had that taken away."

She nodded. "Yeah, um..." Sal turned her eyes on Nya. "To be honest, that's why I didn't come to see you before. I had to work through my jealousy."

Nya reached out to grab Sal's hand. "It's ok. Like the last cruel twist of ayati, right? We thought we were fooling around, and now we're about to be parents. You thought you were making a world where you could build a future, and you lost the ability. It's just not fair."

"No," Sal agreed, "it's not, but it's right. This is what Anglia needs right now, to see our species coming together without prejudice for our differences. And Nya, you're the Orassae's heir. Jarl, you're the King's. You're not just some kids who no one will ever hear about. The pair of you doing this? You're going to make a difference, and a good one."

"But that doesn't mean we'll be good parents," Nya countered. "What if I'm too hard on them? If I snap out of instinct and hurt my own children? What if they're too fast or agile for Jarl to catch?"

"You'll make it work the way it needs to," Sal assured her. "And you happen to have the luxury of an entire Palace and two packs to help whenever you need it. Even if that's sending the kids to me for a week so you can just get away."

"You'd watch them?" Jarl asked.

Sal sighed, turning her eyes to the ground. "Jarl, you could've been my brother. I gave you that choice, and you know it." Slowly, she lifted her eyes to meet his. "You opted to do something even more important, but that doesn't erase the fact that you're still one of us. The only children I will ever have are my pack's, so yes. I will gladly watch your babies. I will love them regardless, my mates will spoil them, and the Blades will train them. Doesn't matter what species they are. "

Jarl nodded slowly. "You would've been a good amma, Sal. No, fuck that. You *are* a good amma. I kinda feel like you helped raise me as much as Dom did, you know? I grew up in this Palace as a bastard, and now I'm supposed to be the next to own it. And in all that time, people have sneered at me, groveled to me, and laughed behind my back, but never you."

"And you never doubted my ability to be the Raewar," Nya added. "You didn't care that I'm young. You gave me the same responsibility you would have given my mother. You made me feel like I could actually do what had to be done."

"And you did," Sal assured her. "Both of you. Yes, you're young, but everyone was once." She reached over to pat Nya's leg. "Unfortunately, there's not too much I can do to shield you from Rragri's paranoia, but if you need a break, I'm sure I can intervene. My mates have her stalled outside right now. I kinda had a feeling you could use the peace and quiet."

Nya groaned. "I think I'll nap when she comes in."

"You going to kill me if I go do some more research?" Jarl asked. "Your amma is getting snappish, and my skin's too thin to take her teeth."

"Not if you tell me about it later," Nya promised. Then she sighed. "I am tired though, Sal. If you want to let my amma in, it's ok."

Which meant she was very politely asking Sal to let her rest. Sal could take a hint, so stood and reminded them to let her know when the pups came, then made her way out. Just like she expected, Rragri was right outside the door, sitting on her haunches to talk to Sal's mates. Naturally, the topic was the inter-species babies.

They are bigger than a grauori pup, Rragri explained, including Sal the moment she was in sight. *I do not know the size of iliri at birth, but these are not large enough to be humans. Not yet, and I hope that she has them before they get there.*

"Iliri are na as big," Jase told her, "but na much smaller. Two or three kilos. How big are humans?"

"Three to four," Gage told him. "I heard Keeya talking about it the other day."

Rragri said, *They seem to have a link, too, which means they will have abilities. In the next few days, they should know their names.*

"Iliri typically do na," Jase warned her. "Our names are chosen by our ammas and imprinted. Nya may need ta name them, and then whisper it ta them as they grow."

Rragri nodded. *I know that humans learn them over time, so I told the children to consider name options. Jarl's adamant that they'll pick their own, but he agreed. Nya had some horrible suggestions, but that just proves how young they are.*

"How bad?" Zep asked.

Dagger was one, Rragri admitted. *Fresh snow, but in our language. Jarl wanted to use family names. That's what has always been done with the people he knows.*

"Well, it'll probably all change when the kids arrive," Kolt said. "I know Las tilted my entire world. Everything I thought I would and would not do went out the window. That little boy became the center of my existence."

Those two will be the same, Rragri agreed. *They are so in love, and so excited about the babies, but also scared. The good kind of scared, though. The type that means they will make the right decisions for their children, and that they will stop and finally think about what they are doing.*

"And grow up too fast," Blaz said. "Because becoming a parent at that age can't be any easier for a grauori than a human. The last of their childhood just vanished."

"I think war took that from them already," Tyr said. "Let's be honest here, people. Jarl was an acting ruler before most of us even understood girls, let alone politics. Nya? She organized an entire army. Well, the grauori part of it, but still! I never would've guessed she was just a kid when I first met her, and that just means she had to grow up to survive. I really don't think they're losing anything. Instead, they're gaining it."

Kolt nodded. "How many other kids out there lost their chance at an innocent youth over the last decade?"

"How many never lived that long?" Gage asked.

I never thought about it like that, Rragri admitted. *Unfortunately, that is one thing I can't give to her. She will never get her childhood back, but at least this way she will have her own pups to make sure she doesn't miss it.*

"So do na look backwards, Rragri," Jase said. "Ya are gonna be a kauvwae. Look ahead ta that, and trust that those two will be as impressive with these pups as they have been with ever'thing else."

Rragri reached up to press her paw over his hand. *Thank you, cousin. I can always count on the Blades to remind me how good we truly have it. The pups are healthy. They seem to be ready now. All that is left is the birthing.*

"And we'll be here to lean on, Rragri," Sal promised. "It's kinda what friends do."

CHAPTER FORTY-SIX

YELLOW

The dining hall in the Dorton Palace had been set up to accommodate the leaders of every country. Tables were adjusted to fit multiple mates, yet keep the leaders side by side. The colors of each country were displayed proudly. Dom had given his staff a day to make it happen, and they'd come through wonderfully. When Sal saw the room, she was honestly impressed.

This was a state dinner, with Anglia hosting the rest of the world. Everyone in attendance was dressed formally - even the soldiers. At one of the lower tables, most of the 112th Mounted wore their dress uniforms in Conglomerate blue with brown trim. The Viraenovan guards were dressed in an impressive, shimmering ivory cloth. Myrosica's men wore the black and yellow checker. Unav's uniforms were less impressive, a sign of that country's near-complete destruction, but the Rebels wearing the jade and wine colors looked proud. As always, the Esceans didn't care about matching, but their size made them impressive regardless.

Then there was Narnx. He was the only Terran in the country. He had no guards, no national symbols except for one swath of purple and black where he would sit, and his recognized advisor as his partner. The man was announced right before Sal, and she watched him walk in with his head held high. Everyone around the room glared at him, but Dom stood to greet him. The King didn't just shake his hand, he pulled Narnx close enough to share a few private words and a smile that everyone in the room noticed.

Then it was Sal's turn. The herald stepped into the hall and pounded his staff against the floor the same way he had for everyone else. "The Kaisae of Anglia, Salryc Luxx; her Ahnor, Jassant Cynortas; her Dernor, Valcor Zepyr; her Taunor, Syrik Kolton; her Cinnor, Gage Dico; her Viernor, Blaz Eason; and her Kernor, Tyr Aristel."

Sal was honestly impressed that he made it through the entire list without fumbling a single title. But when the man turned to wave her in, he was fighting not to smile, which meant he'd probably been practicing. Sal nodded at him slightly as she walked past, careful not to displace the circlet on her head.

The silver and green dress flowed across her body with each step. Jase placed his hand gently on her lower back, guiding her forward. Behind them came the rest of her mates, with Tyr at the end. Every noble in the room watched. The women let their eyes roam, the men looked bored, and the leaders of the allied nations sat a little straighter.

Because tonight, she was not a soldier. Sal looked like a queen, and she knew it. Her men were dressed in black - even Tyr, although he also wore grey trim and accents. These weren't uniforms, though. It was formal attire designed specifically for these sorts of functions, and Sal knew just how good they looked.

When they reached the table, Sal and Jase moved to the far side where Dom sat. Her Ahnor held her chair, helped her scoot it into place, and then bent to kiss her cheek before walking around to his chair on the opposite side. Narnx sat to Sal's right, which meant across from his brothers. Beside him were Grenso, then Anis, Sherin, and Jakin from the CFC.

That left only one chair still vacant, and the herald was banging his staff again. "The Orassae Rragri, her ahnor Arrgro, and her dernor Harrgra."

The grauori had also dressed up for the meal. Rragri wore a cloth collar in green with small white stones decorating the edge. Quartz, maybe? Sal wasn't sure, but it looked lovely against her white coat. Her mates wore something similar but silver, lined with jade. They walked on all fours with Rragri in front and her men's heads swinging from side to side to scan the crowd. To Sal, they looked almost feral, but in the most beautiful way possible.

The Orassae took the spot on Dom's left, hopping up on her couch-like chair with ease. Her mates sat beside Rayna, who offered all of them a damp cloth for their hands. Rragri accepted hers first, her mates a moment later, but they looked confused.

"The floor is horrendous," Rayna whispered. "Do you know where some of these people's feet have been?"

Rragri ducked her head and whuffed a laugh. "Rai do na. Rai do na wanna."

"Just making sure you don't have to taste it," Rayna teased.

But the act of wiping their paws clean seemed to entrance the Myrosican Justice. "Is that inconvenient?" he asked. "Would gloves of some kind help more?"

"No," Harrgra told him. "We live in the wilds and our idea of proper is different from yours. Normally, we care less. We also do not eat with our hands in most cases."

The man nodded. "Well, feel free to be yourselves. I will admit that I am curious, so you shouldn't feel the need to mimic my culture when I'm visiting yours."

"Rragri thanks you," Harrgra told him. "She does not like to speak Glish much, since our tongues are too long for many of the letters, but I translate for her."

"How do you manage so well?" Krex asked.

Harrgra glanced over at Sal. "I heard our native words spoken with a tongue like yours. I heard how the sounds change, and so I practiced." He paused. "Rragri says I'm also young enough to still have a malleable mouth."

Rayna nearly snorted into her drink, barely preventing herself from spitting her wine. "Is that what we're calling it now?"

Harrgra's eyes went wide and his ears drooped when he recognized what Rayna was talking about. "Rraz," he hissed.

Thankfully, Krex was just as amused, and his roar of laughter made the entire table look. The Justice waved it off, but he was still chuckling when Dom stood to address them all. Thankfully, the King was used to Rayna's jokes, and the smile on his face was honest.

"Yesterday, the leaders of the world gathered to air our grievances. Today, let us make friendships. Please, relax and enjoy yourselves."

The moment he sat back down, the food began to arrive. The platters were color-coded for typical species preferences, and the servers moved from group to group, skipping the people who would have no interest in their dish. In the lull of conversation, Jase leaned closer.

"Please tell me there will na be too many more of these?" he begged.

Sal flicked her ears at him. "You wanted to be my Ahnor. This is the price you pay."

"I did na know what I asked," he teased. "Ya look amazing, though. I remember the first time I saw ya in that dress."

"And you never got to take me out of it," Sal whispered.

Down the row, Gage's head snapped over. "Please tell me that's a joint offer?"

Jase scoffed. "Yeh, but keep yer hand on yer daggers, cuz when Sal looks this good, someone allus tries ta kill her."

Dom leaned over toward her. "He does have a point, Sal."

She gestured to the lower tables. "See all those people in black? Yeah, I think I'm good this time."

"All I have to say," Zep told them, "is that someone else can die this time."

"No dying," Sal hissed. "Guys, really?"

"Really," Blaz said. "The way I hear it, the Spring Ball ended with Terrans storming Anglia. The Myrosican dress was ruined when the Widows jumped you. I mean, you're kinda oh for two."

Rayna leaned back to see them. "Guys, it's just a practice run for the wedding. You know, to break the bad luck, because I really do not want any assassins to jump me in the middle of saying, 'I do.'"

Shift jerked his chin at Dom. "What I'm hearing is that we need a lot more reasons for her to dress up."

"And wear the crown," Dom added. "Sal, do you have any idea how much work it was to get that thing for you?"

"About five minutes?" Rayna asked. "I mean, where do you come up with a resin circlet in the middle of Myrosica?"

"Uh..." Dom looked quickly at Justice Krex.

"The Conglomerate camp is in the middle of nowhere," the man agreed. "Although now I'm curious. Did a Myrosican make the Kaisae's crown?"

"No," Dom admitted. "We actually recycled a few Terran swords. They issue black ones, so I added a green Anglian dagger and liked the color. Sal, I made that before we left Anglia. I, um... I thought it was fitting for you to have a crown made from the weapons of your enemy."

"It is," Grenso said, proving he was paying attention. "It's the sort of thing that needs to be mentioned in a book."

"Book?" Dom asked.

Jase nodded. "Professor Molis is writin' the *History of Salryc Luxx.* She is the first Kaisae ta survive the conflict that activated her powers. Her life needs ta be recorded. He is talkin' ta ever'one that helped her get here."

"Tell him I'll ride over when he wants my perspective," Dom said.

Zep shook his head. "No. Dom, I think you need to invite him here. Probably to the Dorton library. He's a proud little man - and a strong-willed one - but I am willing to bet he's never been shown the respect he's due. Bring him to the Palace and change that?"

Dom nodded. "Yeah. I'll send out the invitation tomorrow. The formal kind. I just hope it's not too hard to get copies of this book, because I'd like to put one in there. My library, I mean. I think it's as much human history as iliri."

Narnx nodded. "All of this is, sire."

"Dom."

Narnx leaned over to look at him and lifted a brow. "So you're on a first-name basis with the Emperor of Terric now?"

"I am, Narnx," Dom said. "Mostly because I can never remember if you're supposed to be called Your Eminence or Your Grace. I try to avoid the need to use it, so how about we just ignore all that bullshit, huh?"

"You know I'm not going back, right?" Narnx asked.

Dom nodded slowly. "Heard that was the price we paid for winning: we get one more iliri who I respect. Narnx, I don't care where you were born, who your sire was, or anything else. And no, I won't say that Anglia is an ally of Terric, but you aren't Terric. If you want to renounce the title and swear to Anglia, I'll be glad to have you. If you don't, then you don't, but know that none of us hold you responsible."

Narnx let out a heavy breath. "It's hard." His gaze shifted to Sal. "All my life, it's been my fault. Didn't matter what it was or if I was actually to blame. I was the beast, and so I must've made it happen. The last few months here? I've met people I care about now. I have a family. I just don't want to be that burden anymore."

"You're not," Sal assured him.

Dom shook his head at her. "It's not that easy, Sal. I remember when the crown landed on my head. I was so worried that I'd never measure up to my grandfather. For Narnx, it has to be even worse." Leaning onto his elbows, he met Narnx's eyes. "But we're not Terric, you're not a beast, and you have nothing to apologize for. Own it, Narnx."

"If you're going to fail," Sal quoted softly, "then fail as big as you can. They'll forgive you for anything you do with gusto, and it won't even matter if they *like* you." She huffed once. "That's what I told Reko long ago, and it's still true. Narnx, don't ever regret what you've done. That's not an emotion you're supposed to have."

"And yet I managed to learn it," he pointed out.

Tseri chose that moment to join the conversation. "Of course you did, because it was one of the strongest leashes humans used on us. That's why *we* closed our borders, because they don't just use chains and cages. They twisted words around until we had to learn the same lesson. You are an impressive ruler, Narnx. I sat across from you as we signed the peace agreement, and I saw you meet Sal's eyes without flinching. I promise it's not something I can do. That means you *deserve* the title of Emperor, and I, for one, hope you'll keep it. Because the longer you're in control, even if you're not there, the more time they'll have to forget why they thought fighting was a good idea. Believe it or not, time really will heal these wounds. Yours and your nation's."

"Thank you, Kaeen," he said softly.

"Tseri," she told him. "Because I honestly hope that you and I can become friends."

He nodded. "Thank you, Kae.. uh, Tseri. I'd like that."

"And," Tyr said, "it's also nice to see an iliri male in a position of power. Never know, might bring about a little gender equality, right? Own this shit, Narnx."

He rolled his eyes at the Kernor. "Sal, remind me again what you see in that one?"

"Well," she said, "it's pretty hard to feel sorry for yourself with him around."

"Uh-huh," Narnx said, a devious little smile twisting his lips. "So he's hung, huh?"

"Fuck yeah, I am," Tyr agreed. "See, you know what's *really* important."

CHAPTER FORTY-SEVEN

ORANGE

*T*hat dinner was just enough to get the other allies talking to each other. Dom said he saw the Unavi senators laughing with the Conglomerate Representatives at breakfast. The Myrosican Justice somehow ended up in the library with Tseri. And Vilko invited the Unavi out riding with her. Dom had no idea what they'd all talked about, but to Sal, it was good news.

Because the more the leaders of these nations talked, the less likely they were to give up. Everyone knew that the last part of this summit would be the hardest. First, Sal had to get them all to agree that iliri and grauori were people, not just livestock or pets. Then they all had to find limitations on combat which wouldn't be prejudiced against any of the three species. Easier said than done. Anything mentioned would have to have some kind of precedent behind it.

Currently, the Conventions of War document listed things like desecration of bodies as an international crime. So was torture. The iliri and grauori could be accused of both. Currently, only the humans were bound by those laws, which Sal had used to her advantage. Yes, she'd tortured men to get information. She'd also ignored the human rules for prisoners of war, but she'd give all of that up to be recognized as a legitimate person.

And then, two days later, Sal needed a break. She'd looked over laws, traditions, and more. There was a stack of books on her desk ready to topple, and she was sick of it all. She needed to get away from this for just a bit and play. Rayna did too, and as the maid of honor at the wedding, Sal knew exactly what to do. First, she told Tseri and Vilko they were going to Dorton. No fancy clothes. No guards. This was just the girls, and they were taking Rayna out for a good time. The kind of good that would make her hate them all in the morning.

Then, she enlisted Jase's help. He told Shift to get Dom out without turning it into a parade. From there, Sal's other mates wanted to help. If they were having a pre-wedding party for all of them, then they were doing it right. This was *not* a state function. It was just a few soldiers and their friends going out on the town.

Tyr told Sal he was going with the girls. Rayna was like a sister to him, if not his best friend, and he didn't care if he was the only one there with a dick. Naturally, she had him start inviting as many women as he could. The rest of her mates got to work on telling the men. And then, Blaz had the best idea of them all. He suggested sneaking out the other leaders as well.

Tyr reached out to Brisa. She was more than willing to deliver handwritten notes to both of the Unavi senators and Representative Anis. She also enlisted a couple of guys from her unit to talk to the men. Pig and Keeya were still in Dorton, so they were told to arrange everything, and to keep Dom from following Rayna. Since Shift was in on it, that shouldn't be too hard.

Just over an hour later, they were ready. Tensa and some of the girls who used to work for her agreed to look after any kids who weren't up at the school. Inessi declined to go because of them, and Ran claimed that he was sure she'd need help with something, using it as a weak excuse for the new couple to be alone. Combined, it meant the adults were free to have as much fun as they wanted, for as long as they wanted. But when the group headed out of the stables, it looked more like an army than a party.

Everyone had chosen comfortable clothes. All of the women wore pants - except Roo. Plenty of them were armed - but only with daggers.

Still, that was lethal for this group. There were no uniforms, and yet everyone still had a trace of their colors somewhere. The best part, though, were the smiles.

When they finally made it into the city, they didn't head for the Palace. The streets were filled with citizens having their own celebration, and the path to the King's home would be packed. Instead, Tilso suggested a stable where he knew a few guys. All of the horses were boarded for the night with explicit instructions to take any that hadn't been claimed to the Dorton Palace in the morning, and Sal handed out her first official token.

It was a small thing, made of black ceramic and stamped with the symbol of the Kaisae. Combined with a receipt, it would get the bill paid in full. This was how nobles in Anglia avoided carrying around large amounts of coin, and every international leader would have been assigned something similar. Dom would pay the bills from the treasury later, so his citizens wouldn't risk any loss, and then bill the owner of the token afterward.

From there, they all split up. Sal's mates paused to kiss her, and she saw Jase give Tyr one of those looks that said he'd just assigned her a guard. Thankfully, Tyr laughed it off. Sal knew she'd be fine. First off, she was in Anglia, and secondly, she would be surrounded by the most lethal women in the world.

And then they headed to the bar Rayna liked. They'd tried a few, but stopping in for drinks before dinner was very different from going there at night. This was not the good side of town. It was where working people lived, so no one should recognize most of their faces. Except for Sal. Her ears tended to give her away, but she could live with that.

They arrived before Rayna, but Vilko stopped Sal before she could find the owner. "I got this," she said, lifting up her own token. "I figure the next one's on Tseri."

"I can handle that," Tseri said. "Vilko, just pay for the house?"

The Escean looked back with a mischievous smile. "Oh yeah."

Too bad the owner didn't recognize her though. "No weapons!" he bellowed when she was only steps away. "You want to drink here, then you leave your swords outside."

"Daggers," Vilko corrected, "and that's not going to happen." Then she slapped her credit token onto the counter. "I'm paying for everything between now and midnight. You still want me to leave?"

"Your husband approve this?" the man asked.

She leaned over the counter. "My husband is dead. I'm also better with my fists than he ever was. Look at that thing again, *sir*, because we aren't exactly gentle in Escea."

"Is this..." He looked at the women taking over one entire side of his bar. "That's the Kaisae?"

"Yup," Vilko said, popping her lips on the P. "So, we good?"

The man nodded. "We're good."

"Then let's get the fun started." Vilko marched over to the closest table, and stepped onto a chair so she could be seen. "Drinks are on the house until midnight. My friends want to have a good time, so enjoy it while it lasts."

A laugh rang out, sounding like the perfect punctuation to the statement, and Rayna walked in through the door. "I see you got started without me."

"Oh, we're trying to," Sal assured her. "So, you bring any friends? Because I did."

Right on cue, Anis, the two senators from Unav, and a large group of soldiers entered the bar. The only person who didn't look like she belonged was Keeya, thanks to her comfortable dress and *very* round belly. Sal waved her over towards the empty space beside Shade, making sure she had a place to sit.

"I wasn't sure you'd come," Sal said while flagging down one of the servers.

Keeya laughed. "Pig made me *promise* not to drink, but I said you'd all need a clear head in the group, so he eventually relented. It works out, though, because I hate wine, beer smells disgusting, and the strong stuff turns my stomach."

"I'm not drinking either," Shade said. "Don't want to take *any* risks with the baby."

So Sal looked at the server. "I need the biggest glass of juice you have for my two sisters. Rum for me - "

"Fuck, Sal," Rayna gasped. "Going hard right from the start?"

Sal grinned. "Hopefully, I won't bite anyone. Who else wants a drink?"

All of the girls started ordering, and Anis just waved them off. "Glasses," she told the man. "And bottles. Just bring entire bottles of everything. And a whole pitcher of juice or milk."

"Milk!" Keeya groaned, sounding like that was a delicacy.

"Proves my point," Anis said. "Ok, which ones here aren't drinking? I know Keeya, but I'm sure she's not the only one expecting."

"I'm not," a woman said from the door. Everyone turned to see Vanica walk in. "Still nursing, so can't overindulge."

"Nica!" Sal squealed, hurrying over to give her a hug. "Where have you been hiding?"

"I have three kids, Sal," Dom's sister reminded her. "Two are still at home, and the third's about to have a few of his own. I've been stuck in a nursery. Trust me, there was no way I'd pass this up."

"So, I heard..." Meia said, leaning between Sal and Tseri, "that we don't have to be royal, noble, appropriate, or even respectable tonight. Is that true?"

"It is," Rayna said, answering before Sal could. "This is the last time I'll be out on the town as a normal person, so fuck acting proper."

"Good." And Meia offered her hand to Tseri. "Care to dance? I mean, just so I have something to brag about."

"We'd need music," Tseri pointed out.

Meia just pointed at Rayna. "You gonna start it?"

"Oh, Meia," Rayna groaned. "Really?"

"Do it!" Tyr told her.

"Yeah, really," Meia insisted. "Sing, woman!"

"Ok," Rayna said, glancing over at Teya and Tyr. "The sun is shinin', the horses grained. The road is long and we're ridin' again..." she bellowed out, sounding surprisingly good.

Then Teya joined in. "My armor's shined, my ration's in my pack. The road is long and we aren't riding back."

Tyr took the third verse. "My sword is sharp, my lance is straight. The road is long and we can't wait."

This was one Sal actually knew. It was an old Conglomerate military song. She joined in for the chorus, and others began to try. By the second time through, the girls were all singing loudly, drawing a lot of attention to themselves, and Meia had Tseri swirling with her around the only empty space. Tyr had claimed Shaden, and they were trying to keep up, but neither of them had a clue how to dance to this tune.

Across the room, a man whooped at the entertainment, and even the servers were smiling. But when Tseri was done, Sal demanded her turn with Meia, and the Devil Dog was happy to comply. This time, Brisa picked the tune, and it wasn't nearly as polite. The best part was that the Unavi senators joined in. Not just with the singing, but also the dancing. Tyr had a line of partners, being the only guy in their group. And because she couldn't be outdone, Rayna walked over to an older gentleman just trying to finish his beer and offered her hand.

"Dance with me, sir?"

"Ma'am, my wife might not like that."

She leaned a little closer. "I'm getting married in a few days. Be the last man I dance with while I'm still single?"

"Oh, so this is a hen party, is it?" he asked, looking over at the other men who looked like regulars. "Guys. The girls are celebrating an upcoming wedding. Dance with 'em."

At first, the guys looked a little unsure, but another round of drinks convinced them. One by one, they picked out a woman and began dancing - which was more like swaying. Even Keeya was out there, and the songs just kept getting worse. When Sal bowed out to let someone else dance with her partner, Anis patted the top of the long table she was sitting on.

"So this is what you do, huh?" she asked. "Just pretend to be one of them when you need to get away?"

"Deina," Sal said, flagging down a server for her third glass of rum, as she was too far away from the bottles ordered, and feeling a little tipsy. "I'm not pretending. Here? This is me. Out there? In those meetings? That's the person I'm supposed to be, but I'm not a queen."

"You're a Kaisae," Anis told her, slurring the word just enough to prove she was also feeling her liquor. "That's more than a queen."

"Didn't use to be," Sal said, leaning back on her hands. "Used to be worth a collar around my neck and a cell in a basement."

"Ok, good point," Anis said. "But tell me something, Sal? How come you didn't turn out like the emperor? Not this Emperor, but that one. The fucking asshole one."

"Makiel," Sal said, knowing what she meant. "And why would I wanna be like him?"

"Everyone loved him. They all love you. They followed him blindly. They follow you. How come, when you could rule the world, you haven't tried to?"

Sal blew out a big breath and reached for her glass. Taking a long drink, she thought about that. "I prolly could."

"Oh, you definitely could," Anis assured her. "You have this thing about you. It makes people feel good when you're around. Like happy, or brave. Natyn and I were talkin' about it."

"Grenso?" Sal asked. "And he didn't tell you?"

"Tell me what?"

"It's the vis," Sal said. "Pheromones. It's why the iliri say I smell like hope. That's how they describe it."

"Ahh... " She nodded. "But why don't you wanna rule the world?"

"Where's the fun in that?" Sal asked.

"No," Anis insisted. "I'm serious. Kinda drunk, but serious. Why don't you wanna?"

Sal draped her arm around the Representative's shoulders. "Because my idea of a happy ending is when I retire. I don't wanna do paperwork for the rest of my life, and I *hate* talking in front of everyone. You all stare at me like I'm a freak. I mean, it's better now, but I'm the 'other,' Deina. The freak. I don't wanna be a freak. And I don't really care if I'm rich or powerful. I just wanna live with my men and become a very old and grumpy iliri. I kinda wanna be normal, you know? That's why we're here, like this. Rayna's going to be the Queen.

I'm the Kaisae. Tseri's the Kaeen. You're a Representative, and those are senators. I mean, it's kinda nice to not be that for a bit. To just..."

"Be a real person," Anis finished for her. "I'm gonna vote yes. So's Grenso."

"Yes?"

"For the iliri and grauori," Anis explained. "Pretty sure Jakin's gonna, too. That means the CFC is gonna sign it."

Sal's breath fell out of her lungs. She looked at her glass, wondering if she was drunk enough to be hallucinating. "Really?"

"Mhm," Anis assured her. "Has to be unanimous, but ya got Anglia, Viraenova, Escea, Unav, and Terric. Pretty sure Myrosica is for it. Means you've been wondering how the CFC's gonna go, and that was the only thing holdin' me back. I don't wanna have 'nother Emperor."

"You know," Sal said, leaning over to bump Anis with her shoulder, "Makiel always tried to pretend he was human. Ever wonder why?"

"Shit," Anis breathed. "Because he wanted to be normal too?"

"Pretty sure," Sal told her. "Being the Emperor was the only way he could stop being a scrubber."

"I'm gonna vote yes," Anis said again, this time with emphasis. "And I need 'nother drink."

At the same time, Tseri waved down the singers, making everyone look at her. The Kaeen's eyes were glassy, proving she'd been enjoying the alcohol too.

"You know what we need?" she asked.

Vilko laughed from where she was leaning against a wall. "What do we need, Tseri?"

"We need more men! Ones with less clothes." And she turned - staggering a bit - to face the side where the men were sitting. "Does this town have a place with lots of sexy young men?"

The older man coughed in shock, spewing out a mouthful of beer, but one of the younger guys was nodding. "There's a place, but it's kinda shady."

"Fuck," Rayna laughed. "We're kinda shady."

"Wrong kind of shady, miss. The lower end has some clubs where you'll get a view of the guys, but most of them will stick a blade in you or run off with your guilders. Not worth it, and not a safe way to celebrate your hen party."

"Sounds like a bar fight," Tyr said, but his tone made it clear that could be a good thing.

"Except they know how to win those," the older man said.

Vilko pushed herself away from the wall. "Yeah, well, so do we. Let's do it, Ray."

Rayna turned to look at the pack of women. "You all wanna?"

It was the Unavi senators who nodded first. Then Anis yelled, "Oh yeah!"

It didn't even matter that she had no idea what she was agreeing to, it was enough. This bar was only so much fun, and a few drinks in, the ladies were ready to take on the world. After all, they'd already done it once before.

"Then let's do this!" Rayna said.

But the man she'd first danced with lifted his voice. "Miss Ray? Before you go, when's your wedding? I figured we could send you a little gift or something."

She walked over and hugged him. "Oh, that's so sweet. It's next week, but you don't have to get me anything."

"I wanna get you *something*. Just a little thing. All I need to know is your husband's last name."

Rayna smiled. "It's Jens. I'm going to be Rayna Jens, and the only thing I want is for you and your wife to be there."

His eyes went wide when he recognized the name. "Like..."

"Shhh," she told him. "It's our secret. But do come."

CHAPTER FORTY-EIGHT

BROWN

Zep shoved open the door of the pub they'd chosen and stepped inside. A three-person band played music in the corner, a few of the patrons were tossing darts at a board on the wall, and plenty of people were moving. It looked a little tame, but it did have plenty of space for the crowd they'd brought.

Looks good enough, he told the rest and stepped all the way in.

A moment later, the other Black Blades followed him, making people turn to look. That worked out, though, because then they didn't pay attention to Dom or Ilija. That those two were buried in the middle of the Verdant Shields made it even easier, and none of them had been dumb enough to wear white. The Devil Dogs, most of Dark Heart, and an insane number of Anglian soldiers all came in shortly after.

Zep noticed the staff perk up. They'd just turned this into a very busy night, the kind where the servers would make a killing. Kinetry headed over to the band, leaning in to whisper something - probably a request for more lively music. Everyone else just began to claim tables.

Ilija broke off, heading to the main counter, but Justice Krex hurried after him. Just before Ilija could hand over the King's token, Krex dropped his yellow and black one on the counter.

"Open bar tonight," he told the man staring at it. "Easiest if you just

361

put everyone's drinks on my tab so we don't have to prove which ones are with us."

"You don't have to do that," Ilija told him.

Krex chuckled. "I'm not spending *my* money. That's just a fraction of my allotment. Let me buy a few drinks."

The man behind the counter lifted up the token to look at it. "This is one of the King's credits?"

"It is," Ilija said. "Just deliver it and the receipt to the Palace gates and you'll get paid in full."

"Why's it yellow?"

Ilija gave Krex a warning look, then said, "Helps keep track of the budget. Don't worry about it."

"You got some of those international guards with you?" the man asked.

"Yeah," Ilija said. "Just a couple of war vets spending some time catching up. How about you get those drinks coming, huh?"

"Yes, sir!"

Ilija turned, dropping his arm over Krex's shoulders to steer the man back to their line of tables. "Tonight is not about politics, Krex. It's all about having fun. My brother-in-law is getting married to two amazing people. Let's show the guys a good time?"

Krex nodded his agreement. "Just don't be surprised when I can't hold my liquor. And don't tell me about it tomorrow. I tend to do stupid things."

"And you're among friends," Ilija promised.

Zep lifted his chin to ask, "Ilija, you having whiskey, brandy, or mead?"

"Fuck that," Ilija said. "I'm drinking ale."

"Whiskey," Jase said, making Zep turn to look at him.

"You sure, little brother?"

"Oh, yeh," Jase told him. "And I wanna see Blaz drunk."

Blaz pointed at Gage. "If I'm going there, then so are you."

"You sure about that?" Gage asked him. "Because I drink whiskey."

"Na iliri enough ta get fucked up on it," Jase teased.

"Kiss my ass," Gage told him.

"Later," Kolt said. "And don't worry, Blaz, I'm a fucking lightweight, but I do like a good glass of whiskey."

"Rum," Blaz said to the man who'd come over to take their orders.

Dom lifted his hand. "I want the strongest thing in the house."

"Me too," Shift said.

Arctic groaned. "Then I'm going with mead."

"You are not," Shift told him. "Ghost, help me out here?"

"Brandy for him," Ghost said, "and whiskey for me."

The server paused, his eyes running over Ghost. "You're one of those iliri, right?"

"I am," he said, and all of the Blades grew quiet.

"So am I," Risk said.

Arctic just pointed at his eyes. "A few of us are. That going to be a problem?"

"Was told your kind can't hold their alcohol. That you turn into *beasts*." From his tone, this man was a bit more than just a server. Or at least he wasn't worried about keeping his job.

"Nope!" Zep said, shoving himself to his feet. "That is not a word you use with my brothers, you get me? And the four-legged guy over there? He's not a beast either. So, how about we try this again?"

"You lookin' to get kicked out?" the man asked. "We don't need any rowdy soldiers in here causing problems. Been stuck with too many bills after a bar fight."

"We're looking to laugh, relax, and have some fun. That's it. Would prefer that doesn't come with a fight, because I've had my fair share of them, but if it does, you'll just bill that to the King's credit over there. So how about you get my friends their drinks?"

"How about it?" Ilija asked, moving to his side.

"Because," Blaz said, falling in on Zep's other side, "we'll take that pretty little token back and leave. Or you can be a bit less of a dick and make a few hundred guilders tonight. See, my friends are in the mood to spend a *lot* of money, but if you're going to act like some self-righteous prick, we won't feel like spending it *here*."

"You're not from around here, are ya?" the man asked.

Blaz smiled. "Arhhawen, so no, not really."

The guy looked at him again, then Zep. Finally, his eyes jumped over to Ilija. "You three going to keep the rest in line?"

"Nope," Ilija said. "Nobody keeps the iliri in line but the iliri."

"We didn't ask for them to come," the man pointed out. "Not here, and not to Anglia."

Ilija shrugged. "*You* didn't. I did. In fact, I chased a few down so I could beg. Know what? I made it all the way back from Terric City because of them and our little furry friends."

"And that *woman*," the man snapped, "gave our wives the idea that they're all equal. They got the King by his balls, you know."

"Really?" That came out loud enough to make everyone else fall silent. Clenching his jaw, Dom walked up to stand beside Ilija. "You think the iliri have your King by his balls? How so? Please, I'm *dying* to hear."

"That man's in bed with one."

Shift chuckled. "I heard that rumor too."

"Pretty sure he's fucking the Kaisae," the guy went on.

"Pretty sure he's not," Dom said. "I mean, you know they bite, right?"

"Which means they're beasts!"

Dom just smiled. "You know I bite, right? Not as well, but I give it a good effort. What about you, Zep? Blaz?"

"Oh, I bite," Blaz assured him. "All the time."

Dom just leaned a little closer. "So how about you tell me who's gonna serve my little friends, huh? Is it going to be you? Another guy in here? Or are we getting that token back and going somewhere else?"

"There's a place on the south side that will serve them," the man taunted. "Don't want their kind in my bar, and you're an idiot if you think I'm giving the token back. I can charge anything I want with that."

Dom sighed. "You realize that's not only theft but also fraud, right?"

"And who's going to prove it? You? A bunch of drunken soldiers?"

Blaz just lifted his hand. "So you know, I'm the Viernor."

"Dernor," Zep said.

Ilija grinned. "Sergeant at Arms. And just wait for the title my brother uses."

"King," Dom said. "And it sounds like this is your place? You the owner of this establishment?"

"This is a joke, right?" the guy asked.

"Answer the question," Ilija demanded.

"Yeah, it's my place. And?"

Dom just nodded. "Ilija, send the inspector over here tomorrow. I want the books checked over to make sure he's not skimping on taxes, and have the food inspectors do a sweep as well. If they don't find anything, keep going until this man figures out that hate isn't tolerated in Anglia."

"You can't do that!" he hissed.

But the guy behind the bar was holding up the token like he was offering it as a way to keep himself out of trouble. He was standing behind the owner, so the arrogant fool didn't notice, but it was enough for Kolt. With a thought, he pulled the item, fetching it into his own palm.

"Krex, I think this is yours. Now, where do we want to go for some fun?"

Dom laughed. "I think we're going to the south side. Might be a little rougher than some of you are used to, but I think we'll be *just* fine. Not interested in having my bachelor party in a place where my husband isn't welcome. *Or* his pack."

Pig looked over at one of the other patrons. "Hey? You! Yeah. Where's a bar that can hold this many of us, doesn't mind iliri or grauori, and won't give a shit when men start making out with men?"

"Sounds like a party," the guy teased.

"Was hoping for one," Pig assured him. "You know a place?"

"Yep, take this road south three blocks, then turn left. Another block, and there's one on the right. Big stone building with a faded sign out front. I mean, it's the kind of place where *anything* goes, so yeah."

"Perfect," Pig said, tossing out a bill onto the table. "Kolt? Fetch me one of those bottles? We need something for the walk."

Kolt looked over at the money and nodded. "Yep, that should cover at least two."

And he pulled. The first bottle he handed to Pig. The second he passed to Dom. The King held it up in thanks and then turned for the door. Like a wave, the rest of their group followed. When they were outside, they looked more like a mob, but no one cared. Dom opened his bottle, took a pull from it, and passed it back without looking.

Pig did the same, and quite a few of the guys accepted. Unlike Sal, Dom had left most of the politicians at home. He'd refused to bring along his fellow noblemen, saying they'd ruin the mood. Grenso, from the Conglomerate, had gotten an invite, but not the other two. Since he was iliri, he wouldn't have a problem at all with how Dom reacted to the hate in there. That meant the only person who might get the wrong impression was Krex.

"You ok with that?" Zep asked as he offered the man one of the bottles.

Krex tipped it up and took a long chug. "I watched you die, you know." He turned to hand the bottle to the next man in line. "I was in that room while you were bleeding out, with Blaec Doll the only thing between Myrosica's government and the Terrans. And then two little grauori pups ran in and brought you back."

"So I've been told," Zep said, wondering what this had to do with his question, or if the man really was *that* much of a lightweight.

Krex just turned to look up at him. "I watched Anglia and Viraenova stand side by side and fight for you. Your wife and the Ahnor fought for you. Mr. Zepyr, if that's how the iliri treat their friends, then I think the *least* we can do is fight back like the King just did. It's not going to be easy to get iliri accepted, and not everyone is going to like it, but it's the fair thing to do."

"They're good people, you know," Zep said. "The iliri? I mean, they're just a bit different from what most people expect, but once you get to know them, they're just... good."

"The grauori too," Krex agreed. "Yes, sir. I noticed that. I'm just worried I'm going to use the wrong words and upset them. Like 'beasts' is offensive, but is 'predators'? Can we call them the non-human species? We don't have a lot of iliri in Myrosica, and the ones we do have aren't a big deal. The same isn't true in the rest of the world, though."

"It *wasn't*," Zep agreed. "I think that's changing, though."

"I hope so," Krex said. "And so you know, I was sent here for one reason and one reason only. The Justices of Myrosica want to make sure that iliri and grauori have the same rights as everyone else. If you're worried that the King's stunt in there is going to offend me, don't be. If anything, he just made me more determined to push this through. The way I see it, you died to protect all of us in that meeting. I think I can stand up and vote to protect you and your family."

"Thank you, Justice Krex," Zep said softly. "I honestly wasn't sure why Dom invited you tonight, but I'm kinda glad he did."

"Because I asked him to help me get to know the other leaders. You see, Myrosica and Anglia have always been allies. I'd like to keep it that way, but I barely know your Kaisae or the Orassae. So, um..." He chuckled. "Can we just not count tonight in the political stuff? I assure you that I will end up making a fool out of myself."

"Me too," Zep told him. "And my little brother over there?" He pointed to where Jase was walking with Dom. "He gets *really* friendly when he's drunk, but don't tell him I told you that. He likes to pretend he's a vicious monster."

Krex laughed. "Then I will be sure to buy him a lot of drinks. And you, Mr. Zepyr."

"It's just Zep," he corrected. "Valcor Zepyr is the name my human parents gave me. Zep's the one the iliri use. Well, and my friends."

"So does that mean I'm included in that group?" Krex asked.

"Definitely," Zep said. "And if you want to get on Sal's shortlist? The trick is to get these guys on your side. I'll even tell you what they like to drink."

"Perfect," Krex said. "I guess you all get pretty close, being married to the same woman, huh?"

Zep laughed once. "Yeah, you could say that."

"Rumors say you all share a bed."

"Makes the sleeping a bit easier," Zep agreed.

"Is it weird?" Krex asked. "I know I probably shouldn't even bring it up, but I'm amazingly curious. I mean, is it weird for you to sleep beside them? And how does that even work with your wife? I mean, do you have set days?"

"You really want to know?" Zep asked.

Krex made a face, scrunching up his nose. "Is that wrong?"

"Nope, but the answer may not be something you're ready for."

"Oh, I assure you, I've heard just about everything. I've presided over some pretty unimaginable cases. I think that's why I'm so curious."

Zep leaned closer. "We don't just share the bed. We share her. Two, three, six of us on her at the same time. Usually not *all* of us, but still. We share a bed because we share her, and sex for iliri is mostly in our minds. The more people involved, the more amazing it gets. And then there's the part about their pack mentality. They like to touch each other. Not just sexually, but always."

"Because their skills are often based on physical contact, right?" Krex asked.

Zep nodded. "And because it reminds them that they are not alone. That's really all they ever wanted, and for the first time in their lives, they're finally able to have it."

Krex reached up to pat Zep's arm. "And Myrosica is going to make sure you keep it. The world is changing, Zep. We're living in a brand new age, and I think your wife made it possible."

"Yeah, but do you really think we can keep it?" Zep asked.

Krex chuckled. "Oh, I think that if anyone tries to take it from you, there's a whole lot of people willing to re-join your army. A lot more than I expected, in all honesty. Then again, it could be because your King is so free with his drinks. I heard he carried crates of alcohol all the way across the continent."

"He most certainly did," Zep laughed. "So what's your drink of choice, Krex?"

"Whiskey, if I have a way to get home. Tea, if not."

"Then I'm buying you as much whiskey as you can hold," Zep

decided. "And if you can't walk back, I'll fucking carry you there myself. I want to see what a drunk Myrosican Justice looks like."

"Only if I get to see a drunk Anglian iliri," Krex agreed, looking at Zep to make it clear who he meant.

"Oh, that is definitely going to happen," Zep promised.

CHAPTER FORTY-NINE

ORANGE

*S*al was dancing in circles with some man who'd managed to lose his shirt. She had her hands on his chest, a smile on her face, and the world was all blurry around the edges. Beside her, Rayna was making a scene with Tyr, the pair of them laughing like little kids. The best part, though, was Rragri dancing with Meia. Yes, on her hind legs. No, it *wasn't* pretty.

The Stone Man Pub was exactly the kind of place the girls needed. Tseri had slapped down her token this time, and made sure the entire bar knew the drinks were paid for, but she expected someone to dance with her friends. That had been all it took. The place was packed, and most of the patrons appeared to be labor workers of some kind. Free drinks were a rare treat that they intended to enjoy.

And so almost everyone had ended up with a dance partner, a few too many drinks, and a lot of fun. Mostly, the kind of fun Rayna really shouldn't be starting, but Tyr, Sal, and Vilko were definitely encouraging it. Surprisingly, Deina Anis was almost as bad.

"Twenty krits for you to lose the shirt," she yelled at someone.

"Guilders!" Shaden yelled at her. "Krits don't work here."

"Ok, what's twenty krits in guilders?"

Tseri laughed. "I have no idea. Like 200 guilders?"

"No!" Telyra, the senator from Unav giggled. "Anglia money's worth more than it used to be. It's like eighty, I think."

"Fuck," Anis muttered, digging into her pocket. "Anyone wanna trade krits for guilders?"

Ryali just lifted her hand. "I got a hundred guilders fer that big guy ta take off his shirt and dance fer her!"

The man in question turned, caught Ryali's eye, and reached over his head to yank his shirt up and off. "Pay up," he teased.

Ryali lifted a bill and waved the end of it. "Ya gotta do the dancin' part too. My friend does na get a lot a fun where she's from."

"Yeah?" he asked, looking over at Anis. "And where you from, sweetie?"

"Prin," she said, her eyes raking over the guy's body. "Oh my. You look like one of the soldiers."

"Nah, just work in a warehouse." And he offered his hand. "Come dance."

Sal laughed when Anis accepted and the Anglian pulled her in close, pushing one of her hands against his chest. The Representative was blushing rather impressively, but she also didn't try to pull away. The man just moved his hands to her hips and started grinding - and the entire group of women cheered him on.

"Oh?" the man Sal was dancing with asked. "Is that how I'm supposed to be doing this?"

He spun Sal around and slapped her ass before pressing his hips tight against hers. Tyr laughed, clearly paying attention, but when Sal managed to get her eyes to focus on him, he looked like he was enjoying the view a little too much. She crooked a finger at him.

"You gonna come play?" Sal teased.

"Oh, damn," the man behind her groaned. "I heard you iliri were kinky, but fuck. Stealing your friend's man?"

"Her man," Tyr said, turning Rayna to give her a push toward Sal. "And sure, Sal. I'll dance with him, but you gotta dance with Ray. Trust me, I've spent a lot of time waiting to see it."

Rayna closed the distance in something only barely more controlled than a stagger and pushed at the man's shoulder. He let Sal go and stepped back, putting on a show about it, even though Rayna had barely pushed. Then Rayna bowed low and offered her hand to Sal.

"That worked?" the guy asked.

Tyr moved beside him, grinning a little too much. "Trust me, those two don't take a lot of encouraging." Then he raised his voice. "I want some grinding, ladies. Little making out wouldn't hurt either."

"Oh yeah?" Rayna asked.

Sal stepped into her, pressing their bodies together. Tyr groaned, reaching down to adjust himself without shame. The guy beside him couldn't pull his eyes away as the women writhed together seductively. The only problem was that they couldn't stop laughing, which totally destroyed the image.

Then Sal felt something. A rush of surprise, but not the warning kind. This came with happiness. She flicked her ears up and looked around just in time to see Shift sneak in behind Rayna, wrapping his arms around her without pulling her away from Sal. And then a hand moved Sal's hair away from her neck. A second later, sharp teeth teased her skin.

I did na know ya would be here, Jase thought before changing his touch on her neck to a kiss. *Seems we picked the right place.*

"Yeah," Sal breathed as she leaned into him. "You definitely did."

"Who's buying?" someone called out. Sal thought it sounded like the Myrosican Justice.

"That's me," Tseri said.

Sal turned to see Krex with his arm in the air, clutching a yellow token. "I'll split the tab."

"I want in on that," Grenso said.

"I already used mine," Vilko grumbled.

The Unavi senators smiled at each other, then Vinx produced hers. "I like this place. Let's see if we can drink everything on the shelves tonight."

They cornered one of the servers, all pushing their tokens at her. The woman had no idea what to do with them, but kept nodding even as she backed towards the bar. The man on the other side didn't have that problem. He swept all of the brightly-colored tokens together and waved for the band to kick it up a notch. As the music grew louder, the apparent owner began pulling bottles from the shelves and setting them down on the counter.

"We've got some rich friends tonight," he bellowed. "How about we show them all how the commoners play in Anglia?"

That was when things truly started to get out of hand. Sal ended up with another drink. She couldn't put a name to it, but it burned nicely as it went down. Jase had one hand wrapped around the neck of a bottle and the other holding her against him. Somehow Krex from Myrosica ended up dancing with Vilko. His face was a dark color from blushing, and Vilko kept pressing into him, making it turn ever brighter.

"Shots!" Sal's last dance partner called out. "I'm buying one for my friend's guys. C'mon, I know there's more than one of you."

"That's me," Jase said, hauling Sal after him as he stumbled toward the man's voice.

"Let 'em through," the guy yelled, because a crowd was starting to form. "You drinking with us, Miss Sal?"

"Just Sal," she said, "and yes."

"I *knew* it!" He laughed. "You're really her, huh?"

Blaz fell in at her side. "She's really her."

"So what number are you?"

Instead of answering, Blaz started pointing. "That's one, he's two, three is... there. Four is on her other side. I'm five, and that one is six."

"Ok." Sal's new friend set out eight tiny glasses. "And what are we celebrating?"

"My best friend is getting married to my brothers," Sal said, moving to the edge of the table.

"So, you?" he asked, jerking his chin at Rayna.

"Yep," she agreed, nodding her head too much.

"And the guy - or guys - you're marrying?" He looked up, scanning the crowd.

"That's me," Shift said, thrusting his arm up as he pushed closer for his own shot of alcohol.

Somehow, Dom managed to slip in behind him. "I'm the other. What's your name, friend?"

"Carbis," the man said as he turned. Then he saw the King. "Oh, shit. I mean... You're the...."

Dom lifted a finger to his lips. "Just Dom. I get one of those too?"

"Yes, sir," Carbis agreed, looking over his new friends with awe. "You all done shots before?"

"Plenty of times," Dom assured him as he reached for a glass. "Last one finished buys the next round?"

They all reached for their little glasses. None of them pointed out that drinks were already paid for. They simply started counting. "One, two... Three!" the group yelled as one, and then they all tilted their drinks back and swallowed.

Sal slammed her glass back to the table first, but Rayna was only a split-second behind her. Carbis tied with Jase, of all people, but Blaz was last. With a shrug, he gestured for someone to hand him a bottle and began pouring again, and the onlookers began to cheer them on.

"Gonna need a lot more glasses," Blaz yelled, looking over to the bar.

But a woman was already heading over with them, plus two more bottles. "Owner says we're closing the doors to new customers tonight, so the whole place is yours." She started lining up shot glasses. "So which one's the lucky bride?"

"Me!" Rayna said. "Oh, that is so me."

The waitress grinned at her. "Congratulations, Your Highness."

That made a few people gasp in surprise - the ones who hadn't figured it out yet, but Rayna was just waving for the waitress to hush. "Shh, don't tell. This is the only place in town where we don't have to be stuffy. Our new little hiding spot with some *real* people."

"Then drink up," Carbis told her. "Never shared a table with nobility before."

Vilko pushed in and slammed down her glass. "Fill that up, boy? And you're not just with nobility. You have almost all the world leaders here."

"Most fun I've ever had," Anis said, pushing closer to hold out her own glass. "Someone fill me up so I can dance with Myrosica."

"Unav's dancing with him," Vilko told her. "I dunno which one, but one of them." She made a point of blinking. "Damn, but Anglians know how to have fun."

Carbis just looked her over, his eyes hanging a little too long on her body. "And what do you do, honey?"

"Careful," Rayna warned. "That's the Chieftain of Escea. She'll kick your ass, boy."

"Not tonight," Vilko assured him. "Sal, I'm taking your party favor."

"Then I'm stealing one too," Rayna said. "Tseri!"

The Kaeen's eyes lit up and she turned. "Kesh!"

Dom just grabbed the bottle and started pouring. "Go dance. I think some of these guys will help me catch up on the drinks."

"I need one," Shift told him.

"Guys," Dom said, grabbing Shift's arm to pull him around the edge of the table and into Dom's side. "This is the new Royal Consort. I mean, he will be. Might as well be. Help me show my future husband a good time?"

"Husband?" someone asked.

Dom nodded. "I'm marrying that sexy woman over there and him. I mean, we're both marrying her, technically."

"Iliri?" asked a woman with a little too much makeup on her face and a dress that was *much* too short.

Shift nodded. "I am. They're human."

The woman - who looked like a prostitute - grinned. "Someone needs to give them some South Street wine. I bet the Consort ends up naked before the night's over, and I wouldn't mind seeing that."

"Is that a dare?" Shift asked.

Dom answered before she could. "Oh yeah. I'm daring you. First one of us naked is the last one in her bed tonight."

"It's on," Shift said, pointing to the glasses. "You all heard it. We're going to drink until we're *naked!*"

Hearing that, Sal turned in Jase's arms to grab his shirt and tug. "Figure we can start slow," she said.

"Ya just wanna see my tattoos," he teased, but he was helping. As his shirt came over his head, he tossed it toward the tables at the side of the room. "Whacha got under the shirt?" he asked Sal.

She grabbed both sides and lifted, revealing a black, military-style tank. "Just this."

"That shows off a whole lot more a yer skin," Jase purred, pulling her shirt from her hands just to fling it the same direction as his. But he looked up. "Ya wanna play, ya gotta lose the shirt, big brother."

"Sounds good to me," Zep promised. "But I think we're about to make a scene." And he pointed to the men moving in on both sides of Sal, each of them bare-chested. "Care to dance, kitten?" Zep asked.

Sal flicked her ears forward, feeling her head tilt in confusion. "Huh?" He never called her that!

Zep just stepped in to press her up against Jase. "I'm willing to bet that's exactly what Jase's thinking right about now."

"Dancing was na quite what I had in mind," Jase countered as he cupped her face. "Maybe somethan a little more... fun. Because this party is a lot better when we do na have ta play nice."

Just as he kissed her, she felt her other mates move in. And yes, they danced, but only enough so that each one of them could sneak in to kiss her. Some part of her, and they didn't even care which one. The best part, though, was that no one in the pub cared at all.

CHAPTER FIFTY

PURPLE

*A*round the time the barkeep started listing off things he'd run out of, the music began to slow down. Sal was drunk. Not a little tipsy, but staggeringly so, and so was everyone else in the pub with her. When one of the regular patrons fell over a stool on his way to the door, claiming he should probably get home, Dom called in some help.

The man swore he was fine, but he clearly wasn't. Like everyone else, he'd had too much to drink, and too much fun to consider it a bad thing. It took a bit, but where Dom couldn't convince him to sit down and rest up, Rayna found a way. The man smiled at her with adoration, but the healthy kind. After all, this was the woman who was about to become his Queen.

Around them, the party was slowly winding down, but it wasn't quite done. Still, most of their new friends had work in the morning, so they couldn't stay all night. Dom convinced them to wait for just a bit longer. He swore he had a reason, and then an Anglian soldier banged on the door. With a wave from the King, one of the Devil Dogs opened it, and the soldier stepped in. Sal was pretty sure she recognized him.

"I have three wagons, Dom. You want us to make sure everyone gets home, right?"

"Yep," Dom said. "Help them all the way to their beds if you have to." He sighed, blowing out a breath. "Because they started before me, and I'm fucking *drunk*, Dalyr."

The grauori ambassador began to chuckle. "I see. Is *anyone* in here sober?"

Sal pointed toward one side of the room. It happened to be the wrong one, but she didn't care. "The ammas aren't."

"What do you need?" Vanica asked. "We've made sure they didn't destroy everything."

Dalyr groaned in relief. "Someone who isn't stupid. Um, you want me to come back for everyone here?"

"Horses!" Tilso said. "We have horses. They're in a barn, with a guy. We can use those to get home."

"Yeah," Dalyr said. "Pretty sure you won't be riding them. At least not for very long. Nica? Don't let anyone leave. I've got my whole unit and a few drivers out there. We'll keep making trips until you're all ready to leave - so no one gets mugged because the King got them drunk."

"How many can a cart hold?" Vanica asked.

Dalyr wobbled his head from side to side. "Ten or so. I was told you have about thirty people here from the Palace."

"And more from Arhhawen," Vanica pointed out.

"We'll make it work," Dalyr assured her. "Even if I have to ask for another cart."

"Good idea," Dom mumbled his way. "You do that, Dalyr." He paused, looking over to the side. "I am not taking over your man, Rragri. I just knew he had a cart. He said he'd handle it."

"I did," Dalyr told her, then paused. "Drink more, Orassae. Your thoughts aren't muddled enough yet." But he grinned. "Close, but you can do better. And anyone who wants to go home, let me know! I'll be back in half an hour if you're not ready."

A few accepted his offer, but it wasn't enough to kill the fun. Sal decided it was time to experiment, so she made her way to the bar, bouncing off something hard that she quickly realized was Gage. He caught her and turned them both the right way, but misjudged the distance. They thumped up against the wooden counter side by side.

"What's your poison, Sal?" the barkeep asked.

"I want somethan new," she slurred. "Not rum. No mead! I want somethan yummy."

"Ok." The man set a glass before her. "But one condition. You make sure those guys over there don't go all the way in my bar, ok?"

Sal turned, yelling, "Risk!"

But the man she was yelling at wasn't Risk. *He* was on the other side. "What?" he called back.

"Are you naked?" Sal asked.

Perin answered. "Close. I think I lost his shirt. Tilso's too."

"Pants open?" Sal asked.

"Nope," Perin said. "Figured we didn't need to get messy."

"I got 'em," Arianna said, proving she was hovering around that group. "Niran's mostly sober."

"She means I can still walk," he clarified.

"Ok," Sal said tapping the bar for her drink, assuming she was done.

The barkeep just pointed back to the men he'd actually been talking about. "Them. I'm guessing they're yours? They have that funny gold-blonde hair that usually means iliri, right?"

Gage leaned back - and then started laughing. "Kinetry?" he asked, sounding incredulous.

"What? Where!" Sal followed where Gage pointed to find her old friend holding a guy against the rough, plank-wood wall, with another pressing into his back. "Kinetry?!"

His head snapped over with a drunken smile, but so did his friends. Sal knew she'd seen them before, but it was Gage who gasped in shock. "Exton?" he asked. "I think I got that right."

"Zaedyn," the man at the back told him. Then he pointed at the one against the wall. "That's Exton."

"Ok," Gage said before he started laughing again. "Um, all three of you still have your pants on?"

Exton began fumbling at the front of Kinetry's, but the bodies blocked the view. "Mostly!" he said. "I'm putting it back."

Sal didn't want to know what "it" was. She could guess, though. And then, while Exton pulled his lover's pants back in place, Kinetry leaned closer to kiss him. Zaedyn chuckled and pulled him back.

"The Kaisae said you have to get dressed," he explained, his voice tender.

"Keep it respectable," Gage told them. "At least until you get to a room."

Sal just looked at Gage, doing her best to whisper - which wasn't very good. "Kinetry's onsyc?"

"Um..." Gage just chuckled. "Looks that way. I guess he made some friends in Viraenova. Those two are the lookouts Tseri had working with Shaden. Sounds like Exton's completely into men, but his mate isn't as limited in his preference. I have no idea where Kinetry falls, but... I'm not actually opposed. Would be even better if we could convince those two to stay."

"Only if Tseri won't kill me for taking her best talent," Sal said.

For once, iliri hearing worked against her, because Tseri heard her name. "What talent?" the Kaeen called at her.

Sal pointed toward Kinetry, Exton, and Zaedyn. "Shade's friends."

Tseri lifted her glass at them in a toast. "Exton! You wanna be iliri or nuvani?"

"Same thing," he said. "Mostly, I was just wanting to get laid."

"Well, let me know if you want to extend your visit," Tseri told him.

Zaedyn slid his hands over Kinetry's ass. "At least a few months, Kaeen. Maybe more."

"Works for me," Tseri laughed, "Here's to some Viraenovan ambassadors in Arhhawen."

"Wait," Gage muttered as he swung his head back to the barkeep. "It ok if they keep kissing?"

"Don't care about the kissing or the groping," the man assured them. "Just gotta make sure it doesn't get to the fucking, because that causes some problems." Then he leaned closer. "We don't ask a lot of questions here. Now, how about something fruity?" Because he still hadn't made Sal's drink.

"Mm," she said. "I can do fruity."

He began pouring, adding a few things together to make layers in the glass. "And you, sir?"

Gage shook his head. "Surprise me. I'm not as picky as her."

"Cinnamon," the bartender decided, and grabbed another glass.

Once they had their drinks in hand, Gage led Sal back toward their table. Kolt and Ghost were lying more than sitting, and clearly feeling it. Jase had a massive smile on his face, but Blaz was still going, matching Tyr drink for drink. Arctic had Shade out on the dance floor, holding her close as they swayed to some slow, soft tune.

Across the room, Narnx was laughing with a couple of humans. He was smiling wide enough to show all of his teeth without shame, and none of his friends seemed to care at all. Sal lifted her glass, taking a small sip as she watched, thankful that this idea had been a success instead of a massive failure. It could've gone either way, but it seemed that a little alcohol had been what they really needed to get the world leaders to finally communicate.

And everyone else, it seemed.

Just as Narnx began to explain some point or other, he gestured with his arms. One of them held a drink. The problem was that he reached out just as Baeli tried to get around him, most likely heading for the restroom on the other side. Narnx's hand caught her arm, his drink tilted, and she squeaked as the cool liquid splashed across her chest.

A second later, the empty glass fell to the floor and shattered. It wasn't enough to stop the rest of the party, but Narnx's fingers lay touching her bare skin, and he'd forgotten about everything else in the room.

"Baeli," he breathed.

She tilted her head. "Pretty sure you just soaked my shirt, brother."

"I'm really not your brother," he told her.

"I'm pretty sure my shirt's still soaked," she teased.

He just nodded. "Yeah. I'm so sorry." His eyes dropped to her chest, then jumped right back up. "Take mine." Before she could answer, he pulled his off like so many of the men had throughout the night and thrust it toward her. "I'm so sorry," he said again.

Baeli just let her eyes roam across his chest, ignoring the shirt. Slowly, she reached up to trace a scar that ran from below his nipple down beside his belly button. He caught her wrist, stopping the caress.

"My father's wife did that," he said softly.

"Then I'm glad Keeya killed her. What about that one?" She looked at a puckered spot beside his shoulder.

The corner of his lip curled upward. "I think it was Arctic. I'm not a healer."

"And this one?" she asked, moving her hand - and his since he still held her wrist - to a point just at the edge of his waistband. "Looks like it was bad."

His eyes were locked on hers. "Your brother did that. A backhanded slash at a full gallop, but it's why I wasn't in the caves when they killed the rest of my squad."

"The ones at Skyline Creek?" she asked. "In Escea? They told me about that."

"Yeah," Narnx said softly. "I used to be the enemy, Baeli."

She slowly reached over to accept his shirt. "And some of us used to be slaves. We're allowed to change now."

Then, right before his eyes, she pulled off her wet shirt and traded it for his dry one. Narnx's eyes dropped to her chest, taking in the bare flesh she'd exposed. He leaned in, his hand reaching for her before he stopped himself, but he was breathing hard enough to make the rise and fall of his chest visible.

"I have a mate," she told him as she pulled his shirt over her head.

He nodded. "I've talked to him."

"I won't set him aside as my ahnor."

"I wouldn't ask you to. He's my brother."

"Good." And Baeli grabbed the back of Narnx's neck and pulled his mouth to hers.

For a moment, he froze, but his mind quickly remembered what to do. When his hands landed on her waist, he pulled her closer, until there was no space left between them, and he kissed her like an iliri. Their teeth flashed, lips and jaws were nipped, while around them, Narnx's new friends cheered him on.

But Geo had seen it all. Without a word, he got up and crossed the room. Stepping behind Baeli, he grabbed a fistful of her hair, pulled it aside, and bit her neck hard. She pulled back with a gasp, but Narnx wasn't ready to let go. He did, however, smile.

"I've never had another iliri around to share," he warned her.

"Oh, we'll figure it out," Baeli promised as she reached for his mouth again.

Where she sat watching the whole thing, Sal leaned over toward Gage. "So," she asked, "is that the last prophecy?"

"Narnx's vision was about a child, and they're a long way from that," he reminded her.

"But we're on the right path," Sal told him.

Kolt managed to lift his head to smile at her. "The best path, Sal. We're on the best path now."

CHAPTER FIFTY-ONE

BLUE

*T*he next day was quiet. Very, very quiet. A few healers slipped through Dorton Palace to help with the hangovers, but that did nothing for the exhaustion of staying up until nearly dawn. The best part was that none of those who'd been out with Dom, Shift, and Rayna the night before said a single word to those who hadn't. It was almost like it had been little more than a figment of their imagination.

But it was also the balm Sal needed to get back on track. Zep told her what Krex had said about the iliri. She told him what Anis had talked about. So, unless Unav went against their own interests or Vilko betrayed Sal's offer of friendship, the law for recognition would pass. That meant she needed to be prepared when it came time to counter the restrictions for her species in battle.

That kept her busy until the next Alliance Meeting, exactly one week after the first. The King's wedding was supposed to be held the day after a treaty and the new Conventions of War were agreed upon and signed. Sal hoped that would be sooner rather than later. Mostly because the less time they spent arguing about it, the more likely it was for this to actually go through.

So, on the morning of the summit, she once again rode into Dorton, making a procession of it all. This time, she came "armed." Her weapons were books, and it took all of her mates, plus Arctic and Ghost, to carry them in. One by one, the men stacked them up behind the Anglian leaders. Small strips of colored paper peeked from between the pages, marking the spots Sal would need most, and everyone else noticed.

"I see you came prepared," Senator Telyra said as she made her way to her own chair.

Sal smiled over at her. "I came with hope," she corrected. "Those won't help any of us if we can't make this vote."

Representative Sherin came down the stairs and gestured to the miniature library. "Precedent?" he asked.

"That's the idea," Sal said. "Iliri precedent."

He met her eyes and smiled. "I had a feeling you'd be overly prepared. While the rest of us are making it up as we go, you always have a plan, a back-up plan, and a dozen more contingencies, don't you?"

"It's how my kind stay alive," she reminded him, all too aware that his was the only vote she couldn't predict.

"There's irony there," he mumbled to himself as he turned for his seat beside Jakin.

Next, it was Anis, but she didn't care about the books. "Did I do anything stupid?" she whispered as she paused beside Sal.

"Lots," Sal assured her.

Anis chuckled. "So, that shirtless man really happened?"

"The head of my Peacekeepers paid him a hundred guilders to take off his shirt and dance with you."

"What happens in Anglia stays in Anglia, right?" Anis begged.

"You'll have to talk to Grenso about that," Sal told her. "I'm pretty sure he saw most of it."

"Lucky for her," Grenso said, walking up to join them, "in my culture, it's not a man's place. The woman gets to choose, as often and as varied as she prefers. It's also not my story to tell. It stays in Anglia, Deina."

He patted her shoulder and they both moved to sit down with their peers. Tseri came in not long after, with an armload of journals hugged to her chest. She passed those to her mates as she claimed her chair. The last one to arrive, oddly enough, was Vilko. Like Sal, she had books, but that wasn't all. Two tubes looked like they were meant to hold maps, and there was a box of something else that two of her warriors lugged between them.

That meant they were ready. This looked like it was going to happen. When the entire group was where they belonged, with their chairs pulled up to the table, and most of their hands folded on top of it, Dom finally stood. In the stands surrounding the amphitheater, the crowd stilled until there was complete and total silence.

"I would like to call the second day of the meeting of the Continental Alliance of Nations to order," Dom said. "Our first thing on the agenda today is a vote. The rest of the schedule is dependent upon the outcome of this vote. As you all know, my co-rulers, both the Kaisae and the Orassae, have asked for their species to be listed as sentient and sovereign species, equal to humans under international law." He paused, his eyes moving over to Tseri. "Kaeen? As the person who made it possible for both species to have a voice, would you like to call the vote?"

"I would be honored, sire," she said as she stood. "Ladies and gentlemen of the alliance, I would like to remind you all that for centuries, you have begged Viraenova to participate in these meetings. You heard of our technologies and assumed we had machines to make such things happen. Instead, we have people. Iliri people, for that is what the nuvani are. Viraenova is an entire country of iliri-human crossbreds, and we are proof that not only can those two species coexist, but that the grauori can thrive among us as well."

She paused to tip her head toward Rragri. "It is due to the Orassae's influence that I felt it was time to leave my country's borders. If my close friend could brave the world of humans, then Viraenova could do the same, and yet we still have our walls. Depending upon the outcome of this vote, my people may very well return to our home and lock those gates again. So I now stand before you to ask if you, as representatives of your nations, will agree that the iliri and grauori, plus all crossbred offspring who descend from them, are people equal to humans, with both the sentience and the inherent authority to control their own lives?"

"And how does Viraenova vote?" Dom asked.

Tseri smiled. "Viraenova votes yes."

He moved down the table. "Senators of Unav? How does your nation vote?"

Vinx eased herself to her feet. "Sire, since the people of Unav are predominantly iliri and human, and because this was the reason given when we long ago requested aid from our allies and received none, we think that yes, iliri and grauori are just as sentient and sovereign as humans. Unav votes yes."

"Justice Krex?" Dom nodded to the man. "How does your nation vote?"

"Myrosica is a nation founded on the idea of justice," Krex announced. "Therefore, supporting this change is the only fair and just thing we can do. Myrosica votes yes, and declares ourselves a sanctuary for all species."

Dom turned to Narnx. "Emperor Zaryn-Geirr? How does the nation of Terric vote?"

Narnx stood proudly. "As an iliri myself, and a man who has seen the destruction of hatred firsthand, Terric votes yes."

Dom let out a deep sigh, and shifted to the other side of the table. "Chieftain Vilko? How does your nation vote?"

The leader of Escea took her turn to stand. "Escea," she said, "is a nation founded on the idea that those who are strong enough deserve the right to rule. I have seen no people stronger or more capable than the iliri and grauori, nor more willing to forgive. A woman who could've destroyed my country taught me that humanity does not only belong to humans. It is a trait common among all three of the sentient species of Ogun. Escea is *proud* to vote yes."

Sal let out a breath, relief flooding her body. She'd hoped Vilko wouldn't betray her, but she hadn't been completely sure. With Gallicor and Namisa abstaining from attending, that left only one more country to cast their vote, and somehow Dom had seated them so they would be the last. Clutching her hands together, Sal closed her eyes and waited.

"Representatives of the Conglomerate of Free Citizens?" Dom asked. "How does your nation vote?"

It wasn't Anis who stood up. It wasn't even Grenso. Representative Sherin slowly pushed himself to his feet and leaned over the table, the impact of his hands sending a vibration through the wood. "Kaisae?" he asked. "Will you look at me?"

Pulling in a breath, she lifted her lids and glanced to where the man stood braced. "I see you, Representative Sherin."

"It was early fall when we met. I'd been raised to believe that the non-human species were beastly things who'd turn on me. The problem was that you never denied it. You tried to explain it, but not once did you try to lie to me and say that your people, or the grauori, were harmless victims. Do you remember that?"

"I do, Representative," she assured him.

"I asked the Kaisae how I could be sure that we could trust them, and she answered. Not in any way I'd expect from a human. Instead, she let me into her mind. For a few seconds that felt more like an eternity, I experienced life as an iliri. I was suffocated with the hopelessness of subjugation. I was enraged at the unfair treatment - and *abuse* - heaped on me for no reason. I felt the complete and utter despair of having no options, and then the agony of losing another person I loved. She told me she'd tried to limit the pain, but it felt like my own mother had died all over again while having my mind pierced through with daggers. No, I didn't feel it, but I felt the memory of it, and then she said something to me. Salryc Luxx said that was happening over and over again across the world. Each time a loved one was ripped from a pack, they suffered that kind of pain. Would you say that's a fair description of events, Kaisae?"

Sal nodded. "It is, Representative."

"And yet," Sherin went on, "buried in all of that was a complete lack of interest in any sort of revenge against humanity as a whole. She wanted to end the war that killed her friends - iliri, human, and grauori alike. And she had a *plan*, one so complicated that I lived through it and still can't quite explain all the pieces she put into play. If we're asking about sentience? I cannot deny that the iliri are not only sentient, but more so than any human I've ever met. Sovereign? Well, while this is a highly contested topic in my own country, we are the Conglomerate of *Free* Citizens. If the two species who made the end of the Terran War possible aren't capable of wielding the power over their own lives, then none of us are.

"Kaisae, King, and Orassae," he went on, "The Conglomerate of Free Citizens proudly votes yes." Then he pointed at the stack of books Sal had brought. "The irony I spoke of, Kaisae? It was your plan, the back-up plan, and all the additional contingencies that made us unable to vote any other way. I'm glad you brought the books. Let me be the first to congratulate the iliri and grauori on your real independence."

"Thank you," she mouthed, because the words just wouldn't come out.

With his words, this was really happening. Every nation in the Alliance Meeting had unanimously voted to recognize both iliri and grauori as real people, capable of controlling their own lives and smart enough to be treated as equals. Slowly, Sal looked down the table to Rragri.

We did it?

The Orassae was bobbing her head. *They can't take it back, either. I don't think there's any precedent for taking it away from us. Not now, and not in the future!*

There's not, Sal agreed. *That means it's done. We're....*

Real, Rragri finished for her. *We're finally real people.*

Sal huffed a laugh, a look on her face that was part smile and part open-mouthed shock. The Unavi senators looked just as dumbstruck as she did, but Tseri was smiling proudly. Then Sal looked over at Narnx. Her brother had a fist pressed to his lips and was breathing slowly.

You ok? she asked him.

He flicked his pale green eyes up to meet hers. They were glassy. *Please tell me not to cry? I'm human enough that I can, but not here. Not now?*

You. Will. Not. Cry, she ordered. *This is not something to cry about. It's a reason to laugh and be proud. You are the Emperor of Terric, the Kaisae's brother, and an impressive ilus. You* deserve *this.*

A smile flickered across his lips. *We all do. Thank you, sister. Thank you, my Kaisae.*

Vilko leaned back in her chair and laughed softly. "Do we need a little break for our allies to celebrate?"

"No," Sal assured her. "My kind of celebrations usually take a while, and I think the King wants to finish soon so he can finally have his wedding." Sal cleared her throat. "Which means that the next thing on the docket is to discuss changes to the Conventions of War to accommodate the addition of two new species to the rules of warfare. Does anyone have a point they would like to address?"

Vilko lifted her hand. "Desecration of bodies. That has to come out, since humans are a food source for iliri and grauori."

"But we can't condone cannibalism," Anis pointed out.

Vilko groaned and reached back for one of her books. Her warrior slapped it into her palm and she spread it open on the table before her. "According to our records, grauori are more closely related - genetically speaking - to a monkey-type primate called a tamarin." She turned the book so everyone could see the image. "Humans trace back to apes. While apes and monkeys do share some genetic similarities, they are not the same species."

"But iliri are hybrids, aren't they?" Krex asked.

Sal shook her head. "Genetically modified organisms. Under normal circumstances, grauori and humans would not be capable of producing a hybrid. Records found in Arhhawen suggest that a mutation that occurred from long-term exposure to stellar radiation..." Sal shrugged. "I'm quoting here, so please don't ask me how that works, but that's what made one single bloodline viable. The woman's name was Njeri Zepyr. She lived over three thousand years ago, which is why hybridization is *now* possible, but otherwise, the original humans and grauori would not be able to cross-breed."

"Wait," Tseri said, "so does that mean our crossbreds carry the Kaisae gene?"

Sal groaned. "Not necessarily. The ability to produce a viable child was the mutation. The Kaisae gene is separate. Both could be inherited, or only the reproductive ability. But yes, some crossbreds could inherit our nearly-lost gender from their human ancestors, in theory."

"Which means," Krex said, "that iliri are chimeras of human and grauori genetics, not hybrids. I was told that mineral deficiencies are the reason for the craving of human meat - for the iron in our blood. That means *we* made them this way, so we must deal with it. We have to take desecration of bodies off the list."

"Define it," Anis offered. "Consumption would not be included, but acts of terror could still be prevented."

"I like that," Vilko said. "I know a few Warlords who'd take advantage of it if you tried to remove this. So, we can't limit cutting, devouring, or removing the bodies. I would think that acts of display would be our main focus?"

"So long as our preparation areas aren't considered display," Tseri pointed out. "And while we have non-human options in peacetime, the mineral-rich meat comes from a creature indigenous to the Ahnian Ridge. There is nothing over by - "

Rragri suddenly surged to her feet, cutting off Tseri mid-sentence. The Orassae's head whipped around to her mates and the hair on the back of her neck began to rise. A moment later, Dom gasped.

"Nya," he breathed. "Rragri, go!"

"What?" Sal asked. "Is she ok?"

Dom nodded. "She just started active labor, but the healer says the babies won't take turns. They asked for help."

From the stands, Blaz yelled, "I'm going, Sal!"

He didn't wait, just raced for the door, but Kolt was only a step behind him. Her Taunor sent back a half-formed thought that he'd watch Blaz's back, then they were gone. So were Rragri and her mates, the three of them scrambling away on all fours as fast as they could move. And that was very, very fast.

"Ilija!" Dom yelled at the stands. "Go! You're about to be a grandfather, so *go!*"

Vilko shoved to her feet and thrust her arm to the stairs. "Dom, you and Sal go too."

"This can wait," Tseri told him. "That's your family."

Sal looked back at her books. "We need to - "

"No," Narnx said. "You *need* to go help Nya. Leave the books."

Sal jiggled her head in agreement, torn between what she wanted to do and what she should be doing. "I color-coded the tabs, but you can't read them. Not well enough."

"Iliran?" Anis asked.

"Most of those are from the Iliri University," she explained. "I assumed that we all know human precedent, but the point here is how to make the laws for those of us who aren't human, so I brought as much of our history as I could."

"Looks like all of it," Jakin muttered.

"Not even close," Sal told him. "These are just the parts about war. It explains *why* we do so many of the things humans can't understand, so we can find a way to make the Conventions fair."

Vinx growled as she shoved herself up. "And I can read Iliran. So can Telyra and the Kaeen. We know the colors and we'll teach the humans. The King is leaving, but the meeting was not closed. You go. We will work on this, and we cannot sign until the King calls a vote. Kaisae, trust your allies for *once.* Go be with your pack. All of your pack."

"C'mon, kitten," Jase said. "Zep's bringing the horses around ta the front. This is na a war, it's a birth, and Nya needs ya too."

"Trust us," Vilko whispered. "I know it's hard, but give us a chance to prove that things have changed."

Sal nodded at everyone sitting before her. "We'll let you know about the babies, and I'll send a time for us to try again."

But Jase had come down the stairs to grab her arm. "Sal," he begged.

The pleading in his voice was enough. Spinning in place, ignoring the books, she turned to run, and the Blades came with her. Arctic, Shaden, Gage, Tyr, and more. Behind them, the crowd clapped encouragement, everyone having heard the Orassae say that her daughter was finally having her children.

CHAPTER FIFTY-TWO

GREEN

It was taking too long. Nya didn't make a sound, but Sal knew that was Blaz's healing. Raast was on her way from Arhhawen to help, but she hadn't made it here yet. Tensa was coming with her, just in case they needed an iliri midwife, even though Nya had a grauori one from her amma's pack. Then there were the doctors. Sal had seen three different humans enter the suite, only for two of them to come back out.

Eventually, Jarl gave up on pacing and leaned against the wall beside her door. Slowly, he slid down until his rump rested on the marble floor. Ilija immediately scooted over to sit beside him.

"She's going to be fine," he promised. "We have the best of everything here for her."

"But what about the kids?" Jarl asked. "Dad, we don't even know what they are!"

"Doesn't matter," Ilija assured him. "Those are my grandchildren, and you have all three kingdoms here to make sure they are taken care of, ok? We can't predict the future - well, not anymore - but we're going to do everything we can. It just takes a while. Trust me, Jarl. You kids like to drive us fathers crazy before making a grand appearance."

Jarl flopped over, letting his head rest on his Dad's arm. "Where's Amma?"

Ilija laughed once. "She's with your sisters. When did you start calling her amma?"

"When we left for war," Jarl admitted. "That's what Nya calls her mother, and what the pups called Sal. I dunno, it just sounded better than *Mom*."

"When do I get to be dava?" Ilija asked.

"I dunno," Jarl mumbled. "You're too..."

"Human," Sal finished for him from where she sat across the hall. "You're a dad, Ilija. Dom could be a dava, but you're a little too human."

"Good thing, or a bad one?" Ilija asked.

"It's just a thing," she assured him. "And Jarl, Blaz promised that he will tell me if there are any problems. Even the minor ones. Last I heard, they were hoping the babies could come naturally, but they aren't cooperating. Seems they aren't interested in waiting their turn. I'd say like their dava, but I think their amma's the same way."

Jarl slowly nodded. "She really is. And Dad, I know you still don't get it, but I love her, ok?"

"I know," Ilija assured him. "Trust me, I've been there. I *know*. Everyone tells you it's stupid until you feel a little too defensive, and you try to do everything to prove you mean it, but they're still going to talk. Thing is, none of that matters, ok? You and Nya are still young." Ilija paused to let out a heavy sigh. "*Too* young, but you've got a good head on your shoulders. If you think you love her, then don't let anyone else change your mind for you. I was in love with your amma at the same age."

"You just didn't screw it up as fast," Jarl muttered under his breath.

Sal flicked her ears forward. "Is it a fuck-up if you didn't know?" she asked.

Jarl thrust his arm out at Jase. "He *warned* me, Sal. That first time he caught me, Jase took me to have that talk, and he warned me, Dad warned me, and Dom did too. I just... I didn't want to listen."

"I did na warn ya about this," Jase said. "I warned ya that ya might na be able ta touch a human. That yer heir could be a problem. This? I did na know it was possible either. We did na know ya had the gene."

"We didn't even know about the gene," Tyr pointed out. "Besides, anyone who gives you shit? Well, they just got lucky, because I can assure you that every guy sitting in this hall?" He wagged his finger in both directions, pointing out the Shields, Dogs, and Blades waiting for news. "They were all trying to get their dicks wet at your age too. Some of them struck out. Some of them got lucky. Not *one* of us thought about pregnancy back then. Oh, the girls did. They took their pills, chased us off, and all of that, but the boys? Nah. They don't have any room to talk."

Sal looked over at Jase. "Is that so?"

"I was na that young," he admitted. "Eighteen."

"Fifteen," Zep said. "So, yeah. Tyr's right."

"Kolt?" Gage asked. "How about you?"

"Seventeen," Kolt said. "You?"

"Same. Well, the day before. Was supposed to be my present, she said." Gage shrugged. "I thought it was pretty good. She didn't."

"What about you, Tyr?" Sal asked.

He sighed. "Sal, you don't wanna know that."

"You don't have to tell me if you don't want to," she told him.

"Fourteen, ok?" He leaned his head back against the wall. "She was sixteen, so it's not quite *that* gross, but still pretty gross."

Ilija looked across the doorway to where Dom sat. "What about you?"

"I think I was about sixteen," Dom said. "Maybe fifteen. Didn't realize for a very long time that she was hoping we'd get caught so she could end up the Marquess of Valmere, though."

"That merchant's girl?" Ilija asked. "The one with the fucked-up nose?"

"That's the one," Dom said. "Hey, Zep? You ever do a human?"

"Once," Zep said. "Swore never again."

"C'mon," Rayna groaned. "We're not that bad."

"*You* got a link," Zep told her.

"Didn't when I started hitting on you," she countered.

"And I wasn't interested either," Zep pointed out. "You're a damned good soldier, Ray, and a better friend, but not my type." He smiled over at Sal. "I kinda knew what I wanted."

"You hated me when we met," Sal said.

"No, I didn't like that my entire unit had turned stupid. I didn't blame *you* for it. I just thought their dicks were starting to shrivel up and it was affecting their brains. I wanted to make it clear that you weren't anything special." He smiled, his eyes dropping to the floor. "Except that you were."

From down the hall, Geo scooted forward so he could see. "Hey, Zep? They tell you she was a Kaisae?"

"Not exactly," Zep said. "I'm pretty sure they weren't quite sure either."

"Couldn't believe it, actually," Arctic said. "This purebred girl, who'd been in Fort Landing and the Stonewater Stables for years, and not a single one of us had caught a hint of her? Kaisaes had been gone for years by then, and she'd been right under our noses the whole time?"

Gage pulled his knees up to his chest and wrapped his arms around them. "We were all so sure she had to be fucked up. Too tame or too feral, you know? And none of you can imagine what she was like back then."

"Wild?" Dom asked.

"No," Arctic breathed. "No, she was almost meek. Her military protocol was impeccable. Her manners were perfectly human. She didn't smile. Sal didn't even expose her teeth when she talked, and she wore a cap every chance she could to hide her ears. Our new recruit didn't flinch when we looked in her eyes. No, Private Salryc Luxx was something no one had ever seen before."

"Really?" Sal asked. "I was just trying to stay out of trouble."

Jase laughed once as he reached out for her hand. "Until that idiot hit ya?"

"He split my lip," she explained. "Not enough to throw me into maast, but close. I felt that first rush of invincibility, and the switch flipped."

"Switch?" Tyr asked.

Sal nodded. "Yeah, the one that controls the rational part of my mind, I guess? All I knew was that he'd hurt me, I was cornered in a place where I was at his mercy, and it wasn't going to ever stop. I lunged, aiming for his throat."

"She woulda got him too," Jase said. "But we started movin' in when those two headed her way."

"And the moment you hit the ground," Zep added, "Jase was determined to protect you. Arctic had to scream in his head. Well, our heads."

"Was gonna kill that fucker," Jase grumbled. "He did na realize who he was trying ta shove around."

"Damn," Tyr teased. "She had you by the balls back then?"

"From the moment I saw her," Jase admitted. "I had never seen a thing so perfect in all my life. And then the way she smelled?"

"What's it like?" Jarl asked. "I know you and Kolt are meant for her, but what's that even like?"

"Yeah," Tyr said, sounding as if he'd just realized what he was missing out on. "I mean, you say she smells like hope, and that she reminded you of flowers or snow, but is that what hope smells like?"

"Ya really wanna know?" Jase asked, looking between them.

Jarl nodded. "I only get perceptions like that from Nya, and she's female. I'm not sure how my senses work in comparison."

"I really want to know," Tyr told him.

Jase smiled and tossed a memory at all of his cessivi, as well as Jarl. Sal felt it, but the bright flame in her mind blocked out everything else. Carefully, she reached for it, and everything else faded to the background.

Back then, Sal had lunged at Bardus, intending to make him pay for hurting her, and Jase had rushed in. He grabbed Sal before she could get herself in trouble, his arms wrapping around her chest, careful not to touch her bare skin, because he knew. With his head so close to the back of her neck, her long braid waving in his face, all he could smell was the overwhelming scent of endless possibilities. The scent was sharp but smooth, like a blade made of glass, but it wasn't subtle. It flooded his senses, waking every single nerve in his body.

She smelled like everything he wanted, all at once. Slowly, his mind tried to find a correlation, anything he could compare it to. The rush of emotions pounding in his chest was nearly euphoric, and being near her, everything in the world seemed clear. Perfectly clear, as if amplified. It was a place he never wanted to leave.

When she stopped struggling, he snuck in one more breath of her before he let go. That was when he realized it was snow. Like waking up to find that the entire world had turned as white as her skin and was filled with all the subtle colors reflected by her eyes. Her scent was perfection made into a woman, and one designed just for him, but there were no words for that. The best he could use was hope and fresh snow.

Sal blinked her awareness back to the present and lifted their linked hands to her lips to kiss his skin. "I thought you smelled like home. I'd never had one, but it was the best I had."

Jase tipped his head over to Kolt. "Ya thought he smelled like hope."

"I just thought he smelled good."

"Na, kitten, ya did na. Yer officer spent so many years in yer dreams because ya knew he smelled like hope, and ya dared ta believe it. Ya just did na know that yer path would take a little longer."

"And end up a little better," she agreed, then paused as Blaz touched her mind. *Sal, send Jarl in? The pups are almost here, and Nya wants him to be here. Everything's good. She just wants him with her like they talked about.*

"What?" Jarl demanded, seeing her attention shift. "Is she ok?"

"She's fine," Sal promised, "but she's asking for you. The pups are finally ready and Nya wants you to be with her."

"Go," Ilija said, "and if Rragri growls at you, growl back, boy."

Jarl scampered up, racing the handful of steps to the door like he was on fire, yet he slipped through it gently. When the latch clicked behind him, the entire hall fell silent. Everyone's eyes were on the door. All ears were straining for some hint of a sound. Minutes ticked past, the iliri tensed as if ready to pounce, but nothing. Then a few more.

Finally, a child wailed.

Sal felt her breath burst out, only then realizing that she'd been holding it. But that wasn't the mewl of a grauori pup. It was higher, clearer, and much more human-sounding. Moments later, a second joined it, and laughter began to fill the hall. Two babies, both of them healthy enough to cry. Even Risk breathed a sigh of relief, because so long as they were breathing, he could keep them alive, and Blaz could handle the rest.

"Boys or girls?" Shade asked, looking at Ilija.

He shrugged. "They wouldn't tell anyone. I'm not completely sure they knew, but when I asked, Nya said she didn't want to make any guesses because they weren't like any pups she'd felt before."

"But they're finally here," Sal sighed. "How do we help, Ilija?"

He just tossed both hands into the air. "I told Vanica, and she's coming this way. Besides that? I honestly have no idea. Tell the new parents that they're cute?"

Tyr grunted. "What if they aren't?"

"Then lie, Tyr." Ilija shook his head in disgust. "You always say they're cute. Fuck, man. Don't you know anything about women?"

"Not kids," Tyr admitted.

Ilija opened his mouth to respond, but the door cracked open. There was a brief pause, and then it swung inward far enough for Jarl to step out, juggling two very squirmy bundles of cloth.

"Sal?" he begged. "Can you hold one?"

"Yeah," she breathed, hopping to her feet to take the one closest to her.

She also dared to peek inside the swaddling. Looking back at her was snow-white skin and bleary blue eyes. Pale blue, though, the kind that would fade enough to end up white. Surprisingly, there was no fur. For a moment she just smiled at the little one, trying to take it all in.

"Can I look?" she asked Jarl.

"They're iliri, Sal," he said, his eyes welling up. "Two boys. That one is Nykarl and this is Nassim. They knew their names, but they're completely iliri. I mean, mostly."

"Mostly?" Jase asked, moving toward the child Jarl held. "What do ya mean?"

Jarl eased the blanket away from the child to reveal two very small ears set high on the little boy's head. The edges of them were golden, along with a hint of the same color by the boy's head.

"Rafrezzi," Jase whispered. "They got yer color, Jarl. Is Nykarl the same?"

"They're identical," he explained. "One placenta, the healer said. That means they're exact copies, right? I mean, genetically. Nassim's hair is a little more yellow, and I think Nykarl has bluer eyes, but I could be wrong. I..." He laughed, looking at all the iliri around him. "I have two sons, and they're both iliri."

"Purebred iliri," Sal realized. "More than pure, if that's even possible. They're gorgeous, Jarl. You and Nya have beautiful babies." She ducked her head to the little man in her arms. "We're going to make sure you grow up to be big, strong, and very proud of your dava and amma. And so happy, Nyk. I'll even play your prey, sweetie."

"Nyk?" Jarl said as if sampling how it sounded. "Then I guess this is Nas, huh? You were the first one, weren't ya. Beat out your brother by three whole minutes." Then he paused. "Ok, I have to take them back, but Nya said you can all see them whenever you want."

"Tomorrow," Sal assured him. "For tonight, you two just spend time together as a family."

Carefully, she and Jase helped Jarl get both babies balanced in his arms and Sal walked with him to get the door. She didn't make it.

Rayna had her head bent to Dom. "We need to push back the wedding. I'm sure the leaders will understand, and the staff knows it's a variable date, but tomorrow's too soon."

"No," Jarl said. "You three are getting married tomorrow. Nya wants to go. Blaz healed her up, and she's perfectly fine. Rragri said that the babies won't get sick because we have healers. So she wants to get out of that bed, and please let her? I mean, I can't promise they won't cry, but - "

"I don't care if they cry," Rayna swore. "Those are my nephews, Jarl. I'm going to be Aunty Ray-Ray, and if my little men want to interrupt my wedding, then they're allowed. I just didn't want to get married without you or Nya, and you're going to have a long night."

He just turned so she could look at one of the boys. "Your wedding anniversary will be the day after their birthday. Means they'll always get a royal party, right? Don't put off the wedding, Rayna."

She bent to kiss the cloth over Nas's head, then reached up to rumple Jarl's hair. "Ok. Let's make this the best week of all of our lives, huh?"

"That's pretty much what Nya said too," Jarl admitted.

Sal moved to open the door, letting him back in, and Nyk grumbled about it. The problem was that it didn't sound vicious yet. It sounded cute, exactly how she'd imagined an iliri infant to sound, and her heart hung for a split second. "Congratulations," she breathed as she forced herself to step back out and close the door behind her.

Rayna was there when she turned to wrap Sal in a hug. "He's going to be a good dava," she said before dropping her voice to a whisper. "And it's ok to be jealous. It is, Sal. No one will blame you at all."

She dropped her forehead onto Rayna's shoulder. "It's hard to be jealous when I'm so happy for him, though."

"That's because you are too good of a person for the rest of us." Rayna leaned back to look at her face. "But it's still ok, and I'm always here if you want to talk."

"I know," Sal promised. "You always have been, but I'm ok. I just didn't expect their ears. They're..."

"Adorable little golden iliri?" Rayna finished for her. "Yeah. The best part is that I get to send them home when I'm done spoiling them."

"Oh, and I'm going to spoil all four of them," Sal decided. "The way they all deserve to be."

CHAPTER FIFTY-THREE

WHITE

Sal and Tyr had to leave Arhhawen early the next morning to help Rayna get everything ready for her wedding. As part of the bridal party, Meia and Teya rode down to Dorton with them. The group had an appointment to get primped and finished by the best stylists in Dorton, and as a 'bridesmaid,' Tyr was included in that. He seemed oddly excited about it.

The rest of Sal's mates promised they'd be there on time, and Gage said he'd get them moving. Arctic was coming down later with Ran and Pig to make sure Shift had everything he needed. Sal's guys said they'd just ride with them. They also joked that they were going to have a little more coffee first.

Because it was annoyingly early. The grass was still wet with dew, and fog hung in the topmost peaks of the mountains. In the air over Dorton, the sky shimmered. Probably ice crystals or condensation, but it created a beautiful effect. Almost like an array of miniature rainbows in the air, but they weren't quite that vibrant.

Thankfully, Dorton had declared the day an official holiday. Most of the shops were closed, and the streets were peacefully empty. The sound of their horses' hooves clicked against the cobbles, but they didn't need to hurry. Even at the gate to the Palace, they were waved in with a smile from the guard stationed there.

After the chaos of the last week, it felt good. Everything was finally coming together, and in the very best way. The staff took their horses. The additional guards held the door, and Rayna's wedding party jogged up the stairs to find the room where they would all be turned beautiful enough to impress the masses.

Rayna was already there, wearing little more than a cloth robe, and an older woman hovered over her hair. "Come in, girls," she told them. "Close the door behind you. I'm Madam Slatin, and I'll be helping with your hair and cosmetics."

"Not wearing makeup," Tyr told her.

The woman spun with a gasp. "You can't be in here, sir!"

"Yes he can," Rayna said. "He's one of my bridesmaids."

"It's improper," she huffed.

"Trust me," Rayna said, "he's not really worried about seeing me naked. The pale one's his wife. The tallest? That's the pervert."

"Yes, I am," Meia agreed.

Teya just shrugged. "I'm chopped liver?"

"So, meat?" Rayna asked. "Because I'll treat you like a piece of meat if you want me to." She grinned, looking in the mirror to see them. "Madam Slatin, I'm not a virgin, I'm marrying two men who know all about my past, and I'm not about to become some delicate or fainting little lady. I'm a soldier. I taught this King how to use his sword. Well, so did the Kaisae, but a different sword. Now, if you're done clutching at your pearls, can we make today something kinda fun and a little less judgey?"

"I've just never had a man in a bridal party before," Madam Slatin mumbled, sounding like that was her attempt at an apology.

"Or an iliri, I bet," Rayna told her. "Probably not soldiers. Pretty sure you haven't had a girl marrying two men either."

"Aren't you worried about what people will say?" she asked.

"Nope," Rayna assured her. "Oh no, I'm sleeping with both of them? Fuck yeah, I am. They can be jealous. Sal has six men of her own. That I'm indecent, a slut, loose, a floozy? Those are all things people say to take away our power. See, I learned something from my friends. They love us when we win, and we won the fuck out of this."

"Yeah we did," Tyr agreed, moving closer to the mirror. "Whatcha need, Ray?"

"I'm shaved. I'm getting my hair fixed. I'll do makeup in a second. Oh! Tyr, can you make sure my dress isn't wrinkled?" She pointed to a wardrobe at the side.

Tyr headed over to open the door, then paused. "That's gorgeous!" And he pulled out the dress of every girl's dreams.

Gems sparkled on it like droplets of water, shifting in color from clear at the top to green at the hem. Silver silk lay beneath it, with a trim of delicate white pearls along the neck and sleeves. The thing clearly cost a fortune, but it definitely looked like the right dress for a queen.

The bridesmaids were all in green and black. The brocade of their dresses - and Tyr's suit - was subtle, but dark. While the girls had their faces painted, Tyr took time to shave, leaving a close-cropped beard across his jaw with crisp lines. Then Madam Slatin sat him down to work on his hair.

She was just closing Rayna into the dress when a tap came at the door. "It's time," Linella Piet said, peeking her head in.

"Ten minutes," Rayna told her. "Start getting everyone in their seats?"

"I will. Sal, just follow the carpet, ok? You know where we're going, but there's a reason for the carpet."

Sal nodded to show she understood, because they'd planned this out. Linella was just fretting about last-minute details. Granted, the woman looked more worried about all of this than Rayna did. The soon-to-be queen was as calm as she'd ever been.

"No cold feet?" Sal asked.

"None," Rayna assured her. "I mean, the idea of being a *Queen* scares the shit out of me, but the marriage? No, they're already my mates. This just makes everyone else accept it." Then she turned as Madam Slatin secured the last toggle. "And?" she asked.

Sal lifted the hem of her own gown and curtsied, lowering her eyes to the ground. "Your Highness," she breathed.

"Get the fuck up," Rayna warned her. "Don't *ever* do that again."

"Just had to do it once," Sal told her. "I've bowed to Dom, so I'll bow to you, but only because you've earned the respect. Now, are we ready to do this?"

"Wait, my garter!" Rayna said, grabbing something to slide it up her leg. "That's my broken and new piece. The dress is gifted, and the clips for my veil are borrowed. I think I'm good."

"I got the train," Tyr said, gathering the back of Rayna's gown to keep it from dragging.

And as a unit, they marched from the room, making their way down the stairs, toward the back, and out to the carpet Linella had warned them about. It was green, weaving in lazy arcs toward the pasture and pond Sal had recommended. The moment Rayna stepped on it, Sal sent a thought to Cillian, letting him know to get the music started.

But this wedding would be different. They'd tried to think of everything, hoping to make sure the presentation showed them all as equals in the relationship. That was why, just before Rayna made the last turn, Tyr arranged her dress out behind her. Meia pulled her veil down over her face and neck, temporarily covering the bite scars that were proof of her relationship with Shift. When that was done, Teya handed her the bouquet of silver flowers. Sal just stood on her left, opposite Tyr on her right, ready to handle anything.

Together, they walked into the meadow and paused where the carpet turned to silver. Just beyond sat all the guests, arrayed in three rows. One was designated for Dom, another for Shift, and the last for Rayna, allowing space for their families. Past that, held back by the paddock fence, everyone in Dorton was welcome to view the entire thing, and it looked like quite a few had come.

That was why the carpet changed colors *here*. Between a group of trees on one side, a decorative arch before them, and something which resembled a dressing screen on the other side, Rayna was mostly out of sight, yet still able to see her men at the end of this long, romantic trail.

"And who today is here to claim this woman as his wife?" Cillian called out in the traditional phrase.

Both Shift and Dom answered, "I am."

"And by what right do you have a claim to her?" Cillian asked.

This time, Dom answered first. "I will be her husband, the King of Anglia, claiming her as my Queen."

"I will be her dernor, as is my right as an iliri," Shift said, "claiming her as my mate and our Queen."

"Then will you, Kayden Savis, accept this man as your brother?" He paused, dropping his eyes to the book held before him. "He has no pack of his own except for you. He has no claim to another without you. Will you share your kills, your blood, your mate, and your very life with him? Will you treat him as your equal and partner in all things?"

The last part was the section for the Iliran ceremony, but it was spoken in Glish. Doing so would make it even easier to include the other alterations, including the parts to bind the three of them together legally. Plus, the Anglian citizens would all understand the promises they were making.

"I will," Shift said, "and I have."

"And you, Dominik Jens, will you claim this man's pack as your own, and make him your husband, granting him your name, your property, and all the possessions of your mind and body?"

"I will," Dom swore. "I have."

What's the 'I have,' part about? Rayna asked.

That's for the iliri part, Sal explained. *Proof they have already demonstrated that the pack is made, but simply needs to be recognized.*

Does this make Dom a Black Blade? she asked, glancing over.

Sal smiled. *He hasn't quite figured that bit out yet. Don't spoil our fun.*

Nope. No, this is going to be too good to ruin.

"Then," Cillian said, "as brothers and joint mates, I grant you both authority to claim this woman as your own."

The music started again, which was Rayna's signal to move into view. Shift stepped over to the same side of the small stage as Dom, leaving the far side for Rayna, but first, her and her bridesmaids had to make it through the crowd. As they passed, Rayna scanned the crowd, her eyes searching for something.

Which section is for me? she asked.

The one filled with grey, Sal told her. *All the Dogs are in dress uniforms for you. Tseri's there, and Vilko. The group in the middle is for Shift, and Dom's are on the right.*

There's Jarl! Rayna thought.

And Nya was beside him. Each of them held one of the babies, and they were grinning at Rayna proudly. They weren't the only ones. Pig and Keeya sat at the very front of Rayna's section, their hands clasped between them. Unlike the rest of the Dogs, they both wore silver. Then there was Arctic, Shade, and Ghost. Beside them were all of Sal's mates. In the row behind them was Geo, Baeli, and Narnx - who wore the black and purple of Terric.

The four Representatives of the Conglomerate had chosen to sit in Rayna's section as well. Myrosica had claimed a seat in Shift's, along with the Unavi senators. Dom's side was crowded with every noble who could squeeze his way in, which made it a jumble of fancy cloth and brilliant colors, but everyone important was here. Even the Verdant Shields had elected to sit in for Rayna instead of their King, although it was likely that no one would notice that gesture of support. Having the men of the 112th and the entire Lightning Brigade stacked in behind them made it a bit less obvious.

Sal also noticed Nyurin sitting beside Marnia. She held the baby that had given her the right to defect and become Anglian, and her mate was smiling down at the cloth-wrapped bundle. On the other side of them were the grauori. Most didn't want to use the chairs - as they weren't made for their joints - so they lay respectfully in the grass at the side of Shift's section. Among them was Gawyrr, but beside him was Raast. Rhyx, Roo, and Hwa had found a spot in front of him.

Even with all of that, there was, however, one couple that stuck out. Dressed in common cotton and pale colors, an older man and his wife had taken a spot in the very last row of Rayna's section. The soon-to-be Queen paused when she saw them, lifting her fingers to wave.

The older man smiled back, revealing himself to be the kind man who'd danced with her at the first pub. The woman beside him was likely his wife.

"Thank you," Rayna mouthed at them before continuing up the two steps to the platform that had been erected as her stage.

"And who," Cillian called out, "gives this woman, Rayna Mel, away to be married?"

Pig stood, smoothing down the front of his suit. "I do. This is my sister, and I give her freely to the men she has chosen."

Cillian nodded and turned his attention to Shift. "And who gives this iliri, Kayden Savis, away to be married?"

Ran eased himself up, wearing a black suit with green accents. "I do. I am his sadava, and I give this ilus freely to the mates he has chosen."

But instead of continuing on, Cillian's lips curled into a smile, and he looked to Dom. "And who gives this man, Dominik Jens, away to be married?"

Ilija snapped up like the soldier he was. "I do. I am his brother, guard, and friend, and I give him freely to his wife and husband, if he so chooses."

Dom began to blink quickly, lifting his chin to hold back his emotions, but Cillian just kept going. Rings were exchanged. Words of love were spoken, but the vows had been changed from the traditional, swapping out the lines about children and heirs with phrases about family and loyalty from the Iliran traditions. The words made it clear that this was an alliance of power, and that not all of it was Dom's. Rayna's strength, Dom's rank, and Shift's abilities were sworn to be used for the good of the human kingdom, merging them into a single Royal Family.

And then, finally, came the part everyone had been hoping for. "I now pronounce you, King Dominik Jens, Consort Kayden Jens, and Queen Rayna Jens, married. You may both kiss the bride."

Dom stepped in to press his lips to her mouth, but Shift caught her hand and bent to kiss her neck. There was a moment where no one was quite sure what to do, and then Kesh stood to cheer and clap. That was all it took to convince the rest to join him. Dom tilted his head back to smile against her lips.

"I love you, Ray," he whispered. "And you, my brother."

"I love you both," Shift promised.

"Forever," Rayna breathed. "Nothing can tear us apart now."

"Nothing ever could before," Shift whispered. "We are ayati. All of us."

Behind them, Sal reached over for Tyr's hand. *All of us,* she repeated to him.

Even if we're a bit thick and take a while to figure it out. Welcome to the happily ever after part, beautiful. I think we've finally done it.

CHAPTER FIFTY-FOUR

PURPLE

*A*fter the wedding came the reception. Sal caught the man from the pub to drag him along, making sure he and his wife knew just how much their presence meant to Rayna. Neither of them could believe they'd actually been allowed inside. Still, Jerold - which Sal found out was his name - had honestly wanted to give the Queen a wedding present, so Sal made sure he got the chance.

A thought pulled Rayna aside, and she greeted the gentleman with a warm hug, then clasped his wife's hand, surprising them both. But Jerold wasn't done. He gestured and his wife pulled a ceramic mug from her bag. It was silver with a beautiful green triad painted across one side, and a crude attempt at the Iliran word for future on the other. Jerold explained that he made things like that now that he was retired, and he thought she could use it for her coffee when she needed to recover from her hangovers.

The gesture had nearly ruined Rayna's eye makeup. She'd also made the older man swear he'd stick around long enough to share a dance with her. It was the third one of the night - Dom and Shift both taking up the first two - and his wife certainly hadn't expected the King to ask her as well. After that, Dom claimed Sal, Shift stole Shaden, and

411

Rayna claimed Kesh. Toasts were made, food was served, and eventually, the crowns were brought out.

For the King, this wasn't a coronation, but by tradition, he donned his first - having avoided wearing it until now. Naturally, it was the biggest, and the same one that had been bestowed upon him when he took the throne. As the monarch, he set Rayna's crown on her head and named her the official Queen of Anglia. Covered in a myriad of jewels, hers was almost as impressive as Dom's, but thankfully smaller and much more feminine.

Then she picked up the last crown. Shift's had most likely been made for a prince, but it suited him. When Rayna set it upon her dernor's head, she named him the official Royal Consort. Because their titles were granted through marriage, this was all the coronation they'd get, but it was enough. The entire ceremony had turned out perfectly.

Although whatever words Rayna had planned for Shift were only spoken in their minds, something clearly passed between them. Shift met her eyes and nodded, and Dom wore a wistful smile, so evidently they were good ones. After that, all that was left were the gifts and the drunkenness. The Royal Family was swarmed with people wanting to offer their congratulations. Soon, it would become more of a political affair than a wedding reception, so Sal decided she was sneaking out early, sending one last thought of congratulations to her best friend and her new husbands.

Rayna agreed that Sal should go before it got boring. That was the last excuse Sal and her mates needed. First they made a stop to the suite where Tyr and Sal had gotten dressed. There was no way she could ride home in this gown - although Zep really thought she should try. So, with the guys' help, they got re-dressed quickly, but when Sal stepped back into the hall, a sound made her pause. Not an audible one, but the mental kind.

"What?" Jase asked, seeing the look on her face.

"You guys want to stop and see the pups before we go?" Because she swore she could hear them.

"Yes!" Blaz said, overly adamant about it.

The others readily agreed. After all, Nya had begged out before the reception. Jarl had made an appearance, but he'd left as soon as he could. This would be one of the few chances Sal had to fawn over them without a circus around her. Everyone wanted to see the little ones, but at least the young couple would have no problem finding someone willing to give them a break.

Jarl? Sal thought as she knocked lightly at the door.

"Come!" The voice was Nya's.

Sal peeked her head in. "You in the mood for company?" she asked.

"Sal!" Nya whuffed. "Yes. Come! Bring your mates."

All seven of them piled into the room. Jase and Blaz made straight lines for the bassinets, but Sal headed to Nya. The little bitch sat on a couch with a book in Glish before her. When Sal offered a hug, she took it, clasping tightly.

"Did you get to see them?" she asked.

"They're beautiful," Sal told her. "Perfect little iliri."

Nya jiggled her head. "So, they're not messed up because they're rafrezzi?"

"Iliri don't care about colors, Nya. Blaec was rafrezzi. Risk, Roo, and so many of us are. No, they're most definitely not messed up."

She sighed, her eyes closing in relief. "I wasn't sure where they'd be welcome if they weren't right. Did Jarl tell you that they knew their names? When my labor started, they began thinking them to each other. I think they were worried and making sure they didn't get split up, but I heard them."

"I did too," Jarl said, walking out of the bedroom with a handful of clean diaper cloths. "They're so little, but they can already link!"

"It is na abnormal fer purebreds," Jase told him. "Sal came with the switch on. All she needed was a willing mind and she could reach us."

"Hey, um..." Jarl looked at the guys. "Can I borrow Sal for a second and get you guys to help feed and change the pups - kids, I mean?"

"Pups," Jase assured him, holding out a hand for the diapers. "There is na a thing wrong with callin' 'em that."

"Ok. Well, we're still figuring out how to manage them, and I know a few of you have done this."

"I got it," Kolt promised. "Everyone's still at the reception, so take your time."

"Thanks," Jarl said, tilting his head for Sal to step outside with him.

She followed, wondering what could be on his mind, but when they reached the hall, he didn't stop, turning to walk a few more doors down, well out of iliri hearing. His anxiety was obvious, the scent of fear, excitement, and love all blurring together.

"Ok," he finally said, turning to face her.

"Is everything ok?" she asked.

He nodded. "I hope so. Um..." And he sighed. "For all I know, I could be fucking this up completely, but um... " He paused again, this time to swallow. "Nya and I have been talking. Like, since she told me she was pregnant we have, you know? About this. Us, staying together, living apart, where we'll raise the babies, and we came up with some options, right? I mean, I'm only sixteen. She's not even thirteen."

"It's ok to be scared," Sal told him.

"But you never are," he countered. "And yes, I'm scared, but not for me. I'm scared for them. We just want to do the right thing, so, I'm just going to lay it out there, ok? Like, no expectations or anything. So please don't take this wrong?"

"I won't," Sal swore.

He nodded again, a sign of his anxiety. "I know you can't have kids, and I know the guys adore them. The group of you would be amazing parents. Better than Nya and I, and those two little boys are purebred iliri. We..." He had to stop as his voice cracked from the strain. "We want to know if you'd adopt them. I mean, we don't want to lose them, but we couldn't give them what you can. Rayna said you might not want kids, and that's ok, but you'd be the perfect mother, so I wanted to ask you where the guys couldn't pressure you."

"Me?" Sal asked, lifting her hand to her mouth.

"Yeah. I mean, Nya and I kinda hoped that you'd let us be in their lives a little, but we get it if that's not an option. It's just that... I mean... How can I raise them right while living in the Palace? There's nowhere for them to run, hunt, growl, and tackle each other. And Nya? They're going to be infants for a long time. She lives in a cliff face! They won't be able to climb when their friends do. What if they get hurt?"

"You know you're welcome to raise them in Arhhawen yourselves," Sal told him.

"I know," he said, reaching up to grab her arms, "but that won't make me anything more than a sixteen-year-old boy with no clue how to get my own shit right, let alone theirs. I'm trying to do the right thing, Sal - for my boys - and I think you're it. I don't want to make you feel like you have to, but you've always been our first choice. If not you, then we're going to ask Arctic. I mean, Risk was an option, but they've got the girls now, so I dunno. But we need to do this. We know we do, and while we don't like it, that doesn't make it any less right. I just wanted to ask you alone so you could say no if you wanted to."

Sal pushed out a breath, feeling like her mind was spinning. "And you're sure this is what you both want?"

"This is what our sons need," he repeated. "They deserve to live like real iliri, Sal. The only question is if you want to be their amma?"

"Yes," she breathed. "The first time I saw them I was so jealous. Yes, Jarl," she gasped.

He stepped into her and smothered her in a hug. "Oh, thank fuck," he breathed. "Thank you, Sal. Thank you so much."

"I'm gonna be an amma?" she asked, feeling like she couldn't quite catch her breath. "You're going to let me?"

"Yeah, because you're the best amma I can imagine. Now, did you want to think about it for a bit before telling them?"

"Cessivi," Sal said, reminding him of their bond. "My mates are already wondering what's going on. They'll ask as soon as we go back in there, and I'm having to reassure Jase that I'm ok."

"And that," Jarl told her, "is why we wanted you. Just imagine how safe Nyk and Nas are going to be?" He cocked out his elbow and offered his arm to her. "Let's go have a family discussion, huh? I'm kinda getting good at these."

"I still think you'd make a wonderful dava," Sal told him.

"I hope to one day," he said. "I dunno, and maybe when I'm older,

I'll get to explain to them why we thought this was best. I mean, at least iliri are used to a dozen ammas and davas, right?"

"That they are," Sal promised just as they reached the door.

The moment Jarl opened it, all of Sal's mates turned to look. "Ya ok?" Jase asked.

Jarl held up his hand and his eyes shifted to Nya. For a moment the young mother watched him, and then she sighed in relief. "Yeh," she breathed. "Ask 'em?"

"Ok," Jarl said. "So, um, I just talked to Sal because I wasn't sure if she wanted kids. I mean, we all know she can't have them, but that's a lot different than wanting them. And even though I know most of you guys are on board for the idea, I wanted to check with her first. So, now that I have her answer, um... Nya and I want you all to adopt our boys. We want you to take them home, raise them as your own, give them the last name of Luxx, and have their birth records formalized to show you as the parents."

Blaz's knees buckled, and he sat down on the couch, hard. "You don't want them?" he asked.

"We're not ready to be parents, Blaz. Nya and I know it - and if you stop and think for a second, all of you do too. I'm sure you've said it. Everyone else has. We'll be good parents, but we'll need help. It won't be easy. We're so young, but we have the right resources. I promise you, we've heard it all, and we're trying to be responsible. It's a little late, but not for them." He looked over at the baby Jase was holding.

"Are ya gonna want 'em back?" he asked. "Because I could na love them fer a bit and then ferget them."

"No," Nya said. "We want to be involved, but like you'll be with Shaden's baby. We want to make sure they know they're loved, but we understand that this is forever. We still think it's what they need, and you would give them the lives they deserve."

"They're pure iliri," Jarl said. "Jase, you and Sal are some of the few who'll understand. I won't! How will I explain being meant for someone, or the urge to growl? We've been talking about this the whole time, but we didn't really believe they'd be so..."

"Perfect," Nya finished. "They're perfect for you, Sal. Not for me.

The only way I could raise them would be in a cage, and I will not let my boys have anything but the freedom they deserve."

Zep looked over at Sal. "Are you ok with this, demon?"

"I am," she told him. "No. Fuck that. The idea of us finally having babies together? I want this, I just didn't think I could have it. We're free! We have a home, a pack, and everything laid out before us. I want to have pups too, but I can't."

"And now you can," Nya said softly, looking over at the child Gage was offering to his mate.

Sal took him, smiling down at the pale eyes watching her. "Hello, Nas," she whispered.

"You can even tell them apart," Jarl pointed out.

Gage chuckled once. "It's the smell, Jarl. They're completely different to us."

Sal stroked the little boy's cheek with her finger. "Tyr? If you're not ok with this, then we're not going to do it. Jarl says he has a backup plan, so they didn't want to pressure us."

"I'm not changing diapers," Tyr told her. "I mean, maybe the wet ones, but not the poopy ones. And someone's going to have to show me how to hold them so I don't screw up their necks or anything."

"Lemme guess," Kolt said, "and you're not going to get up at night to feed them?"

"Nah, I'm down for that part. It's the easy bit. But you can't laugh at me when I don't know how to dress them."

"I'll show you," Kolt promised, turning to Jase to hold out his arms, asking for little Nyk. Like the experienced father he was, he cradled the child before him and moved him to Tyr. "Now, hook your arm out, and just keep his head up so he can see you, and make sure you don't let go." Gently, he laid the little boy in Tyr's arm.

"He's so white," Tyr breathed, smiling down at the baby.

"You seen his ears?" Gage asked, pulling back the blanket to show the top of his head.

"You're just like a puppy!" Tyr told him. "Oh, aren't you so cute. Now, no puking on Daddy Tyr, ok?"

"He doesn't love you until he pukes on you," Zep teased.

Tyr never looked away from the child. "You can puke all over Daddy Tyr, little man. I'm going to be the best daddy."

"Only daddy," Gage fake coughed.

"Exactly," Tyr said. "A dozen davas and one daddy."

Jarl looked over at Sal. "So, I guess I should get their things?"

"Are you sure?" Sal asked.

"Yes," Nya said. "And the sooner you bond with them, the easier it will be. The less I do..." She clasped her paws together before her and twisted them together. "Congratulations, Sal. You're going to be a perfect amma."

"Any time," Sal told her. "Middle of the night, when you're sure we won't want you, I don't care. Any time you want to see them, you are welcome. Both of you. They deserve to know where they came from, and you deserve to be a part of their lives. You don't have to pretend this is easy."

"It's not," Nya said, "but you deserve the family you've fought so hard for. They deserve an amma who can truly care for them. Thank you, sister."

"Il bax genause, Nya," Sal told her. "Il bax genause, Jarl. You have both changed my life, and I will never forget this."

CHAPTER FIFTY-FIVE

SILVER

*W*hile the guys gathered everything the children would need, Sal sent a thought to Rayna, letting her know what had happened. She was *thrilled* with the news, then admitted she'd suspected that was what the kids were planning. They'd asked enough questions to make her wonder. Then she countered with her own piece of good news.

It seemed that the Alliance had presented their own wedding present. While the Anglians had been busy with Nya giving birth and the wedding, the allies had all put in an honest effort to write a fair and equitable version of the Conventions of War. They'd made liberal use of Sal's books, Vilko's records, and everything else they could. No one had tried to catch any of the non-human species in a loophole. In fact, they'd even added a clause that allowed amendments as cultures changed over time. Dom and Rragri had looked over it, and both felt it was more than fair. All they had to do now was sign it.

But that would come later. Tomorrow, maybe the day after. It didn't matter, and the allies were not pressuring them to get it done. While Sal and her men got their two new bundles of joy onto horses for the trip home, Rayna made sure Rragri knew about the adoption. She said Nya had told her about it, and she was honestly relieved to know the babies would be where they truly belonged. She sent a thought to Sal thanking her for allowing Nya and Jarl to have the best of both worlds: their youth and their children.

The trip home felt like it took even longer with two newborns being held on horseback. Sal's maternal instincts were starting to kick into overdrive, and she looked over constantly, but Blaz and Zep had them. Those two had claimed that as the best riders, they were the most capable of getting them home safely, and they did. The only problem was that so many people from Arhhawen were still down in Dorton, enjoying the last of the King's wedding celebration.

Tyr and Gage offered to take the horses. Kolt said he'd find something to work as a temporary crib for them. Zep was convinced that his boy had shit himself halfway up the hill, and Jase said he knew how to change a diaper. Well, he'd read about it. Sal headed to Tensa's kitchen to ask about milk, thankful that iliri didn't need a complicated formula, just something with higher sugar like what horses produced, which Tensa was known to keep.

Bottles were easy. Plenty of the iliri women had an extra they were willing to offer, and one of them said her son had just outgrown his crib. She'd be honored if the Kaisae wanted to use it. In less than an hour, Sal and her mates had one of the smaller bedrooms off the main suite converted into a makeshift nursery, and they finally got to pause and appreciate the boys.

"Nas, right?" Zep asked as he unwrapped the swaddling so he could change the kid's diaper.

"Yeh," Jase said. "Nyk has the blonde streak more ta the side."

Zep nodded, his complete attention on removing the cloth diaper. Jase had a clean one ready to swap out, and Sal stood there watching them work together. It was the most adorable thing she could imagine. In their bedroom behind her, Tyr had Nyk leaned against his chest, and he was humming a little song.

"This won't be easy," Sal said, mostly to herself.

Tyr heard. "But it'll be worth it, right? Sal, we already have a few kids. Lyzzi, Lasryn, all four of Roo's pups, Valri? We got this, and Jarl's right. It's hard for a guy that young to grow up so fast. Oh, he'll try, but he'll have moments, because as wise as he is, he's still just a kid himself. Us? We're adults and we're going to be asking for backup at times. And two boys? Trust me, they're going to run all seven of us ragged."

"Yeah," Sal agreed, "but I thought you didn't want kids."

He sighed and turned for the main room. "Gage? Your turn."

"My turn!" Gage said, hopping up to steal a little time with Nyk.

Tyr released the infant and turned to grab Sal, pulling her with him toward the balcony. He didn't stop until they were outside, and then he pointed straight out to the east.

"How far can you see, Sal? With your iliri eyes, how far can you actually see?"

Sal looked, her eyes making out the road down from Arhhawen, the twists and curves it took until it came to Dorton. From here, the city looked like a child's toy, but she could make out the Palace and the green area around it that was the King's lands. Beyond that, the world kept going, turning hazy with distance until it met the curved horizon.

"I can see about halfway to Valmere," she admitted, "but I can't make out more than land."

"Know why?" he asked.

"Why?"

"Because we're on top of the world, Sal. We're standing here on your balcony, looking at your land, with your family. We both have spent our entire lives picking fights and losing many of them, and we finally came out ahead. Here's the thing that's kinda hard for you to get. I *don't* just think of myself. I became a soldier because I wanted to help others. I convinced the Dogs to defect because I wanted to help the Blades. I rode all the way to the Emperor's front door because I wanted to do the right fucking thing."

"I know," Sal assured him.

He moved behind her, grabbing the stone railing on either side of her body to cage her there. That put his lips beside her ear. "And somewhere along the way, I fell in love with you. I still didn't think of myself. I started thinking of you, of what you wanted, of what was best for you, and how I could take the beating for a bit so you didn't have to.

Sal, I tried to push you away because I didn't want to tear you apart the way Blaec did. I honestly thought that if I ended things before they began, then it wouldn't hurt - but it did. It hurt so bad, so when I realized that you were trying to ignore the pain of being unable to have kids, you know what I did?"

She turned in his arms to face him. "You told me you didn't want kids?"

"Yeah. I took the blame, giving you an excuse so you could feel better about it. But the thing is, I kinda do. I want to get out of bed and make bottles. I want to sew them little soft swords, and teach them how to fight humans, iliri, and grauori. I want to cheer them on when they learn how to ride, and hold them when they cry. More than all of that, I want to see that smile on your face, Sal. The one where you glow with pride because now, as of today, you are *our* little boys' amma, and it's honestly ok for you to hold them, to love them, and to just let this happen, because no matter what, I'm always going to be the one to take the blame so that you never, ever have to."

"I love you, Tyr," Sal breathed.

"I love you so much, baby, so how about you turn back around and look at that again, because we are *on top of the fucking world.* You hear me? We deserve this, and the King of Anglia gave you the best view in the world. The Prince gave you a family. The Orassae gave you an army to make this possible." He paused to kiss the side of her neck. "And this is where our sons are going to grow up, Sal. Up here, sitting at the top of it all, right where they belong."

But something caught her eye. Just at the edge of her vision, she swore she saw an orange flare. Nothing bright enough to be blamed on the sun, and it glistened. It was too light out still to be the aurora, and when she looked at it, the color went away, only for blue to be visible on the other side.

"Tyr?" she asked softly. "Do you see that?"

"The view I was just telling you about?" he teased.

"No, that. The ice in the atmosphere."

"Sal?" He leaned back, then stepped to her side to look at her. "The sky's perfectly clear. The exact weather Rayna was hoping for on her wedding day. There's not even a cloud, let alone *ice* up there."

Guys? Sal asked, calling her mates out there with her. *Can you come look at something for me?*

One by one, they all made their way out to the stone balcony set above the main entrance to Arhhawen. Jase had Nas, Gage still had Nyk, and the rest followed behind. And then Zep stepped out.

"Fuck," he breathed, gaping at the sky in shock. "When did that happen?"

"You see it?" Sal asked.

"Link us, Sal," Jase told her. "Let us see what he can."

She had to close her eyes to do it, the transparent shimmering almost hypnotic as it wove together, but she felt when her mates all merged into one. Then, she opened her eyes. From Zep, she could see it even clearer than she could from her own eyes. Those weren't just shimmers of colors, they were strands, and they were moving.

"Ayati," Jase breathed.

"It's in color," Sal told them. "And it's not tangled!"

But Zep was focused on something else. Feeling it, she turned to find him looking at the boys. "Did anyone ever look at those blood tests?"

"No," Gage said. "We were a little busy. Why?"

"But Ashir sent them, right? He did them all?"

"Yeah?" Gage said, dragging the word out to make it a question.

"Because I have a feeling," Zep said.

That was all it took to have Kolt hurrying back inside to rifle through the stack of papers in the main room. When he found it, he came out, reading them off from the top down.

"Sal is double Kaisae," he said. "Jase has one copy. I have one copy -"

"Doesn't that make you onsyc?" Tyr asked.

"Technically," Kolt said, still reading.

"So you do men?" Tyr asked.

"Are na disgusted by them," Jase clarified. "It is na an either or thing. Who else, Kolt?"

"Zep has one copy. But he's human?"

Sal was nodding. "And the right bloodline. Who else?"

"Gage has none, Tyr has none, Blaz has one? Huh. Oh, and Las has one!" Then he paused. "Valri has two. Ryali has one. How did Ryali get one?"

"From her human ancestor," Zep realized. "And these boys got one from Jarl. I don't even need to look; I'm sure of it." He glanced up at the sky. "The pattern's back, Sal. They're the last piece. You had to give the iliri one more bloodline so the cycle could reform. I can fucking feel ayati again!"

"And I can see it," Sal told them. "And guys, it wasn't like this last time."

"How'd it change?" Tyr asked. "Is this a good thing, or should we brace for something else to go wrong?"

"No," Sal told him. "It's not tangled. I think it's... weaving? And it's in the right colors. Orange, green, blue, they're all up there! I can see black, brown, and pink as well, but there's not very much of them." And then she paused as her own words hit her.

"What?" Jase demanded.

"Blaec said that he had to die to change the pattern. He didn't mean just for me," she realized, pointing up at the colors shifting above. "He meant he was going to change all of ayati. He died so that we would never have to fight like that again."

"So our next Kaisae - whether that's Lyzzi, Valri, or both - won't have to fight, die, and suffer the way every other one has before," Gage said.

"Both," Sal decided. "Because for the first time, we *can* have two Kaisaes at once. They can rule their lands without needing to fight about it. One for the east, one for the west. Or even Namisa, if Lyzzi eventually wants to go back there." She began to smile. "And we can live."

"Yeah," Tyr said, reaching over to slap Blaz on the back. "Blaec found a way to put us on top of the fucking world."

Jase passed Nas to Tyr, then stepped to the rail and leaned out, his eyes hanging on the sky. "*This*, Sal. This is how it's all supposed ta finally end. I just do na know how I am gonna describe this when we put it in yer book."

"You won't need to," Sal promised. "Because every Kaisae who comes after me will live to old age, and she'll be able to see the pattern the entire time, written in the colors of our words."

EPILOGUE

Orange, blue, white, cyan, green, and more. Color after color, he lined up the threads. All fifty-five of them. For months, he'd collected every scrap of possibility that he could, twisting them together until they were threads. Each one was tinted by the emotions of the moment, finally giving something back to the pattern. They were all hung on two old lines. Two completely unrelated lines, except that they'd been in the right place to catch what was left of his soul when he pulled himself apart.

One tasted like Kolt, but it wasn't him. It was his son's future, promising him peace. The other bore a dead man's name - his name. The child of a lost sibling and a man who should've been the enemy. Together, they would be the foundation of an entirely new world. One where the options didn't all have to be bad. Where humans weren't the only ones who could look forward to tomorrow.

Those lines were the only things holding him together, allowing him to remember what had come before. He was as tied to them as everything else in reality, and he planned to stay in this abyss until she was done. Because this was the price of his sacrifice.

She'd live for many more decades. Her children would grow, have children of their own, and forget that iliri were supposed to only be white. Already, the lines were blurring, and it was all because she'd helped to change the rules. Fibers from grauori had blended with humans, and were woven in with iliri. Day after day, month after month, he worked on this masterpiece. It was all he had left, but it was also all he needed.

He could no longer remember his own name, but that didn't matter. He knew hers. He knew the colors of the men she would surround herself with. Combining them all, he slowly wove them together into the most complicated tapestry. This was life. It was the past, the present, and the future, all written in a way that didn't remove control. It was made so that once they reached the end, it turned to send them back up to the beginning.

Over and over, they would be trapped in this cycle, so he wanted to make it a good one. The last had been made of love and death, with little else in between. This one had joy, faith, knowledge, hope, and more. He finally had all the pieces, but completing it would take him years. Decades even. Ideally, as long as it would take for her to grow old, so they could all start together again.

Slowly, he focused on weaving his lines together, wondering what his next life would be like. He wanted joy. He dreamed of love - the kind so strong it couldn't be broken. Knowledge would be nice, but would it matter without the strength of life or pride? Everything was important, and he would have no way to know which thread would be his. He did, however, know it would be gold.

However, the first one she loved should be blue, because everyone deserved someone to believe in them. The second should be life, so that she could live in safety. The third would be pride, since that would prevent her from crumbling under the pressure. Fourth would be knowledge. The fifth would need to know pain so that she never had to. And last, he'd give her joy.

Slowly, a pattern began to form. The man beside the void watched as the knots shifted into place. Some threads wanted to drift apart, others begged to slide closer. Every twist released smaller threads which dangled down to start new lives, although it didn't take much to move them out of the way. But slowly, in the middle of it all, one symbol began to form.

This would be her name. It would be her greatest power and her weakness, all tied up together. It would ensure that she, more than anyone else, was never lost completely. Lifting the purple thread, he twisted it around one more time. He couldn't remember where he'd learned this, and he knew he'd be taught it again. Still, he knew the word.

Before him, it was starting to be legible, but only from this side. Below, in the fabric of reality, there would only be colors and emotions. Up here, however, he could read the most important thing of all.

This was the name of the woman he still loved, and one she would remember no matter how many times she was thrown back into the pattern. Her name was Hope, and she was the reason for it all. In Iliran, it was pronounced, "Kaisae."

THE END

GLOSSARY

The Iliran language is a constantly evolving one. The letters p, j, q, and the combinations of th, ch, sh, and ph are not native to the original language but have slowly become used through the association with humans. Due to the inability of humans to understand pack hierarchy, many new titles have been created to aid in interspecies and international relations.

ahnam: first
ahnor: first mate; also a title for the Kaisae's husband (capitalized when used as a title)
ahvir: eternally
aitae: help
akerna: dam or birthmother, does not imply a relationship nor exclude one
alous: always
amma: mother or mom
ankan: spread
arhha: north
Arhhawen: North Wind
arn: and

arzionah: evening

ast: are

aufrio: grey, typically used to describe a color pattern on grauori

aussah: thank you

auxec: save

avixa: tell

ayamae: help me

ayati: the nature of things, fate, and used as slang to mean joy/happiness

bax: earn

berrn: leave

brerror: loner or outcast from society

bynor: eleventh mate; also a title for the Kaisae's husband (capitalized when used as a title)

ca: with

canzara: distance (away)

cenla: slate

cessivi: soulmate; and a title for a partner bonded in such a manner

cinnor: fourth mate; also a title for the Kaisae's husband (capitalized when used as a title)

corvae: love

dargo: dominate

dava: father

denn: home

denwar: blocks

derc: two

dernor: second mate; also a title for the Kaisae's husband (capitalized when used as a title)

derza: right

dregor: sire or birthfather, does not imply a relationship nor exclude one

dru: you (plural)

e: the or to, depending on how used

ed: be

edst: is

einay: they

gan: does

gar: my

gara: most often translated as "uncle", but refers to a male pack member or caretaker, not related to the child. Used as a term of endearment.

garn: mine

gavwor: father-in-law; can be used as a title of respect

gehwah: show

genause: soul or direction of one's life path

gern: do

gerus: those grauori deemed successful enough to contribute to the species and allowed to breed; implies respect

gernor: ninth mate; also a title for the Kaisae's husband (capitalized when used as a title)

grae: know

gru: babies

grunae: pup

ihrend: word

il: you

ilnae: an iliri child

ilus: derived from the grauori idea of proving one's worth, now used as a title of respect similar to sir or ma'am

inurga: wrong

Kaeen: female leader of Viraenova

kai: her

kaisae: leader (female); one of the four genders of iliri, when capitalized it refers to the chosen female ruler of the species

kaisor: leader (male); a title created to show respect to Blaec Doll

kaizen: leaders or rulers (plural)

kalargi: brother

kanae: his

kanna: name

kano: he

kauvwae: grandmother

kernor: sixth mate; also a title for the Kaisae's husband (capitalized when used as a title)

khemma: daughter

kierna: she

koleri: sister

laetus: reverence

lannae (lannar): emotional sex, to make love

liall: dog

lor: for

loura: missed

lursarati: devil or demon, a personification of evil

lynnor: thirteenth mate; also a title for the Kaisae's husband (capitalized when used as a title)

lyrva: revenge

maargra: grauori soldier, literally means "one who protects"

maast: bloodlust, can be used as a profanity

maerte: the meat derived from humans

moxero: bravery

nacione: white, often used to describe a color pattern on grauori

nas: not

nee: please

nieur: die

novi: new

onsa: same

onsyc: homosexual or pansexual gender of iliri

Orassae: grauori queen, literally means "leader of the people"

ortas: intelligence

raergah: respect

raewar: strength of the pack, recently made into a title for military leadership

rafrezzi: gold, typically used to describe a color pattern on grauori

rahdreg: pride

raz: stop

rocrra: force

rornnae (rornnar): carnal sex for physical pleasure, to fuck *rylnor:* eighth mate; also a title for the Kaisae's husband (capitalized when used as a title)

sadava: adopted father

sae: I

sahn: us

sahna: we

settivo: place

sevic: hunt

sinna: this

sivex: friend, not to be confused with acquaintance which has no specific word

suma: that

sussa: need

sylnor: seventh mate; also a title for the Kaisae's husband (capitalized when used as a title)

taunor: third mate; also a title for the Kaisae's husband (capitalized when used as a title)

tola: all

umso: submit

unes: where

va: am

vaera: life

van: will

vargwar: voice, recently made into a title for an official translator

vau: have

vau: was

vaun: are (plural)

verg: freeze

viernor: fifth mate; also a title for the Kaisae's husband (capitalized when used as a title)

yllnor: tenth mate; also a title for the Kaisae's husband (capitalized when used as a title)

wen: wind

wohanna: honor

wona: true

xernor: twelfth mate; also a title for the Kaisae's husband (capitalized when used as a title)

xie: ridge

za: of

za: what

zan na: slang equivalent to "of course"

zar: in

BOOKS BY AURYN HADLEY

Contemporary Romance: *Standalone Book*

One More Day

End of Days - Auryn Hadley & Kitty Cox writing as Cerise Cole
(Paranormal RH): *Completed Series*

Still of the Night

Tainted Love

Enter Sandman

Highway to Hell

Gamer Girls - co-written w/ Kitty Cox

(Contemporary Romance): *Completed Series*

Flawed

Challenge Accepted

Virtual Reality

Fragged

Collateral Damage

For The Win

Game Over

Rise of the Iliri (Epic Science Fantasy):

Completed Series

BloodLust

Instinctual

Defiance

Inseparable

Tenacity

Resilience

Dissent

Upheaval

Havoc

Risen

Hope

The Dark Orchid (Fantasy RH / Poly):

Completed Series

Power of Lies

Magic of Lust

Spell of Love

The Demons' Muse (Paranormal RH):

Completed Series

The Kiss of Death

For Love of Evil

The Sins of Desire

The Lure of the Devil

The Wrath of Angels

The Eidolon Chronicles (Paranormal Poly):

In Progress

Not A Vampire

Not A Ghost

Not A Succubus

The Path of Temptation (Fantasy RH / Poly):

Completed Series

The Price We Pay

The Paths We Lay

The Games We Play

The Ways We Betray

The Prayers We Pray

The Gods We Obey

The Wolf of Oberhame (Fantasy):

Completed Series

When We Were Kings

When We Were Dancing

When We Were Crowned

Wolves Next Door (Paranormal RH / Poly):

Completed Series

Wolf's Bane

Wolf's Call

Wolf's Pack

ABOUT THE AUTHOR

Auryn Hadley is happily married with three canine children and a herd of feral cats that her husband keeps feeding. Between her love for animals, video games, and a good book, she has enough ideas to spend the rest of her life trying to get them out. They all live in Texas, land of the blistering sun, where she spends her days feeding her addictions – including drinking way too much coffee.

For a complete list of books by Auryn Hadley, visit:

My website -
aurynhadley.com

Amazon Author Page -
amazon.com/author/aurynhadley

Books2Read Reading List -
books2read.com/rl/AurynHadley

———

You can also join the fun on Discord -
https://discord.gg/Auryn-Kitty

Visit our Patreon site
www.patreon.com/Auryn_Kitty

Facebook readers group -
www.facebook.com/groups/TheLiteraryArmy/

Merchandise is available from -
Etsy Shop (signed books) - The Book Muse -
www.etsy.com/shop/TheBookMuse

Threadless (clothes, etc) - The Book Muse -
https://thebookmuse.threadless.com/

Also visit any of the other sites below:

facebook.com/AurynHadleyAuthor
twitter.com/AurynHadley
amazon.com/author/aurynhadley
goodreads.com/AurynHadley
bookbub.com/profile/auryn-hadley
patreon.com/Auryn_Kitty

Made in United States
Troutdale, OR
10/22/2023